Also by Karim Dimechkie

Lifted by the Great Nothing

The Uproar

The Uproar

Karim Dimechkie

Little, Brown and Company
New York Boston London

Copyright © 2025 by Karim Dimechkie

Hachette Book Group supports the right to free expression and the value of copyright. The purpose of copyright is to encourage writers and artists to produce the creative works that enrich our culture.

The scanning, uploading, and distribution of this book without permission is a theft of the author's intellectual property. If you would like permission to use material from the book (other than for review purposes), please contact permissions@hbgusa.com. Thank you for your support of the author's rights.

Little, Brown and Company
Hachette Book Group
1290 Avenue of the Americas, New York, NY 10104
littlebrown.com

First Edition: June 2025

Little, Brown and Company is a division of Hachette Book Group, Inc. The Little, Brown name and logo are trademarks of Hachette Book Group, Inc.

The publisher is not responsible for websites (or their content) that are not owned by the publisher.

The Hachette Speakers Bureau provides a wide range of authors for speaking events. To find out more, go to hachettespeakersbureau.com or email hachettespeakers@hbgusa.com.

Little, Brown and Company books may be purchased in bulk for business, educational, or promotional use. For information, please contact your local bookseller or the Hachette Book Group Special Markets Department at special.markets@hbgusa.com.

Print book interior design by Bart Dawson.

ISBN 9780316581189
Library of Congress Control Number: 2025931369

Printing 1, 2025

LSC-C

Printed in the United States of America

For Nana Afua

Part I
WITHDRAWAL

1.

SHARIF'S PREGNANT WIFE, Adjoua, had been distant for over a week. Her warmth and humor and affection stayed hidden behind a wall of invulnerability. So it surprised him when she lay on the park bench that morning and rested her head on his lap. Knowing better than to spoil the moment with a reaction, he sat perfectly still, letting the physical contact fill him with a bright and cleansing air. Her box braids were tied in a top bun that poked out of her green and gold headscarf, a few strays spilling over his thigh. Pretty as the braids were, he quietly missed the natural hair they protected. When unbound, her hair was a resplendent halo of vitality. But he knew the halo required a complex, labor-intensive morning and night routine for which she had lost patience.

The couple's 150-pound, brown and white pit-bullmastiff lay at Sharif's feet. Through the park fence, across Essex Street, and up on the sixth floor of a prewar building hung their small, dim apartment. Behind them, in the center of the park on an inactive ground fountain, were a dozen elderly Chinese women rehearsing a choreographed dance. They twirled, stomped, and snapped their red folding fans to the drum and fiddle music playing from a tinny stereo.

Sharif had eighteen minutes to finish the email on his phone before heading to work.

Subject: Dog Care

Hi Everyone,

Sharif here, Workforce Development Case Worker II. Forgive me
for the group email out of the blue, but Merjem gave me the green
light to reach out about a personal matter. At 36 weeks pregnant,
my wife and I learned that our unborn daughter has leukemia. It's
certainly not what we hoped for, but we're lucky to have caught the
disease prenatally. Our doctors project an extremely high chance
(98%) of full remission after the two-year treatment. I share this
because our doctors have advised us to rehome our dog for the
duration of the treatment to minimize any risk of infection.

The name our dog had when adopted was Judas, but that
was unbefitting such a sweet and loyal boy, so now he's Judy. He's
on the waitlist of every no-kill shelter and foster-care provider we
know of, but we hope someone from our community will provide
him with a loving home for that critical two-year treatment period.
Judy is 8 years old, 150 lbs., and the most wonderfully lazy and
affectionate companion imaginable.

This should have been easier. But unlike the friends and family he'd
written to about this, none of his coworkers had met Judy, and Sharif struggled to present the dog's less appealing characteristics in a way that wasn't
instantly off-putting.

Judy was cute in the way of big, slow-moving, sullen-faced creatures,
but he was also an unusually burdensome housemate. Aside from his stack
of physical issues — arthritis that required his 150-pound body to be carried up and down stairs; the unconquerable smell of urine on his pink and
brown mottled belly, resurfacing minutes after a bath; frequent and poi-
sonous gas regardless of diet or how they slowed his inhalation eating style
(a tennis ball in the bowl, pouring his kibble onto the floor, hand feeding,
etc.); chronic dry mouth that caused incessant tongue clucking, making it
impossible for anyone but Adjoua to sleep in the same room as him — the

real problem was his propensity for violence around nonhuman animals. So, no animal lovers or foster-care providers who already had a pet, which turned out to be all of them so far, were viable rehoming options.

About a year earlier, Judy woke up with a new core desire to annihilate any domestic pet within ten feet of him. His hackles ridged along his back. His tail turned stick straight. He bared his teeth and growled a brief warning before transitioning to death-battle lunges against his leash. The vet said this happened sometimes in old age. Sharif and Adjoua hadn't heard of murderousness as a symptom of aging but didn't have a better explanation.

In solidarity, Adjoua expressed contempt for any dog or cat Judy wished to destroy. When he growled at his confused enemies, Adjoua's eyes went heavy and small, her lip Elvis-curled, and she muttered a mobster impersonation, saying, "Fugthatguy," as she pulled Judy to the other side of the street. When Judy kept looking over his shoulder at the other animal, she'd switch to "Walk away, bro, walk away. He's not worth it." Whether Judy gnawed Adjoua's shoes to death or stole the roasted Cornish hens cooling on the stovetop, he was blameless to her. She might scold him, but then she'd immediately apologize for scaring him and proceed to shower him with love, inadvertently rewarding his crimes. Like God, Judy was only accountable for the good he did, which was limited to sleeping, getting carried up six flights of stairs without fuss, shitting on the sidewalk, eating his breakfast and dinner, cuddling, playing, and being funny. Sharif perceived no sense of humor in their dog, but Adjoua said Judy's self-seriousness was the funniest thing about him; besides, cuteness is inherently funny.

Sharif passed his phone to Adjoua, and asked, "Does the part about minimizing the risk of infection make Judy sound dirty?"

Adjoua held the phone above her face, grimacing at the screen like it showed a graphic image. He shouldn't have involved her. Aside from her restless fatigue, upper abdominal and back pain, anxieties around caring for a sick child, and financial worries, learning they had to rehome Judy was what nearly broke her. After skimming the email, she passed it back and clenched her eyes in silent pain. Sharif felt the trees and buildings around them increase toward the sky, creating a sinking feeling.

Before Adjoua adopted Judy on her twenty-ninth birthday, people warned her that having a huge dog in a tiny apartment was a bad, even inhumane, idea. They were wrong. She met Judy at a kill shelter in the Bronx the day before he was to be put down, and had since provided him with seven additional, love-filled years in numerous tiny apartments. Judy was her prince. Her first and only unconditional love. She reflected on past romantic relationships as dishonest, imbalanced, or transactional in one form or another. Her friendships had somewhat rigid boundaries — polite, with limited capacity for addressing miscommunication or hard feelings. And her parents' expression of love had always been conditioned on her achievements. They had emigrated from Côte d'Ivoire when she was four, leaving everything familiar and safe to transfer the sum of their aspirations into their only child, unable to have more. Praise and affection were given when academic benchmarks were met, Adjoua's writing was published somewhere they or someone they knew had heard of, and when she got pregnant and married a nice man. Adjoua said her mother's description of Sharif as "a nice man" was a euphemism for "a white man," which corresponded with her mother's white-is-right worldview.

Sharif and his brother, Walid, had fair skin, dirty blond hair, and light brown eyes. Their father was a Lebanese man who had progressively adopted total integrationism — cutting ties with his native country — and their mother was a redhead from an Illinois coal mining family. Sharif and Walid had a predominantly white bread American experience growing up in Shoreview, Minnesota, only occasionally reminded of their father's Arabness. Adjoua's mother had held in a big breath when asking Sharif if he was a practicing Muslim, making no attempt to conceal the magnitude of her relief when he answered no. Adjoua congratulated Sharif in front of her mother for being both "nice" *and* non-Muslim.

Out of a cultural avoidance for acknowledging illness and an extreme power-of-positive-thinking attitude, Sharif's in-laws never appeared concerned by their future granddaughter's cancer diagnosis. The only worry they let slip was about how little money Adjoua and Sharif seemed to make. Hadn't they both been well educated, healthy, beloved upper-middle-class kids given every opportunity for economic advancement? Why were they so poor? Both sets of parents would have surely been willing to help with rent and whatever else was needed for the baby's well-being, but the couple agreed that asking them for money at this age constituted a failure too great to stomach.

Before the pregnancy, Adjoua had no reservations about their professional paths as a social worker and fiction writer. They had been hard up but fulfilled in careers that had net societal value. They felt proud telling people what they did. But by the time of the diagnosis, Adjoua felt betrayed by her pre-pregnancy self: that idealist who believed if she pursued her dreams, the money would follow. *How's that for irony,* Sharif heard her tell a friend on the phone the other day, *as a result of refusing to shape my life around money all these years, all I think about is money. How could I have relied on something as fickle as the publishing industry?* It was now urgent to her that they do whatever it took to give their baby the same safeguards and advantages they enjoyed as children—high-quality food, healthcare, schools, tutors, proper vacations, housing stability, and parents who weren't stressed about bills.

Sharif was shaken by the drastic shift in his wife's priorities, and her sudden dissatisfaction with their life. It was hard not to imagine this dissatisfaction spilling over into her choice of partner. He committed to asking for a raise at his nonprofit, but even if he secured the maximum possible raise, which was far from guaranteed, they'd still be one mistake, one stroke of bad luck, from being no different from his poverty-stricken clients when the baby came (the unspoken difference being that their parents would probably intervene if the threat of total ruin presented itself). So, in addition to Sharif needing that raise, Adjoua planned to double down as a freelance advertising copywriter, work that she hated. She had only resorted to copywriting once or twice to pay off towering credit card debts, which her adjunct writing instructor's salary at Mercy College could do nothing about. She planned to build a copywriting portfolio strong enough to pitch to the big, evil Manhattan firms that offered big, evil compensation packages.

It saddened Sharif that Adjoua put her fiction writing on the backburner. Aside from it being an existential anchor for her, every signpost suggested her second book was going to be huge. She had published her first novel, *Red-Out*, a year and a half earlier. It was about a nine-year-old girl in Abidjan who ends up being the only living witness to her father's violent crime. It came out with a small press for a $5,000 advance, which continued to be the entirety of the couple's savings. It had a small launch and readership, but an unexpected review from the most important New York critic was triumphant. This attracted a new, high-powered literary agent and eagerness about her next book from prominent editors at major publishing houses. But her physical discomfort, brain fog, and financial stress had made the idea of writing a novel seem ridiculous.

Sharif felt inadequate for not earning more money. He dreamed of affording her the time and resources she needed to work on the new book. But social services was all he knew. It's not like he could quit and join a hedge fund even if he wanted to, and besides, his low-paying job provided the health insurance they couldn't risk interrupting now.

Sharif was glad when Adjoua's new agent put her on the hook with the *New York Times* behind her back. Adjoua received an email out of the blue from the editor saying they looked forward to receiving her op-ed by Monday on the Daniels case, the latest high-profile trial of a police officer who'd killed an unarmed Black man. Adjoua was shocked that her agent didn't check in with her first, especially for a subject she'd never written about or had any direct experience with, but it was impossible to pass on such an opportunity. She told her agent she would take this one assignment but then immediately return to her awful advertising plan. No more surprises, please.

A mask of tree-dappled sunlight shifted on Adjoua's face, and Sharif pictured the sick baby floating inside her. Adjoua then rolled her face into his stomach, as if seeking to smother her reality. He looked at the sky, which sometimes broke up the helplessness that collected in his chest when Adjoua's sadness entered him. He counted ten breaths while staring at a cloud that looked exactly like a brain. Two seagulls rode the air with outstretched wings, rocking side to side. A decade in New York City and it still momentarily confused him to spot seagulls. The city hid the ocean so well.

Adjoua spoke a muffled sentence into his gut. He said, "Sorry, my love. I didn't catch that."

Rolling her mouth out of him, she repeated, "Yes, the email needs to make it clear that Judy's clean. That there's nothing wrong with him."

"Right. Yeah."

She twisted further away to peek in on Judy—first with melancholy, then with doting amusement. Judy's chin lay on his white-socked legs. His forlorn whale-eyes scanned left to right, eyebrows bobbing in turn. She caressed his massive head once before pulling her hand away to tend to an itch on her belly. Scratching at her stretched skin, sunlight shattered and reconstructed her wedding band over and over.

Sharif searched old emails Adjoua had written asking friends to dog-sit over the low-budget holidays they used to take. They'd managed to never pay a stranger to look after Judy, one of the many frugalities that allowed them to make rent. They had discussed leaving the Lower East Side for a neighborhood that didn't devour 75 percent of their combined income on the first of the month. But moving itself was prohibitively expensive: penalties for breaking the lease, moving costs, first and last months' rent, security deposit. Besides, even if a new landlord would accept such financially precarious tenants, the only places Sharif and Adjoua could afford now were so far outside the city that they might as well leave New York altogether.

Each time Sharif and Adjoua had found Judy a weekend caretaker, always at the eleventh hour, it was a tiny miracle. Now all those tiny miracles resulted in a pool of friends who would never take Judy again. Everyone found Judy instantly lovable, but no one who'd lived with him signed up for a second tour. Adjoua's parents weren't an option because they spent over half the year in Côte d'Ivoire, and Sharif's parents and brother lived out of state with pets of their own that they preferred Judy not kill.

Sharif copied and pasted a paragraph Adjoua had written a year earlier, prefacing it with,

> My wife wanted to add this:
> Judy is so cuddly and sweet. He barks, but rarely. He's not so great with dogs, cats, rabbits, ferrets, or any other domestic animal really (in fact, he wants to kill every one he sees). Speaking of killing, he kills mice and cockroaches. Really well.
> He responds to "come here," "no," and "sit" — treats (included in his bin) greatly increase his response time to these commands.
> Sometimes he dreams about chasing things and will woof in his sleep. It's alarming at first, then endearing.
> He's super housebroken (we take him out every 8 to 10 hours). Oh, and last thing, you'll notice he has a lipoma on his upper left shoulder — it doesn't hurt him and you should pretend it's not there. We had it aspirated and it's non-cancerous, just unsightly!

He attached a few pictures of Judy, then closed out the message:

> Sharif again. If you have any interest in meeting the old bear, or any questions or leads, please don't hesitate to reach out. Thanks so much for reading, and I'll see you around the office!
>
> Sharif Safadi
> Case Manager II
> 2242 Church Avenue, 4th Floor
> Brooklyn, New York 11226
> (718) 282-0108 Ext. 66125
> www.CAPPA.org

Sharif hit send, looked up, and was startled by a man standing two feet in front of them, staring down at Adjoua. The man's chest, neck, face, and head were a carbon copy of a Lenin bust, his bald head shining like white marble. Sharif bounced his thigh to get Adjoua to open her eyes and witness the live Lenin bust in their personal space, but she grumbled, No, I'm not ready. The man walked off. Sharif said Damn it, Adjoua opened her eyes and said What, and he said Never mind. He then skimmed two news notifications that confirmed the world was still run by sociopaths and their president was still that amoral man.

The sun had been eclipsed at some point. An edge of it now slipped past the cloud that used to resemble a brain and was now a brain on fire. Light struck Sharif in the eyes, and heat pounded his chest. Time to march the flock out of the park, get everyone safely across the street, and trail Adjoua up six flights of stairs while carrying 150 pounds of dog. Adjoua would ascend, holding her belly like a prize-winning pumpkin. She'd work on two pieces of writing today. One, an op-ed for the *New York Times* about racist police; the other, online copy for a to-go sushi restaurant called No More Mr. Rice Guy.

To Adjoua, he said, "Okay, my love. Message sent. Shall we get going?"

Adjoua's eyes had clenched again. "You're going to ask for your raise today?"

"Definitely," he said. He waited a beat before reiterating, in as spirited a voice he could muster, that it was time to seize the day. That's when he heard Adjoua, who never cried, make a whimpering sound.

2.

SHARIF WALKED DOWN Grand Street through Chinatown to catch his train. It was trash day, and the city air had a wounded aspect. Foul smells hung in pockets of humidity that clung to his face. His phone alerted him to another rejection to the friends and family version of his Dog Care email:

> I'm so sorry you guys are going through this. You know we loved looking after Judy last time, but sadly things are a little cramped at the apartment since the twins came . . .

On the sidewalk, streams of commuters flowed around piles of garbage bags, slow-moving seniors, Russian and French tourists, and phone-distracted locals. Live eels were laid out to suffocate on a bed of crushed ice. A fishmonger slung a bucket of brown water at the remnants of a shrimp stir-fry on the ground, splashing Sharif's shoes.

Sharif said, "Come on, man, make an effort," but the fishmonger showed no sign of hearing.

The weather turned with cartoonish rapidity, clouds multiplying and meshing and abscessing a heavy gray. Sharif made it underground into the Grand and Chrystie station at the first boom of thunder. The clouds dumped on the city floor above. He could hear it was the kind of sharp rain that bounced off the street and up to the height of your shirt. At this point, it made no sense to run back for his umbrella and raincoat. He'd be soaked and late. He had already been taking a lot of time off for medical appointments. Missing work meant rescheduling with clients who were in crisis or asking overburdened coworkers to cover his caseload. All he seemed to do lately was ask for favors. It didn't feel good, and certainly didn't bode well for the raise he needed.

Sharif always got a seat on the Brooklyn-bound B train since most commuters were headed the opposite direction into Manhattan. The same riders sat in his car every morning, sitting in their usual configuration to align with the street exit at their respective stop. He tunneled underground with these familiar strangers, then clacked along the Manhattan Bridge. The rain obscured both boroughs on either side of the East River. He thought of Adjoua's weeping face from earlier that morning.

The Church Avenue station was muggy. The uneven cement floors made puddles with the leaking ceiling. People who'd thought to check the weather were wrapped in shapeless ponchos, plastic bags, and raincoats. They shuffled together, forming the collective hobble of wet city-dwellers headed for a narrow staircase.

On the ground-level floor of the station, he assumed the three sets of double door exits were bottlenecked because people needed extra time to prepare before stepping into the rain. But as he inched closer, he saw the other reason. Just beyond the second exit door window stood a man in a hoodie blocking the door with his back. Sharif felt a surge of indignation powerful enough to give him a small shock. Working to subdue his overreaction, he told himself that no one is that brazenly inconsiderate. The man is keeping dry under the station's awning and is unaware that he's blocking traffic. A simple oversight. Sharif pushed his way through the crowd to tell the man he could come inside and keep dry by the MetroCard machines until the rain passed. He knocked on the glass and said, "Excuse me, sir," while pushing the door until it tapped the man's heels.

The man glanced over his shoulder at Sharif. Backlit by the bright gray sky with his hoodie up, he was faceless. He shook his head and said, "No, no," as if batting away an irrelevant idea.

Sharif's indignation resurged. Injustices, even minor ones, maybe especially minor ones, turned him hot. The words that came out next didn't reflect the boiling happening inside, but his tone came close: "That's all *right!*" he said, pushing the door harder.

The man dropped out of view so quickly it was like a trapdoor had opened beneath him. Sharif opened the door further, revealing the calamity he'd triggered. A tower of newspapers this man clearly intended to sell today had been tipped off the short stoop under the awning and into a massive puddle. The man was crouched, reaching for his day's livelihood, half of which was underwater while the rest got pelted by rain.

Sharif squeezed onto the other side of the door and dropped down next to him. Both men managed to hook their fingers into the strings binding the newspapers. They heaved the stack up, but the strings snapped. Papers spilled like entrails back into the puddle. The man and Sharif yelled *No, no* to commuters pushing from behind.

3.

THE FLOW OF foot traffic ceased between trains. Ten graceless seconds later, Sharif and the man were staring at the wads of newspaper they'd dragged into the station. Unable to look at the man directly, Sharif slapped at his pant legs, as if that might dry and clean them at once. Sharif was mostly feeling his own embarrassment and guilt.

"I'm sorry about this."

Speaking more to himself than to Sharif, the man said, "What can I do?" His Haitian accent was in the slight forward-pushing, francophone sound of "do."

Sharif asked how much the newspapers would set him back. The man said, "I believe my boss invested twenty. He wanted me to sell for forty."

They finally looked at each other head-on under the station's fluorescent lights. The man's concern softened.

"Hey, it's you," he said with a touch of bemusement, lowering his hood.

"Yeah, hey," Sharif said, unable to place him right away. Of an unguessable age, the man had shorn hair and large wide-set eyes. Sharif would have believed him to be in his thirties as easily as his sixties. There was a baby-faced roundness to his cheeks, but he also had deep lines in his forehead, as if he was constantly looking up. His bulbous nose, cheeks, and far apart eyes created the illusion of a fish-eye view, even as the man stood at appropriate conversational distance. The effect contributed to the friendliness of his face. Yes, Sharif had definitely seen him before. At work, maybe?

Smiling in the way of someone who is a step ahead of you, the man said, "I was the one with the Idaho potato, remember?" He waited. "You thought it was a yam."

In rushed the complete memory. "Yes, of course!" Sharif had been doing intake at work that day, screening up to ten walk-ins an hour for program eligibility. His nonprofit, Church Avenue Professional Pathways Association (CAPPA), provided economic development services to low-income, unemployed New Yorkers. Most people came through their doors for help as a last resort, so Sharif always searched for a personalized icebreaker to put them at ease.

For this man—Emmanuel was his name—Sharif had commented on the foil-wrapped yam he held. Sharif said it looked like a good one, or maybe a big one, something that didn't make much sense but was delivered in a playful, hopefully stress-reducing tone. Emmanuel chuckled and said it was actually an Idaho russet potato. He'd baked it in a crockpot with a pinch of salt, two pats of butter, and finely chopped scallion—one of his favorite treats. Before Sharif had time to reflect on his yam assumption, Emmanuel explained that he hadn't come in today for help with employment. In fact, he currently had two jobs: one, as a delivery person (the soaked newspapers were for the bodega across the street from the station); the second, as a wheelchair escort at LaGuardia Airport. Emmanuel came to CAPPA because he'd heard of their referral network that included free immigration legal services. Sharif confirmed this was true, pulled the legal provider's folder from his cabinet, and was briefly taken aback by the discovery of Aberto Barbosa's business card pinned inside. Aberto was a highly regarded immigration attorney who also happened to be Adjoua's ex-boyfriend.

Sharif had met Aberto two weeks earlier at a work function. Aberto's firm had received its nonprofit accreditation and a private $2 million grant, making him someone who improved society and had loads of money. Sharif's exact professional fantasy. Sharif's boss, Merjem, called Aberto the rising star of his field. He's got all the necessary ingredients to be an influential player, she said. He's talented, hardworking, tall, handsome, and arrogant. More threatening to Sharif than any of this was the confounding fact that Aberto had been the one to end things with Adjoua. After Aberto left her heartbroken, only a month before Adjoua met Sharif, she trained Judy to climb a stepladder into bed with her. Judy would be the only man she needed. He'd lie under the covers with his head on his pillow and look back at her when he was ready for spooning. She put her chin on his thick neck and breathed him in, the top of his head always smelling of a wheat field.

Sharif never told Adjoua that Aberto was something of a bogeyman to him. He knew such insecurity would make him less attractive, and there were few things he avoided more than what might make him less attractive to his wife.

Lately, feeling unattractive seemed inevitable, given how inward, and ultimately distant, Adjoua became when stressed. They were opposites in this way. The more stress she felt, the deeper her libido got buried. When he was stressed, sex was the quickest path to alleviation and reconnection. It was perhaps the only activity that guaranteed a respite from anxiety, where for a short time his mind was occupied by only one thing. The less she was open to sex, the more he wandered into an insecurity that increased his desire for its reassuring effects. He'd made the mistake of giving voice to this dynamic the week before. She seemed to receive the topic as pressure she simply couldn't take on right now, but also as evidence of his obliviousness, as if he were proposing a meaningless diversion in the middle of an emergency, like offering to play video games during a house fire. Moments like these, the baby became a paradox; it unglued them day by day while seeming to be the only thing that kept her from leaving.

Sharif had clipped her ex-boyfriend Aberto's business card to the usual list of legal providers and handed it to Emmanuel because it was the right thing to do, and because he wouldn't have to see the card again. He only noticed the Idaho potato had been left on his desk when Emmanuel was already halfway out the door. He called after him, but Emmanuel told him to enjoy it, thanking him again for the list of resources. Sharif did peek into the foil a couple hours later when he was off intake. After a moment's hesitation, he bit into the soft, lightly salted, buttery, still-warm potato. He found himself closing his eyes and chewing slowly, almost sensually. It was the most satisfying potato he'd ever had.

"Oh my God," Sharif said to Emmanuel now. "What a crazy way to bump into you. How have you been?"

"Well"—he shrugged at his newspapers—"ups and downs, you know. This is life. How are things with you?"

"Fine, fine. I never thanked you for that potato. It was delicious. I keep meaning to get one of those crockpots."

"You won't regret it. I cook everything in this."

They nodded at each other for a while. Sharif started thinking out loud about money before deciding what he thought the fairest solution was for the newspapers: "I only have a couple dollars on me at the moment, but maybe—"

"Oh, no no. I should have brought the papers in right away. This wasn't your mistake."

Emmanuel's generous interpretation of events triggered an outsize sense of reciprocity, deciding it for Sharif. "No, I want to reimburse you. My bank is up the street." He could see Emmanuel hesitating, which made him all the more determined. "Look, it's cleared up outside. Come on. We'll only be a minute."

4.

Re: Dog Care

I pitched this to Dylan but he found some nonsense on the Internet about big dogs eating babies and . . .

THE WORST OF the rain moved west, still falling in curtains a block from the station. Sharif's shoulders and face relaxed in acceptance of the remaining drizzle as he and Emmanuel walked down Church Avenue, passing the Checkers, T-Mobile, Meat Palace, Palm Jewelry, a soul food buffet, a beauty shop, and sneaker stores that seemed replicated in hundred-yard intervals. Dollar cabs honked and slowed for people who were identifiably Caribbean, West African, Bengali, and Pakistani. Past and current clients greeted Sharif with warm smiles, fraternal head nods, and waves.

The sidewalk in front of the fruit and vegetable market was crowded enough for Sharif and Emmanuel to get separated. Emmanuel was trapped between a man pushing a shopping cart of eggplants and an old woman sitting at a card table smoking a cigarillo and selling bags of black-eyed and pigeon peas. Sharif waited for him between a blighted building and an empty lot littered with plastic wrappers, Styrofoam cups, and chicken bones. As Emmanuel navigated the jam, Sharif saw something in the weary kindness of his face that contained both goodness and disappointment. He felt a push of kinship toward him, for he too was good and disappointed.

Sharif's disappointment was accompanied by his resistance to a world that did not reward goodness as it should. If Sharif had created the world, people would be exactly as healthy and prosperous and celebrated as they were kind, honest, and generous. Intellectually, he knew this was a childish fantasy, but on a deep emotional level he could not accept the unfair order of real life. Of late, this nonacceptance seemed to rumble beneath everything, amplified by Adjoua's growing disquiet and the countdown to their baby's arrival.

Re: Dog Care

If I traveled less, I'd totally take Judy-pie. But it would be unfair to him . . .

Emmanuel extracted himself from the jam-up of local commerce by hopping down into the street between parked cars and traffic and walking around a small construction site encircling a manhole. His hoodie was unzipped now, and Sharif saw his T-shirt had Dragon Ball Z characters on it that had clearly been drawn with markers. Sharif asked about it, and Emmanuel was visibly pleased by the question. "My boy made that himself."

"Wow, he's really good."

Emmanuel glowed. "It is one of his talents."

Across the street stood a man named Carlos who was nearly seven feet tall. Shirtless and glistening from the rain, Carlos maintained his crooked smile as he leaned on his multiple-point cane, wearing a red Kangol faux-fur bucket hat and plaid pajama bottoms. His rib cage was both broad and pointy, the width of two barrel-chested men's, but he was also severely pigeon-chested. A sharp point of bone, like the bow of a boat, jutted out about a foot. He called to Sharif in his giant's voice, "Hey, buddy! Got some work for me today?"

"Sure!" Sharif said. "Come to the office, I'm headed there now." They went through this whenever they crossed paths.

Carlos said, "Ah, for sure, man! Tomorrow! You'll see me there tomorrow without fail!" He laughed. Sharif gave him a dollar through their ritual hand slap. Carlos said, "All right, fam, good lookin' out." He laughed again and the ritual was complete. Sharif's hand sustained the physical memory of Carlos's long, thin fingers for a block or two.

As Sharif and Emmanuel walked by a restaurant called Chinese Food, Sharif asked if he managed to get in touch with any of those legal service providers he'd given him. It turned out Emmanuel had started working with Adjoua's ex-boyfriend, Aberto. "He's a good, successful, brilliant man," Emmanuel said. "He's helping me a lot."

While Sharif sincerely wanted Emmanuel to solve whatever immigration problem he had, he also noticed the chugging of his heartbeat he felt when reminded of Aberto. It happened every time he saw Aberto's name light up Adjoua's phone. Early on in their relationship, Sharif had asked how often she still spoke to Aberto. She said she didn't know, maybe twice a month or so? Sharif knew it was considerably more than that. He later asked if she still shared early drafts of her writing with Aberto, and she said yes. She then studied his face before sharing that she wasn't one of those people who pretended her exes were dead. That's not going to be an issue, is it? He acted surprised and mildly offended by her feeling the need to say that. And then said, Of course not. I'm not like that. I was just curious.

Between a pawnshop and a copy store doubling as a bilingual tax-assistance business, an old guy wearing a pink T-shirt that said #CRAYCRAY in glittery blue handed Emmanuel a flyer. It advertised a high-paying career in the private security sector after an initial investment of $399 for a Security Guard Certification. Sharif told Emmanuel, "New York residents can get the same certification for free through a city program and a handful of community-based organizations. That guy's employer is profiting off the information gap in this community." As soon as it was out of his mouth, he felt foolish. He'd heard the arrogance in his tone and understood it was linked to a stupid sense of competition with Aberto. Despite this self-awareness, his mind immediately searched for ways to mine Emmanuel for more information on Aberto without sounding insecure to his new friend. Then his phone rang. Adjoua.

"Excuse me for a second," Sharif said while answering.

People shuffled and chattered on Adjoua's end, which was explained when she said, "I'm in the hospital."

"What? Why?" He had stopped and said these words both into the phone and to a small man walking by. The man held an extra-large movie theater popcorn bucket and stopped too, locking eyes with Sharif.

Adjoua said, "My water broke."

Sharif said, "But we've still got four weeks," as though this logically overrode what she'd conveyed. The small man grabbed a handful of some type of groundnut from his popcorn bucket, threw them in his mouth, and carried on with his day. Thoughts of Adjoua's body betraying her swirled and crashed in Sharif's head. "Are you at New York–Presbyterian? You took a car?"

"Yeah. They say it'll be a while before the baby actually comes, so there's no need to rush here or anything." She sounded heavily weighted by apathy. Her fear sometimes expressed itself as exaggerated indifference.

"I'll be right there."

"Can you go to the apartment first and put together my labor kit? The list of what I need is on the fridge."

"Of course. Why didn't you call me from the cab? Will you put the doctor on the phone for a second?"

"I haven't seen a doctor."

"But your water broke."

"No one seems impressed by that."

He was punched with the smell of fried food as someone exited the Texas Chicken & Burgers he and Emmanuel stood in front of now. "Well, I'm impressed. I'll get your stuff and come as soon as I can."

"You have time. Really. The nurses think I'm many hours from delivery." This flew in the face of everything Sharif understood about water breaking. How did he still know so little about pregnancy? If he couldn't be a partner who provided financial stability for his family, couldn't he at least be a knowledgeable one? She said, "I don't know what we're going to do about Judy." Her shell of indifference cracked, exposing raw fear that seemed to say to him: Why can't you protect me?

At this, a kind of daze fleeced over Sharif, and his mind stalled out underneath. He lost control over his body next. It floated slowly down the sidewalk like a sleeping fish. A home recording of a man with an accent that Sharif would have guessed was Indian played on loop through a blown speaker, promising to repair any, Any, ANY, broken phone for five dollars. Sharif was at risk of sitting down where he stood. Then came a to-and-fro between helplessness and a refusal to give in. Adjoua needed a decisive, problem-solving partner. The back and forth of yes and no, and fight and quit, filled his head up and down and side to side, whirling like a cloud of gnats.

A yellow-eyed pigeon walked by in that jerky, stop-motion style of walking birds. The intensity of reality was somehow distancing him from reality. He looked up at the sky, hoping to ground himself. The sun, even from behind gray clouds, strained his eyes, and he dropped his gaze. Emmanuel's face was there, friendly, with that fish-eye lens quality. Sharif stared at the tip of his nose. The storm clouds mapping Sharif's brain started to clear. The parts of him that wanted to quit were slipping away, losing, and he became increasingly focused and numb, reduced to a simple and narrow point of view. Depersonalized but mission-driven.

Adjoua said, "Hello?"

"I'll handle Judy."

"Well, okay, but we need an actual plan."

Putting Judy in any of the humane boarding kennels for more than a couple of nights would decimate their monthly budget. He looked at Emmanuel and thought, What about him? Could he do it? No. That's an insane idea. Cars and pedestrians paused, others hastened. They all looked ridiculous moving around the city like this, rolling in their boxes or swinging their arms, enacting their days without intention. He said to Adjoua, "I said, I'll handle it. I'll call you when I'm on my way to you."

"Oh. Okay," she said, sounding both reassured and a little intimidated by his assertiveness.

They hung up, and Emmanuel asked if everything was all right. With a strange, dispassionate force, Sharif said, "My wife is having a baby earlier than expected."

Emmanuel nodded, having picked up on that from the call. "Congratulations. Will this be your first?"

"Yeah." A purple ring of light strobed in his field of vision and then fucked off.

"Go be with her. Don't worry about this money."

"The bank's right there," he said, pointing across the street. As they waited for the white walk signal, a group of adolescent boys approached the opposite crosswalk with an overstated swagger that betrayed their wish to be older. When the leader stopped at the crosswalk, the others bumped into his backpack like a row of ducklings.

Chandice, the Bank of America security guard, held the door for them. She had been Sharif's client a week after emigrating from Jamaica. She extended a fist bump, and Sharif reciprocated without feeling.

He inserted his card and punched in his pin, wondering how to broach the subject of dog care with Emmanuel. The ATM did its rumbling as he stared into the mirror strips above the machine. The skin under his eyes was thin and bluish with skin-colored bumps. He thought of raw chicken and looked away. Facing Emmanuel as the ATM spat cash, he said, "The baby. My daughter. She's got cancer." The statement came out as a cold, anesthetized fact, like death itself.

A grave empathy furrowed Emmanuel's brow. He stepped in closer, offering a sense of privacy, which magnified the fish-eye effect and friendliness of his features. Sharif said, "I need someone to take my dog."

Emmanuel looked confused. "Let's move out of the way."

"What? Oh." A lady stood waiting for her turn at the ATM. Sharif took his money, and the two men moved aside. Without fully realizing the crazy request he was leading up to, Sharif said, "My wife and I aren't supposed to keep the dog during our daughter's treatment. I need him out of the apartment before bringing the baby home." He'd come this far. Why not ask. "Is there any chance you—or maybe someone you know and really trust—could look after him until I find a longer-term solution?"

Emmanuel was still catching up. "A dog."

Sharif pushed on, "I would pay you of course. Or, whoever looked after him. Sixty dollars a week? I'll pay two weeks up front. If I find something else before the two weeks are up, you'd keep the money. He's a great dog. All he needs is a place without other animals. Do you have pets?"

A scream hurtled through the floor-to-ceiling bank windows. An emaciated woman stood directly behind the window, screaming, *They'll do you in! They'll do you in! DO YOU IN!*

The bank's staff and customers stiffened. To the outside world, they must have looked like a glassed-in museum display. There was a collective exhalation of relief, followed by a few chuckles. It was merely an unarmed person in the throes of a mental health crisis. Chandice, the security guard, watched the woman with a flat affect. The screaming woman wore an oversize, faded black T-shirt with an image of the *Titanic* film poster on the front. She gestured wildly with an unlit, bent Newport 100 in her hand after she'd completed her warning. The scream and gesticulations were two distinct actions. Total tranquility came next, smoothing her features and slackening her arms and shoulders. She carried on down the sidewalk with a performative grace, walking aggressively on sunshine.

Emmanuel said, "Do you have a name for your daughter?"

"Zora," he answered. Emmanuel was the first person outside of the couple to hear the name.

Emmanuel smiled. "This is beautiful." He looked out the window where the screaming woman had been, and then at Chandice, who gently swayed as if hearing a pretty melody, before saying, "So what would I need to feed this dog?"

5.

EMMANUEL'S APARTMENT WAS a few blocks from CAPPA, which was a few blocks from the bank, but of course they needed to get Judy. Sharif ordered a car from his phone then went to withdraw another $120 from the ATM for Emmanuel, on top of the $40 he'd already given him for the newspapers. Seeing his $589.19 balance, he remembered he'd incur a penalty if he dropped below $500. The bank's logic never failed to embitter him: *We're afraid we have to charge you for running desperately low on funds.* He explained his predicament to Emmanuel and asked to pay $60 now and the second half in two days, after his next paycheck, reiterating that he'd pay in full even if he picked Judy up before the two-week period was over. Emmanuel accepted easily, as if money played no role in their zero-hour arrangement.

Sharif had already obliterated his daily budget. Anything beyond thirty dollars meant dipping into Adjoua's five thousand dollars of book advance savings later in the month. They had maintained her book money for over a year, borrowing against it, paying it back eventually, but never bumping it above five. After calculating the hundred-dollar weekly increase in expenses when the baby arrived, plus 20 percent of the $6,000 cost of Adjoua's delivery that their insurance didn't cover, he should be able to contribute seventy-five a month to their savings account if he secured the maximum possible raise at work of $10,000.

Last year, his job promotion from Case Manager I to Case Manager II had landed in his lap without him asking for it two days after Adjoua sold her book. In an irreverent celebration of their carefree and auspicious love, they eloped at City Hall that weekend. They were invincible. Life was full of rewards for happy, hardworking, in-love people like them. While Adjoua's faith in their good luck had dwindled precipitously in recent weeks, Sharif still held on to a belief that with grit, intention, and honesty, the luck of an easy life would be returned to them, perhaps even better than before, as a reward for what they endured. He half expected a doctor to call and say Zora's tests had been reviewed and the cancer was miraculously gone.

Sharif stood still while waiting for the car, but his heart pumped like he was running. Peripherally, he saw an animal carcass glistening in the road, a bird or squirrel. When he looked at it head-on, it proved to be a can of beans exploded by a car. He and Emmanuel got in the back of the Toyota Camry that pulled up, the driver's pop radio playing low, Mardi Gras beads clicking against the front windshield. iPads on the backs of the headrests baited them with multiple choice trivia: *The Eiffel Tower is in which of these cities...?* Sharif gave Emmanuel a cursory overview of Judy responsibilities: walks, meals, medications, supplements.

"He's unwell?" asked Emmanuel.

"Just old, creaky joints and whatnot. He's really hardy for his age, size, and breed actually. The most important thing to remember is to never let him near other animals. Dog owners are going to approach you and insist that everybody gets along with Bella or Lucky or Sparky or whoever. And it must be firmly communicated that Judy is dangerous."

"Okay." Then: "Is he really dangerous?"

"Yes. No. I mean. Only with nonhuman animals. He's never so much as growled at a human. You'll see, he's a teddy bear."

Emmanuel considered this for a moment, seeming to realize this wasn't as straightforward as he'd thought. "All right."

Surrounded by redbrick housing blocks, they rolled up Ocean Avenue too slowly for Sharif's liking. The southeast entrance of Prospect Park finally opened to their left. A bit further, a group of Rastafarians clustered around a bench on the sidewalk. A large, sunburned redheaded woman jaywalked in front of them with a baby tied to her back. She looked like Sharif's Aunt Cheryl who had drunk too much at Thanksgiving last year and went on and on about how beautiful Adjoua was, nearly shouting the words "*so* beautiful" at her. On the train home, Adjoua had told Sharif that "so beautiful" meant Black. As in, "I'm so excited to be in a comfortable environment with a friendly Black person! I always knew I wasn't racist!" Sharif had chuckled and said, But you are beautiful, so maybe that is what she meant. Adjoua shrugged and started reading her book. He didn't know what had just happened, if anything. Did she feel gaslit by his literal interpretation of Aunt Cheryl's drunken proclamation? Would it really have been better to agree that Cheryl didn't mean Adjoua was beautiful? Rationalizing that he had no reason to assume this was a particularly meaningful or uncomfortable exchange for her, and not wanting to interrupt her reading to force meaning or discomfort, Sharif let it go. He should have shut up in the first place.

Outside of the car, people walked and sat and talked as if this were some ordinary day. Sharif rehearsed the next twenty minutes of his life on loop: *Pick up Judy and labor kit stuff, bring everything to Emmanuel's, go to the hospital, be positive, be supportive, be confident, inspire calm.* While on loop, he simultaneously anticipated turns the driver would make, tracking the route on his phone while also batting away the parts of his mind that imagined how shocked Adjoua would be to learn Sharif had entrusted Judy to a man he'd known for an aggregate of fifteen minutes. What other option did I have under the circumstances, he eventually asked the image of her in his mind. I'm sorry I can't throw money at the problem. I'm sorry I'm not as financially successful as you'd suddenly like me to be, okay?

They cut between the park down Flatbush Avenue, passing the zoo and rose garden. A cardboard home on the sidewalk had the entangled legs of two lovers poking out.

Emmanuel spoke to Sharif with calm: "You know, I was quite nervous the day my son, Junior, was born. But I can tell you. Even if it's difficult raising a child, my life makes more sense than before. I feel at least twice as much purpose and care and fulfillment. This isn't so bad, right?"

Sharif stared at him, wondering how he had been so fortunate as to run into this angel of a man when he did.

The iPad trivia game asked, *Which following U.S. president never married and declined to run for a second term in office . . . ?* Emmanuel clicked on "James Buchanan" for a correct answer.

They took the roundabout at the Grand Army Plaza arc and exited down a stretch of one-story buildings peppered with markers of gentrification. Smoke shop, liquor store, all-organic grocer. Blighted building, Yemeni bodega, espresso bar. Begrimed deli, liquor store, yoga studio. And then construction, always construction. A permanent facet of the city. Adjoua had once mused out loud about what New York would be without its ongoing newness; its scaffolding, netted buildings, orange and yellow cranes posing like industrial artwork; boarded-off blocks with 150-foot holes for new foundations. She said if all signs of perpetual change ceased abruptly — no more alteration, preservation, growth — the city wouldn't be itself. There'd be an eerie quality, the source of which would take a while to put your finger on, like if suddenly all the pigeons disappeared. Whoa, Sharif said, that would be spooky. You should write a story about that. About what, she said. About New York City without construction or pigeons, he said. That's not really a story in and of itself, she said. I guess you're right, he said, but a super-interesting detail anyway. Thanks, baby. She smiled and kissed his cheek. That felt like a long time ago now. But even then, when Adjoua was buoyant and spontaneously kissing her husband, it was her ex-boyfriend, Aberto, who was her first reader of all her fiction drafts.

A text came in from Sharif's boss, Merjem. Sharif had completely forgotten he was due at work. He was meant to ask for a raise today. Instead, he was a no-show.

Merjem's message read: . . . Hey . . . you okay . . . ? Planning on coming in today . . . ?

All of the middle-aged immigrants in Sharif's life—his boss, coworkers, in-laws, father—used an abundance of ellipses in written communication. But Merjem took the crown. She never wrote a line without those impatient dots.

> I'm so sorry I didn't have a chance to reach out, Merjem! Adjoua went into labor this morning. I'm rushing to the hospital now.

> Wow!!! . . . Oh my God, congratulations!!! . . . She doing okay . . . ? . . . And what about the dog. . . . ?!?!!?

> Sorting it out now! Adjoua is great — more soon!

6.

EMMANUEL ENTERED THE apartment behind Sharif only to immediately step back out into the hall and shut the door. Sharif had not adequately prepared him for Judy's size, which was emphasized by the small space.

"He's really friendly, Emmanuel!" Sharif called through the door, trying to sound more jovial than desperate. He had dropped to his knees to intercept Judy, grabbing his midsection and flipping him so that his back lay against Sharif's chest and his legs splayed open on the floor. Sharif whispered, "Please be good, bubba." To Emmanuel he called again, "He's incredibly gentle, really! Come in whenever you're ready. The door's unlocked." He gave Judy a few loud pats, his thoughts coaching his other thoughts to conceal his impatience. He needed to make this experience easy and gratifying for Emmanuel.

The doorknob turned slowly, and Emmanuel poked his head back in. Sharif said, "He loves all people. Truly." Emmanuel smiled nervously, his body still shielded by the door. Putting on a show, Sharif spun Judy around so they were nose to snout and made some jaw-jutting caveman sounds. Judy sniffed the caveman's mouth once before slinging his tongue at it. After a direct hit, Sharif pulled back, laughing and congratulating Judy on getting him. Sharif hugged Judy around the neck, sincerely grateful for his dog's playful mood and corn chip breath, the most pleasant (and inexplicable) iteration Judy's breath took.

The left half of Emmanuel's body entered the apartment, right hand still on the outside knob. Sharif said, "You can even do annoying things to him, and he'll love it. Watch." He stuck three fingers between the black side-fat of Judy's mouth and jiggled it around, then inverted Judy's ears to give him an elfin look, then created a funnel around Judy's snout with his hands and forcefully blew air up his nose, causing Judy's eyes to blast open and his cheeks to flap rapidly. Adjoua called this the schnoz-blow. Sharif then squeezed Judy's head between his forearms. Judy pulled free from Sharif's trap, turned in a tail-chasing circle, sneezed, and returned for more, pummeling his giant crown into Sharif's chest. Nearly floored from Judy's headbutt, Sharif said, "He embraces any and all kinds of human touch. Come on, Emmanuel, you try." He worried Emmanuel had heard his pleading undertone.

"It's, wow. He's—I did not imagine he'd be so large," Emmanuel said as he made himself reenter fully, keeping the door cracked and his hand on the inside knob.

Sharif recognized the progress being made but was also feeling oppressed by the passage of time. His wife could be in active labor right now. Sharif said, "I'm going to let him come to you. He wants to say hello. Is that okay?" As soon as Emmanuel agreed, if only with a dubious head movement, Sharif released Judy, who moved quickly on their guest. Judy's entire back side wagged as his head gyrated ecstatically. Sharif saw how this could resemble a beast's approach to what it intended to eat. Judy nestled his neck against his new friend's shins and properly smeared the side of his body against Emmanuel's pants, leaving a streak of hair. Emmanuel had pinned himself against the door, thereby shutting himself in with little choice but to surrender. Sharif was glad for Judy's bullying affection. Emmanuel eventually bent toward Judy and touched the top of his neck with the back of his wrist. Judy then went for his best crowd-pleaser and flopped to his back on top of Emmanuel's feet, exposing his naked belly. This would be the moment Adjoua called him a little piggie-pie and began using all manner of baby talk. Sharif said, "He's making himself vulnerable to you. He feels safe."

Emmanuel took the bait and reached down to pat the pig belly with his fingertips. Judy wriggled left to right on his back, snorting like a gleeful ogre as gravity pulled down his top lips to reveal his canines. Emmanuel began to gain confidence, eventually crouching down fully. With increased fascination, he said, "It's like a bear. But also like a cow. Or pig."

"I know exactly what you mean!" Sharif stood and checked his phone for any updates from Adjoua. "I see him as those animals and a bunch of others. Rarely a dog."

Judy stopped snarling and shimmying to roll to his belly. He looked up at Emmanuel, who said, "In the eyes he looks like a sad child though. So human."

"Yeah." The two men pondered this for a quiet moment. Sharif said, "For reasons I don't understand, a lot of his cuteness and lovability seems to emanate from that sadness."

Snapping out of whatever social mode Sharif had briefly slipped into, his mind resumed its focused emergency setting. He texted Adjoua asking for an update, then dragged Judy's translucent bin of toys, food, bowl, meds, and dog bed to the door. Next, he moved through the labor kit list on the fridge: water spray, handheld fan, comfy white sneakers, sweat suit for Sharif, bendy paper straws, phone, charger, headphones, laptop, two hard-boiled eggs, granola bar, two dark color gowns, slippers, wool socks, old nightdress, old T-shirt, massage oil, birth ball and pump, lip balm, 2 silk head scarves, face creams + serums, toothbrush + Sensodyne, V-shaped pillow + two regular pillows.

Sharif found everything relatively easily, including the hard-boiled eggs in the fridge that Adjoua routinely restocked. He stuffed all that would fit into two backpacks, used a garbage bag for the pillows, and then called Adjoua. Landing on her voicemail twice while shuttling everything downstairs, he cycled through possibilities: She could be pushing out the baby right now, or having an emergency C-section for some reason; maybe she's just having a clarifying conversation with the doctor, or is in the restroom without her phone. He thought of calling his in-laws to ask if they had any updates, but they probably didn't, and asking would only make them worry. After leaving everything on the sidewalk for Emmanuel to load in the car he'd called, he searched for the hospital number online and called the front desk. Just then Adjoua texted: On the phone with my parents. Everything's fine. Still a ways to go before delivering. Where's Judy?

He hung up the call and replied, Oh good. I'm taking him to a friend's now. What friend?

From work. Hands are full. I'll fill you in when I'm there. It's a great situation!

Emmanuel sat up front in the idling car. Across the street, a man stood in a parking space to block the car that was clearly angling to take it. The man shouted at the car's windshield, "Bring it the fuck on then!"

Sharif and Judy squeezed into the back next to the birth ball. Presumably, the dog bin, dog bed, backpacks, and garbage bag of pillows were in the trunk. He had warned the driver that he'd be traveling with "a dog and some bags," but the driver was visibly displeased by how they had overwhelmed his space. Sharif couldn't rig up the seat cover he usually used to prevent Judy's hair from sticking to the upholstery. The cover was made to connect to the front and back seat headrests, creating a little hammock that kept Judy and all of his shedding neatly contained. But it was too crowded to clip into place as designed. As they pulled out, the car across the street was blaring its horn at the man standing in the parking space with his arms outstretched. The guy holding down the horn in his car used his free hand to point at his opponent with a thrusting motion, then flipped him off, then pointed and flipped him off again. The repeated gesture communicated, *You. Fuck you. You. Fuck you. You. Fuck you.*

Sharif usually thought of this as a friendly city. New Yorkers were quick to smile and help strangers, undeserving of their reputation as rude and abrasive. But today this was a place of belligerence.

Judy began whimpering and readjusting compulsively, making a wet clicking sound at the top of his inhalations where his nasal cavity and throat met. It was disgusting even to Sharif. The thirty-minute ride felt so much longer and was increasingly claustrophobic. He was sure Emmanuel was having second thoughts.

Unloading at Emmanuel's, it became clear that the driver's annoyance had multiplied. Sharif asked him to wait downstairs nonetheless, assuring him that he'd return alone. He needed to get to Adjoua without further delay. The driver didn't respond at first. By the time Sharif and Emmanuel brought Judy and all of the dog gear to the entrance of the building, the driver was on all fours in his back seat, slapping at Judy's hair with a rag and shaking his head in dismay. Sharif knew those hairs would merely pop up in the air, do some slow flips and spins, and stick to the upholstery elsewhere. Only an industrial vacuum cleaner, a lint roller, and forty-five minutes could make this right.

Sharif made a show of scolding Judy, "Look at the mess you made!"

Showing no sign of remorse, Judy yawned and gave a vigorous body shake, relieved to be out of the car.

Still on all fours, the driver looked over his shoulder. "Please get the rest of your things out. I won't wait for you."

Re: Dog Care

You're still in need, right? I have a really promising candidate in mind who FUCKING LOVES DOGS!!! I'll circle back as soon as I get deets!

Sharif typed a response with one hand: Amazing, standing by!

The lobby walls in Emmanuel's building were a glossy brown reminiscent of Yoo-hoo. Judy rode the elevator to the fourteenth floor without fuss. Emmanuel said, "Good boy," to him, relieving Sharif of his fear that Emmanuel could still back out.

Sharif sometimes teased Adjoua for calling Judy a good boy for standing or lying there. She'd come home and her face would light up at the sight of Judy snoring on the kitchen floor like some drunk in a bear costume. She'd drop her bags, do a controlled fall into child's pose, nestle her face into his neck rolls, and tell him what a good boy he was. Judy's goodness had nothing to do with his behavior. He was good because his mere presence filled Adjoua with a purifying love. Sharif wished that he could have this same effect on Adjoua.

Re: Dog Care

Shit, SHIT, *SHIT!!!* Please disregard my last email! False lead. Just learned my "promising candidate" joined the Peace Corps and is moving to Nepal next month. I SUCK.

The elevator opened on the fourteenth floor with a tired bing.

7.

THERE WAS A POWERFUL stew smell on Emmanuel's floor. Every third ceiling light worked, creating long stretches of dimness. Sharif imagined Adjoua shaking her head.

Once at Emmanuel's door, a little girl in the apartment across the hall poked her head out. She stared at Judy with enormous eyes of fascination and terror. Emmanuel said hello, but she didn't reply. All of her focus was on Judy. There was no sign of her even registering the two men's presence. She had thin braids and a circle of a face. All of her features were circles, in fact. Circle eyes, nose, ears, mouth. She reminded Sharif of photos he'd seen of Adjoua as a child, before womanhood sharpened her cheekbones, elongated her eyes into slightly asymmetrical feline shapes, and strengthened her nose (among his favorite and Adjoua's least favorite traits). Judy's old, slow-moving head turned to face the girl, causing her to gasp and slam the door. Emmanuel whispered to Sharif that he shouldn't be offended. She had never once acknowledged him in the six months she'd lived there with her foster mother. He said, "I think she's a little . . ." and then, not unkindly, made a hand gesture by his head that suggested she might be touched.

The first thing Sharif noticed when they entered Emmanuel's apartment was the giant water stain on the wall facing them. Starting at the baseboard and intersecting with an electrical socket, the dark stain climbed the wall like a gnarled spine. When the spine hit the ceiling, it splayed out into moth wings, spanning at least twelve feet, swelling the ceiling paint into thousands of blister-like bubbles. It looked alive and dead at once. Adjoua's face returned, her wide eyes glaring a light on how terrible she found Sharif's idea. No, he pushed back, he had gotten a clear signal that Emmanuel was a good and trustworthy man. That's what you go on. That's what matters. Judy's well-being is in no way impacted by an ugly water stain, or a mildew smell. He needs kindness, food, water, relief walks, and a pet-free space. He'll get all of that here.

A small kitchen with linoleum flooring occupied the right side of the interior. The left side was the living room space covered in brown wall-to-wall carpeting. Judy was mashing his nose against Emmanuel's carpet now, vacuuming for information. To the left of the water stain was a small window and fire escape, facing the identical NYCHA building across the alley. Against the living room wall was a cat-tattered black pleather sofa with a pillow and blankets crammed to one end. A small coffee table stood in front of it with a ten-inch TV on top, its wire crawling across the carpet to plug into the outlet intersecting the water stain. There were two doors on either side of the sofa. One was shut and decorated with coloring book pages of Dragon Ball Z characters and a bubble letter sign that read, *Junior's Room*. The other had an unfinished wooden cross hanging on it and was left ajar, revealing bathroom tiles. Emmanuel probably slept out here on the sofa, which meant he or his son would be subjected to Judy's all-night tongue-clucking marathons. Sharif felt guilty that he had not warned Emmanuel about that, yet he didn't warn him now either.

Judy finished aspirating the carpet and collapsed with a satisfied sigh. Chin resting on his wrists, clucking his tongue already, he'd adapted to his new environment. Sharif spoke to the Adjoua in his mind: See? He's fine.

He disrupted Judy's contentment to show Emmanuel how to put on the no-pull harness, then removed it and asked Emmanuel to give it a try. Emmanuel understood where all the straps and buckles went on his first attempt. Sharif had needed to watch three videos to make sense of the S&M-looking rig. Continuing to be as thorough as Adjoua would have expected, they took Judy out for a practice walk. The little Adjoua look-alike from across the hall peeked her head out again, having surely heard the jangling of Judy's harness. This time, she aimed a phone as tall as her face at Judy. Her jaw hanging open, she carefully filmed the behemoth mere feet from her home.

Downstairs, Sharif checked his phone for updates from his wife. He showed Emmanuel how to wear the poo bag like a glove. Seeing that Emmanuel hadn't considered picking up Judy's shit before now, he felt a twinge of guilt. He then reiterated the importance of avoiding other animals, especially big dogs. He also said that it might feel cruel to deprive Judy of whatever bone or sludge or pizza crust he had rightfully discovered on their walks, but it was imperative that Judy only eat the food from his bin: the raw freeze-dried grain-free organic bison kibble ($79 per three-week supply) and the organic Blue Buffalo trail treats ($23 per pack of six). Despite how anxious Adjoua had been about their finances, it never seemed to cross her mind to stop buying Judy the most expensive version of everything.

Back upstairs, the little Adjoua across the hall poked her head out again to film Judy. She still kept most of her body behind the door, in case Judy blitzed her. Sharif said, "You can come say hi if you want. He's really friendly." But it was as if Sharif hadn't spoken at all. Her attention remained solely fixed on Judy through the camera's viewfinder. Judy gave her a glance, and she slammed the door on him. This time, a woman's voice from inside could be heard saying, "What is it, sweetie?" The peephole darkened and the woman drew a sharp breath. "Oh, Jesus."

As Sharif showed Emmanuel how to feed Judy and in what order to mix in the supplements ($2.07 per meal), he asked, "You think Junior will be comfortable around him?"

Emmanuel said, "I'm more worried about how he'll react when you take him away." He laughed. "My son loves animals and has the biggest heart. Too big sometimes."

"That doesn't sound like the worst problem to have in a son."

"No," he said, smiling, "I guess not. My wife used to say her goal was to raise a compassionate man. And Junior is well on this path."

Sharif understood now that Emmanuel's wife was dead. It somehow increased Sharif's connection to him. "That's beautiful." The two men nodded and shared the eye contact of bonded strangers. Sharif said, "Well, if you don't have any questions, I'd better get going. I'm truly grateful for your help. Oh, we should probably exchange numbers."

"Of course. I'll get my phone reconnected today," he said, patting the pocket with the cash Sharif had given him.

He again saw Adjoua staring at him like he'd condemned their dog to a terrible fate.

After trading numbers, the men shook hands, and Sharif told Judy to be a good boy. In the hall, walking through dark patches between functioning lights, Adjoua's judgmental expression reappeared. In the elevator, he mumbled, "This is what we could afford, okay? I'm doing my best. I never promised you I'd be rich."

8.

AS SHARIF WALKED through the metal detector in the hospital lobby, a security guard poked around his backpacks and garbage bags with a metal stick, then gave the birth ball a whack. The information desk person directed Sharif to Adjoua, and he rode to the eighteenth floor. He found her in a curtained-off space, still pregnant and intact. In his relief, he allowed himself a moment to take her in through the gap in the curtain before announcing his presence.

The weight she'd gained from the pregnancy suited her, giving her skin a subtle stretch that made her cheeks seem to emit even more light than usual. She stood with her palms on her lower back, bent forward, looking over her ballooned midsection at the floor. She was absorbed in some anxious corner of her big, beautiful head. It wasn't long ago that he could make her giggle by calling her head big. She'd respond in a childlike tone, "My grandmother made it!" Which was partly true. At birth, Adjoua had been handed to her Grand-mère Mariam for head shaping. Grand-mère Mariam had gently worked Adjoua's soft skull into the desired shape for a couple hours every day over a few months. Sharif was amazed that anyone could have the gumption to shape a human head by hand. Had Grand-mère Mariam received training? Was there consensus on the ideal shape? As it turned out, Adjoua's head was Grand-mère Mariam's first. And while Sharif was a great admirer of Grand-mère Mariam's work, he was not open to her or anyone else molding Zora's head.

Whatever was happening in Adjoua's head now caused her shoulders to tense up nearly to her ears. Sharif couldn't have said when his love for her had coalesced with those shoulders and the soft neck they protected, and her head, and her perfect nose and thighs and stumpy toes. When had he lost the distinction between her physicality and her personhood? When had he started getting absorbed in her wholeness through her individual body parts? As these parts swelled or discolored throughout the pregnancy, he found himself cherishing them more. And when he imagined them aging, he loved them more still. Change exposed vulnerability, and her vulnerability deepened his attachment.

A barely perceptible scar ran vertically from the right side of Adjoua's top lip. Climbing halfway to her nose, it was the width of a light pencil line and gently raised. She got it when she was three, in Côte d'Ivoire. She'd been standing on the patio of her family's compound, eating cubed mango that her father cut for her. Only he prepared her fruit properly. At the end of meals, their cook would come out with a cutting board, knife, and fruit. Her father would announce, "Ah, yes, my duties are incomplete," and laugh. Adjoua examined the way he peeled and sliced as though it were a precise choreography that required her supervision. He loved when she chastised him for peeling too quickly or slowly, cutting a piece unevenly or in the wrong shape.

After one of these fruit preparation sessions, she tottered out front with her mango bowl. The compound's guard dog, a Doberman Adjoua's parents had let her name Toutou, walked up to investigate. Toutou wasn't allowed on the patio, but he and Adjoua had a secret friendship. Or, at least, Adjoua's toddler mind was under the impression it was secret. She gave him a piece of mango from her bowl that he rapidly swallowed. After Adjoua gave him another, giggling at his animalness, she brought a third piece to her lips and hummed at him through the fruit like a kazoo. Toutou understood the gesture as another offering and quickly grabbed the mango resting on her lips. They repeated this, Adjoua's giddiness expanding each time Toutou's hot breath and wet nose and lips and whiskers touched her. His excitement increased too, and whether she leaned forward or puckered her lips, or he overshot his mark on his own, the result was pierced skin. The bowl shattered on the patio. Toutou started whimpering before Adjoua screamed. Her father appeared with the fruit knife, grabbed the scruff of Toutou's neck and plunged the blade beneath his jaw. It was only after her father had dropped to his knees and stabbed twice more, ending Toutou's shocked life, that he looked up at Adjoua's bleeding face.

This was her earliest memory. Subsequent events — the rush to the hospital, the two stitches, her parents' fear of uneven scarring — were a mishmash of Adjoua's imagination, photographs from that period, and the story her parents recounted. Only her playful feeding of Toutou and her father's aberrant loss of control remained true and vivid in her memory. She'd never seen her father so much as raise his voice before or since then.

Her parents said it didn't happen like that. They said Toutou had gone crazy, rabies maybe. Another time they said the compound's foreman abused Toutou, and that's why he snapped. Her father had saved her life. Adjoua didn't insist, but she was certain their narrative was false. It was her father who had lost himself, she knew. Sharif couldn't imagine being so confident about a memory from age three, but he perceived no trace of doubt in her.

She had included a variant of this memory in her debut novel, *Red-Out*. She changed the mango cubes to chicken shreds, the Doberman to a German shepherd, Toutou to Empereur, and the killer of the dog to the family cook. Despite her parents' pride at her publishing a book, and the two hundred copies they bought and distributed among friends and family (single-handedly earning back her book advance), they never suggested they recognized details in the book from their life. It remained unclear whether they didn't want to talk about what they found or hadn't read it. Adjoua had never known them to read novels. Her mother occasionally read books about Catholic saints, and her father self-help books about corporate leadership.

It was when Adjoua told Sharif the story behind her scar, on their fourth date, that he admitted to himself that he'd fallen in love. There are few things that more clearly reveal how you feel about someone than imagining them hurt, scared, or alone.

Re: Dog Care
You know I would take Judy in a heartbeat if he wouldn't try to kill Pepper or Dolly . . .

Sharif again thought of how uneasy it would make Adjoua to learn where he'd left Judy. He felt the strain of their finances, the fact that he hadn't more urgently asked for the raise he needed, the sick baby arriving a month early. His anxiety circled his concern for Adjoua's health and began its descent to that ugly runway in his mind reserved for his fear of losing her in this absurd world where unfairness struck at random. A runway that exposed that he would never feel he'd gotten enough time with her.

It was the guarantee of loss inherent to love, of being shortchanged, that Sharif found viscerally unacceptable. He'd been approaching this unacceptable fact with increasing frequency, but also brevity. He couldn't stand it for long. He thought love was supposed to give you strength. But nothing weakened him more. One moment he'd be enraptured in Adjoua's necessary existence, and the next it was as if he were chained to a tree out of reach from where she sank in a pit of quicksand. Powerless, useless, imploding. Adjoua had dismantled his faith system that all lives had equal intrinsic value. No, he now understood, some were much more valuable than others.

9.

WHEN SHARIF ANNOUNCED himself, it had no discernible influence on Adjoua's mental state. It was like he'd been with her all morning. Back when she was less stressed, and less distant, he enjoyed being taken for granted every once in a while. Her thoughtless expectation that he'd always be present and of service to her reduced him to a secure fact in her life, creating the warm illusion of permanence. Now he felt a bite of disappointment. They'd both had such rocky mornings on this high-stakes day, and he wished their reunion inspired relief, if not a minor celebration.

He closed the curtains around them as a throng of nurses and doctors flew by like Broadway dancers clearing a stage. Adjoua neither refused nor reciprocated his hug. She just let it happen to her. She smelled strongly in a way that made him miss her more. There was a unique ache to missing the person you were holding. Years ago, his first encounter with her body odor acted as an affirmation that he'd always be attracted to her. A salty, woody, delicately coarse odor that had the ability to intoxicate him into wild idiocy, devotion, and now desperation. She asked if he'd brought her deodorant. He said yes but held her a moment longer.

Speaking over the braids poking out of her headscarf, he said, "So what's the doctor saying?"

"I still haven't seen the doctor." She pushed him away. "But the nurses are saying two things that seem vaguely contradictory." She fished the

45

deodorant out of a backpack and applied it punishingly, flashing her taut balloon of a belly. "One, that I came here way too early. Two, that my blood pressure is high and I shouldn't go home."

"How high is it?"

"Pretty high. They said it could be stress."

"Right. That's okay. We'll just camp out then."

"I hate camping."

"You've never been, have you? Anyway, you know what I mean. Are your parents on the way?"

She finished the second armpit and lobbed the deodorant on the bed. "They'll be here in an hour." Adjoua's parents would be driving from their Farmington, New Jersey, residence. "They asked when your parents are getting here."

Sharif's parents had just started a thirty-day silent meditation retreat in Twentynine Palms, California. "I'll try them, but I know they're not checking phones or email."

Adjoua said, "You could call the meditation center."

"Yeah, let's see the doctor first and get some more information."

He felt lucky that his parents were off grid. He didn't have the bandwidth for them. They incessantly asked unhelpful, fear-based questions about the pregnancy, about Zora's future medical treatments and how hard that will be for their baby girl, and about Sharif and Adjoua's finances, as if constantly reminding Sharif of his challenges ("But aren't you worried, especially now, about how little you're earning?") assisted him in overcoming them. As visitors of New York City they required hand-holding. He had to find them a place to stay, recommend restaurants and activities daily, and give them step-by-step directions everywhere because they refused to learn how GPS worked. All of it was made worse by their refrain of not wanting to be a burden and asking how they could be of more help. This required Sharif and Adjoua to think up inessential tasks for them (like bringing Judy outside for a brushing when he'd just had one), for which his parents would have a dozen follow-up questions that doubled as thinly veiled suggestions to do things differently. Then they'd fish for more assurances that they weren't a nuisance to him and his wife. They were sweet, caring, well-meaning people who were too much work for Sharif.

He harbored guilt for his intolerance of them. They'd never wronged him in any way. They had provided him and his brother with far beyond the basics throughout childhood. And yet Sharif couldn't help but find their voices and mannerisms and humor and opinions and the way they ate irritating. It went without saying that he would be there for them if they needed any real, practical help. He wasn't a complete ingrate. But as long as they were healthy and safe, he preferred to not have them around, never missed them, and wished they could be very happy people who stayed very far away.

He hid his rejection of his parents from Adjoua. Her mom and dad exasperated her too, but it had no impact on how much she included them in her life. It didn't seem to matter to her whether she got credit for her inclusiveness either. For example, she called them every other week to say, "So, I need your advice on something," when she absolutely did not need their advice. It was a purely devotional gesture. She'd tell them about a personal or professional issue she was dealing with, then patiently listen to their guidance that was reliably off the mark, either because they didn't have the generational, social, or cultural points of reference, or because they suggested she apply their Catholic faith to her situation. She could resolve her issues more efficiently without their hours of input, but it was her way of sharing what was going on in her life while making them feel they played an important role in it. Sharif was in awe of this generous and thankless gift she repeatedly gave them. It was the most loving thing.

Their happiness was a priority to her, and he knew she wished he felt the same way about his parents. She'd told him it was a red flag on their first date when he said he wasn't close to his family. But at the time she wasn't looking for a serious relationship. It was still too soon after her breakup with Aberto, so she had disregarded her concern and told herself to have some fun.

Adjoua was now sitting slumped and sullen on the end of the bed. Sharif said, "Want to bounce on the birth ball a little?"

She was biting her nails. "No. Thank you." She looked at him. "I'm nervous to ask."

"What?"

"About Judy."

"Oh, I found him a place with this really nice and interesting guy I know from work. It's perfect." He sat next to her on the thin bed then immediately stood back up. "He can keep Judy for at least two weeks, so that buys me plenty of time to find something longer term."

"A guy from work? Where does he live?"

Under any other circumstances, Emmanuel's unclear immigration status, single fatherhood, poverty, and public housing residency would have been details that opened Adjoua up to Emmanuel, causing her to root for him and give him the benefit of the doubt to a nearly irrational extent. Sharif was the same way about virtually any socially, politically, or economically disadvantaged individual, especially when they were people of color. But since Adjoua sought maximum security and comfort for Judy — an animal she described as her heart walking outside of her body — he omitted details that could be interpreted as risk factors.

"Let's see. His name's Emmanuel." The Dragon Ball Z drawings sprang to mind: "Oh, he's got a little boy, Junior, who absolutely adores dogs." He actually couldn't remember if Emmanuel had said anything to that effect, but it must have come from somewhere.

"How old is Junior?"

"I'm guessing seven, eight?"

"You didn't ask?" Now she got off the bed and sat on the birth ball.

"Are you always supposed to ask? There wasn't a whole lot of chitchat to be honest. Things were moving pretty fast."

Adjoua rocked back and forth on the ball with a faraway look. "I'm going to miss him so much."

He said, "We'll visit him all the time."

Because she had not been a crier before this morning, there were still a few seconds of delay in Sharif's comprehension when it started. The way it came on so suddenly. How she stuck out her bottom lip and dropped her head and clenched her eyes. It seemed like an imitation of crying, a joke, as if her next words might be: *Oh, boo-hoo.* Sharif's initial reaction was bafflement. Why is my wife spontaneously fake crying? The bafflement was quickly replaced by a second surprise: She really is crying. This surprise was then replaced by an overwhelming urge to make her stop hurting.

Adjoua sobbed quietly: "Judy won't be around much longer. He's old. And so fat."

"Oh, my love, he's really not that old or fat," he said, crouching next to her, rubbing her back as she bounced sadly on the ball, feeling that swirling, sucking helplessness that took him when he couldn't relieve her pain. He attempted to hold her but it proved awkward to embrace someone sitting on a bouncy ball. He found himself hovering his mouth at the tiny, soft curls at her temple. "Thanks to the diet you keep him on, he's fit as a fiddle, okay?" He pulled back. "You should have seen Judy sauntering around today. He looked so great."

"Really? Tell me more about this person looking after him. What makes him nice?"

"He's funny and wise and kind, and he really bonded with Judy. They seemed to totally get each other, you know?"

She stopped bouncing and crying. A look of suspicion flashed in her eyes before she firmed up. "We need to do things differently, Sharif. I'm basically forty, and our baby has cancer. We need more security. The stress of barely hanging on is too much."

"You're thirty-six, and Zora is going to be fine. Every doctor says so."

"We live in a shoebox," she said. "We're two educated, healthy, privileged, hardworking people living hand to mouth." Speaking to herself now she said, "How did I let myself get into such a compromised position?"

It was impossible not to hear this as her saying she'd married the wrong man.

He responded sharply, "I said, we're going to be fine." His tone surprised them both. She looked up at him, waiting for him to say more. He got a handle on his defensiveness, and said, "I'll get my raise. You'll do your advertising thing if that's what you want. On your own time, you'll finish your book, which is going to be huge and open all kinds of doors for you. We're climbing that ladder slow and steady for now. I wish you wouldn't worry so much. We got this; I know it."

"Please, stop doing that. I don't want Band-Aids on everything. I don't want you to tell me things are fine when they aren't. We are not in a good position, Sharif. I need you to at least acknowledge that." She held her belly with both hands and looked down at the top of it. "We're not prepared for this." She sighed. "And now we've given away my best friend in the world." This retriggered her crying.

Somehow, inexcusably at this point, he didn't understand what she was doing at first. Then, "Oh, baby. I know this hasn't been easy. I'm sorry for that. And I get that I probably sound like a broken record, but I truly see this as a rough patch. People manage with much less than what we have, you know that——"

"I don't want to just manage."

"——and we'll visit Judy every day if you want. Breathe, Adjoua. There's no sense in thinking too big-picture right now. One breath at a time, okay? Let's get through today."

Turning his last words into a mantra, she repeated, "Get through today, get through today, get through today," as she recommenced rocking back and forth on the ball.

Needing a break from her pain, he glanced at his phone.

Re: Dog Care

Sorry, man, my mother-in-law moved in with us to help Abida with the baby and you know how Saudis are about keeping dogs! Haha!

Slipping the phone back into his pocket, he tried for some levity: "Maybe in a few months we'll get your agent to find Zora representation so she can do baby commercials and contribute to our monthly expenses."

Adjoua did not smile. She abruptly stopped the mantra and the rocking, and said, "Wait. I still don't have a clear sense of where Judy is exactly."

He sighed like they'd already exhausted the topic but was willing to revisit it one final time if it made her feel better. "He's with a really nice man who I met through work, remember?"

"What do you mean, through work? A coworker? Not a client, right?"

"No, not a client," he said as if that were a ridiculous idea. "He's an affiliate of the agency."

She thought for a moment. "An affiliate? I don't think I understand how you're using that word."

"Look, I left Judy in amazing hands. Please trust my judgment. He's in a spacious apartment——"

"But where? Give me some basic information."

"Flatbush. Right by CAPPA. Sorry, I thought I said that."

"Oh, no." She put her hand on her forehead. "People throw chicken bones on the sidewalk there. You know he can't eat those."

"I've never noticed chicken bones."

"What's this guy's schedule like? What does he do for a living?"

He thought of Emmanuel's jobs as a delivery person and a wheelchair escort at LaGuardia. "He works in sales. And the service industry as well."

"Why do you sound sketchy?"

"I don't know!" He laughed. "You're making me nervous. Judy seemed comfortable in the apartment. The guy was excited. I trust him. He lives five minutes from CAPPA and five minutes from Prospect Park. Judy will be able to run and play there every day."

She said, "He can't be off-leash in Prospect Park, Sharif. You know that." She stood and looked at the white wall behind the bed, as if gazing out a window. "I want to talk to him."

"Who?"

"What do you mean, who? The man looking after Judy."

"Okay, fine," he said. She waited long enough for him to understand she expected him to call right now. He called Emmanuel and a recording said the number had been disconnected. He'd forgotten about that. "Went straight to voicemail," he said. "I'll try him again in a bit."

"You couldn't have left a message?"

"Adjoua, I literally just dropped Judy off. I don't want to freak the guy out, okay? He's doing us a really huge favor."

"For free?"

"I mean, I offered him a little money, but still."

"How much?"

"Sixty a week."

She shook her head. "I really hate that sixty dollars sounds like a lot of money to me. That shouldn't sound like a lot of money. My parents worked their asses off to put me through prep school and get me into an Ivy. And sixty dollars sounds like a lot."

"Please, let's not worry about money today. Can we focus on what's going on with you and Zora?"

"Okay. I'm sorry. I trust you," she said as if she had no choice. "I'm sure Judy's fine."

"He is. That's the thing. He really is."

She nodded for a while, then slipped right back into her investigative tone: "You brought all of his stuff to the guy's place?"

"Adjoua."

"Just tell me."

"Of course I did."

"His food, meds, toys?"

"Yes. Everything."

"Bed, bowls, scat mat?"

"Yes."

"The guy knows how to mix the supplements into the food so Judy doesn't eat around them?"

"Yes."

"What about the harness?"

"Totally gets the harness. We even did a practice walk. He knows everything."

"Judy's probiotics. From the fridge."

Shit, he thought. The probiotics.

She whipped her head toward him. Catching his hesitation in her flood-light eyes, she became animated, almost thrilled by his failure. "Sharif, he needs those. His gut flares up without them."

"Adjoua, please. One minute you're worried about sixty dollars and the next you're fixated on our dog's overpriced probiotics."

She was stepping side to side in the tiny space as she spoke now. "They're so important. Especially since he's much more likely to eat random shit off the street when we're not around."

"I explained to Emmanuel about not letting him —"

"And all those chicken bones."

"What chicken bones?" Sharif was buying time, debating on whether there was still room to lie about the probiotics. He technically hadn't confessed that he'd forgotten to bring them. But no way, he'd been too slow. He couldn't lie to her face now. "You're right. You're one hundred percent right. I'll bring the probiotics over as soon as you deliver this baby and we get you home."

"No, no. No." She shook her head absolutely. "Who knows when that'll be. And after the delivery, they'll keep me here for at least a couple of days. Zora is going straight to the NICU. Go do it now, please.'"

"You're kidding, right? I'm not leaving you here alone."

"I've been here alone all morning. And you'll need to leave me here a bunch more over the course of this hell."

"No. I won't. I'll be here the whole time." He stared, dumbstruck, at her. "Are you serious? There's no way I'm leaving."

Adjoua's face cycled through a few shades of frustration before she spoke in a forced calm, "Sharif. I'll feel a lot better if I know Judy has everything he needs. And take pictures this time. So I get a proper sense of his new space. Actually, video please."

"I'm not going."

"I know you think I'm being crazy. I am being a little crazy. But I don't care. This is what I need."

Her wide-eyed, open-mouthed stare stayed aimed at his face. He couldn't believe how ridiculous this was. Neither Sharif nor Adjoua took probiotics. They were incredibly expensive and there was no scientific consensus that they even worked. And yet Judy going a day without them was unthinkable? He of course understood this wasn't really about the probiotics. She was grasping for any small sense of control over her life. But he also couldn't help but dread that this is how it would be with the baby. The pregnancy and diagnosis would be the beginning of the end. Adjoua's stress, desire for control, and emotional withdrawal from him would only increase. Their relationship would be reduced to arguing or his being chastised over the parameters of Zora's care — what and when she ate or what laundry detergent was best for her skin. Every inconsequential decision would take on grave proportions. The tiny failures and disappointments and disagreements would add up to a crushing mass. The thing he had loved most in the world, his relationship with his wife, would be squashed like a bug, and for what? A sick, screaming baby who never asked to be here?

He said, "Adjoua. Maybe, *maybe,* I'll get him the probiotics after your parents get here. But I don't want you here alone. Okay?"

"I'm not alone. I'm surrounded by hundreds of medical professionals."

He snapped, "You have an answer for everything, don't you!"

Her head cocked to the side. "Are you telling me to not talk back now? Is that what you're saying?"

"No." He felt ashamed. "I'm saying I'm waiting for your parents, okay?"

For the next forty-five minutes, she paced and sat and bounced, loudly ignoring him, acting like she couldn't bear to look in his direction. It oppressed Sharif. He left to find one of Adjoua's nurses, who said Dr. Ballou was in surgery and would be in to see Adjoua as soon as possible. He asked for a rough estimate on timing, and the nurse said the surgery was scheduled to go on for another two and a half hours. Sharif was gobsmacked by this news and reminded the nurse that his wife's water broke. The nurse told him not to worry, Adjoua had time. If there was cause for serious concern, another doctor would step in. Sharif went back to report what he'd learned to Adjoua and she shrugged. She stared at her phone until her parents arrived, making the point that Sharif's presence had been entirely unnecessary.

10.

ADJOUA'S PARENTS WENT by their European names, Charles and Sylvie. When they moved to the U.S., which happened the same year as Adjoua's dog bite, they also started calling Adjoua by her European name, Lisa. Afraid that she wouldn't learn English, they stopped speaking français de Moussa or French around her. She attended public school for the first ten years while her parents saved enough to send her to a boarding preparatory high school. There she met multilingual West African students who went by their African names. While she had previously been embarrassed by her parents' accents and comportment, she now regretted her disconnection to her origins, struggling not to judge her parents' choice of erasure.

She also struggled not to judge their refusal to acknowledge the racism they experienced. Did her father know that his white neighbors didn't make sure to carry ID on them when going for a jog? He responded to this question with a laugh and said he must be more orderly than their neighbors, what's wrong with that? When Adjoua complained of being followed around a store or getting hushed in an all-white movie theater when she wasn't the one talking, her parents called it bad luck and then segued to the importance of her dressing better, walking and talking more lightly, and never allowing anger into her heart, or at least show on her face.

She took French in high school but it did little to help her understand the pidgin French of her home country. Before starting college, she retired the name Lisa and reclaimed Adjoua. It took nearly five years to get her parents to start using it again too, and they did so only briefly before transitioning to Addie. Adjoua still intended to learn français de Moussa, and had paid for online lessons here and there, but she didn't have the capacity or budget to take it on with the devotion necessary to properly learn a language.

Her parents had used all of their savings and some borrowed money from relatives to move to the U.S. in 1990. Adjoua's father, Charles, had been working in Côte d'Ivoire's Ministry of Technology and was well on his way to becoming a key aide to the minister. It would have only been a matter of time before he'd be an important and connected person of means, a Big Man. His family, friends, and colleagues were perplexed that he wanted to leave. But Charles had romanticized the U.S. his whole life and when he won the green card lottery, he couldn't pass up the chance to go. He was confident he would achieve even higher status and reverence in America, and find better opportunities for his daughter.

After four months of searching for a job from his uncle's house in New Jersey, Charles landed an entry-level position at Dell Technologies and sent for his wife and daughter. He worked long and hard hours, climbing as high as a Black man with a foreign accent and limited cultural points of reference could, which, after twenty-five years, amounted to middle management. Although he probably thought he concealed it well, his career was a source of great shame and frustration.

Adjoua's mother, Sylvie, had signed up for free small business training workshops at a nonprofit in Trenton. Within six months of completing the course, she had taken out a low-interest loan from a Community Development Financial Institution and launched an HVAC company. Her husband, and anyone else who knew her, reminded Sylvie that she had neither HVAC experience, business management experience, nor really any other kind of professional work experience. She was undeterred. God had lit this path for her, and she was going to follow it. She worked eighteen-hour days, six days a week, building this HVAC business, and God's path turned out to be lucrative. In fact, her income far outpaced her husband's. By the time she sold the company for a handsome profit around her sixtieth birthday, she had twenty-two full-time employees. Now she was bored out of her mind. She went to church every day, praying for another path to be lit by God so she could know what to do with the next thirty years before heaven started.

Legacy was of primordial importance to Adjoua's parents, and the pregnancy provided them great existential alleviation and optimism. Charles claimed becoming a grandfather was the only unmet goal left in his life. Sylvie had always been candid about her impatience for Adjoua to get on with it.

When Charles and Sylvie entered the hospital, they appeared to have time traveled from a 1993 corporate event. Charles wore a navy suit with an oversize and boxy silhouette, wide pants that pooled around highly polished square-toed shoes, and a wide traditional red and blue striped necktie on a billowing dress shirt. He had a bearlike softness and strength, and an easy smile that made the thought of him stabbing a Doberman to death unimaginable.

Sylvie was heavily made up and perfumed, and wore a royal blue puff-sleeve dress, opaque white stockings, and cream-colored heels. There was a beautiful severity to her face. Her small, wide-set eyes always looked half shut, and she kept her head tipped back, giving the impression of perpetually looking down her nose at everything, despite being only five feet tall. Adjoua had inherited her high and broad cheekbones from her mother and her nose and darker complexion from her father. Her large feline eyes and long lashes came from someone in their lineage no one alive could account for.

Sharif greeted his father-in-law, a jovial but invulnerable man who never admitted to fatigue, illness, overwhelming emotion of any kind, or error. Complaining or venting seemed all but impossible for Charles. Such pride would be an obnoxious trait in anyone else. But with Charles it felt like exactly who he was meant to be. There was an inevitability to his arrogance that made it earnest. And it wasn't the sort of arrogance that relied on putting others down. It was an arrogance that expressed his idea of dignified maleness: unflappability, self-sufficiency, and chivalry. It was his honor to help out his seemingly infinite number of family members with money and the advice attached. He would have loved it if Adjoua and Sharif asked him for money.

To Sharif's initial surprise, Charles turned out to be the deepest and best hugger he had ever encountered. So astonished by it the first time, Sharif's knees weakened and he sort of collapsed against Charles's simultaneously soft and dense body, reminiscent of refrigerated pizza dough. Charles enveloped Sharif in his big strong arms, holding him more closely and tightly and for longer than was typical. All concern melted away. There was nothing in the world but the security of this embrace. Being released was like coming out of a deep, replenishing nap. Sharif looked forward to these hugs with near-inappropriate eagerness. Adjoua once reported that he had let out a kind of groan during one of the hugs. She warned that anything remotely homoerotic risked making her dad uncomfortable, jeopardizing the hugs Sharif cherished so much. Sylvie's hugs, on the other hand, were quick, stiff, and punctuated with three rapid pats on the back. But that felt right too. Sylvie was the cool, refreshing shower after the warm bath of Charles.

The greetings behind everyone now, Charles and Sylvie expressed dissatisfaction that their daughter wasn't in a private room. Charles put on his man-of-action hat, slung open the curtain, and took a step toward a nurse frowning at her clipboard.

The nurse, who was not assigned to Adjoua, looked up at the staring man in the suit. "Yes?"

Charles jovially announced, "Look, my wife and I arrived to be with our daughter on her big day, and we're trying to catch up!" He laughed loudly and warmly, in his surprisingly high pitch, for a long time.

The non sequitur between what he'd said and how he reacted to what he'd said worked as it always did. The nurse smiled and was soon laughing with Charles, forgetting about her clipboard and telling him she'd go check up on the exact status of Dr. Ballou's surgery right away, something Sharif had not managed to inspire in Adjoua's actual nurse. Charles's ability to get strangers to laugh with him despite no one having said or done anything funny was such an effective shortcut to human connection that Sharif questioned the point of real humor. Sharif had seen Charles leverage his contagious laughter apropos of nothing with staff and managers at restaurants and shops, and one other time at a hospital in Trenton where Sylvie was getting a hernia surgery.

The only time Charles did not use this technique was with West Africans in service positions. He was unsmiling with the staff at La Savane, an Ivorian restaurant in Harlem. He'd give the server a small tip up front and say, in a rumbling alpha tone, that he expected attentive service. From that point on, the waiter would respond to everything with *Oui, Monsieur* and make a show of speed-walking to and from the kitchen. Adjoua was ashamed of her father's transformation. How jolly he was with Americans versus this Big Man act with his countrymen. Capitalizing on the rigid socioeconomic hierarchy among Ivorians was a perpetuation of a culture borne of colonial dominance, of grinding people down by constantly reminding them of their rank. Sylvie rebutted her daughter's "liberal" claims (a word she only ever said in air quotes, as if the label itself were a myth) by saying Adjoua didn't understand their culture; this is how it works over there, she'd said, and everyone in this restaurant knows that. Adjoua was indignant. This not only reminded her of how hierarchical, classist, and racist her parents could be toward other black people, but also how they denied her access to Ivorian culture throughout her childhood only to now make her feel like an outsider when it suited them.

Sylvie's approach to getting the service she wanted was more consistent than her husband's. She was Napoleonic no matter the audience or cultural context. At the hospital now, she called out orders to anyone wearing hospital garb, and once even to another patient out for a walk: "Hey. What's your name? Come here." This too was an effective technique. She got another nurse to confirm that Adjoua wouldn't go into labor for a long time, then insisted on a concrete estimate. The nurse finally guessed, "Four hours?"

Sharif took advantage of the nurse's presence to ask, "What about her high blood pressure?"

She answered that's what the nurses were here for, and that she'd continue checking Mom's BP hourly, making sure Dr. Ballou received regular updates while in surgery.

Neither of Adjoua's parents seemed hung up on the high blood pressure or why Sharif was leaving his hospitalized wife to deliver probiotics to the dog. They were singularly focused on their mission of getting a private room. Sharif had asked Adjoua three times if she really, truly still absolutely needed him to do this. With unwavering resolve, she said, "Yes."

Before he left, she softened and added, "Thank you. This means a lot." She then whispered, "One last thing. Can you ask my mom to rinse off her perfume before you go? It's making me feel ill."

Sharif was relieved when he saw she was mostly joking. She thanked him again, and he left her and her project-managing parents in the tight, curtained-off space.

11.

DESPITE BEING TOLD he had at least four hours before the baby came, he was too anxious to risk taking public transportation. What if the nurse was wrong, or he got stuck underground, or simply missed an urgent call while not in cell service? So he took a car, yet again, from New York–Presbyterian Weill Cornell Medical Center to the Lower East Side to get the probiotics, then back to Flatbush, struggling to silence the accountant in his head who was calculating all the money he'd been spending over budget today.

At Emmanuel's, Sharif asked the driver to wait for him again. There were five young men, in their early twenties or late teens, between him and the entrance of the building this time. Drill music played from a cell phone while one of them practiced his dance moves. The merriness of this rap dance usually tickled Sharif, but now that it was something he had to circumnavigate on the walkway, it made him a little nervous. Two of the other young men were play-boxing while another filmed them. Sharif caught eyes with the fifth guy leaning against the building next to the intercom. This guy had a cinnamon stick in his mouth and his knee drawn up with a foot pressed flat against the wall. He wore a Brooklyn Nets jersey, light-colored jeans, white high-tops, and a white Nike sweatband. Sharif finished zigzagging through the drill dancing and boxing and filming to get to the intercom, which was a few inches from the cinnamon stick guy's head. Sharif gave him a downward nod and received a faint upward nod. He buzzed Emmanuel's apartment a few times and waited. The cinnamon stick guy asked who he was looking for. Sharif said Emmanuel, and the guy said Emmanuel who.

"I actually don't know his last name," Sharif said. "He's around my age, I think. About this tall. He's got a son who draws Dragon Ball Z cartoons on shirts."

The drill-dancing guy said, "Oh yeah, Junior's dad. Haitian dude, right? He got some huge dog."

"Yes, that's him!" Sharif said.

After some more nodding, Sharif's enthusiasm passed. They had simply established that the man he knew to live here had been seen living here, walking the dog Sharif had left with him. No mysteries solved there. He asked, "Did you see him leave with the dog recently?"

The guy said, "No, that was a while back."

"And you guys have been here since you saw him? All morning?"

The guys exchanged glances, and Sharif realized his questions about their whereabouts were intrusive. The cinnamon stick guy said, "What do you want with Emmanuel? He a friend of yours?"

"Yeah, I mean, yeah. He's looking after my dog," Sharif said.

"Half the buzzers here don't work," the guy said. "Just go up." He rolled himself off the wall like it was a bed, used his key fob to unlock the door, then opened and held it for Sharif.

"Oh, thanks. I really appreciate it. Thank you," Sharif said.

On the fourteenth floor, a television blared a game show one door down from Emmanuel's at a nearly incredible volume. After knocking a few times with no response, he imagined Emmanuel and his little boy, Junior, were playing with Judy in Prospect Park. No—he looked at the time on his phone—Junior would be in school still.

Re: Dog Care

... my landlord doesn't allow dogs over 25lbs, but I'll ask around ...

Sharif jostled the bottle of probiotics in his pocket and sucked in his lip, wondering how to produce a note for the pills he intended to leave at the door and hope for the best. During a brief interval of silence in the game show on the neighbor's TV, Sharif caught the unmistakable sound of Judy whimpering.

The TV recommenced its racket, and Sharif knocked louder at Emmanuel's door. That's when Judy started barking. Questioningly at first, then with increasing urgency. Why wasn't he coming to the door? He always came to the door. His barks grew more desperate, but still muffled and distant. They must have shut Judy up in Junior's bedroom or the bathroom. But why? Sharif had told Emmanuel that if he didn't want Judy on the couch, he could use the scat mat in the dog bin.

He started knocking at the neighbor's where the TV blared. After what felt like a whole minute, an old white man in a ribbed tank top opened the door slowly but fully. He had thin arms and a potbelly so defined it was as if he'd slipped a fruit bowl under his tank top. His silver hair appeared slicked back with grease and slept on. He was unshaven and dry-lipped. The daytime television host shouted about a big prize through the audience's downpouring applause. It sounded like the speakers were about to break. Judy's barks became higher and more distressed. Something about the distance of the barks made even less sense. It was now as if they came from behind a closed door in this man's apartment.

Sharif spoke fast. "Hello, sir, I'm sorry to bother you. Your neighbors are looking after my dog. I need to use your fire escape to check in on him through their window." The old man's mouth opened and froze, as if expecting to be fed. Sharif said, "You hear that barking? That's my dog. I need to check on him. Sir? Hello?" Sharif registered the man's pinpoint pupils and understood he was high on opioids. "Excuse me, I have to do this," he said while moving carefully around the man and letting himself in. Sharif beelined through the brown-carpeted living room littered with fast food wrappers and soda cans toward the window. The barking sounded like it was coming from next door again. But as soon as he opened the window, he saw his dog.

Judy was standing on his bed on the fire escape. The bed was too big for the landing so it drooped partially over the stairs leading to the next landing. The new forty-pound bag of dog food had been crammed out there too, now ripped and half emptied. Judy's water bowl was upturned, the bed soaked. Judy rushed toward Sharif but was blocked by his leash, which must have been tied to the radiator in Emmanuel's apartment, the window shut on it. "No! Stop!" Sharif shouted, afraid Judy would slip off the part of the bed hanging over the stairs.

Sharif pulled back inside the old man's apartment so he could exit leg first. His momentary disappearance caused Judy to panic and fight harder against the leash. As Sharif straddled the sill, his left knee pressing into the fire escape grating, the old man jabbed him in the ribs with a finger. Sharif jumped and hit his head against the bottom of the open window. He grabbed his head and squinted in pain at the old man. The man grinned and put his hands up, as though Sharif were a child pointing a water pistol at him. He finally spoke, in a dry rumble: "Who sent you?"

Judy's anxious attempts to get to Sharif caused his right foot to slip off the bed and down the stairs. He fell hard, cracking his chin against a step and making an awful yelp. The harness and leash prevented him from falling the rest of the way, but also incapacitated him. His hind legs were still on the bed, one of them bending unnaturally far back. His left foreleg was trapped under his body, and his right paw punched and slipped against a step in a futile struggle to reverse. When Sharif made it all the way onto the fire escape, he saw that the landing Judy's body was aimed toward had no vertical bars on the handrail. It was an empty frame, an opening into the fourteen-story drop to the alleyway. Sharif crawled onto the bed and caught ahold of Judy's leash to pull him back. Judy writhed and moaned. White stress points spread across the plastic buckles of the harness. Knowing they wouldn't hold, Sharif reached for the scruff of his dog's neck. As he made contact, one of the buckles snapped, spinning Judy out of the harness and away. Sharif lunged to catch the scruff in time. Fully extended, the weight of Judy's fall brought Sharif flat to his stomach on the stairs. Judy's bottom half was off the ledge now. His instinct was to break free of Sharif's one-handed grip and regain control by twitching and kicking into the open space fourteen floors over the alley. Sharif roared *No!* as he used his free hand to grab the nearest handrail bar and pull himself and Judy back, dragging them both up the stairs.

He opened Emmanuel's window, shouted *Hey, help!* and climbed in while keeping a firm hold on Judy's scruff. Once inside, he cradled Judy and brought him in, placing him on the floor. Judy's legs gave out immediately. Something was broken, maybe his wrist, his shoulder from the harness, the hind leg that had gotten jammed back. He whimpered in rapid succession while Sharif frantically repeated, You're okay, you're all right, you're going to be okay. Sharif found a cereal bowl in the kitchen sink and filled it with water, but Judy wouldn't stop crying long enough to drink.

Sharif was sweating abundantly. The room spun. After a few blurry seconds, he took out his phone. Another dog care rejection email. Two missed calls and a text from Adjoua: Where's my boy? Send video, please! He swiped it all away and dialed 911. That didn't make sense. He needed a vet. He hung up and stared at the screen, his body vibrating as he tried to remember how to search for contacts in this fucking thing. His cognition cleared up enough to find Dr. Cohen's number. Pacing the living room, he shouted at the secretary that he had an emergency. She put Sharif on hold to see if the doctor could squeeze him in ASAP. Sharif glanced at the door covered in Dragon Ball Z drawings, then at the horror-show water stain on the wall, then the open window, then the leash dangling off the radiator, then down at his broken dog. To Dr. Cohen's absurd hold music, which hadn't been changed since the holiday jingles of December, Sharif said *Fuck this* and decided to go straight to the vet. He moved back and forth between the door and Judy, experiencing another lapse in cognition, unable to decide what should come first, opening the door or picking up his injured dog. He unlocked the door and returned to Judy.

Things started moving even faster, becoming more hysterical and distorted when Emmanuel's front door swung open, revealing a young man. Sharif perceived his tallness, cornrows, and sparkling cube-shaped earring all at once. The first words out of the young man's mouth were the same ones in Sharif's head: "Who are you?"

Sharif was still shouting everything. "This is my dog!"

The young man looked down at Judy. "What's wrong with him?"

"Someone put him on the fire escape, and he fell!"

"But I tied him up."

"You did this? Who are you?"

"Wait, where's my dad?" He scanned the apartment. "How did you get in here?"

This took a moment to compute since Sharif had previously decided Emmanuel's only son, Junior, was a little boy. He didn't have time for this.

"I have to get to the vet," Sharif said as he took a step toward the exit. Junior stepped into the doorframe and put his hands up to signal Sharif should go no further.

Junior said, "We're supposed to get another sixty."

"Are you out of your mind? You hurt my dog and expect money?"

Junior now looked offended, disgusted even. "I put him outside in case he had to pee."

Judy's bucking and twisting started up again, straining Sharif's arms and back. When his head faced Junior, he growled. Judy had never growled at a human before. Sharif commanded, "Move out of my way. We're leaving."

"My dad said you owe sixty no matter what."

Judy was kicking harder, wanting to be put down, wanting to be able to defend himself from this guy. What else had Junior done to him? Sharif yelled, "Get out of my way!"

"You can't take him without paying."

"Move!" Sharif strode toward the door with his panicking dog, but Junior didn't make space. Sharif had to barge Junior aside to get out. All three bodies briefly pressed together in the doorframe. Sharif stumbled into the corridor, barely catching his fall to prevent Judy from crashing to the ground. He looked up and saw the little girl with the camera. Junior yelled, "Hey! Come back here!" as Sharif was halfway down the hall. Then he was in the elevator, panting, still hearing Junior call for him to come back. The doors closed. He was going down.

12.

THE DRIVER SAID, "Whoa whoa, what's going on, what's the matter, what's this dog?"

Sharif's adrenaline was still making him shout everything, "He's hurt! Go straight and take a right on Church! Go, go! We're going to Avenue A in Manhattan. I'm punching in the address now!"

Judy was a mess. Crying and fear-slobbering, unable to be still.

Like the driver, the young men in front of Emmanuel's building must have thought Sharif was fleeing a crime scene. The guy who'd filmed the play-fighting now filmed Sharif speeding off. The driver accelerated through turns, shaking his head, as if disagreeing with himself for getting swept up in his passenger's drama. Adjoua called again, but Sharif texted instead of picking up: Everything okay?

Yeah, I'm fine. Why aren't you answering? Don't forget the Judy video please. About to see the doctor now.

He sent a yellow thumbs-up.

Judy had always hated the vet's office, unable to stop crying even when pumped with treats and praise during routine checkups.

Sharif burst into the lobby with his crying dog. The waiting room was full of pet owners, cats and birds and dogs with shaved sides, stitches, splints, casts, and cones. Judy started growling, and Sharif squeezed him harder to his chest. The secretary shot up from her desk and led Sharif through a door, a narrow hallway, another door, and into a cold operating room, telling him to place Judy on the metal table while she got the doctor. As he lay Judy down, Sharif murmured, It's going to be all right, bubba, don't worry, I got you, I love you. You'll be okay.

A different doctor from Dr. Cohen entered, looking no older than twenty-five. He conducted a physical exam with such relaxed confidence that it was patronizing. In under a minute, he airily posited that Judy had minor bruising. Nothing broken or torn. He followed up with a full body X-ray that confirmed his nonchalant assessment. The bruises, in combination with Judy's arthritis, were why he didn't want to stand at the moment. The vet, who sounded like a kid impersonating an adult he admired, said, "With a little pain management and TLC he'll be up and at 'em in no time. The old fella is a little sore is all. Isn't that right, old man?" He smiled at Judy. Sharif found it rude when people called his old dog old but was relieved there was no serious damage.

Judy gagged around the first pain pill the boyish vet crammed down his throat while saying "That's a good boy," as if goodness were synonymous with suffering.

The initial exam cost $30, the X-ray $135, and the seven-day supply of pills $85. Sharif put it all on the credit card, feeling his life force sliced out of him as the card swiped through the machine. He carried Judy outside and placed him on the sidewalk to order yet another car he couldn't afford. Judy was able to stand all of a sudden. After shaking his body like he'd had a swim, he took a couple of sniffs over each shoulder then looked at Sharif, as if to say *Okay, boss, what's next?* It couldn't have been the pill since the vet said it took twenty to forty minutes to take effect. Sharif was a little annoyed that Judy acted like nothing out of the ordinary had happened, but was also a little proud of his resilience.

He wondered what other forms of neglect or abuse Judy would have endured had he not come to drop the probiotics. What else *did* Judy endure for him to growl at Junior like that? After ordering the car, he distracted himself from a mental image of Junior kicking his dog by looking up the $85 pain medication. Maybe the pill was responsible for Judy's miraculous recovery after all. He found himself wanting that boy vet to be wrong. The internet confirmed that it did take at least twenty minutes for the medication to work. It also turned out to be the exact same chemical compound as over-the-counter aspirin. Looking up from his phone, the world around him appeared more dangerous. Passersby seemed selfish, avaricious, cruel, but also dull somehow, like emotionally deadened kids who dismember insects. Junior seemed like one of those kids. Sharif remembered a recent news story of a massive dogfighting ring spanning Long Island, New York City, Connecticut, and Massachusetts. Pessimism was winning him over. He'd have to shake this off before returning to Adjoua. If Judy could do it, so must he. Adjoua needed a positive, reassuring, solutions-oriented partner.

He returned to his phone in search of contacts who might take Judy for a few nights, but it was a useless exercise. He'd all but begged everyone in his network. Someone would have taken him by now if they could. A pang of shame shot through him. When was he going to stop expecting others to save him? When would he stop relying on luck to get by?

A middle-aged man walked up to him with a panting smile and his arms spread wide. "Look around, my dude! Ha ha! Look at the beauty all around you! Ha ha!" Sharif watched him zigzag down the sidewalk with the optimism of a dog. The man paused for a moment to tilt his head up and moan at the beauty of the sky.

With Zora's imminent arrival, Adjoua's mounting stress, and Judy's day of abuse, Sharif had to opt for the sure, if unaffordable, option: the Doggy Hotel in Midtown.

Instead of calling Adjoua, he called his mother-in-law. Sylvie's formality would make it easier for him to suppress any negativity. Also, Sylvie was unlikely to ask about Judy.

"Aye!" Sylvie answered. "Where have you been?" Sharif could hear that she was in a light, teasing mood.

"I'm on the way. Any updates?"

"About Addie? Oh, she's doing fine!" She laughed at her daughter. "Still a long way from delivering any baby."

In the background, Adjoua responded, "O*kay*, Mom," in the regressive adolescent tone she only used with her parents that usually made Sharif smile.

Sharif asked, "And her blood pressure?"

"Mildly high, they're saying."

Adjoua asked, "Is that Sharif or not? Where is he?"

"Uh-oh, did you hear Wifey?" Sylvie said into the phone, still amused.

"Sure did." Sharif hadn't yet decided how much to share with Adjoua. If Judy was totally fine, why make her feel sad and helpless by telling her he had suffered? He said to Sylvie, "Tell her I'm coming as quickly as I can. Traffic has been crazy. I should be there in about forty-five minutes."

"Oh, don't worry, there's plenty of time." She cackled. "Hold on, she wants to talk to you." Sylvie passed the phone before Sharif could object.

Adjoua said, "Why didn't you call me back?"

"Hey, how are you feeling?"

"Fine, but did you hear me?"

"Yeah, I'm sorry. My hands have been really full up until now. A lot of running around, you know. I thought I'd check in with your mom first in case you were busy or stressed or something."

"Okay." There was a silence that expressed his explanation was insufficient. She moved on. "How's Judy?"

He looked at their dog, who sat on the sidewalk, leaning on a haunch and coiled inward to lick his groin. "Good. Really good."

"It's just that you weren't responding. And now you sound weird."

"I know. I'm sorry."

"That's it?"

"What do you mean?"

"I mean you're not allowed to be cagey with me. Did you make a video like I asked?"

Adjoua's father could be heard in the background: "Who's being cagey with you?"

Sylvie answered, "She's on the phone with Sharif, Charles. Where have you been?"

"Looking for the doctor," Charles said. "He's still in surgery."

Sharif said to Adjoua, "Getting to our place and then Flatbush took a while. I completely forgot about the video. I'm sorry. And maybe I sound different because today is such a different day. I don't know. But Judy's doing really well, and I'll be there soon, okay?"

She sighed. "All right." Judy was now licking some brown sludge dripping out of the bottom of a trash can. Sharif tugged hard to pull him away. "What was that?"

"What was what?"

"Never mind. I thought I heard the jangling of his harness. I'm going crazy."

Sharif looked up at the sky. "How much time do they estimate before labor now?"

"No updates since they said four hours. They started doing urine and blood tests."

"What for?"

"Checking for protein and other stuff, I'm not sure. Doctor Ballou will do a proper test between his scheduled surgeries."

"A proper test? This is pretty confusing. Do you want to see if we can change to a doctor who's not so busy today?"

"No, I actually find it reassuring how unconcerned everyone is with me. And my dad is enjoying the chase of it all."

Sharif could hear Charles smiling when he said, "What are you saying about me now?"

Sylvie said, "The doctor, Charles! The doctor! You were looking for the doctor, remember?" Occasionally, Sylvie treated Charles like he was senile, which was not the case. Underneath her hammed-up exasperation for her husband's nonexistent senility—and whatever motives she had for portraying him as helpless — was devotion: *When your mind and body betray you, I will frequently complain but never leave you alone.*

Sharif said, "Okay, can you tell me what kind of test the doctor will do when he's available?"

"It's to see if my water broke."

"But it did, I thought." It was like every new piece of information distanced him from understanding.

"I don't know, Sharif. They want to do a test for some reason, okay?" Then, "I think I messed up."

"What do you mean?"

"I think I came here way too early." Her tone had turned vulnerable.

"Going in was definitely the right move, my love. Especially with this high blood pressure business, you know?"

"I made you miss work again. On the day you were meant to ask for your raise."

"Oh, please don't worry about that."

"And everyone here is kind of laughing at me."

"Fuggum."

Sharif could hear her sheepish smile, the one that came when she wanted to feel small and cared for. "You won't laugh at me?"

He never thought much of the expression "bursting with love" before Adjoua, but some clichés were so resonant. He really did feel he was swelling beyond capacity at times. "I would never."

The car he had ordered arrived. Adjoua asked, "Where are you now? Did you show the guy how to give Judy the probiotics?"

He needed to get off the phone before she heard him hefting Judy into the car, where the whining marathon would start. He felt the bottle of probiotics bulging his pocket. "Yep, Judy's all set up. I should let you go. I'll be there soon."

"Okay. Bye."

He got in the car with Judy and clapped the door shut. Through the rearview mirror he registered another driver who wasn't charmed in the least by his huge, whimpering, throat-clicking, shedding dog. Sharif patted his carsick buddy's head, and Judy blinked with every pat.

Re: Dog Care

I know it's not what you want to hear, but the shelter option, if it comes to it, isn't necessarily a death sentence. There are amazing organizations that really do everything possible to ensure dogs are matched and not put down . . .

Sharif decided never to speak to that person again. Then he contemplated the cost of replacing Judy's bed, dog bin, and supplies. It could easily set them back another three hundred dollars. He flashed on Emmanuel's son, Junior, and experienced the focus of anger. It activated him to call Emmanuel and demand that the dog bed and bin be delivered to his apartment by the end of the day. He also wanted a full reimbursement for the lost food, vet expenses, and additional car rides. But Emmanuel's number was still disconnected. He found himself getting more and more worked up about Emmanuel failing to keep Judy safe, and being impossible to reach even though he'd said he would reconnect his phone today.

Once at the Doggy Hotel, Judy leapt out of the car without assistance. The driver yanked the emergency brake, threw off his seat belt, and got up to inspect the damage in the back.

Sharif and Judy were halfway to the Doggy Hotel entrance when the driver called out.

Sharif turned and saw he'd finished his inspection. The driver huffed as he said, "I must give you a negative review now." The two men locked eyes. The driver continued, "You did not warn me about the dog and took no precautions to protect my car. This is my livelihood. And that," he said, pointing at Judy, "is not a service animal."

"I never said whether he was."

"Well, is he?"

Sharif wanted to ask if he had any idea what he'd been through today. He wanted to shout that his dog had been abused. How the idiot kid responsible tried to hold him hostage for sixty dollars. How his wife was giving premature birth to a baby girl with cancer. How he was a good person who didn't deserve any of this. How the world was so fucking ugly and stupid. And how his wife gave him a fraction of the warmth and affection he needed. It took Sharif a few breaths to decouple his indignation from the driver who had nothing to do with it. His anger simmered to sadness, then wilting exhaustion. He blinked slowly and said, "He's not a service dog. I deserve a bad review."

13.

"**WHO DO WE** have here!" said the Doggy Hotel receptionist whose name tag read *Katherine N.*

Sharif answered that we have a dog who cannot tolerate other dogs. She gave a sympathetic frowny face. Her desk had two multitiered resin rock fountains that you'd expect to find at a spa. But the bright lighting and pop music was more befitting a gym. She explained that they were nearly at capacity since so many Doggy moms and dads were on vacation, which meant Judy could not be offered his own fenced-in AstroTurf garden today. The only available option was the Spacious Kennel.

He and Judy followed her through the glass doors and around the fenced-in dog run. The Spacious Kennel looked only twice as spacious as the one at the cheaper boarding place he and Adjoua had brought Judy to years ago. Unwilling to leave him in such a dark and cramped space, they canceled their flight to Austin for a friend's wedding and went home.

In this kennel, Judy could only stand, turn, and take a couple of steps in any direction. Sharif hated the way Judy looked at him from behind the closed gate, surrounded by the sound of a dozen ecstatic dogs playing in the indoor dog run a few feet away.

"Forget about them," Sharif whispered as he crouched down. "You're number one, okay, bubba? You're so loved, do you understand?" Judy tried to get his snout through the bars. Sharif put his nose closer and received a few pleading licks. "I promise I'll do better, sweet boy. I'm so sorry." Judy responded with a look of uncomprehending sorrow.

He ended up putting $110 on his credit card for Judy's overnight stay plus two meals, two walks, and the administration of the probiotics and $85 aspirin. As he left the Doggy Hotel, he berated himself. He needed to be smarter and more discerning to protect his growing family. But how could he have ever guessed that Junior was such a heartless, greedy kid? Emmanuel had seemed so kind and responsible.

The memory of Junior trying to hold Sharif hostage for sixty dollars whipped itself into renewed anger. The anger was good and energizing. He fantasized about telling Junior off, then Junior physically attacking him, which gave Sharif no choice but to put him in a headlock, drop him to the ground, and force him to apologize to his dog. He edited and cycled through the fantasy a few times before ordering himself to forget about Emmanuel and his idiot son. The only thing that mattered now was getting his family to a safe and stable enough place to experience happiness. He would ask his boss for a raise as soon as he got back to work. No, he'd email her about it tonight. And he wouldn't ask her. He'd tell her. He simply required more money to meet his family's basic needs. No apologies and no begging.

He knew that if he got a respectable raise and was on a clear path to another one in a year or two, Adjoua's optimism and warmth would return. They didn't need some massive windfall; they needed to reconnect with a sense of possibility and gradual progress. Yes, if he got the raise and showed he was on an ascending career track, Adjoua would become light and enthusiastic again. He smiled at the thought of Adjoua smiling more, her heart opening back up to him and the beauty of the world, letting herself get caught up in her imagination and big dreams, returning to her fiction with a sense of urgency. He missed her romanticism, the sliver of pride he heard in her voice when she laughingly told friends about the vow of poverty she'd taken. The provocation he heard when she said similar things to her parents, flaunting her freedom from their expectations. She'd committed to art and humanism over any spiritless illusion of security. Sharif trusted that her magnificent hubris and romance was merely in hibernation. It would return with a little good news.

He received two more rejections from his Dog Care email. One came from a coworker as a reply all: Sorry, good luck.

Then another coworker he didn't know well replied all to the first reply all: No response is better than a cold response, Boo.

Sharif was flattered to be defended publicly.

Things got more exciting when the first reply all coworker replied all again: Since when is saying "Sorry" and "Good Luck" cold? Never got the memo, "Boo." Mind your judgments. Please and thank you.

The small thrill of being fought over vanished when Merjem, his boss, replied all to say: Please do not reply all on this email thread again...

The fact that his email led to his boss's annoyance felt like a threat to his raise. He succeeded at discarding the negative thought and chose to stick with his previous line of optimistic thinking. In that moment, happiness did feel like a choice.

Three drivers accepted and immediately canceled his request for a pickup. When a fourth driver accepted, Sharif called him before he could cancel. He explained that his poor profile rating was due to his dog, but he would be riding alone this time.

The first thing Sharif noticed when Hamid rolled up was that his forehead was unusually short. Sharif then realized this only appeared to be the case because Hamid's hairline was unusually low and thick. He asked Hamid if he minded him making a quick phone call and rang Adjoua. "Hey, I'm twenty minutes out. Any news?"

"They did the test. We're waiting on the results. Dr. Ballou seemed pretty convinced that my water did not break. But he wants to induce labor anyway because of my blood pressure. They're going to start me on some kind of steroid to prep Zora."

"This is — We need a second opinion, right?"

"Yeah, he's having his colleagues weigh in too. Can you just get here?"

He had the overwhelming desire to hold her, to give her the chance to let all of her weight go in his arms. "I'll be there soon."

Sharif noticed Hamid glancing at him in the rearview a few times before saying, "Sharif aism Aarby. Enta min wen?"

Sharif spoke the only Arabic sentence he knew, which was that he didn't speak Arabic. But like many Arabs in Sharif's experience, Hamid was excited to hear him speak Arabic and continued speaking Arabic. So Sharif had to clarify, "No, saying I can't speak Arabic is really all I know how to say."

"But you say it so well!"

"Practice."

"But your name is Muslim name!"

"I know."

"Haram aadameh. It means like 'king' or maybe 'noble one.' You understand?"

This also happened a lot. When an Arab accepted that he didn't speak Arabic, they then assumed he'd never learned the meaning of his name. After a few moments Hamid said, "You know, habibi, I have to tell you. I almost canceled you."

"Yeah, that's why I called."

He smiled. "So you know what is your problem."

"I do."

"And you will stop bringing fat and hairy dogs that are always crying in cars."

"I'll certainly try."

"It cost us one entire hour of work, plus detailing charges, and so forth. Some of your drivers today did not like your riding style at all."

Sharif nodded. "I regret today's riding style too."

At a stoplight, Hamid and Sharif observed a man in a tattered and lopsided wheelchair begin his unhurried trek across Sixth Avenue with one second left on the walk sign. As rushed as Sharif had felt today, he now admired the comfort in which this man seemed to be operating at his own pace.

When the man finished crossing, Hamid said, "Yes, if the dog is nicely behaved, okay, it's no problem. If you tell us it's your service animal, halas, we must accept. Bas if the dog is a big, smelly animal who is always dropping hairs and crying and spitting and so forth, providing no service, drivers will tell other drivers you are a dirty rider."

"They mentioned my dog's smell on the app? Can I see that?"

"La, I'm helping you, habibi."

"Well, I didn't know how to move my smelly dog around this city without a car. So."

"They have special car companies for these kinds of animals. Don't call on people like us for this, really." He nodded at Sharif in the rearview and added, "Really."

"I know. Today was a series of emergencies." Sharif couldn't understand why he was keeping this conversation going, but he also felt some relief talking about today's Judy emergencies as a thing of the past.

Hamid seemed to only register half of his statement. "Yes, it's so much better to be calling the other companies for this kind of help." He nodded some more. "Really."

"I got it. By the way, is there any mention on the app of the seat cover I used all those years?"

Hamid shook his head, not knowing what Sharif was talking about.

A young man was sweeping the sidewalk in front of Radio City Music Hall, and Sharif again flashed on Junior. What was that kid thinking trying to block him from leaving like that? Sharif had always been a bit frightened of teenagers. But now he experienced a touch of pride for not being afraid to stand up to Emmanuel's teenager. He'd won a fight he hadn't started. He felt tough and noble.

The car turned on Sixty-Eighth and pulled up to the severe, white, art deco tower of New York–Presbyterian Weill Cornell Medical Center.

Sharif started getting out of the car with the sense of a new and brave beginning. "Thank you, Hamid."

"Anytime, habibi. Remember, when you are with the dog —"

Sharif shut the door before he could finish. He peered into the jaws of the hospital's high, glass-ceilinged lobby, and walked tall toward the entrance.

14.

Re: Dog Care

. . . I wish we were in a position to help out with Judy, my man.

Keep us in the loop about how this all plays out . . .

ADJOUA LAY IN BED in the same curtained-off space. She wore a gown and purple hospital socks shaped like pillowcases with rubber grips. Her feet poked out the end of the thin blanket that couldn't possibly influence a person's temperature. She looked tired. Defenses down. Sharif once fantasized of shrinking Adjoua and placing her in his mouth, holding her in the safety and warmth of his cheek. He'd told her about this vision, and she giggled, saying it would be too wet and dark.

Sylvie and Charles were getting tea from the Au Bon Pain on the ground floor. Adjoua had requested they leave her so she could have a moment to herself. Before Sharif could ask if she wanted him to come back later too, Dr. Ballou tore open the curtain and said, "Hello there!"

"Hi," Sharif said, taking a half step back. Despite having presumably just come out of surgery, Ballou's breath smelled of ham.

Dr. Ballou was tall enough to always look a little out of place. He had the round, curly hair of a clown and a long, stooping neck. Adjoua once called him "a bit of a brontosaurus." However, the silliness of his appearance really centered around his tiny, pale Cheerio of a mouth. Adjoua joked about the miniature sandwiches his bitty mouth required. But now his silly physicality contributed no levity.

"So!" Dr. Ballou said. "I was telling Mom that it's been confirmed that what she imagined was her water breaking was actually vaginal discharge, and some urine." He chuckled, and Adjoua nodded in shame. Sharif imagined grabbing Dr. Ballou by the throat and forcing him to apologize.

"But it's good that she came in, given her blood pressure. Since it's only mildly high now, we have the opportunity to administer Betamethasone steroid twenty-four hours apart to get Baby's lung maturity, intestinal track, and all other vital organs up to snuff for us to induce labor tomorrow at six p.m.!"

The baby comes tomorrow, Sharif said to himself, absorbing this as a second chance to rehome Judy and get a raise before starting fatherhood. "And why do you think Adjoua's blood pressure has been elevated when that's never been the case before?"

"Great question! The good news is that we've ruled out gestational diabetes and any placental abruption. Could be preeclampsia, could be stress. Those are my competing guesstimates at the moment, but we'll know more with continued monitoring and testing for a couple of things as we go."

Sharif did not want a doctor who used guesstimates. "Right. What 'couple of things' will you be testing for exactly?"

"Sure! Blood pressure, obviously. CBC, liver function testing, BNP panel, twenty-four-hour urine protein collection."

"That's about five things. Did you mean you'll be testing for five things when you said a couple of things?"

"Sharif," Adjoua said.

Sharif took a breath to bridle himself. "Doctor. As you can probably tell, we're a little on edge. So we're counting on you to be as precise as possible."

Ballou slowly slid his legs apart to lower himself to Sharif's height, crossing his arms and putting his hands in his armpits. "I completely understand. Believe me. I think the main thing is to relax as much as possible."

Sharif closed his eyes and said, *"What?"*

"If stress is causing Mom's hypertension, relaxing is the single most important thing to do. Keeping that blood pressure down will help Baby get the oxygen and nutrients she needs for tomorrow. Trust the process. This continues to be a healthy pregnancy."

Adjoua said, "Healthy aside from the high blood pressure, induction at thirty-six weeks, cancer, and false labor, you mean."

Dr. Ballou said, "Whoa, whoa, let me stop you right there, Mom." He laughed, then snuck a quick peek at his wristwatch. "First of all, nothing unhealthy whatsoever about false labor. Second, our steroid and induction strategy is tried and true. And third, we have a phenomenal plan in place for Baby's leukemia. Like I said, the absolute best thing you can do now is chill."

Adjoua must have seen Sharif flinch at the word "chill." "It's okay," she whispered to him.

"Doctor," Sharif said, "what will help me chill is getting straightforward answers to basic questions."

Adjoua said, "Sharif. Leave it."

Without taking his eyes off the doctor, he said, "No, he's telling us everything is perfectly okay but that you need to spend the night in the hospital getting regular tests and steroids before inducing preterm. It's not coherent."

The doctor squinted at Sharif and pursed his lips, impatience beginning to show through.

Adjoua cut in. "It's all standard best practice under the circumstances, right, Doctor?"

Dr. Ballou nodded slowly at Sharif. "Exactly right."

"Fine," Sharif said, even though he felt Adjoua was doing this man's job for him. "Does this mean she'll get a private room?"

"Entirely your call."

"Meaning whether we want to pay nine hundred dollars."

"Eight eighty-nine. Correct." He was staring dead into Sharif's eyes, their dynamic having turned mutually adversarial.

Before the tension could come to a head, Sylvie entered and announced, "Charles is in the bathroom again!" and rolled her eyes. Then she asked Dr. Ballou, "Can my daughter have her own room now?" Apparently it had been decided that Charles and Sylvie would pay for that.

The doctor smiled at Sylvie. "Absolutely. I'll send someone in to settle that now."

When he left, Sylvie asked Sharif, "You okay, big guy?"

"Yeah. I'm going to head to the store to get a toothbrush. Do either of you need anything?"

Adjoua said, "Oh, I don't think you can stay over."

"Why not? Isn't that one of the main benefits of a private room?"

"They said there isn't room for three visitors."

He put his hands on his hips and looked at the ground for a second before asking, "Are you punishing me for standing up to the doctor?"

Sylvie chuckled. "Why? What did you do to the doctor?"

Adjoua asked Sylvie if they could have a moment of privacy.

"Again?" Sylvie asked, then shrugged and stepped to the other side of the curtain, where she could obviously still hear everything.

Adjoua said to Sharif, "I'm not punishing you. But yes, I do wish you were a little more diplomatic with our doctor. He could turn out to play a fairly important role in this movie."

Sharif said, "The standard of care shouldn't depend on how likable I am. And believe it or not, I was using all the restraint I had. I've had such bad luck with doctors today," he said, remembering Judy's boy vet.

"What do you mean? What other doctors?"

God, he was bad at hiding things from her. "I just mean Dr. Ballou should be clear and professional."

Sylvie spoke from behind the curtain, "What was he unprofessional about?"

They ignored her. Adjoua said to Sharif, "Doctors are human. And Zora's and my well-being happens to be in that human's hands today. So I think general deference and amiability is best."

Sylvie burst back in. "*Zara?* Like the store? *That's* the name?"

Adjoua said, "Shit." Then, "Yes. I mean, no. Zora, Mom, not Zara."

Sylvie froze, then shot a betrayed look at Sharif. "A Muslim name."

Adjoua said, "Mom, please. The name is not up for debate." Back to Sharif: "The nurse said we get one cot and one chair. Since my parents came all this way, I think they should be the ones to stay."

"Eight eighty-nine and they can't give us three cots?"

"It's not a matter of how many cots they're willing to give us, but of physical space in the room."

Sylvie said, "And don't worry about the money, Sharif. It's no big deal for us. But now do you mean to tell me that you are going to raise your daughter Muslim?"

"No," Sharif said. "Why would we?"

Adjoua said, "Zora Neale Hurston wasn't Muslim, Mom."

"People will assume she's Muslim," Sylvie said.

"Let them!" Adjoua said. "People have assumed my name is Muslim before."

"Aye!" Sylvie said, putting her hand on her heart. "Addie, who said that about you?"

Back to Sharif, Adjoua said, "You know what would make me happy?"

"Tell me."

She reached for his hand and squeezed his fingers. "If you went and picked Judy up and brought him home. I get induced tomorrow night, but they'll keep us here for at least a few days. Knowing my guys were together, sound asleep tonight, would be so nice. Maybe the guy can take Judy back in a couple days if we don't find something else?"

Sharif swallowed and gave a vague nod.

Adjoua asked Sylvie, "Mom, could you give us a minute alone, please? A full minute this time."

Sylvie was staring at the floor, still shaking her head about her granddaughter's name. She walked out mumbling, "You're making a big mistake."

Adjoua motioned for Sharif to come closer and whispered, "So you'll go get him?"

"Yeah. Sure."

"Thank you. Come closer." Even more quietly she said, "You've seemed angry."

"Have I?" he said. She looked back at him wordlessly. "I do get worried sometimes, but I'm not *angry*. Not that I'm aware of anyway."

"That's kind of what I'm worried about."

"Okay. So either I admit to having a sudden anger problem or I'm delusional *and* have an anger problem? Those are my options?"

Her face softened with a pitying tenderness that said his reaction proved her point. "I love you. Call me as soon as you and Judy are home, okay?" Then, "Hey, we meet our daughter tomorrow."

He gave a half smile, unsure if this was a celebratory statement or a plea for him to do better.

Outside the hospital, he called the Doggy Hotel. Despite their twenty-four-hour booking cancellation policy, Katherine N. offered a majority refund as a one-time courtesy, charging only thirty for the hour and a half of Judy's care. Somehow, it then made the most sense to use their Doggy Chauffeur service and meet Judy at home. Quoted at $89.99, the grand total now exceeded the cost of the overnight stay. "Would you like to leave a tip for Judy's Chauffeur?" she asked.

"I'd absolutely love to." He regretted the sarcasm. None of this was Katherine N.'s fault. "I'm sorry. Yes, I would like to leave a tip."

"Oh my God, please don't worry! Are you having one of those days?"

"Sort of."

"Do you want to talk about it?"

He wondered if she could possibly be serious. "Oh, no, thank you. So, what kind of tip do people usually leave?"

She made a humming sound, followed by a series of other thinking sounds — tongue clicking, then *doo doo dooooo?* — then, "*Mmm,* twenty percent is pretty standard I guess?"

"Let's do that then."

He hung up and commanded himself to let go of all the money spent today. He'd make up for it by staying under budget the next few weeks, skipping coffee and lunch and other unnecessary expenses, and by securing his raise. Besides, Judy would be so thrilled to come home, and Adjoua would be comforted. And comforting Adjoua made Sharif's self-esteem rise like a red balloon out of a loud city.

15.

HE TOOK THE M15 Select bus down First Avenue and listened to a podcast about the depraved president. What impressed Sharif most about the guy was his seemingly infinite energy for behaviors that would exhaust Sharif: publicly whining and lying and blaming with transparent self-interest. There was something almost superhuman about his unlimited capacity to broadcast desperation and narcissism. For every minute in his shoes, Sharif would need a week's bed rest. Just hearing others talk about him now had a sedating effect. So he switched to a podcast about relationship dynamics that was typically light and entertaining. This episode, however, centered on infidelity, a topic that caused Sharif to conjure Aberto, Adjoua's ex, and trigger a race-against-loss feeling in his chest, as if some essential inner structure was turning to sand.

He'd never managed to eliminate, or even weaken, his underlying fear that Adjoua wished Aberto hadn't left her. Aberto had a flashy and lucrative career success as a do-gooder, and was more confident, traditionally masculine, and better-looking than Sharif. As stupid as it would sound, Sharif was even jealous of Aberto's skin color.

Sharif knew his whiteness took some effort for Adjoua to accept, which she never quite did. Instead, she redefined him as "white presenting" because of his Lebanese father. It was clearly important to her that her partner not be *only* white. Sharif was embarrassed when she referred to him as "white presenting" to friends, because anyone could see he'd been afforded the full privileges of a white man. It was disingenuous to go along with the suggestion that he had any lived insight on the nonwhite experience, but go along with it he did. He feared challenging this part of her narrative would loosen one of the few screws keeping them together.

Also connected to this was how she reacted to Black people she knew partnering with white people. She might say things like "Of course, why am I surprised" when she learned of it, and even "That's disappointing." Her biggest eye rolls were reserved for Black men who seemed to exclusively date white women. While Sharif had an intellectual understanding of the betrayal she was alluding to, a small inner voice still said, "But we're an interracial couple."

Adjoua was wrecked when Aberto left her. She had dated Sharif as a kind of distraction, which led to cohabitation, then marriage, then pregnancy. Meanwhile, it was obvious that Aberto wanted her back. Sharif knew this from reading Adjoua's emails from him in the middle of the night: Aberto's tone, the kinds of questions he asked her about her marriage, his continual use of the pet names he'd had for her when they were together. Adjoua never reciprocated Aberto's flirtations, which were usually veiled as fraternal affection or humor, but she never shut them down either. Sharif suspected she felt empowered by both the flattery of his inappropriate comments and her lack of reciprocity, a kind of drawn-out vindication for his original sin of leaving a damn good woman.

But with Adjoua's growing dissatisfaction in the life she shared with him, Sharif thought she must be asking herself why she'd rushed into a lifelong commitment with the first guy she dated after losing her big love. Was it some shortsighted way of punishing Aberto? Had her heartbreak made her tired and careless? Had she been worn down by her parents' pressure to have a kid, feeling her age and willing to settle?

The guest psychologist on the dating podcast said it usually took longer for the victim of cheating to recover than the cheater. The cheater has control over their future, able to decide whether to stop or repeat cheating behaviors down the road. The cheated, however, have little grasp on what they could have done differently and live in paranoia of another betrayal.

The bus was at full capacity when a heavyset woman with short silver hair came on and stood next to where Sharif sat. He couldn't discern whether she was elderly or not, so he didn't know if it would be rude to offer his seat or rude not to offer it. The two other youngish people on the bus stared at their phones. Sharif looked up at her, waited for her eyes, then made a subtle gesture with his head toward his seat, offering it while also maintaining plausible deniability. She smiled down at him and gently shook her head. Sharif's sense of clarity was short-lived. She may have been smiling politely because a stranger made eye contact. And her head may have been shaking from the swaying of the bus. To free himself from this ambiguity, he stood and walked to the middle of the bus. He grabbed a bar for balance as the psychologist in his headphones kept on about how good betrayers have it. When he looked back, he saw that the woman was still standing there next to his empty seat, and felt cheated.

16.

AWAITING JUDY'S DROPOFF, Sharif leaned against his building next to the intercom, his knee drawn up with a foot pressed flat against the wall. He realized he was posing exactly like the helpful young man with the cinnamon stick outside of Emmanuel's. His mind then proved too tired to reapproach the drama with Junior again. The whole thing was already as fragmented and distant as a dream. No matter, Junior and Emmanuel were out of his life forever. It was all a bizarre blip.

A black van with the Doggy Hotel insignia pulled up. The driver was an unsmiling, long-haired guy wearing a *Corey M.* name tag. He had a chauffeur's hat that read, *I Drive on Doggy Time*, with a stuffed dog tail sewn on the back that looked like a floppy carrot. Someone's job was justified by coming up with this nonsense, and they surely got paid a lot more than Sharif. For the first time, he felt truly angry about how little society valued his job. He'd always felt at peace, occasionally even a bit superior, about his commitment to a low-paying profession that made a meaningful impact on people's lives. Choosing this career despite how underpaid it was only made his sacrifice more noble. But now the idea of getting paid less than whoever came up with *I Drive on Doggy Time*, which literally connoted nothing, disgusted him.

It wasn't Corey M.'s fault for wearing a work uniform that triggered Sharif's unprecedented bitterness toward capitalism. In fact, the clash between Corey M.'s deadpan and his silly hat caused Sharif to victimize him, repeating the words *Sorry* and *Thanks* more than made sense as Corey unloaded Judy. Corey put Judy on the sidewalk. "Is she sick or something?"

Sharif immediately pictured Adjoua's pregnant belly, then understood Corey was of course talking about Judy. People often thought Judy was female, even without learning his name, most likely because of the winged black eyeliner coloration around his eyes. "No, he's not sick. At least, I hope not."

He shrugged. "Cries a lot."

Sharif felt himself getting defensive. "He's a bit of a weeper in the car, that's true." They both looked down at Judy, who glanced between the two men.

"I don't know," Corey M. said. "I drive a lot of dogs. Something's wrong with this one. You should get him checked out."

"Oh yeah?" Sharif's sarcasm resurfaced. "You recommend that I drive him to the vet to ask why he doesn't like being driven?"

Corey M. shrugged the exact same way as the first time. "I'd probably call first."

"Okay, Corey M. You have a great night."

He carried Judy up the stairs, kissing the white patch at the back of his fat neck. Dog hair stuck to Sharif's nose and right eye, crosshatching his eyelashes. He said, "Is it true, bubba? Did you cry in that stupid car? You were deep in your feelings, weren't you?" He tried to get the hair off his eyelash by lightly catching it on Judy's neck, but rubbing it against more hair didn't help. "What happened in that terrible apartment, sweet boy? What else did that psychotic teenager do to you? I'm so sorry I left you there." With one eye shut from the dog hair, he imagined Adjoua tottering a few steps ahead of them. The image of her, combined with a neighbor's footsteps echoing in the stairwell, was so vivid that it frightened him, briefly compromising his balance. He couldn't remember ever feeling so tired and unsteady.

In the apartment, he was faced with the absence of Judy's dog bin and bed. It inspired renewed anger at Emmanuel for delegating Judy's care to his careless son. Judy sniffed at a dead fly in the rectangle of dust his dog bin had left. He picked it up with his tongue, smacked at it a bit, spat it out, then sniffed the soaked carcass like it was something new. He looked at Sharif: *This isn't how it used to be around here.*

"I know, man," Sharif said. "I'm working on it." What he also needed to work on was that email to his boss about a raise. Pumping himself up to do that as he opened a can of wet food for Judy that they kept stashed in the cupboard, he caught himself actually using the phrase "man up." It was embarrassing to ask for a raise when he'd been so flaky and needy lately. And if his boss said no, he'd have to wait at least six months to ask again. But he had to risk it now. By this time tomorrow he'd be a father.

He watched Judy's food slowly plop into a cereal bowl. These cheap cans of wet food dated back to when Adjoua wasn't constantly worried about Judy's health. She now referred to them as Judy's McDonald's. Nutritionally flawed as they were, Judy turned into a demon as he inhaled and snorted the gelatinous meat like it was the best stuff on earth. After cleaning the bowl with his tongue so hard that Sharif expected the ceramic to crack, Judy looked imploringly at him again, licking his chops, ready for the main course. Sharif crouched down to say, "If once in your life, you could intimate the slightest thanks, a simple pause followed by a nod maybe, this relationship would be even more gratifying for me." They held each other's eyes. "Bark once if you understand. Come on, bubba. Use your words."

Stalling before opening his laptop to write to his boss, Sharif made himself an omelet that he didn't really want in front of Judy's wide, eager eyes, then dumped the whole thing into Judy's cereal bowl. He gave him a second can of wet food after that. "You really are a piggie-pie."

He finally opened his laptop on the kitchen island, and began and deleted the first words of the first sentence many times over:

Hi, I think

What I'm beginning to think is

I feel

How are you

Here's a curveball for you

So I've been working at CAPPA for nearly three

With a caseload of 40 clients, and the capacity to take on more, I believe

First, I want to say how much I appreciate

Hi

Hi there

I know it's late

Weird time to be on work email but

Things have been tough

I've been struggling

Our sick baby is coming prematurely tomorrow

We need more money to live

Honestly, my wife is freaking out

I deserve a raise because

I hope this email finds you well

What a night!

It's been a long day

It's been a JOURNEY

Adjoua's doing really well

Adjoua's blood pressure was pretty high

They're keeping Adjoua in the hospital overnight

The Gods have gifted us 24 more hours before it all comes crashing

This will seem out of the blue but do you think we could

Do you ever feel like giving up?

Judy growled at someone today

That kid was physically barring my exit

Emmanuel was so nice, how could he have such a defective child

What if my daughter is a dickhead
Or maybe Emmanuel is a dick and I completely misjudged him
My instincts suck
Why am I still thinking about those people
What am I going to do with this poor dog
The point is
What's the point?
What is the point, Sharif?
Fuck you
Fuck fuck fuck and fuck you
My wife shuts down
She's drifting away
Shouldn't life make more sense and be easier with age?
I don't get why she's even with me
I spaced out for a minute there
Okay, this isn't working for me
I think I'm ready to move on
I need time to think, more than I have

Judy had been watching Sharif as if the frenzied clacking at the keyboard was the sound of more food being prepared.

"I know what I'll do," he said to Judy. Instead of the email, he sent a calendar invite to meet with his boss tomorrow. The subject of the meeting was Discussion of Future.

Within ten seconds she accepted the invite and wrote him: Kind of a cryptic subject line...Hope I shouldn't worry...Did you have your baby...Is Adjoua okay...?

He forgot she didn't have any context since he'd texted her that Adjoua was in labor. He responded: Nothing worrisome, she's fine! Baby's now due to come tomorrow night! Just wanted to share some thoughts!

Okay...sure...

Still gazing hopefully at Sharif, Judy's left leg slipped out from under him. He landed hard on his hip, and Sharif thought his heart would break right then and there. He got a pill from the $85 dog aspirin bottle, opened Judy's jaws, and forced one to the back of his throat, then clamped his mouth shut through eye-bulging gags until he swallowed. It never ceased to amaze Sharif that Judy didn't hold a grudge for what must seem like a random act of abuse. He forgave everything instantly.

Not long ago, on a day when Adjoua was teaching at Mercy College, Sharif rolled the top three-quarters of their dog's body up in a carpet and sat on him to cut his toenails. Sharif's brilliant idea was to avoid paying for transportation and the twenty dollars that Dr. Cohen charged for something Sharif was certain he could do himself if Judy remained still. Once inside the carpet, Judy wailed like a kidnapped victim. A sound that haunted Sharif to this day. But having gone this far, Sharif decided to see it through as quickly as possible. He cut a cuticle on the first clip. A shocking quantity of bright blood poured across the wooden floor. Dr. Cohen instructed Sharif by phone to dunk the bleeding toe in hydrogen peroxide, then flour to stanch the blood, put a sock and a condom over the foot, and tape it tightly. Mere seconds after Sharif managed the steps, Judy was kissing him on the same mouth that was begging forgiveness for causing such unnecessary suffering. Sharif successfully stopped the bleeding and removed any signs of injury before Adjoua came home.

After his shower, he hesitated on which bed to take for himself and which to give Judy. He and Adjoua had been sleeping separately since before Zora's diagnosis. Sharing a bed had gotten increasingly dangerous as Adjoua's belly grew, resulting in the second episode of bloodshed at home. The only place their double bed would fit was wedged against three brick walls, meaning Sharif, who slept on the inside, had brick crumbs fall on him at night. And because the bed was raised high off the ground to give them the storage space they needed underneath, climbing over Adjoua in the middle of the night to use the bathroom was an unreasonable feat of athleticism. While he was trying to climb over her one night, Adjoua woke up and reflexively palm-struck Sharif in the nose. He bled like a faucet onto her face, and she began screaming and flailing. Judy charged in, barking at the bodies panicking in the dark.

Thirty seconds later, everyone had crossed over into full consciousness, the lights were on, and Adjoua and Sharif were overcome with delirious laughter. The two of them tried to mime what had occurred but couldn't make it through the convulsive laughing. Any effort to speak made them more hysterical. Covered in blood, they moaned, wiping at their watering eyes with the backs of wrists, before having the wherewithal to clean up. It was the hardest either of them had ever laughed, and they slept apart from that night on.

When Zora arrived, there would be even less sense in Sharif and Adjoua sharing the big bed, since the crib would be pushed against it. Sharif would stay in the half bedroom where the baby stuff would pile up and he'd change diapers on his bed. They couldn't justify buying a changing table.

Throughout the first half of the pregnancy, Sharif gave Adjoua ritual foot massages in bed. She would almost always conk out before he got to the second foot, so he alternated which one he started with every night. It fascinated him what put her to sleep. He could never sleep with someone touching him like that. Just like he could never fall asleep the way she did in front of movies.

"Come on, baby," Sharif used to say as she woke up during the end credits. "I've specifically been wanting you to see that one."

"I know! I tried, I'm sorry!"

They watched films extra loudly and with all the lights on, but to no effect. She would put her head on his lap, and he would warn, "That right there is not a promising move."

Five minutes in, her eyelids batted heavily. Sharif curled forward to hover over her cheek and whisper, "Baby, it's barely even started."

Her eyes shot open. "What, I'm awake," she said, looking dazed and feigning offense.

Her fibbing made him love her more. "Okay," he said, "I hope you like it," and watched her big, beautiful eyes grow heavy again. The scar on her lip would be more pronounced in the glow of the computer screen, pulsating in the blue light. He liked to tease her afterward by asking what she thought of the movie and whether she had any favorite scenes. Struggling to maintain a straight face, she'd say something like she absolutely loved the part in the middle when the main guy shows up at that place with the other characters. He'd say, Yeah that part was amazing.

Movies were an opportunity for her to stop thinking, planning, worrying, and processing to-do lists. The emails she needed to write, the coursework she needed to prepare and student stories or essays she needed to read, Judy's healthcare regimen she needed to manage and improve, the copywriting deadlines and pitches, the novel outline, the daily journaling and free writing. She was not someone who could sit and let her mind wander without purpose. She was intentional to a fault. Her three modes seemed to be Planning Action, Taking Action, and Sleep. But movies offered a liminal space between these modes, a sweet spot where she could vaguely follow the unimportant happenings on the screen for a few minutes, successfully diverting her attention from the Planning Action or Taking Action mode, awake and checked out at once, all while feeling physically close to Sharif, before entering Sleep mode. A childlike brightness came into her eyes when he suggested watching a movie. She had claimed movie night with him was her favorite thing ever.

Since the diagnosis, Adjoua had refused foot massages and movie nights. She could no longer tolerate planned distractions or pleasures. Sharif worried she'd lose her mind if she didn't take a break from her disappointment and fear. But what threatened him most was her lack of communication about her shutdown response to their circumstances. Weren't they in this together?

Lately, he'd been waking her with his dream-state cursing from the half bedroom on the other side of the kitchen. The first time it happened, she teased him with exaggerated imitations. She scrunched up her face and made fitful head movements along with sudden outbursts — *Fucker! Shithead! I'll kill da muddafucka!* Sharif told her he would never believe that he'd said that. She said if it happened again, she'd film it on her phone. But she never did, because it was no longer a funny anomaly when it happened again. Her instinct was to wake him right away, free him from whatever he raged against.

He lay in the daybed now with his waves of worry. Sloshing up and down his chest and head were all the things that could go wrong with the pregnancy, subsequent years of cancer treatment, and their marriage. Then he saw Merjem, his boss, squinting as she listened to him trying to formulate one good reason he deserved a raise right before his paternity leave. He pictured Emmanuel's face at various distances, Judy on the fire escape, Emmanuel's fucked-up teenager, Junior; the cinnamon stick guy, the impatient eyes of drivers in rearview mirrors; Carlos, the pigeon-chested panhandler; Dr. Ballou's tiny mouth; the Dragon Ball Z drawings; then a drawer full of baby scorpions he remembered as an image from a novel; the rain-pocked cement Buddha in his parents' yard in Minnesota.

Then he saw his anxious little mother and father looking pityingly at him. Unlike the pressure Charles and Sylvie had put on Adjoua growing up, Sharif's parents hadn't demanded much of him or his brother. They let Sharif quit ice hockey and piano and the Boy Scouts the moment he wanted to. He now disagreed with how little they pushed him. It had taken him years of concerted effort to overcome his reflex to quit at any sign of discomfort. It still took effort.

Sharif had no memory of seeing his parents work hard. His father had inherited enough money from his parents to buy a small chain of nursing uniform stores called Scrubs & More. His mother had helped his father manage and grow the business for a few years before it ran itself. Sharif's parents hardly ever went to the physical locations anymore and lived comfortably on the biweekly checks they received. And yet, despite their life of leisure — vacations, hobbies, meditation retreats — they existed in a constant state of nervous helplessness.

His brain flipped through disparate images and people until they became rapidly morphing geometric shapes. Before sinking through the bed, falling through the floor, the building's other apartments, the street, and underground into a burying sleep, he felt a whisper of relief that there would be no witness to the foul things he might scream in the night.

17.

JUDY BARKED LIKE a seal inches from his face. Sharif's eyes opened and Judy paused, cocked his head to the side with his ears raised and forehead wrinkled, then exhaled a whimper of relief. Sharif remembered part of his dream. A frozen ocean. Ice skates on his feet, he'd sprinted toward the horizon, racing against the setting sun. The darkening ocean spun under him like a vast treadmill. No matter how hard he skated, everything looked the same, until the cold air dissipated, trading places with his dog's breath. That was all he remembered. Nothing to scream about.

Adjoua had made him an appointment with their primary care provider in Midtown months ago, after the third nighttime spasm. Their doctor had a lethargy to him that inspired little confidence, but he was one of only a handful of doctors who accepted Sharif's insurance. The doctor checked a few glands, Sharif's reflexes, tonsils, shot a light up his nose, announced him generally healthy, and wrote him a referral to an in-network neurologist in Queens, an hour from home by bus with two transfers. The neurologist put Sharif through a CT scan, ran blood and urine tests, said there were no signs of neurological abnormalities, and wrote a referral for the closest in-network therapist. Upon Adjoua's insistence, Sharif traveled an hour and a half into deep Brooklyn, where the therapist listened to him describe his life and what Adjoua reported about the shouting. After two sessions, the therapist concluded Sharif was stressed. He wrote a referral to a psychiatrist

in Washington Heights, another hour and a half from home, who might pre-
scribe antianxiety and sleep-aid medications. Sharif came home and told
Adjoua he was putting a hold on the whole process. He couldn't imagine
traveling to the therapist and the psychiatrist on a regular basis, especially
after Zora came. He also wasn't convinced that he should be taking medication for stress caused by an objectively stressful situation. It wasn't a good
time to be experimenting with mind-altering medications anyway—side
effects, dependency, long-term impacts these psychiatrists don't seem to
know much about. And those thirty-dollar copays had no place in their budget. He promised to reconsider if things didn't improve after Zora's birth.
He said he was convinced all of their current stress was anticipatory, and
there would be a collective sigh of relief when none of it turned out to be as
bad as they feared.

Judy came closer, trying to lick Sharif's face. He couldn't get enough
of Sharif's morning breath. The harsher it was, the more it excited him.
"We're different, you and me," Sharif said with exaggerated breathiness
to taunt him. He then had to turn away quickly to avoid Judy's slingshot
tongue. "Whoa, nice try, buddy, nice try, little buddy, nice try, little buder-
ooney, better luck next time, budderoonsky." Something about this animal
inspired inane repetition. Adjoua became a broken record when she put her
face close to Judy's too. The amusement of these up-close repetitions was
amplified by Judy's deadpan. He was the best straight man they knew.

At a little after seven a.m., Sharif called Adjoua. She told him not to
come to the hospital, to go to work and get that raise, and insisted she was
perfectly fine. Blood pressure had settled, not too much protein in the blood
or urine, no negative reactions to the steroids. On track for six p.m. induction. He said he preferred to come, and she said, "Really, Sharif, there's no
need. Absolutely nothing has happened since last night. I managed to get a
little writing done on my laptop, then fell asleep with my parents. My poor
dad was in a chair all night. Tell me something about Judy."

He looked over at Judy, who pawed at the radiator. There must
have been a bug in there. "He's working on an important bug-hunting

project at the moment. I'm glad you got some writing done. Copywriting or the op-ed?"

"The op-ed."

"Really, that's great! When can I read it?"

"Oh, not yet — it's a mess. Did you hear last night that the police report described the murder victim as an 'unknown male inside the apartment who confronted the officer'? She walked into *his* home uninvited and shot him while he ate a bowl of ice cream on his couch. They're truly shameless," Adjoua said.

He agreed and said something about the ever-mutating cancer of racism in this country, and she talked energetically about the exhaustion it caused in her. He was fired up by their exchange. It was the first time in months that they had weighed in on the same side of an issue with passion. As ugly and tragic as the inspiration for their shared passion was, it filled him with a celebratory, purifying air. He'd known her faith in humanistic principles and justice and writing hadn't disappeared, but actually receiving that energy from her, being invited to participate in it again, feeling it dissolve her shields of stoicism and pragmatism, made him feel like they were running toward each other in an open field.

"God, I want to see you," he said.

"I know. But go to work, my love. Get that raise for the family. I believe in you."

He hung up and followed up with each of the eleven no-kill shelters by email to see if Judy could be bumped to the top of the waitlists under the circumstances.

Part II
WORK

18.

ABOUT FORTY-FIVE MINUTES before Emmanuel reentered his life, Sharif jogged to catch the elevator at work. In the cramped ride to the fourth floor, a CAPPA employee always asked a colleague how they were doing this morning, and the response was invariably related to their proximity to the weekend: Well, it's Monday, they'd say with exasperation, and the others would give a commiserating chuckle, do some shoulder bouncing and head wagging. If it was Tuesday, the person was expected to respond that they can't believe it's only Tuesday. Wednesday warranted a joke about getting over the hump. Thursday received an "almost there" rally. And Friday, which was today, ranged from stating the word Friday in overacted, breathy satisfaction to "Lord, help me survive one more day."

Grateful to those who participated in the script about the days of the week, sparing everyone a silent ride, they spilled out wishing each other good luck. By nine a.m., the lobby was packed with clients or walk-ins, most of whom had probably been there since maintenance unlocked the building an hour earlier. Gathered were the unluckiest New Yorkers, those described in grant proposals as the Most Vulnerable, Most in Need, Economically Disadvantaged, Immigrants, Foreign Born, Refugees, Asylum Seekers, Migrants, Minorities, Illiterate, Low Income, Very Low Income, Rent Burdened, Severely Rent Burdened, Chronically Ill, Chronically Unhoused, Formally Unhoused, Single Parents, Survivors of Domestic

Violence, Individuals of Low Educational Attainment, Public Assistance Recipients, Undocumented, Underemployed, or Unemployed residents of the most economically depressed census tracts of Brooklyn. They had come to pick up the free MetroCard CAPPA provided clients who honored their case management plan, or to meet with their benefits advocate for entitlement enrollment and reporting, or to get help completing a job or housing application, or how to attain MWBE status for their small business. Most were visibly foreign — Eastern Europe, Ethiopia, Bangladesh, Pakistan, Haiti, Senegal, Syria, Venezuela, China, everywhere — living in a New York City that couldn't possibly resemble what they'd dreamed of before making it here.

They had turned to CAPPA because they were straining or failing to meet their basic needs: food, shelter, safety, access to healthcare. Some of the immigrants Sharif worked with had thrived in their home countries as business owners, pastors, councilmen, chiefs, army sergeants, and professors fleeing dictatorships, war, famine, persecution against their ethnic or religious group, their political affiliation, or sexual orientation. Now they worked in low-ceilinged kitchens in Chinatown, underregulated warehouses in Red Hook, construction sites on Wall Street, in rideshares driving college students around all night and manning a cash register at Dunkin' Donuts all day to feed and clothe their children. Many ended up living in crowded and dangerous emergency shelters or squatting in blighted buildings. Others were lucky enough to live with family or friends. Some hoped to relaunch the careers they had built in their home countries and were here to learn how to write an American résumé, perfect the fundamentals of American interviewing, emails, elevator pitches, and work etiquette (how to dress, shake hands, smile) through CAPPA's workforce readiness workshops. Others needed assistance getting ID, a social security card, filing taxes, translating credentials into English, applying and testing for the professional certification required in their field, navigating any other myriad, opaque processes required for their stability and, possibly, advancement. There was a frenetic energy in the lobby that was reminiscent of an ER.

People paced, rocked their babies, and spoke with urgency into phones. One or two always stood up from the bench when the elevator opened, hoping to see their case worker step out.

Re: New Adoption Timeline!

Hi Sharif,

I have processed your request for priority consideration with our Scheduling Manager. Judy is currently number 248 on the waitlist. With this in mind, we hope you will continue to look for alternative options. But, with you, we will keep our fingers crossed . . .

Sharif's desk was in the corner of a white and windowless computer lab down the hall from the lobby. The overhead fluorescents painted everything with a harsh and yellowish pallor, annihilating shadows and flattening dimensions. Sharif's vision had little to grip aside from the rows of black desktops reserved for clients. A few times a day, his eyes strained and dried until they watered heavily, as if rebooting his eyesight. This was especially true in winter when dry heat blasted from the vents.

Being the only employee in the computer lab, he had relatively little contact with his colleagues. Other caseworkers, job developers, workforce readiness instructors, the fundraising team, IT, admin, and others all sat down the hall, in the cubicle farm behind double-paned glass doors that required a key fob to open. There were about 150 employees, a quarter of whom were devoted to CAPPA's mission of helping underserved populations, and the other three-quarters endured various shades of jadedness, as if this was merely a low-paying job in which their own life circumstances had trapped them. He'd overheard the bitterest ones speak to clients with contempt, weaponizing terms of address like "sir" and "ma'am": *I told you, sir, if you don't have the right forms, I cannot enroll you. Please come back when you have collected ALL the necessary documents, sir, thank you.* The majority of the sincerely devoted employees were religious, doing God's work and frequently saying as much. Aside from the lack of windows in the computer lab, Sharif didn't mind the isolation from his coworkers. He even tended to eat lunch alone, since his job required constant dialogue with clients and having that one quiet hour helped him recharge.

What he loved about his job was building trust with clients, and the unrivaled sense of accomplishment when he succeeded at connecting them to opportunities that actually improved their quality of life. Three months earlier, he had closed out his biggest case. It was a group of Sudanese clients he'd worked with for nearly a year — three children, two women, and four men who slept shoulder to shoulder in a 350-square-foot studio in East Flatbush. He'd found them intensive ESL classes, provided referrals to free daycare and a summer youth employment position for the eldest child, rental arrears payment, and assisted in getting the adults on-the-books jobs with a unionized construction outfit in the Brooklyn Navy Yard. He should have asked for a raise immediately after closing out that case.

As essential as this job had become to his identity, he was not excited to be here today. The dread he felt about the ten a.m. meeting he'd requested with his boss was expanding by the minute. He was good at his job, but he had no real argument for deserving a raise. As a caseworker, he could only see so many clients in a day, and his caseload had been maxed out since last year's raise. He had nothing new to contribute in exchange for more money.

Re: New Adoption Timeline!

. . . We appreciate these are extenuating circumstances for you and yours, however, due to shelter policy, Judy remains 189th on the waitlist . . .

While working with his first client of the day, Tanisha, he was aware of not being as present for her as he normally was but couldn't seem to do anything about it. Tanisha was in her early forties and had the wiry physique and sallow skin of some former addicts and lifelong smokers. She walked with wide, mannish steps, the way young people who sag their pants might, but she didn't sag. It seemed to be an affect developed from another time to signal that she wasn't scared of anybody, which Sharif saw as a dead give-away of someone living with a lot of fear in their heart. She wore black Air Force 1 sneakers, khaki pants, and a white long sleeve T-shirt with the brand written across the chest in a teal graffiti font.

During his first session with Tanisha a couple of weeks earlier, she'd spoken without inflection and jammed her few short sentences into single words: *YeahHeyI'mTanisha*. He assumed her monotone mumbling was a defense mechanism like her strut, which he later realized was only half true. The other half was that she was, in fact, bored by Sharif. She'd gone through similar programs before and had come to CAPPA reluctantly, a last resort after a long and fruitless job search. As Sharif talked her through the various program options, everything he said seemed to reinforce her assumption that this would be a drawn-out, patronizing, hoop-jumping experience.

She had come to CAPPA because she needed a paycheck. Yesterday. She wanted a job to make rent and buy the groceries she actually wanted instead of waiting in line at the emergency food pantry for their idea of nutritionally balanced meals. Like everybody, she wanted autonomy in her life. Her work history from before her six years in prison was in building maintenance, and she'd heard from a friend that CAPPA could get her a job in that field after a few weeks of case management bullshit. She did not look forward to CAPPA's "holistic continuum of care."

During that first encounter, the bored frustration on Tanisha's face seemed to harden as Sharif prattled on about the opportunities and support systems she could be enrolled in to meet her hours. He cut himself off mid-sentence to say, "Hey, how are you feeling about all this? I know it's kind of a lot."

"What?" Her expression looked like disgust.

"Did you have any questions or concerns so far?"

"No."

This wasn't going well. He remembered one of his most effective ice-breakers. "Let's back up. Before we go on, I'd like you to tell me what you had for breakfast."

The irrelevance and lightness of the question sometimes amused clients. She looked at him head-on. "What's that got to do with anything?"

Sharif shrugged. It had taken him years to be comfortable with sustained, silent eye contact with an impatient client.

She sighed. "I had a breakfast sandwich," she said, and waited. "You going to write that down in your little file?"

"Hmm. Was it good? What was on it? What kind of bread?"

She quickly looked over her shoulder as if she felt someone sneak up behind her, then back at him. "Are you messing with me right now?"

"I am not. No."

"Egg. Sausage. Cheese," she said in the tone of someone asking what the fuck his problem was. "Oh"—her volume increased—"and I made them toast the bagel extra so the cheese melted how I like. You getting all this?"

Sharif looked at his computer screen. "It says here that if we input the beverage you had with the breakfast sandwich, it'll complete your full psychological profile."

There was a silent, climactic tension between them, a crossroads. After a few long seconds, the subtlest of smiles tugged at the corner of Tanisha's mouth. She tried to fight it off. Then she laughed, then laughed harder, then called him a crazy person. A door opened between them. Her laughter and the ease of their conversation that followed made Sharif feel like he'd summited a mountain. That was Sharif on a good day, doing excellent work.

Two of Sharif's other clients sat in the computer lab with him and Tanisha today. Fadhil, a dapper sixty-five-year-old Iraqi refugee with thick salt-and-pepper hair who had been an orthopedic surgeon in Mosul before it was burned to the ground. And Sherwayne, a rotund man in his mid-thirties living in a men's shelter in East New York. Every day, Sherwayne wore the same enormous Tweety Bird T-shirt with a speech bubble that read, *I tawt I taw a puddy tat!* He continued to wear it after going to the appointment Sharif made for him at the free business attire nonprofit in CAPPA's referral system. Fadhil's task between nine and ten a.m. was to fill out an online application to become a medical interpreter for Arabic-speaking patients at various hospitals and health centers across the boroughs. Sherwayne's task was to find online concierge job descriptions that he could mine for language to use on his résumé. Sharif would check in on their progress after signing Tanisha up for a few workforce readiness workshops.

Adjoua called, and he asked Tanisha to please excuse him for a moment.

"Hey," Adjoua said, "I'm still fine and I know you're at work, but real quick, did you order all new supplies and a new bed for Judy?"

"Uh, yep, I did actually." Sharif had put in the order on their credit card that morning. It ended up costing $287 with the promo code.

"Oh. Okay. Because when I got the email confirmation I thought it must be a mistake." She waited. "Or fraud." When Sharif still didn't say anything, she explicitly asked, "So, why did you do that?"

"I was in such a rush yesterday that I left Judy's stuff on the sidewalk."

"Wouldn't it have been cheaper to go and pick it up? Did you call the guy you left Judy with?"

Wanting to sound distracted, he clicked aimlessly at Tanisha's electronic case file. "Um." *Click.* "What's that?" *Click.* "Yeah." *Click click.* "I did, but the stuff was gone."

"The guy said it was gone?"

Click. "Um, sorry, hold on a sec." *Click.* "Yeah, that's what he said."

"Someone stole a dog bin and bed?"

"I don't know. Possibly." *Click click. Click.* "Or maybe the garbage people took it." *Click.* "I'm really sorry, sweetie, do you mind if I call you back? I'm sort of in the middle of something with a client."

Tanisha said, "I don't mind."

"'Sweetie'?" Adjoua said with suspicion.

It was true, Sharif never called her sweetie. Their standard terms of endearment were baby, my love, some food items and animals with a "y" added to the end, but never sweetie. Weirder still, it was her ex, Aberto, who called her sweetie.

"Can I call you a little later?"

Way too loudly, Tanisha said, "I told you I don't mind."

Adjoua let him off the phone but was clearly not satisfied with the information she'd received.

Sharif did some more aimless clicking, waiting for his mind to come back to the room. He glanced at his cell phone and saw he'd received four more responses from the no-kill shelters saying his circumstances changed nothing for Judy. After a minute of computer sounds and gum chewing and breathing, Tanisha sadly announced that it was her daughter's birthday.

"Oh yeah?" Sharif said, unsure why it sounded like a bad thing. "Any plans?"

"Laquan and I have been planning her dinner for three days, but I doubt she'll come home after school or even sleep at home tonight." She shook her head.

"Isn't Jayda eleven?" he asked.

"Twelve today. She hides at her friend's whenever she's mad at me."

"What happened?"

"The girls were helping Laquan and me make this fancy chocolate mousse for Jayda's birthday, and I was feeling kind of off, like kind of annoyed in general for some reason. I don't know. Just pissed off about parts of my life I guess. And then Jayda asks me out of the blue if singing is easy or hard. And I kind of snapped."

"Singing," Sharif said. "Like singing a song?"

She nodded. "That's what I said to her. I said, 'What do you mean, singing?' But I said it in a foul way. Laquan's daughter was already mad because I scolded her for licking the whisk. She went to her room in her snooty princess way like she does when she's pissed. I don't know why but I got even nastier with my daughter, repeating her question like it was the dumbest thing I ever heard. 'Is singing easy or hard, *Psh*. Are you stupid or something? You open your mouth and sing. What's wrong with you?' And then I did this ugly, 'La la la! How come you don't know that?'" Sharif heard a knot amassing in Tanisha's throat. "I said, 'Why are we paying for your school books if you can't even learn something as basic as that?' And I saw this pain in her face. It surprised me, you know? I knew I was being rude or whatever, but I didn't think it was bad enough to really hurt, you know? She's real mature for her age, so I forget she's a little girl sometimes. I looked away from her and kept my eye on the bowl of chocolate mousse, grating an orange peel into it like Laquan said. He calls it 'zesting.' Thinks he's some kind of top chef or something." She briefly smiled with teasing affection. "But all that time 'zesting' I could feel Jayda's pain, like throbbing next to me. I wanted it to go away so I ignored it. It's like if I addressed it, it meant it was real, or that I'm a bad mother or something, even though I knew she took what I said as, like, proof of another thing that feels hard for her but easy for everybody else. Like there's something broken about her or something. And I'll be completely honest with you all," she looked over her shoulder to include Fadhil and Sher-wayne more deliberately, "I've done things to my daughter you'd probably think sound a hell of a lot worse than that stuff about singing, but for some reason, the way I said it, with the 'la la la' and all that, and the way I could tell she heard it, and how it made her feel something so bad and lonely that it took over her sweet little face and crawled up in her shoulders so high that I even saw it with my head down in the chocolate mousse? I swear. I would have been better off smacking her in the face. I've never laid a hand on her, but I'd bet anything she would have preferred that right then." She wiped at her tears. "And you know what the stupidest part about the whole thing is? I didn't even understand her question in the first place. I could have said 'What do you mean, sweetheart?' I could have said, 'What makes you ask that?' I still don't know if she meant singing in general, or singing well, or singing professionally, or memorizing songs, or what. And you want to know something else? No matter the kind of singing she was asking about, I don't have any fucking idea, excuse my language, whether singing is easy or hard." Here her crying and speaking took on a self-scolding tone. "Like I ever really tried to sing a goddamn thing in my life."

Even though physical contact with clients was forbidden, Sharif rubbed her back when she curled forward to cry fully into her hands.

Fadhil had turned away from his computer to watch Tanisha as she talked. He then spoke in his poised, intentional fashion: "I suppose you could still tell her she can sing. That singing is difficult until it becomes easy with practice, like anything. It could become very comfortable for her to sing later in life."

Tanisha said, "I don't know why I get like that with her. There's no one I love more in this world. But when I mess up with her, all I want is for it to go away, and so I dig my heels in. I get even more aggressive, or defensive. Shit, I don't know the difference anymore." She accepted some tissues from Sharif and patted at her tears. "Man. I hate my aunt to this day for always putting me down when I was little, making me feel like a piece of shit for being curious, like every question I had was shit, like all I did was shit, and everything in my head was shit. And now look at me doing that to my baby."

Sharif floundered for a helpful response: "Jayda definitely knows how much you love her and that everything you do is with her well-being in mind." On top of it being generic, Sharif didn't even believe children thought that way, especially not after a parent hurts their feelings. He struggled to find truer words. He'd been distracted all morning: bad at his job, imprecise.

"It will be okay," Fadhil said. "Children are very resilient. You'll simply use very soft tones next time you speak to her and she will forget this."

Sherwayne weighed in: "Talk to her about it. Go back and tell her you feel bad about how you said that stuff. She'll appreciate that. We got to model that behavior too. Show kids it's strong to apologize."

Tanisha nodded and then said, "You know, I walk around all day worrying someone is doing me wrong. And I forget how much worse it feels when I'm the one doing someone wrong, especially someone who doesn't deserve it. Especially someone I love so hard. Everybody here at CAPPA is always talking about *trauma this* and *PTSD that,* but the trauma you all never talk about is the trauma of hurting someone else. Not being the victim, but being the perpetrator, you get me? All the people I was incarcerated with who were in there because they wronged someone hated themselves for that. People think we're all locked up waiting to get out so we can hurt somebody else, but the truth is, most of us can't stand hurting people. I swear to God, being the perpetrator is worse than being the victim."

Sharif recalled the podcast about infidelity — about how the cheater is better off than the cheated since they can choose to change — and tried adapting this concept for Tanisha. "The silver lining is that you can choose to not repeat any behavior that makes you feel bad. You're in control of how you talk to Jayda in the future. You feel you made a thoughtless mistake. Now you can make it better by apologizing, like Sherwayne said, and committing to not doing it again." His voice rang false. Why was Sharif forcing himself to give advice he wasn't sure about? Tanisha hadn't asked for advice. Why had all three men assumed she wanted their guidance? Maybe all she wanted was to let something painful out.

It was then, at about 9:45 a.m., that Emmanuel entered the room.

19.

EMMANUEL'S PRESENCE FELT supernatural somehow, like a hard wind had blown through the room without actually moving anything. There were two incoherent realities: Emmanuel, the nice man Sharif recognized and who owed him an apology; and Emmanuel, whose body seemed inhabited by some entirely different, cold person. Everyone kept their eyes glued to him as he stood in the doorframe, his chest rising and falling like he'd run to this threshold. As if stepping out of the sky, both radiant and threatening, he approached. He had stubble this morning, a surprising amount of it was gray, and it twinkled under the fluorescent overheads. His voice trembled when he said to Sharif, "He's a child."

Sharif was so taken aback that he couldn't speak above a whisper: "What?"

All heads in the room followed Emmanuel's slow advance toward Sharif, riveted by this man's energy.

"Three bones are broken," Emmanuel said, pain and fury rushing together. "He won't heal back to normal."

"Whoa," said Tanisha, the first to shake out of the trance. She kicked her chair back and sprang up between Emmanuel and Sharif. She thrusted her arm out, pointing a finger at Emmanuel's chest. "Stop right there." He stopped centimeters from her finger, looking past her at Sharif. Tanisha said, "Back up, man."

"You nearly killed him," Emmanuel said to Sharif.

Sherwayne and Fadhil surrounded him from both sides. Fadhil took Emmanuel's arm and told him to step back. Emmanuel ripped free. "Take your hands off me." Two other CAPPA clients who happened to be walking by were suddenly surrounding Emmanuel too. Emmanuel started yelling at an incomprehensible volume, "You almost killed him!" Others grabbed him by the arms. Indignation surged in his eyes as he tried to break free from the entanglement, telling them that they had no right to touch him. CAPPA's two security guards broke into the melee and began pulling Emmanuel toward the exit.

Sharif's vision pounded. Emmanuel struggled with his detainers, shouting, "You should be dragging *him* out!" Clients and coworkers flooded the hallway, where security had Emmanuel now. They cautiously followed as he was forced into the lobby and to the elevators. Sharif followed too, his heart flying, hearing Emmanuel shout, "What kind of man beats a boy!" There were a good forty people in the lobby now: clients from all over the world, staff, maintenance crew, program directors, and security. Emmanuel again tried to shake off the guards physically controlling his body. He was still shouting from inside the elevator with the guards. When the doors shut, everyone turned to Sharif.

20.

SHARIF WITHDREW TO the stairwell of the building to collect himself, walking up two floors to avoid any familiar faces. He paced the sixth-floor landing, trying to wrap his mind around what happened. Emmanuel had of course been referring to his son, Junior. Right? Who else? But why did he think Sharif had hurt him? Sharif didn't want to involve or worry Adjoua, but he had an overwhelming urge to hear her voice.

He called, and as soon as Adjoua picked up, she asked what was wrong.

"What?"

"You sound weird again."

He remembered their recent conversation about his reordering Judy's things. "I'm a little rattled from work stuff."

"What work stuff? She said no to the raise?"

"It's not that. I haven't even gotten to that. I don't know how to explain it."

After a pause, she asked, "Do you want to try?" It was clear that she had intended to sound gentle, but there was impatience there too.

"Okay, but I really don't want you to worry." He chastised himself: If that was so important, why did he call her? He said, "This guy came into my office and started shouting. It escalated really fast. Security had to take him outside."

"Shouting about what? Oh my God, did he hurt you?"

Maybe he did want to hear her worry if it was for him. "No, no. He started yelling stuff that didn't make any sense."

"That sounds awful. Jesus, I'm so sorry that happened. Who was he? A client?"

His phone alarm went off, reminding him of his ten a.m. meeting with his boss to request a raise. He almost had to laugh at the irony of it timing out so perfectly with his unprecedented drama at work. "No, not a client. Sorry, I wanted to hear your voice for a second." He touched the cement walls in the stairwell with the pads of his fingers. There were thin grooves in the cement, as if someone had taken a comb to it when it was still wet. "It's been a rough start. But everything's okay. Tell me how you're feeling."

She said, "I'm fine. Same as when we spoke ten minutes ago. Are you sure you're all right?"

"Yeah. It's just that nothing like that has happened before."

"Can't they set up your desk behind those secure doors with everyone else? Get you out of that computer lab? I don't understand how you can even breathe in there."

"I like being in my own room with the clients."

"They could at least put secure doors on that room."

"Maybe, yeah."

She exhaled. "Another reason to look for something new, I guess."

"What do you mean?"

"Sorry," she said. "That was dumb. I just want you to be safe, and for us to be okay."

"We are okay." They were quiet for a while. He said, "I know you want to be better than okay. And we will be. Just not overnight, you know?"

She was slow to respond: "Yeah." It sounded more like acknowledgment of his having said something than agreement.

He said, "I should go. I'm sure Merjem is looking for me."

"Okay. Please stay safe. We'll talk more about everything tonight, before they induce."

21.

MERJEM'S CORNER OFFICE had the opposite problem as Sharif's windowless computer lab. It received a burdensome amount of natural light. The wraparound floor-to-ceiling windows turned it into a blinding white cube all morning. It reminded Sharif of a pre-afterlife scene he'd seen in a film once. To make out her computer screen or the person in front of her, or to read the grant proposal drafts submerging her desk, she alternated between squinting and wearing sunglasses. He asked her once if she'd considered getting curtains. She said no, the painful quantities of light were a sandblaster to her depression. He also knew Merjem prided herself on not asking for more than she was given.

She was a Bosnian refugee. After fleeing her hometown as a young woman with her family to Srebrenica, which the UN had declared a safe haven, Serbian soldiers overran the place, executing some eight thousand Muslim men and boys, her father, husband, and two brothers among them. The outnumbered UN peacekeepers helplessly watched the massacre. Merjem and her sister managed to slip away in the mayhem, hiding and waiting out the men's executions and the women's shipment to camps. At nightfall, they ran through the woods and walked for two days to government-held territory. Their homes and family gone, the sisters were flown and housed in Italy for a year before receiving refugee status in St. Louis, Missouri. Her sister married into a Bosnian family there, and Merjem moved to New

York, climbing her way up the nonprofit ranks. She must have been in her mid-forties now. Her accent was subtle but present enough for Sharif to be impressed by her vocabulary, which was superior to that of any native English speaker he knew. She also happened to have the appearance of a 1960s supermodel: six feet tall with powder-white, seemingly poreless skin, high and sharp cheekbones, a delicately upturned nose, the piercing blue eyes of a Siberian husky, and red hair so full and vibrant that it made the world behind her monochromatic. Her stunning looks were more preposterous than attractive. When not meeting with funders, auditors, or going to a conference, she tried to beat back her looks with excessively casual dress. Today, she wore her adolescent daughter's dirty Adidas sneakers and oversized GAP hoodie with a pair of grungy, ill-fitting jeans, her hair tied up messily with a rubber band.

It was entirely thanks to Merjem that Sharif had gotten hired. He had been submitting his résumé through a job site without realizing it was getting botched in the upload. He had uploaded a PDF when it should have been a Word doc, or maybe it was the other way around. Regardless, by the time his résumé landed in the thirty or so nonprofit employers' inboxes, the text had transformed into a cipher. It read that he'd gotten his "M#W" license at "The Ci," while working full-time as an "e#L in#trtor" at the "NeWorPubicrary" in the year "2." He found out about this when Merjem, the only hiring manager who'd invited him for an interview, showed him a printed copy of what she'd received and asked him to explain why it looked like a ransom note. After the initial awkwardness, she said she had called him in because she liked his cover letter, which had arrived intact, and was drawn to his ESL teaching experience. She admitted that the agency most desperately needed an adult ed instructor for a new contract with the city starting next week. Would he possibly be amenable to teaching until she found a more permanent instructor for the role? As soon as she did, she'd move Sharif to a caseworker position.

Adjoua would later say that Merjem had been manipulative, or at least opportunistic without considering what was best for Sharif. Merjem could have made him a caseworker right away and spared him the brunt of *her* staffing problem. Sharif understood Adjoua's point, but ultimately saw Merjem's offer as aligning with the all-hands-on-deck culture of the agency. And the workshops he taught ended up being a great introduction to the range of CAPPA clients.

The groups of workforce readiness students he taught were so diverse as to be farcical: a Haitian asylee who stopped school in the seventh grade and hardly spoke English; an Egyptian chemical engineer with a PhD and eight years of high-ranking experience in a power plant in Alexandria turned political refugee; a gay Ukrainian music teacher in a wheelchair persecuted for her sexuality; an ex-gang captain from Brownsville recently released from prison; a seventeen-year-old Nepali boy who'd been the groundskeeper of a tourist lodge on the Annapurna trail; a high school history teacher who'd emigrated from Barbados. Low- and high-skilled workers, unhoused single parents, recovering addicts, victims of human trafficking, cult escapees, and the hyperbolically religious all gathered in the same classroom, learning the same material from a young white guy from an upper-middle-class Minnesota suburb.

When he revealed himself as a Sharif on the first day of class, spelling it out on the whiteboard in case anyone missed it, he took pleasure in the shift he felt in the room, like he had suddenly become intriguing to them.

There was such an assortment of English language skills, educational attainments, work experiences, cultural backgrounds, and career goals among his thirty-plus students that it made lesson-pacing virtually impossible. They had a lot of fun in there nonetheless, shared stories, laughed, and experienced breakthroughs in understanding the invisible stumbling blocks to employment, like how to make sure you don't upload a résumé in the wrong format, a story he shared to the delight of every cohort. Sharif saw enough of his students get placed in promising jobs with opportunities for advancement and family-sustaining wages that he was sure CAPPA was where he wanted to be. It quickly became his most fulfilling job to date.

True to her word, Merjem moved him to Case Manager I after six months of teaching, and then a year later, around the time Adjoua sold her novel, to Case Manager II, which meant he had more paperwork and would be expected to train new case managers — something that hadn't come up due to stagnated and unrenewed budgets. Since his last promotion, CAPPA had been laying people off faster than they were hiring. The city and state still gave the nonprofit some money, but the federal government under the new administration proved determined to starve social service providers that served a lot of immigrants. They did this by mounting impossible requirements to maintain funding, mandating that CAPPA serve a hundred more refugees than the year before, despite the administration allowing a record low number of refugees into the country. There had been twenty NYC organizations with robust refugee programs a decade ago, and today there were three. Merjem said it would be down to one soon, and zero if this president got a second term.

Sharif had always gotten along with Merjem. Their ease and openness about their work and personal lives had led to something resembling friendship. But since planning to ask for a raise, he'd grown nervous around her. The next logical promotion would have been to Supervisor I in a year and a half. There weren't even any current openings for that position anyway. He'd contemplated inventing a new job that he would spearhead. He'd even try his hand at grant writing to get funding. But a new job would only be justified if it solved a specific problem for poor New Yorkers, and the only problems he could think of were far too big for one inexperienced person to tackle. Besides, his underlying motivation was to solve his own problem of being broke. His angle was his need. Implicit would be the suggestion that he'd have to leave CAPPA if that need wasn't met. This was neither something he wanted nor a credible threat in the short term since this job was his family's health insurance. There was no way to do this from a place of strength.

Squinting through the morning light of Merjem's office, Sharif asked her how she was doing.

"Me?" she said. "Forget about me, Sharif. What the hell happened? Are you okay?"

"Yeah, I'm fine. I honestly don't know what happened."

"So, he's not a client?"

For a split second, he contemplated sharing the full background: Emmanuel coming in for a referral; the newspaper mishap; Adjoua's false labor; asking Emmanuel to look after his dog; Judy on the fire escape; Emmanuel's teenager demanding payment. But those details didn't explain why Emmanuel showed up here accusing him of injuring his son, and Sharif wasn't eager to tell his animal-loving boss that he'd entrusted his elderly dog to a virtual stranger who proved irresponsible and volatile. He said, "He came in a few months ago for some legal services referral. He was perfectly friendly then."

"And then he comes back out of the blue and starts screaming about how you crushed his child's bones?" She shook her head. "Scary. Elected officials have been talking about tackling the mental health crisis since I moved here, and I haven't seen a single meaningful improvement in twenty-five years." Her assumption that Emmanuel was mentally ill surprised him, but he supposed he didn't have evidence to the contrary. He didn't know Emmanuel. She said, "We need to set up a key fob door-entry system for that computer lab. Sharif, I am so sorry you went through this."

"It's okay, thank you." His eyes still straining from the direct sunlight, he gave in and grabbed a pair of neon sunglasses from the selection Merjem kept in a wooden bowl for visitors. A green pair. For the first time, it crossed his mind that the lack of curtains was a power move to put visitors on the back foot. About Emmanuel, he felt compelled to add, "When he came in for that referral, I really didn't pick up on any mental health flags. He was cordial and reasonable—nothing seemed off."

"Believe me, the crazy switch can be sudden. Consider Jo." Jovana was Merjem's twelve-year-old daughter whose clothes she was wearing and who was suspected of having borderline personality disorder. "She's an angel all day and then something random triggers her into becoming an incoherent psychopath who wants to claw her mother's eyes out." Merjem got up to fill her mug from the Mr. Coffee that was so backlit that it was compressed into a comma. In her half step to the Mr. Coffee, Sharif was reminded of her marked duck-footedness. It was one of two mismatches to her supermodel glamour. Her only other attribute of physical humility were her rounded shoulders. She had the curled-in posture of a tall adolescent wanting to hide her body; someone who did not enjoy being stared at as much as she surely had been her whole life.

"How is Jo doing?" Sharif asked.

She shrugged, put down her coffee. "Doing her schoolwork, at least." A cloud of sadness passed over her, which caused her to stop squinting, yet this was when she put on her oversize tortoiseshell sunglasses. The glasses with the loose bun and hoodie turned her into a sorority girl. "Anyway," Merjem said, "if this man actually believes you hurt his son, there's a chance he'll come back." She had the look of an epiphany: "Oh my God. I'm an asshole. You're asking me about Jo, but how's Adjoua?" She leaned forward on her desk. "What are you even doing here?"

"She's fine. They're inducing labor tonight at six p.m."

"Wow, so what happened yesterday? Why are they inducing?"

"That's exactly what I wanted to know. Apparently that's an indecent question to ask a doctor. But basically it's because her blood pressure is elevated."

"Okay, I'm sure they know what they're doing." She leaned back, cupping her coffee in both hands. "What an insane couple of days for you guys. And as of tonight, you'll be new parents." She lifted her mug in a cheers gesture, then sipped and rocked in her chair for a bit. "You'll start your paternity leave Monday then?"

He hadn't thought it through. "Well, the baby won't come home right away, so I'd like to delay my leave if possible. I'll find out more tonight and message you."

"Please do," she said, sounding disappointed by the uncertainty. "So even though I'm putting in that request for a secure door in the lab, it'll take at least a week to actually get it installed. I'll set up a desk for you in the main room with the others in the meantime."

"Oh, I really appreciate that, but I'd rather stay in the lab if possible. Pretty much all of the in-person work I've designed with clients revolves around those computers. So I'd be in there all day anyway."

"Sharif. That guy could come back."

"I know to call security if he does." He saw an admirable reflection of himself in Merjem and understood he sounded brave and devoted. "Besides," he continued, "whoever is working the front desk doesn't have secure doors either. Maintenance and anybody else passing through the lobby is technically at risk, and so are the adult ed teachers in the classroom. I'll be fine." This was his opportunity. He took in a big breath, creating a pause and signaling a transition to another topic. He felt as ready as he could to tell her what kind of raise he needed and why. The moment he opened his mouth, he heard two quick knocks at the door.

Shazeeda, from the front desk, poked her head in. With her eyes closed against the light, she said, "Sorry for the interruption, but Officer Dauphne's here to see you." She cracked open her eyes slightly to indicate she was speaking to Sharif, then closed her eyes while awaiting his response.

"Great," Merjem said, "more excitement. Thank you, Z. Have her come in here please."

22.

OFFICER PATRICIA DAUPHNE stepped in and put on her aviators. Patricia's cousin, Fabienne, had been one of Sharif's first clients as a caseworker. Sharif had landed Fabienne — a sweet, shy, twenty-five-year-old Haitian asylee without a high school diploma or formal work experience — a temporary job in a mailroom while helping her get a commercial driver's license and a job as a bus operator. Patricia had since referred many community members to CAPPA, some of whom were recent arrests of hers. She liked to accompany them to the office for a warm handoff, dropping in for a visit with Sharif or Merjem.

Her walkie-talkie made intermittent beeps, followed by white noise and a man mumbling a long series of numbers. She turned the volume down and announced, "My partner is in the process of booking that unruly gentleman who was here."

Sharif was uncomfortable. "Booking him? Why?"

She cocked her head to the side, surprised by the question. "We were on our beat when we saw him screaming his head off at your security guard downstairs. We tried to help calm him down but he got more ornery. A crowd formed, then the cell phones came out and the police brutality taunts started. He was riling everyone up, and next thing you know, the only way to diffuse the situation was to bring him in."

"On what charge?" Sharif asked.

She shifted in her seat to face him more directly, which seemed cumbersome with her police belt and the boxy bulletproof vest under her shirt. "Disorderly conduct, for one. Disobeying a peace officer." Her aviators reflected a thin funhouse version of Sharif's face back at him. It looked like he was being sucked down a black hole wearing neon green sunglasses. "I hear he tried to attack you."

Sharif said, "Oh, no. I don't think he would have attacked me."

"It's best when you don't have to find out. Trust me." Patricia took out a pen and notepad from her breast pocket. "So, what can you tell me about this guy?"

He found himself speaking incredibly slowly, as if his voice itself were on tiptoe. "He came in for a referral a while back." Cornered into sticking to what he'd told Merjem, he cursed himself for not giving her the whole backstory.

"Okay. And it sounds like you have a different take on what happened from the security guards. How would you describe your interaction with this man today?"

"How would I describe it? Um, brief? Surprising. But basically inconsequential."

Patricia and Merjem shared a look. Patricia said, "Inconsequential? I heard he made quite a scene. What was he shouting about? Killing his children or something?"

Merjem answered, "Breaking his child's bones."

"All of them?" Patricia said with the trace of a joke.

Merjem said, "The poor man was obviously having some kind of episode. Patricia, did I ever tell you about that guy who threw a brick at my back? Happened right here on Church."

"When was this?" She leaned back in her chair.

"About ten years ago now." Merjem told the story, and Patricia then shared a story of her own about catching up with a guy who'd pushed four people in front of subway trains at various stations over the course of a week. Merjem repeated her critique of elected officials not doing enough about the mental health crisis, and Patricia couldn't agree more. Merjem then told Patricia that Sharif would be a new dad this evening. Patricia gave a shout of delight, sincerely congratulating him and saying how wonderful it would be. Sharif tried to receive and internalize her enthusiasm but couldn't really feel anything.

Eventually circling back to Emmanuel, Patricia asked, "So, any CCTV monitors catch today's incident?"

Merjem said, "There aren't any in the computer lab where it started."

She turned to Sharif. "That's something else I'll request."

To Patricia she said, "But Shazeeda can share footage from the lobby."

"I probably won't need to dig too deep on this one, but glad to know it's there."

She looked down at her notepad and jotted down a single word that Sharif couldn't see.

"Okay. Good enough for me." She said, "Sharif, please call 911 immediately if this guy messes with you again, and then call my cell."

"Sure, thanks. So what happens to Emmanuel now?"

"That's up to the judge."

"Well, if he's confused or unwell or something, it doesn't seem like he should be in jail. Would it speed up his release if I called the station?"

"You do-gooders are too much." She laughed. "And people say I'm a softie. This guy barges into your place of work and flips out on you so hard he has to get dragged out, and you're worried about how his day is going." She laughed again.

Merjem said, "That's how my people think, I'm afraid."

Patricia said, "Well, don't you worry, Sharif, he'll be fine. Probably out in a couple hours."

"Mind if I call a little later to check in about that?"

"Sure, not at all."

Merjem asked Sharif, "Now, have you talked to any coworkers or clients about what happened today?"

"No. I went straight to the stairwell to collect myself. Then came here."

Merjem took off her sunglasses and turned her squinting eyes to the ceiling, taking in and expelling a lungful of air. "Sorry you have to witness my PR hawkishness, Patricia—but, Sharif, I hope it goes without saying that we must keep this story simple and consistent. That man is clearly unwell. That's all there is to it. We want to avoid any distortions or rumors." She aimed her squint at Sharif. "You know what I mean?"

He nodded. "Of course."

Cultivating trust in this community had taken decades. If even a small number of residents rallied around Emmanuel's claim, maybe getting the press or locally elected officials involved, it could hurt CAPPA's reputation, which would in turn damage their ability to offer critical services, which would then dry up more funding streams and jeopardize the agency's existence. Merjem's boss, CAPPA's president and CEO, was an Irish American woman who had founded the nonprofit with her Irish American friend in this predominantly Black neighborhood in the late seventies. Adjoua pointed out how problematic it was that 95 percent of CAPPA staff and clients were people of color while 98 percent of the executive leadership and board was white. Sharif agreed this was a major problem. But the current leadership was keeping the place afloat during record budget cuts, so he couldn't see how replacing themselves for being white would be to the community's best interest right now.

Merjem had learned the hard way to be hypervigilant about reputational damage. Before her job at CAPPA, she had been the head volunteer coordinator for an international confederation of big charities when it surfaced that three American volunteers they'd placed in rural Colombia were hiring and abusing sex workers. *The Philanthropic Times* disparaged the confederation, painting them as a colonizing force. Donors and partners publicly withdrew support, and in response, the confederation cleaned house. Merjem was among the dozen fired. She directly oversaw the manager who oversaw the manager who oversaw the team in Colombia who oversaw the volunteers from hell. She had no clue about the vile conduct happening on her watch, but it had set her career back ten years before she rebuilt it at CAPPA.

"As a matter of fact, I'll send a staff email right now," Merjem said. She loudly rattled her mouse to wake her computer. She was evidently finished with Sharif and Patricia.

As Patricia stood, Sharif said, "Oh, Merjem. There was that other conversation I wanted to have. The one I sent the calendar invite about?"

Fully in her email now, she spoke absently, "Yeah, let me fire this off before my ten-thirty. Check my calendar and send another invite for later today if you see an opening. Not sure today works off the top of my head. But definitely check."

Doing his best to hide his deflation, he said, "Sounds good, thanks," and started leaving with Patricia.

As they were halfway out the door, Merjem said, "Sharif, wait."

He turned back with an irrational hope in his heart. "Yes?"

"Sunglasses."

"Of course," he said, and returned them to the bowl.

By the time Sharif had gotten back to his desk, Merjem had sent the email. He finished enrolling Tanisha in the workforce readiness workshops but accomplished little else after that. Clients and coworkers kept dropping in to share their experience of the incident. Some were disturbed by what happened but most seemed excited, grateful to have a reason to remember the day. A story to tell back home. Everyone considered Sharif lucky that Tanisha, Fadhil, and Sherwayne had been there to stop that guy from causing any real damage. Although they all responded humbly, making the classic statements about how anyone would have done the same in their position, they clearly felt bonded in their collective heroism.

Without wanting to undermine their bravery, Sharif did mention a few times that he had no reason to think that "the guy" intended any violence. But like with Patricia, the response was thank God Sharif didn't have to find out. The narrative was as simple and unanimously accepted as Merjem could have hoped: Some unhinged stranger tried to commit a random act of violence against a caseworker. It could have happened to any of us. What a relief to know that we are a united front in such emergencies. The ease with which Emmanuel had been reduced to a dangerous lunatic unsettled Sharif as much as it shamed him for being too craven to challenge it. He didn't know much about Emmanuel, or why he did what he did, but he believed the kindness he'd received from Emmanuel after learning Adjoua was in the hospital was real.

Around noon, Adjoua texted to say she was still fine and hoped he was doing better and that his talk with Merjem went well. He wished he had good news to give her, but Merjem had no openings in her calendar to meet again that day, so with defeat in his heart he sent the new request for ten a.m. on Monday. He called Patricia to check in on Emmanuel, prepared to go there on his lunch break to assist in his release in any way he could. She said Emmanuel's lawyer had already secured his release and gotten all the charges dropped. Sharif asked if she had gotten the lawyer's name by chance, and she confirmed that it was the one he was dreading. The man who'd been hounding his imagination for years. Aberto Barbosa.

23.

ON THE TRAIN to the hospital, after quickly stopping off at home to walk Judy, Sharif read through four more replies from animal shelters. All confirming Judy would remain deep on their waitlist. He'd been Googling Aberto and was zooming in on a picture of his face when the train slowed to a complete stop between Times Square and Fifty-Seventh. Five minutes passed underground without cell service, and then ten. Sharif sat with a primal panic, causing him to sweat profusely. The conductor's frequent, lengthy, incomprehensible explanations over the loudspeaker only served to batter Sharif's nerves. Fifteen minutes in, the sighs of other passengers felt hostile. They stood, paced, removed layers of clothing, opened doors between train cars to look down the dark tunnel for clues. The train started moving again nearly an hour later, at six thirty. Pulling up to the Fifty-Seventh and Seventh Avenue stop, Sharif saw the missed calls from Adjoua. She was calling him again right now.

"I'm so sorry," he answered. "The train got stuck underground."

"You're not going to believe this," she said. He was perplexed by the enthusiasm in her voice. "I've been discharged."

"What?"

"The nurse yesterday was using a blood pressure cuff that was too small. That's what gave such high readings."

"You're kidding."

"No, and it's been completely normal since last night and all day today."

"So what does this——"

"It means I go home and wait for natural labor to commence." She expelled little puffs of amused, relieved disbelief. And then: "Hello? You there?"

"Yeah. Sorry. This is so——" But he didn't finish, because the only word he could think of was "good."

"I know, I know." She sounded happy. The train's door-closing chime sounded off, and she added, "Hey, depending on where you are, you might want to switch trains and meet me at home. I'm getting a ride in a minute here."

He leapt up and wedged himself between the closing doors, fighting them off, blackening his hands on the rubber sealing strips.

He was on the platform when she said, "This is a really great opportunity. We can use this time to get our ducks in a row. Find Judy long-term care. Make tracks to improve our finances. You know?"

"Yes," he said, feeling a rush of optimism and relief, like an answered prayer. "I totally agree."

He emailed Merjem with the update right away, explaining that it would probably be another month before he'd need to use his paternity leave. He wasn't shy about sharing his gratitude for the extra time they'd been given in his email. But on the ride home, that gratitude was tainted by thoughts of the medical incompetency that had created it. His gratitude had been borne of the resolution of a false problem. How could he trust the people in charge of his wife's and baby's health? It was a special kind of insecurity to lose confidence in the people who were meant to be the experts. If they had quickly discerned that Adjoua's water hadn't broken and that she was otherwise well, it would have spared them tides of unnecessary stress and expenses. Sharif may not have even had to bring Judy to Emmanuel's at all. He would have simply gone to work and asked for his raise.

Being reminded of Emmanuel and Junior resulted in him Googling images of Aberto again. Eventually ceasing this weird behavior, he then got absorbed in a news story about a long-haul truck driver in Canada who ran a stop sign. The twenty-nine-year-old driver was an immigrant from India who worked long hours to support his family. He had not been under the influence, looking at his cell phone, or even listening to music when he missed the sign. He'd been distracted by a corner of tarp on his truck that flapped loosely in his side-view mirror. This momentary lack of focus resulted in a T-bone crash into a bus full of boys heading to their hockey game. Six of the fourteen- to fifteen-year-olds were killed, and twelve severely injured. So gutted by what happened, the driver pleaded guilty to every charge, even the completely unfair ones, rejecting his lawyer's guidance to go to trial. He refused to put the families of the victims through that. Sharif found the story tragic on multiple levels, but he found his sympathies funneling primarily to the driver. The error itself was so minor. It would have warranted a fifty-dollar fine had pure bad luck not put that bus there. He was expected to get a minimum of ten years in prison followed by deportation.

Adjoua was already slicing tomatoes on the kitchen island when Sharif got home. She wore her faded pink cotton sleeve on her head and the sapphire boubou with a six-inch tear in the side. He affectionately referred to this as her wizard outfit.

She didn't look up from her tomatoes when he came in and said hello, or after he had closed the door, or put down his bag, or greeted Judy, or taken off his shoes.

"Hi," he said again. "Remember me?"

"Hey," she said flatly, without a glance.

Her icy demeanor threw him. He'd anticipated a warm reunion after their phone call about her discharge. "Can you run me through everything the doctor said?"

"You know everything. Small cuff caused false blood pressure readings. Now we wait for labor."

Judy stood so close that his under-neck lay perfectly flush with Sharif's crotch, his chin flat against his abdomen, gazing up at him with open desperation. Sharif envied how passionately Judy wanted things, both because of how purposeful such focused desire feels and because Judy always ended up getting what he desired. The desires could only be one of five things: sustenance, relief walk, play, safety, or affection. He might be made to wait longer than he'd like for any of these five things, but was never denied them. Adjoua disagreed with Sharif's list, convinced there was a sixth thing Judy desired. The antidote to something unnameable and existential. A deeper emotional void that was as big and vague as it was for any human struggling to be still inside their body. She believed in Judy's depth — that an ache of sadness or confusion passed through him with the randomness of weather, as it did with her. To Sharif's mind, her projection onto their dog still fell within his list: a desire for both safety and affection.

While Sharif squatted to be face-to-face with Judy, he wondered if he should mention how his attempt at a raise had been foiled by today's events. Was Adjoua silently, punitively waiting for an update on that? Or did this have nothing to do with Sharif? Maybe she was disturbed by the medical incompetency at the hospital too. Judy retreated only to wallop the top of his big dome into Sharif's inner thigh, coiling into him, panting ecstatically, leaning against him and knocking him back onto his ass. Sharif laughed as he wrestle-hugged his bear. He then flipped Judy on his back and played his belly like a bongo drum. Judy's tail thumped the ground repeatedly. One of the great things about Judy was how he let Sharif exorcise complex emotions on him in ways that were unacceptable between humans: rough touch, hard body patting, schnoz-blows, surprise attacks that might transition into an awkward game of airplane. Judy always went along for the ride.

Adjoua was not smiling down at her boys' reconnection.

He finally ventured, "Okay. Tell me what's the matter."

She stopped slicing. "I thought we were a team."

"We are. What's up?"

She closed her eyes and put the back of her wrist against her forehead, knife dangling in front of her face. "Why did you really get Judy all new stuff?"

Sharif felt a sudden buildup of saliva in his mouth. His instinct was to buy a little time. To pull back so he could think, even if it ultimately meant confessing in the next few seconds. "What do you mean?"

Adjoua dropped her arm and opened her big, spotlighting eyes on him. "What I mean is that I don't believe your earlier explanation."

So much had happened since they'd seen each other that he actually forgot which details he'd omitted. In a sense, this was the most compelling reason to come clean. He had neither the recollection nor the cleverness to save half truths. Yet he dreaded telling her what happened to Judy.

She pinned him to the floor with those spotlight eyes. "You've got nothing to say? Okay, here's another question. Why did Aberto call looking for you?"

"He did?"

"Yeah, Sharif, he did." It was bad that she was repeating his name. "His client is accusing you of hospitalizing his son."

His hands, covered in dog hair, went to his face. "I really don't understand that." He stood from the ground and stepped up to the kitchen island. Judy's eyes followed as if Sharif's every move determined his survival.

Adjoua let the moment linger. "Apparently this guy's son underwent some dangerous surgery. He's claiming you're responsible, Sharif."

"Wait. Let's slow down." He put his hands flat on the island. "What did Aberto say exactly?"

"That this guy looked after Judy, and you got into a fight with his son."

"A fight. Like a physical fight."

"You tell me, Sharif." Her impatience dissipated. She only sounded afraid now.

"What else did he say?"

"That guy who shouted at you at work today. It was about this, wasn't it?"

"To properly fill you in on what's going on, I need to call Aberto and find out for myself. There's too much about this situation I don't have any understanding of yet."

She nodded at him slowly. "Do you lie to me often?"

"No."

"Only when it's important?" After looking away from him for a while, she spoke again, this time all emotion gone from her voice. "He's the last person who called." She motioned toward her phone with steely detachment, then went to the sink to rinse her hands.

Saving Aberto's number to his phone, he said, "I'm going to take Judy out, call Aberto, and clear this whole thing up. Please don't worry about anything."

"Stop telling me not to worry."

"Sorry, I just—don't want you to worry."

24.

SHARIF HAD MET Aberto only once at that work function where he got his business card, which he later gave to Emmanuel, but he'd gleaned Aberto's bio well before then. Aberto had been the star attorney at several nonprofits before starting his own firm, one without the politics and red tape he felt restricted him from doing the greatest good. The legal system was bridling and unevenly handed enough as it was. With the $2 million private grant Aberto secured, he could offer services on his own terms. Adjoua had mentioned Aberto's "insatiable appetite" for lawyering on behalf of the marginalized, and how he had an uncommon disregard for his own financial security. Sharif suspected Adjoua had gotten her line about "taking the vow of poverty" that she'd once used to impress friends and provoke parents, from Aberto. He wondered what salary Aberto took home since getting that $2 million grant. Had he renounced his vow of poverty like Adjoua?

According to social media, when Aberto wasn't feeding his insatiable appetite for lawyering, he was volunteering at food pantries and emergency shelters, writing social justice op-eds, and participating in advocacy efforts: campaigning city council members for after-school funding and literacy programs; lobbying senators for affordable housing rent subsidies or anti–gun violence measures in neglected districts with disproportionately high shooting rates.

He had long curly hair and a bike messenger bag glued to his body, or at least that's how Sharif always pictured him, since Aberto hadn't removed that bag the whole time he was at the CAPPA event where they met. Aberto's parents were Brazilian immigrants. He had light brown skin, a square, permanently stubbled jaw, and small, shiny blue eyes like aquamarine stones stuck in his handsomely weathered face. If Aberto had proposed to Adjoua that morning instead of unexpectedly breaking up with her after more than two years of living together, they'd be the ones married and pregnant today. Sharif knew this alternative reality didn't matter. But occasionally it did.

Aberto was attending events and fundraisers thrown by community-based organizations like CAPPA to build up his new firm's referral network. He would refer job-seeking clients to them, and they would send clients in need of free legal services to him, bringing both parties a step closer to the outcomes they'd promised funders. The demand was high enough for Aberto to get plenty of clients without this relationship-building tour he was on, but he touted a "systems change" approach—something he'd written about for the *Bklyner*—and intended to poach clients from other nonprofit firms. His innovative model of higher and more humane standards would force other firms to elevate their standards. Sharif couldn't discern any methodology behind Aberto's ambitious goal from the *Bklyner* piece, besides leveraging his inspirational personality to hire a team of talented, experienced lawyers for nonprofit wages, but Aberto had defied odds many times before. Merjem, who spoke of Aberto in a simultaneously disdainful and lustful tone, said whether people hated or admired his cavalier, outside-the-box approach, it had won him a handful of precedent-setting cases at an unprecedentedly early stage in his career.

After observing Aberto for an hour at the CAPPA event, Sharif downed his fourth cup of boxed wine, refilled it, and approached. He didn't have to do this. They could have easily spent the evening without interaction, pretending they'd never Googled each other. But Sharif knew he'd be haunted by cowardice if he didn't look into the boogeyman's eyes.

Adjoua only came up once, when Sharif introduced himself as her husband. He regretted it immediately since it begged the question, *Okay, Adjoua's husband, and how do you know who I am to her?* But Aberto didn't ask that. They shook hands and waited for the other to say more. Sharif eventually asked him where he got his T-shirt. It was yellow with the green logo and Arabic writing Sharif recognized as the Hezbollah insignia. Sharif couldn't tell if it was being worn ironically. Aberto explained that his little sister was a journalist who'd brought it back for him after doing a story in southern Lebanon and that he only wore clothes he could guarantee were not made in a sweatshop. Think what you will of Hezbollah, he said, but they don't use child labor for their swag. Sharif said his dad was Lebanese, and Aberto replied, Oh, that's surprising to be honest. He said he'd never met a Lebanese person who looked so European. Before Sharif knew how to respond, Merjem joined them. Her attraction to Aberto was made immediately obvious by how closely she stood to him, and the way she laughed and touched her hair.

They talked at length in front of Sharif about how Aberto had no intention of paying off his law school debt. Aberto didn't mind receiving calls and letters asking for payments, or getting sent to collection, or spoiling his credit. He said no one should owe 150k for an education, let alone one used for a public good like his. Merjem was fascinated by Aberto's ability to disregard these demands for payment without experiencing stress. It was true, Aberto was uncommonly self-assured in his nonconformity. He was definitely full of himself, but like Adjoua's father, there was an inevitability to it. He was singularly himself and no one else, radiating a sincere, if excessive, self-confidence.

At home, when Sharif drunkenly reported meeting Aberto, he included not picking up on any underlying insecurity in Aberto's arrogance. Adjoua laughed a bit caustically and said Aberto was so insecure it wasn't even funny. This would have been reassuring if delivered in a detached tone. A successful, handsome ex who comfortably transcended societal expectations is more intimidating than an insecure blowhard. But the negative light

Adjoua put Aberto in sounded like an attempt to convince herself she was glad he'd left her.

As soon as Sharif went for the leash dangling on the doorknob, Judy started his pleading whine. It annoyed Sharif that Judy began whining moments before he was obviously about to get what he wanted. Sharif's annoyance shifted to painful tenderness when he noticed Judy favoring a hind leg. He brought his work bag with the $85 aspirin on their walk. Adjoua would see the vet bills and everything else on the credit card statement at the end of the month. He'd need to disclose what Judy had gone through before then.

Outside, Sharif forced a pill down Judy's throat and held his mouth shut. "I'm sorry. I wish you understood why I did that to you."

Crossing the street to the park, he made the call. "Hi, Aberto. It's Sharif. Adjoua's husband."

"Hey," said Aberto. "How are you?"

"I'm okay. Eager to figure out what this is about."

"Sure, of course. Basically, I've been working with this guy for a couple months, trying to get his TPS sorted —"

"Yeah, I actually gave Emmanuel your card."

"Oh, well, there you go. So yeah, Emmanuel calls me from jail, and I'm surprised to hear him mention you. Says you beat up his son pretty badly." Sharif felt a kind of relief at the preposterousness of the claim. "Junior's wrist snapped in three spots and there was internal bleeding. He was rushed to the hospital for emergency surgery. They don't know how it's going to heal up yet."

Sharif wasn't sure what to say. "That's . . . terrible."

"Look, I don't think anyone is interested in getting litigious here. So I propose we get together for some informal mediation. Get everyone on the same page, hash it out, and move on."

Judy had been sniffing a small area of a large tree trunk for the past minute. He lifted his leg and peed a full two feet behind the spot he'd been sniffing, missing the tree entirely. Sharif interpreted such inaccuracy as senility. Adjoua's theory of the case was that Judy respected the scent of the other dog on the tree and diplomatically urinated next to, not on top of, the alpha dog's urine.

"I'm really sorry to hear about what happened to Junior. But to be honest, I'm having trouble understanding why he told his father it had anything to do with me."

"Okay." Aberto let time pass, apparently not inspired to sympathize with Sharif's confusion. "So, can you pop by to clear the air with us? Emmanuel is upset, but he's a smart and reasonable guy."

He remembered how everyone at CAPPA had decided Emmanuel was a madman. He said, "That was my impression of him too. And I'm sure any parent who believes their kid was beaten up by an adult would be beside themselves. I also happen to know I had no role in Junior's injury." Judy dropped and rolled over to shimmy on his back against the ground. "May I ask, do they have medical insurance?"

"Yep, they do." Sharif could tell that Aberto had pinched the phone between his ear and shoulder and begun rummaging through his desk with both hands. "Hold on, just grabbing my scheduling book."

Sharif had no desire to meet with Adjoua's ex-boyfriend and two people accusing him of violence, but he didn't see how to turn down an invitation to an informal conversation meant to clear the air. What was he going to do, claim he didn't have a spare hour anytime this month for that? He should get it over with, make sure that no more dramatics related to this circle back to CAPPA. And maybe it would feel good to look Emmanuel in the eye and explain what had really happened between him and Junior. It bothered Sharif to think Emmanuel saw him as some abuser. He'd also get to hear Emmanuel's explanation for why Judy ended up on the fire escape. Maybe Emmanuel didn't even know his son had done that.

Aberto rapidly turned the pages of his scheduling book. "Tomorrow's Saturday, so let's do it at my home office. It's up the street from CAPPA, I'll text you the address. What time is good?"

25.

ADJOUA WAS EVEN more upset about what Sharif had hidden from her than he anticipated. She frantically inspected Judy for signs of pain, pushing on spaces between bones. Judy looked confused. Sharif explained that the only reason behind his reticence to give her the whole story had been to not stress her out more than she already was. This caused her to feel patronized on top of being lied to: two of her least favorite behaviors in men.

He said that things were moving really fast since yesterday, and the two of them barely had any alone time to catch up. She said this was not a catch-up topic. It was potentially life-altering breaking fucking news that he had a responsibility to share as soon as possible. He said he didn't actually think it would end up being a big deal once he sat down with Emmanuel and cleared things up. It's just some crazy misunderstanding. She pointed out that if he didn't think it was a big deal, he wouldn't have been so deliberately evasive. She added, You're being accused of breaking the bones of a minor. How is that not a big deal? Because it's ludicrous, he said. She demanded he never again conceal information like this. He promised he wouldn't. She said they needed to face hardships that impacted their family together, did he understand? He said yes, even though he really didn't think this would impact their family, but he heard and agreed with her.

He said he thought they could apply a little more of her sentiment about facing hardship together to their hardships around Zora. She said, Don't change the subject. She hadn't been hiding basic facts from him, and that's what they're talking about here. Okay, he said. He understood and accepted her request. He sensed they were at the end of the scolding. But then they entered a new argument about whether she'd come to Aberto's tomorrow for the mediation session.

Sharif strongly preferred she not come. She didn't care what he strongly preferred. She was going. This impacted her too. He said aside from getting together with her ex under these uniquely bizarre and uncomfortable circumstances, he didn't like the idea of Emmanuel and Junior meeting her. After Emmanuel's blow-up at CAPPA, and everyone else's certainty that he would have struck Sharif had others not intervened, Sharif wasn't willing to take any risks, however small. At the end of the day, he didn't know these people. Too bad, Adjoua responded. He should have thought of that before handing Judy over to strangers. She wouldn't take no for an answer; besides, Emmanuel already knew where they lived, thanks to him. She turned her position on this topic into an extension of her position that they must face hardships together, to which he had previously acquiesced. She had won that argument, which came to mean she won this one too. It was decided. Tomorrow morning they'd take the train to Aberto's together.

She declined his offer of a foot massage after her shower and invited Judy up in bed with her, saying, "Come on, bubba, up!" while looking only at Judy, as if he could get up there by himself. Judy's eyes anxiously scanned left to right, unsure of how to give her what she wanted. Sharif lifted and placed him next to her. She didn't thank or look at Sharif but called Judy a good boy.

Sharif lay awake, shifting in the squeaky daybed on the other side of their tiny apartment, with Adjoua's statement replaying in his head: *You're being accused of breaking the bones of a minor.* Should he reach out to his brother, Walid, a corporate lawyer in Virginia? Get some preliminary counsel? Sharif hadn't returned Walid's calls in over a month, and he felt a heaviness at the thought of calling only when he needed help. Besides, tomorrow was an informal conversation to clear the air. He wasn't going to court.

The premise of the meeting struck him as odd in a new way. If Emmanuel and Junior are medically insured, then what's the point of this meeting for them? If Sharif was the father of a teenager who he thought had been injured by someone, would he feel it important to have a mediated conversation with that person to clear the air? Was Emmanuel seeking an apology? Or maybe Emmanuel no longer believed Sharif had hurt his son and would make Junior apologize. All possible motivations for Emmanuel wanting this meeting seemed equally unlikely.

Unable to sleep an hour later, he found himself scrolling through Aberto's social media. He'd gotten there after looking at Adjoua's reposted Judy-rehoming pleas, to which Aberto had responded: Thinking of you.

Aberto's most recent pictures represented his latest volunteer work, with some physical activities peppered in: hiking, slacklining, cliff diving, teaching a boy in Rio de Janeiro how to ride a bike. Sharif found the same pictures of Adjoua that had always been there. In one picture, she made an ironic kissy face at the camera. She was in a bar, and her eyes were smoky, drunk, and empowered. From the look in her eyes, Sharif knew she'd have wanted sex that night. Sharif found it creepy that Aberto kept a sexually charged photo of his now-married ex up on his page. Sharif then moved on to Aberto's professional website: Barbosa & Associates Full Service Multilingual Law Firm. His bio highlighted his previous nonprofit legal experience, important cases he'd won, and his involvement with activist groups. Aberto was doing good work, Sharif forced himself to say in his head. It's really important and good work. He then mumbled out loud, "My God, I'm really beginning to hate this man."

Sharif got out of bed, took Adjoua's laptop off the kitchen island, and opened her email. It had been over two weeks since he'd breached her trust in this way. There were some new emails of Aberto and Adjoua sending links to articles back and forth, and one exchange of substance in the side chat bar:

Adjoua: You there?

Aberto: Wow, my heart actually skipped a beat when I saw your name

Adjoua: 😳 Any chance you'll have time to read a draft of something this week? 1000 words the Times wants me to write about the Anthony Augustin murder

Aberto: Of course I have time for that!

Adjoua: Thank you! Still stitching thoughts together but I'll send something soon

Aberto: Can't wait. Btw, I was with Paula tonight and you came up. She has a two-year-old now with a white dude and apparently the learning curve on her man's raising a biracial kid has proven steep and rocky. Cause of major friction at the moment

Adjoua: Yeah?

Aberto: Are you and your dude discussing that stuff at all?

Adjoua: Ha. Discussing child rearing philos sounds like a luxury. I'm exclusively thinking about healthcare, rehoming Judy, getting a free crib, and how to make money

Aberto: Totally makes sense. I guess it's more about whether your guy is doing his homework. Reading books, talking to his black friends (does he have any?), etc.

Adjoua: I'll ask him if he's thought about this. Actually, I probably won't. Asking might require me to explain why I'm asking

Aberto: It shouldn't. It's a reasonable and self-explanatory request

Adjoua: Maybe, but the risk of explaining anything about race right now makes me feel even more exhausted than usual

Aberto: That's why I quit white people, even "white presenting" people. I need someone who just gets it

If anyone was white-presenting it was Aberto, Sharif thought. Even though his mother was half Black, he could easily pass for Sicilian if he wanted.

Adjoua: I've never been with someone who gets everything about me

Aberto: Right, but the race piece is huge

Adjoua: Race piece is huge. Sex and gender pieces are huge. Different brain, class, culture, childhood, sensory experience are pretty big too. I have sadly come to accept that I can't marry a replica of myself

Aberto: Okay, but do you think he's ever contemplated the ways your daily experience as a black woman differs from his?

Adjoua: I thought this was about child rearing a biracial kid

Aberto: It doesn't sound like you guys have talked about that so I'm taking a step back to get a lay of the land

Adjoua: So far, only black women have some sense of my experience as a black woman. But on the balance Sharif shows more interest in understanding my experience, especially on an emotional level (sometimes to an oppressive degree), than anyone before

Aberto: Ouch. I guess I walked into that one. Oppressive how?

Adjoua: Ouch what? You dumped me, dude. Oppressive in that I don't always want to inspect my fears and anxieties with someone

Aberto: You have to stop saying I dumped you. I suggested a short break. You proceeded to ghost me and resurface with this guy. I never closed the door on us. That was all you, sweetie

Adjoua: This is ironic within the context of partners who understand me. Have we met? Did you really think I was a woman who'd wait around for a guy to be done with his "break"?

Aberto: You're right. Probably my biggest error to date

Adjoua: Oh stop

Aberto: Let me ask this. He shows more interest in understanding you than anyone before him, but does that mean he understands you more than anyone, or just that he tries harder? Those aren't the same

There was a two-minute difference in the time stamps between Aberto's question and Adjoua's answer, the longest in their exchange.

Adjoua: I'm not sure what difference it makes.

Aberto: Fine. I can tell you're done with this. Just wanted to make sure you're okay

Adjoua: I'm that happiest girl in the world. Everyone knows that

Aberto: Good. That's what I like to hear. Can't wait to read the op-ed draft xoxo

Sharif's heart raced as he shut and returned the laptop. He lay awake until four a.m. Should he confront Adjoua? Wasn't it emotional cheating to maintain such closeness with an ex who was actively attempting to win her back? She didn't exactly set clear boundaries. And what did she mean when she said I'm not sure what difference it makes to his question about whether Sharif understands her best or just tries the hardest? Did it not make a difference because she felt stuck with him?

He dreamed of being a mite-size man backpacking through one of those ice troughs at fish markets, hiking between gargantuan eel bodies, some chopped in half, others suffocating slowly. Adjoua shook him awake as Judy barked. Both of them sounded out of breath. After everyone calmed down, he asked if she could make out what he was saying this time. She said he kept shouting, *Shut the door, he's coming in! SHUT THE DOOR!*

26.

ABERTO LIVED ON Nostrand Avenue, across from a nineteenth-century-era bank that had been retrofitted into a Burger King. When he opened the door to his apartment, his shoulder-length brown curls glistened with an oil that may have been the source of the cedar and sandalwood odor wafting out. His black wiry chest hair sprang out of his shirt, which was undone to the fourth button. He wore formfitting cuffed jeans. No shoes or socks. His smile was big, white, and intrepid. Those aquamarine eyes shone even brighter than Sharif remembered. Sharif thought: A person of color, maybe, but a Black man? Come on.

Aberto hugged Adjoua like he'd caught her from a fall. He squeezed and tottered her whole body side to side, groaning about how good it was to see her. Sharif scanned Aberto's profile, noting the perfectly sculpted ass of a sprinter. Between Aberto and Adjoua's legs stood Aberto's hefty, small-headed mutt with circular yellowish eyes, named Babs. Aberto asked Adjoua about Judy, and she said he was hanging in there but definitely sensed big change on the horizon. Sharif forgot that Aberto knew Judy; had lived with him even. He imagined Adjoua referring to Aberto as Judy's papa as she now did to Sharif.

The weak smile gelled to Sharif's face was tiring his cheeks. Aberto released Adjoua but wasn't done drinking her in. He looked her up and down while holding her shoulders. His hairy wrists were wrapped with various beaded bracelets, strings, and leather straps. Admiring Adjoua's pregnant beauty, Aberto said, "Unbelievable. It's like you've doubled in size from two weeks ago. You're cooking a whole human bean in there!" They both laughed. A cutesy inside joke. Sharif thought Adjoua was leaning into this endless greeting and fondling as some kind of continued punishment for yesterday.

"Yep, and now scheduled to come out whenever she wants!" Adjoua said, making a circle on her stomach. They laughed, and Sharif understood that Aberto knew about what happened at the hospital.

"I can't wait to meet her," Aberto said. "And I hope it goes without saying that if you don't find anyone to take Judy before her birth, I'll give Babs a residency at my brother's upstate so Judy and I can bunk here for a while."

"That's really kind."

"No," Sharif cut in, receiving smile-interrupting looks. "I've got some great leads on that front." Adjoua furrowed her brow but thankfully didn't ask for specifics. "We'll take care of it," Sharif said to Aberto, "but thank you for the offer, it is kind."

It was then that Aberto addressed Sharif for the first time, looking him in the eye, patting him once on the shoulder. "Thanks for coming in today. Really appreciate it."

"Sure," he said, noticing considerable tightness in that single word.

After an awkward beat, Adjoua said to Aberto, "So this is the new place!"

Aberto said, "I can't tell you how proud of myself I am for unpacking everything within a week of moving in."

They followed Aberto through a modest kitchen to get to his office. Adjoua commented on how clean the place looked, and Aberto said, "You planted the seed, my dear!" Once seated in the office, Babs gave Sharif's pant leg a dry lick and coughed before going to her bed behind Aberto's desk.

The office was lined with waist-high filing cabinets that had wooden bookshelves standing on top of them. Swollen with binders and law books, the shelves leaned forward as if peeking over a ledge, seeming liable to come crashing down on everyone with the slightest bump. Framed portraits of Thurgood Marshall and other accomplished-looking men and women in suits hung on the few available wall spaces. Aberto's desk had a laptop, coffee-stained mugs, stacks of paper and open books smattered with stickynotes, and a gold Buddha statue at the front, facing outward and looking down on the seats Sharif and Adjoua occupied. For the first time, Buddha appeared judgmental. Aberto sat behind his desk on an antique tribal throne of some sort. Sharif decided the throne had a long-winded backstory about an "authentic experience" overseas, but this was corrected when Adjoua spoke to it directly: "Oh my God, my parents will be so happy to hear you're still using that." Understanding it was a gift from Adjoua's parents, Sharif wondered if they'd had it imported from Côte d'Ivoire or got it from a dealer in the city. Either way, he had certainly never received anything that nice from his in-laws. What rankled him most was when Aberto thanked Adjoua for giving them the great idea and picking the throne out herself.

The doorbell interrupted Aberto's blissed-out eye contact with Adjoua. "That must be them!" he said, as if this were some social gathering.

Adjoua and Sharif faced the judgmental Buddha as they heard Aberto greet Emmanuel and Junior. Babs had found the motivation to stand but not to go all the way to the door. She stopped to put her chin on Adjoua's lap, receiving an impersonal, flat-handed pat. Adjoua was stiff and distant with other dogs, as if showing them affection would be a betrayal to Judy. Adjoua smiled and said to Sharif, "Babs and Judy were close once. They shared a bed, can you imagine?"

Babs returned to her bed next to Aberto's throne, plopping down with a sigh. Adjoua ran her hands over her bulging belly as she took in the room with a mystery in her eyes that Sharif interpreted as nostalgia. In addition to the throne, she surely recognized Aberto's other things. Only then did Sharif notice the small corkboard, cluttered with photographs, leaning against the bottom of one of the slanting bookshelves. Photos of Aberto's friends and family at a graduation, a wedding, a dinner, a park, on a couch with popcorn. It was the kind of thing you'd expect in an adolescent's bedroom. Sharif's heart quickened when he spotted the picture of Adjoua pinned into the clutter. She wore a winter hat and stood arm in arm with Aberto and three people Sharif didn't recognize. An empty chairlift floated in the background. He had no idea she'd ever been skiing. Her face had the scrunched expression of mid-hilarity. Sharif pointed the photo out to her, whispering, "Jesus, have you seen this?"

She said, "I know," shaking her head. "I look so young there."

"You look the same." She smiled politely, but he hadn't meant it as a compliment. If anything, he meant it with reproach. Reproach that her unchanged face showed how recently she'd been in love with Aberto. That she might still be in love with him. But for now, all Sharif wanted from Adjoua was acknowledgment of how fucking weird it was that Aberto had this photograph of her here. Old social media posts were one thing, but who the hell has a picture of their ex-girlfriend on a corkboard collage in their home office?

The metal rig on Junior's forearm was captivating. Six teal-tinted pins jutted three inches out of his skin at various angles, all linked by a zigzagging bridge. It looked so cumbersome and painful as to seem like the cause of the injury. The arm resembled a speared animal he cradled with his other arm. Junior was thinner and taller than his father. Their style and body language were dissimilar too. Junior walked with a backward lean in oversize clothes and impeccably white sneakers. His eyes only half open, he was performing either sleepiness or not giving a fuck. Emmanuel had an anxious, forward lean to his walk today. He wore a faded navy suit jacket on top of a button-down. His tubiform khakis, white socks, brown shoes, and tattered briefcase made him look like a struggling salesman. Father and son took the two open seats to Sharif's right.

All eyes stayed on Aberto as he strolled to his throne and hummed random notes that Sharif supposed were meant to communicate light-heartedness. After sitting, Aberto offered each of his guests a moment of individualized eye contact. When Sharif received his, it came from over the shoulder of the judgmental Buddha. And when Aberto beheld Adjoua, he said, "Welcome. Welcome."

27.

"MEDIATION IS MORE humane than the court system," Aberto said. "Here, we're not bound to the hyperspecific, inflexible, inherently dated legal system that's more concerned with legal precedent than common sense and fairness. Today we have the opportunity to address what feels most urgent and true to both parties, whether that means sharing one's personal circumstances, emotions, or any legal questions you might have, if that's where our dialogue organically leads. As everyone communicates their perspective and priorities, I'll guide us toward a mutually acceptable resolution. The goal is for you, not some judge, to be in control of the outcome. That said, people often enter mediation expecting validation. To be proven right. And that's an unrealistic expectation. We're here today because there is disagreement. So in the best-case scenario, both parties should end up feeling some combination of gains and losses. That's compromise, right?" He did a quicker version of the individualized eye contact thing again. "Okay, that's enough from me for now."

Emmanuel didn't skip a beat before announcing, "I brought the medical report, as we talked about." He fished some stapled pages out from his briefcase and handed them to Aberto.

While Aberto read aloud the location and severity of Junior's distal radius and two other breaks, Sharif noticed Adjoua taking furtive glances at Junior's injury. The pin-stabbed forearm was especially dark, misshapen, and swollen just before the wrist, bulging two inches beyond normal proportions. Sharif's mind teleported him to his middle school science classroom, where there was a terrarium with a python whose throat bulged nightmarishly when swallowing a live mouse.

Adjoua touched Sharif's arm to bring him back into the room.

That was when he heard Aberto say, "We don't yet have an exact number for the bills, but we'll have those shortly."

Sharif said, "The bills?"

"Yeah, their insurance plan has a deductible. So we'd need to eventually discuss that plus the copays for follow-ups and prescriptions."

"Eventually?" Emmanuel said. "This is the reason I'm here."

Sharif said to Aberto, "You described this as being about clearing the air."

"That's still the case," Aberto said.

Adjoua asked, "What's the deductible?"

"It's high," Aberto said, almost submissively.

"Meaning?"

"Thirteen thousand, eight hundred dollars."

"Is that a joke?" she said, putting her hands on her belly.

"It's the maximum legal deductible for a family plan in New York. I anticipate the total to climb up to at least fifteen thousand after all the copays."

Sharif's body became a fist. "They'll apply for emergency Medicaid, right?"

Aberto said, "They're just over the benefits cliff to qualify. Emmanuel would have to quit his airport job to be eligible, and that would mean they couldn't make rent. Filing for bankruptcy is off the table too. I've looked into every way to nullify the bills, and I've submitted their file to every medical debt forgiveness organization, but chances of selection are low given the volume of applications. Emmanuel picked the insurance with the premium he could afford at the time."

Emmanuel said, "Fifteen thousand does not include loss of wages. Junior cannot work at the grocer's after school with his arm this way."

"Right," Aberto said. "That's an approximate eleven thousand dollars' loss over the year it'll take for Junior to recover enough to work again. So we're talking about twenty-six thousand. Give or take."

Adjoua started laughing and repeating *Sorry* while sounding less and less able to stop laughing. Sharif saw their sick child floating inside of her, then the snake swallowing the mouse again. Then he saw the $529.19 in his checking account. He'd avoided looking at his credit card, but he knew he owed a few hundred dollars on it. He talked himself out of a cup of coffee on the way here because of how much he'd spent over budget the last few days. He wouldn't receive his biweekly salary — $40k slashed down to $29k after federal, state, and city taxes and health insurance, netting $1,208.33 per paycheck, all of which plus $192.67 of the next one going toward rent — for another eight days.

On the train to Aberto's apartment, Adjoua had asked Sharif whether "we" should consider getting a lawyer. Her use of "we" touched him, but that was undercut by her adding how tricky Aberto could be. She seemed to imply Sharif stood little chance against him. He said he wasn't concerned; this was an informal discussion. Besides, he wouldn't know where to find a quality same-day lawyer to defend them pro bono against a low-income asylum-seeker in an unofficial mediation session at someone's apartment on a Saturday. She said she didn't mean for today, but in case this escalated. He firmly stated it would not.

Adjoua regained her composure, and Aberto said, "Let's not get bogged down in the bills before getting on the same page about what happened. We need to hear from Sharif and Junior. Sharif, why don't you begin by giving us a sense of your experience."

Sharif glanced at the photo of Adjoua in her winter cap, intertwined with Aberto and friends. He quietly echoed, "A sense of my experience." He then leaned forward and turned to face Junior, who sat on the other side of Emmanuel, slouched and staring at the carpet, cradling the bloated and speared arm, legs splayed straight out in front of him.

Sharif said to him, "First, I'm really sorry about what happened to your wrist. I'm also really sorry for any alarm I caused. I can only imagine how jarring it would be to come home to some stranger panicking in my living room." Peripherally he could see Aberto nodding in approval, which he found more irritating than encouraging. Sharif's tone exposed some of that irritation as he continued: "I was scared for my dog. My priority was to get him to a vet. I know I wasn't the calmest version of myself, but—" He paused, preparing to say the next part as diplomatically as possible. "I didn't feel I had time to explain why I was upset about finding him on the fire escape, or why I didn't intend to pay for the second half of his care." Before recounting the events of that day beat by beat, how he entered and left the apartment, he readjusted so that he was looking over Aberto's head and at the brick wall, allowing him to better visualize his memory.

When Sharif finished his detailed account, which included Judy's unprecedented behavior of growling at Junior, Aberto said, "You're telling us you didn't even see Junior fall or get hurt."

"Correct."

"How much physical contact was there between you?"

"Like I said, Junior wouldn't move out of the doorway after I asked multiple times. So our bodies made contact. I couldn't have exited otherwise. I tripped while squeezing myself out and caught my fall in the hallway, nearly dropping Judy in the process. On my way to the elevator, I heard Junior calling for me to come back and pay him. Up until Emmanuel showed up at my job yesterday, there were no clues whatsoever that anyone but Judy had gotten hurt."

Aberto leaned forward on his desk, shooting a quick glance at Emmanuel and then at Adjoua.

There was a long pause where the only sound Sharif could hear was of Emmanuel's leg bouncing up and down. Aberto cleared his throat and said to Sharif, "Judy didn't sustain any serious injuries in the end, correct?"

Sharif said, "He had severe bruising. He still favors one hind leg over the one that got twisted back when he fell down the fire escape steps and cracked his chin. He'll be on a pain management regimen for at least a week." Aberto was squinting and nodding. It looked more like Aberto was listening to the negative assessment of Sharif playing in his head than any of the words coming out of Sharif's mouth. Sharif added more forcefully, "You know, for a dog his age to undergo that kind of neglect, pain, and shock, not to mention the psychological trauma of——"

"Are you out of your brain?" Emmanuel cut in. "Your dog's psychological trauma? What about my son?"

Sharif said, "Emmanuel, I'm sorry he's hurt. But our encounter couldn't be the cause."

Emmanuel looked at Aberto disbelievingly. "This is why he's come here? To say he didn't have anything to do with it?" To Sharif: "Are you serious?"

Aberto suggested, "Why don't we hear from Junior." He nodded at Emmanuel, as if to say, *Don't worry, this is all part of the process.* He turned to Junior and said, "All you, man."

Junior's eyes remained glued to the carpet. There was a long enough silence for Aberto to feel the need to explain. "Junior is on some pretty strong pain management meds."

Emmanuel said, "He can't even do schoolwork on this drug. But he's in so much pain an hour before it's even time for the next dose. On top of this, he cannot draw or play sports or work or even sleep properly. He can't even bathe without help."

Everyone stared at Junior, waiting for him to weigh in for what felt like an entire minute. Scooting her chair up, Adjoua leaned forward to look at him directly. Junior didn't break his spell with the floor when he finally spoke, but his words were inaudible. Aberto looked around the room, understanding others hadn't heard either and asked Junior if he could please repeat that. Only slightly louder, Junior mumbled, "He slammed into me as hard as he could. Sent me flying to the ground. That's when everything broke." He lifted the injured arm a few inches.

Sharif's mouth dangled open. Adjoua said, "He *slammed* into you, and you flew to the ground?"

Mistaking her surprise for sympathy, Emmanuel said, "Tell her what he said after."

Junior's eyes beaded left to right like he was searching for the words on the ground. Unable to locate them, he glanced up for help.

Aberto said, "It's okay, you can say it."

Emmanuel said, "Go on."

After considerable hesitation, Junior said, "G-damn you, mother f-er. But he said the whole thing."

Sharif said, "Why are you saying that?"

Junior stared angrily or sadly or guiltily or indifferently at the floor. Impossible to say. Sharif didn't believe a doctor had prescribed a sixteen-year-old such a high dose of medication as to inhibit basic communication.

Perhaps still believing Adjoua was an ally, Emmanuel turned to her. "When I arrived at the hospital, they said he was under general anesthesia in emergency surgery. That there was hemorrhaging. And for the *six* hours he was in surgery, no one could promise he would survive. Can you imagine? When my boy woke up, thank God, he tells me about what your husband did." Emmanuel pointed at Sharif while looking at Aberto. "And somehow I was the one arrested."

"He wasn't hurt when I left," Sharif said. "He was calling for me to come back and pay him."

"Nah," Junior said.

"Nah?" Sharif said. "You didn't demand money?"

"Hey," Aberto said, "don't mimic him like that again."

Something about this flustered Sharif to the point of needing a few seconds to catch his breath.

Emmanuel said, "He talks about my son like a thug who cares only about money."

Sharif said, "I was pointing out that he was focused on the sixty dollars at the time he was supposedly badly injured."

"Why are *you* so focused on the sixty dollars?" Emmanuel said. "So what if he wanted sixty dollars? I told him he could earn this money, save this money for the video game console he always wanted. Does this mean he deserves to be crippled?" And then Emmanuel was speaking to Adjoua again: "I didn't agree to take this dog because of money. Or because I care for dogs. I did it because I saw a man who was afraid for his wife and child." He gestured toward Adjoua's belly, and Sharif's spine went cold. "This touched me. I know this feeling very well. But now it's his turn to be decent, to take responsibility for what he did to my child."

Sharif said, "I didn't do that to him."

"My son doesn't lie. He's a good, God-fearing boy. Do you understand what this means?" As if remembering that of course Sharif wouldn't understand something like that, he returned to Adjoua. "In your husband's mind, he's protecting you and the baby by saving money. In other circumstances I might sympathize with that. But when putting your own family first, there is a moral limit. I beg you, sister. Help him make this right."

It was in Adjoua's character to remain quiet and attentive, nodding along through Emmanuel's personal appeals, until she was ready to reveal her position. She said, "I really can't imagine how hard this has been on you and your son. But the way you are speaking so certainly about Junior being an honest person is how I feel about Sharif. I'm sure you perceived some of his goodness when you met. Isn't that also part of the reason you were so open to helping him?"

Emmanuel appeared sad for the first time. "You too are insinuating that my son is some greedy liar." He emitted a tired chuckle, as if disappointed with himself for investing so much in Adjoua.

"No," she said, "that's not it. I'm saying there's been a misunderstanding. We know what Sharif's version of events are now. And we've heard from people who weren't there that day. What would be helpful is to hear more from the other person who was there. I know Junior is medicated, and in a lot of discomfort, but do you think it's possible to engage him a little more on the details?" Without waiting for permission, she put her big eyes on his son. "Junior. I want you to take as long as you need to answer me, okay? There's no rush."

Junior nodded vaguely at the floor, his apathy broken by a weird smile.

She said, "And let's put aside all questions of lying and money, okay?"

Junior's smile was reabsorbed into his aloof expression. "I didn't hurt your dog."

"I know," Adjoua said, sounding like a compassionate schoolteacher. "And Judy is doing fine." She nodded. "Now, what I want to focus on is the moment of your injury. That's what's most important. You said Sharif slammed into you, sending you flying to the ground. In which direction did you fall? It sounds like Sharif stumbled into the hallway, so were you thrown into the hallway too?"

"No."

She said, "You fell into the apartment?" He nodded. "Okay. So he slammed into you while holding the dog, ended up in the hall, but you were thrown inside the apartment to the ground. Is that right?"

He nodded.

"Adjie," Aberto said, "those are leading questions."

She ignored him. "Junior, you remember how big Judy is." She smiled. "You're not exactly a small guy either. Help me visualize how Sharif threw you back inside the apartment as he was pushing his way out with the dog." Junior's bizarre, dead-eyed smile briefly ruptured his aloofness again. Adjoua said, "You know, sometimes, when everyone around us is worked up, it feels like we have to stick to what we said originally. Or say what we think they want to hear. You know?"

"That's enough," Emmanuel said.

Adjoua continued, "Junior, if you remember any detail differently than you did at first, no matter how small, or if maybe you're fuzzy on a particular part of it, it's important that you share that with us."

"I said, it's enough," Emmanuel said. "Shame on you for wanting to manipulate him." To the ceiling he asked, "How am I involved with such people?"

"Let's take a short break," Aberto suggested.

"No." Emmanuel stood up. His wide-eyed expression gave him a suspended-in-time appearance. "We're finished here."

"Hold on," Aberto said. "What do you mean?"

"I've had enough of this. Come, Junior, we're going."

Aberto said, "It hasn't even been ten minutes. Let's have a quick chat in private. Then you can decide if you want to use the rest of our time together or not."

Emmanuel seemed to be scrolling through options in his mind before saying, "No, we're turning in circles. Unless we present video evidence of what happened, these people will deny any responsibility whatsoever. And who knows, maybe even then they will manage to deny it."

"That's not true," Sharif said, remembering the little girl across the hall who had filmed Judy. Maybe she did have a recording of the incident. He vaguely remembered seeing her in his periphery on his way out. "I'd definitely embrace video evidence. Trust me."

"Well, I don't," Emmanuel said. He told Aberto, "Let's file this bodily injury claim we talked about. Tell me what you need to proceed. And I'll talk to my other neighbors to see what they heard or saw."

Sharif said to Aberto, "A bodily injury claim?"

Emmanuel said to Sharif, "I cannot accept someone laying their hands on my boy." He nodded rapidly with his own words. "There are things I can take, but not this." He choked up. The nodding seemed to be what kept the tears standing in his eyes from falling. "Get up, Junior. We're going now."

Junior rose languidly to his feet, lifting his pin-stabbed arm with the other, and slowly followed his father. He looked embarrassed. But embarrassed of what? Of creating this mess? Of bringing his father down a dead-end track? Or was it simply the embarrassment a teenager feels in a room of adults?

Aberto followed them out. The front door slammed. Adjoua pinched the bridge of her nose and shut her eyes.

28.

ABERTO RETURNED TO his throne and said, "At least we know where everyone stands."

Sharif stood to leave, and Adjoua said, "Let's give it a few minutes so we don't end up on the same train as them."

"They won't take the train," Sharif said. "They'll walk." He didn't want to be around Aberto any longer.

"Right, I forgot. You know where they live," she said in a weary tone. "I don't want to end up walking behind them either."

"They're going in the opposite direction."

"Sharif. I want to give it a few minutes, okay?"

He sat back down, hating that Aberto had witnessed that.

Adjoua said to Aberto, "You see that Junior's story doesn't make sense, right?"

He nodded. "Yeah, I'll need him to clarify a few things. But you weren't helping with those leading questions."

She said, "I don't think I was doing that." Aberto smiled at her, as if endeared by her minor delusion. She then said, "I can't understand why it's so hard for Emmanuel to entertain the possibility that his teenage son is hiding something. Don't all teenagers lie to their parents? Emmanuel talks like it's impossible."

Aberto said, "They've gone through a lot together. They have a special bond. And while I don't work with many teenagers, I can tell you adults lie a whole lot. Maybe Emmanuel believing his son isn't that different from you believing your husband."

Sharif had a heightened awareness that after what Aberto had just said neither he nor Adjoua glanced at each other. Sharif said, "Come on. Pain medication or not, Junior's a particularly evasive teenager, one with poor enough judgment to put a dog on a fire escape with a gaping hole. And who thinks he can get away with pinning his injury on me."

Aberto said, "Not everyone grew up in the world of friendly dogs, Sharif."

"Okay." Sharif again felt that flustered out-of-breath sensation he had when Aberto told him not to mimic Junior saying "Nah."

Aberto said, "He didn't grow up around pets and assumed dogs were more comfortable outside than cooped up in an apartment. It's not irrational."

"Actually," Sharif said, "it is pretty irrational. None of us grew up around all of the planet's living creatures, but I bet we'd know not to tic any of them up to a dilapidated fourteenth-floor fire escape. And you know what, most people in our situation would demand that Emmanuel pay Judy's exorbitant vet bills. That went virtually unacknowledged."

Aberto said, "We can include that in the conversation moving forward. But from your telling, Judy only fell when you climbed onto their fire escape."

"So it's my fault."

"Arguably. If I balanced my mug at the edge of this desk, and you knocked it over later, who should pay for it?"

Adjoua said, "This isn't some philosophical sparring exercise for us. They're talking about suing now."

"I know, sweetie," Aberto said, making Sharif's face prickle with heat. "But you have to admit, it's pretty unlucky that Emmanuel and Junior didn't come home before Sharif got on their fire escape. Emmanuel would have explained to Junior that dogs shouldn't be put out there. They'd have gently brought him back inside, and that would've been the end of it. A harmless, teachable moment."

Sharif said, "I don't know why you're assuming it would have played out so gently. Judy growled at that kid for a reason."

"His name's Junior. And yeah, I've noticed you trusting your interpretation of your elderly dog's growl more than 'that kid's' word. Is there something inherent to Junior that makes you assume he's a liar?"

Again with that flustered sensation, but lighter and shorter now. He said, "Junior said he didn't hurt our dog a minute after falsely accusing me of terrible violence. Forgive me for not giving him the benefit of the doubt over my dog's unprecedented behavior."

Adjoua said, "Right, this isn't constructive. Aberto, please get the truth from Junior as soon as possible."

"Sure thing, my dear," he said.

"Good." To Sharif she said, "I need to use the bathroom before we go."

Sharif was determined to sit wordlessly until Adjoua came back. But as soon as he heard the bathroom door shut, he said, "Aberto, are you really under the impression that you're helping the Fleurimes? Emmanuel will find out Junior is lying. And he'll have wasted his time and energy for nothing."

"We'll see." Aberto bent down from his seat and started petting Babs, who lay on her dog bed.

"I think you owe your clients better guidance."

"I'll give them my best guidance as soon as I get a handle on the facts."

"One would think you'd have done that already."

"I prefer entering the first mediation relatively cold." Aberto was holding Babs's face and staring into her eyes. "But don't worry. Like with all my clients, I'll explain to Junior why it's in his best interest to be honest with me. Clients usually get that." Babs let herself be rolled over, and Aberto started rubbing her belly. "Most people tell me what part of their story is untruthful or that they're struggling to remember. The rare times they don't, I have a pretty good record of picking up on inconsistencies."

"So you're going on your gut, huh?"

"Instinct is a big part of it, like most professions, I imagine." He stopped playing around with Babs and looked at Sharif. "But to be clear, regardless of what truth I uncover, my job is to give them the best legal protection possible. This pain and debilitation Junior is experiencing, and this medical bill, constitute a life crisis for the Fleurimes."

"I assure you, a bill like that would constitute a serious crisis in our lives too."

Aberto smiled. "If you knew their story, I doubt you'd compare yourself to them. And with this kind of debt and Junior's loss of income, they risk losing the roof over their heads and any shot at remaining in this country legally."

"I'm not comparing myself to anyone, but their background doesn't change what happened between Junior and me. I work with disadvantaged clients too. It doesn't mean I should be assigned their financial burdens at random. I couldn't pay twenty-six thousand dollars if I wanted to."

Aberto snorted lightly. "Come on, man."

Sharif's anger floated from his stomach to his chest. "Come on man what? You want to see my bank statements?"

"You're a young, healthy, white, educated American man. You have access to opportunities and wages of which they could not dream. If it came down to you having to pay part or even all of the bill, you'd figure something out. You could ask your parents for a no-interest loan."

"Excuse me?" Sharif said. "What do you know about my parents?"

Adjoua stood behind Sharif. "What's up?"

"Nothing," Sharif said, fuming. "Can we go?"

Adjoua looked back and forth between the two men. "Yeah, I'm ready."

29.

SHARIF AND ADJOUA stayed in their heads as they walked away from
Aberto's. The unusually humid eleven a.m. June heat weighed heavily on
Church Avenue itself, the sidewalk and street, the trees, the cars. But the
people seemed to channel the heat into a confident, leisurely, almost sensual
way of walking. Not Sharif. He felt disoriented and uncoordinated. The sun
and people and traffic added up to slow chaos. It required concentration for
him to not bump into the unhurried people. The more he concentrated, the
more encumbered he was by his body, as if it were too big for what he was.
Then, abruptly, the others changed, looking encumbered too. The families,
couples, dogs, Adjoua—all were now as confined in their clunky bodies as
he was in his. It did not reassure him to discover he wasn't alone in being
trapped. For it meant no one could save him.

Re: New Adoption Timeline!
Hello, Sharif — all of our waitlisted dogs are in emergency need
of adoption. The circumstances of the parents don't change the
circumstances of the dog . . .

In the simpler, narrower low-ceilinged subway corridor, Sharif's mind
could think beyond the mechanics of safely driving his body. Aberto's

manipulations started to play on a loop, beginning with his failure to mention the $26,000 on their initial phone call or the bodily injury suit he'd discussed with his clients. Sharif then revisited the times Aberto made him sound racially insensitive for expressing shock at Junior's lies; then the *sweeties* and *dears* for Adjoua; then the games about the mug and who was to blame; then the attempted guilt trip around Emmanuel's disadvantages; then that scoffing assertion that Sharif could pay their astronomical bill because of his privilege. What the hell did Aberto know about Sharif's parents? Had Adjoua said something? Sharif himself had no idea what $26,000 meant to his parents. They never talked of finances. He had no memory of them discussing a bill or whether something was affordable or expensive. Sharif and his brother were spared the topic of money, which of course was a sign of high privilege, but it revealed nothing about his parents' capacity to absorb some stranger's medical bills.

Sharif had started thinking about money in college. Not about making his own money, but about its unequal distribution. He became obsessed with the unfair hand some were dealt and understood there was nothing fair or earned about his exceptionally good hand. It was what drove him to social services. But it had never crossed his mind that he owed money he didn't have to resolve someone's problem he didn't cause.

He needed to consult a good lawyer, something he couldn't afford. The inevitability of calling on his brother, Walid, only seemed to deepen Sharif's resistance to it. The thought injected a dread in him that rivaled the circumstances.

By the time he and Adjoua were pacing between pillars on the 2 train platform, he realized they hadn't spoken since leaving Aberto's. He didn't want to process every beat of the meeting with her. That felt premature, even for Sharif, who thought of himself as someone who liked thinking aloud and solving problems collectively. He was still too rattled by the experience to jump back inside it. What he wanted was a moment of reconnection with his wife. Something that said, This is crazy, but at least we're in it together.

He started with "How are you feeling?" nodding toward her belly. "Physically, I mean. You haven't had anything to eat or drink since we left home."

"It hasn't been long. I'm feeling fine." She returned her thinking eyes to the platform floor.

He then said, "Weird photo, huh?"

Pulled out of her thoughts again, she looked up at the subway billboard behind them and said "I guess," before returning to whatever she was working out. The billboard was an ad for nonalcoholic Heineken: a glistening bottle with the text *Baby on Board? Cheers.*

"I meant the photo in Aberto's office." He gave a single, breathy chuckle to communicate it wasn't a serious matter, but something light and amusing. Comic relief. "The one of you on some ski slope?"

"Oh." Her eyes flinched. "Sorry, what about it exactly?"

"Kind of bizarre to have a picture of your ex-girlfriend in your home office."

She furrowed her brow and twisted up her mouth. "I don't really think of myself as his ex-girlfriend. More of an old friend."

"Right, yeah."

He was about to ask if she believed Aberto considered her an old friend too when Adjoua went on to say, "Besides, it's not a photo *of* me. It's a photo of Aberto and his closest friends, which happens to also include me."

A 241st Street–bound 2 train drove in loudly on the opposite tracks. After it came and went, he said, "Did you sound a little annoyed with me there, or was I imagining that?"

"When?"

"Just now."

"About the photo?"

"Yeah."

"I wasn't annoyed. Just confused as to why you brought it up."

"I thought it would be something we could laugh about. I didn't mean to make you defensive."

"I'm not defensive."

"Okay." Wouldn't it have been easier for her to acknowledge the photo was weird? It seemed like an easy, low-stakes way to sympathize with her husband. "It does seem like he's pretty attached to your shared past though."

"Hmm? What?" she said impatiently and with the disingenuous affect of someone who'd moved on, challenging him to insist on recentering the inane topic.

"The photo. It makes it seem like your history is pretty important and . . . *present* for him."

"Well, history is what makes people old friends."

"I guess that settles it then."

"No, go ahead. Is there more to say about the photo?"

"I don't get why you're defensive about this. I was just saying it's weird. Wouldn't you find it weird if I had pictures of my exes on my work desk?"

"I certainly wouldn't be thinking about it right now. If my defenses are up about anything, it's about this horrifying, potentially ruinous situation we're in at the most vulnerable time in our lives. And I cannot see where that photo fits in." She shook her head. "I'm sorry. I'm stressed." She walked to the pillar opposite the one Sharif stood next to. "If we could be quiet for a minute that would— " She shut her eyes. "I need to be quiet, if that's okay."

"Sure. Of course."

The next time he heard her voice, it was as she shook him by the shoulders: "Sharif! Wake up!"

Passengers stared at him. He'd never fallen asleep on a train before. It was dreamless as far as he remembered. He sat straight and wiped at his mouth. "What did I say?"

"It was either 'I don't know you' or 'I don't owe you.'" She put her hand on her forehead and fell back into her seat.

"It was 'I don't owe you,'" said the middle-aged Black man sitting across from Sharif. He'd said it with such unshakable eye contact that Sharif had to look away.

Part III
CONFLICT

30.

SHARIF AND ADJOUA had been moving around each other since getting home. Adjoua simulated privacy by facing the stove and stirring pasta more than pasta needs stirring. WNYC Radio streamed from her phone on the kitchen island at her back. Impatient as Sharif was to know what she was thinking in her walled-off state, their tensions at the train station had reminded him of how counterproductive it was to draw her out of her shell before she was ready. He was annoyed with himself for forgetting that, and even more annoyed with himself for his strong urge to draw her out all over again now. Suppressing his reflexes and desires was an increasingly frequent sensation in this marriage. He guessed it would only get worse with the baby.

So far it was only the unpleasant aspects of parenthood that he found easy to imagine: sleep deprivation, messy home, loud noises, bad smells, loss of freedom, sexless marriage—things one might experience as a child-less person. The positive aspects that made it "all so worth it" as parents reported—your child's first smile—were impossible to imagine as sources of great fulfillment.

Neither he nor Adjoua had yearned to have a child. So how had it come to feel so inevitable? It originated from the lifelong, external, majority consensus messaging: If you don't have children, you will miss out on the deepest meaning available to humankind. In effect, they had decided to upend their perfectly happy life based on persistent endorsement, not personal desire. How deranged to trigger a seismic and permanent disruption to their otherwise love-filled lives — in hopes of what? Preventing their future selves from *maybe* having regrets? Most experiences one tries based on recommendation or FOMO, like new foods or travel destinations or even careers, can be sampled, explored, and abandoned at will. With babies there is no test-drive. Yet somehow it became a foregone conclusion to roll the dice and flip a great life on its head. The alternative had been to not roll the dice and always question if they could have been a little happier, a little more purposeful, had they done it. Neither of them possessed the self-confidence to have a childless life without doubting the choice forever. In other words, bringing a new life into the world was an entirely fear-based decision, one that had so far sparked an unprecedented decline in their happiness.

Judy lay sprawled on his side between the kitchen island and Adjoua. There was sleep buildup in Judy's eyes, so Sharif stepped over him to get to the sink, wet a paper towel with warm water, and gently clean them. Wiping his dog's eyes was Sharif's favorite caretaking activity. Judy always welcomed the moist paper towel like a tongue bath. He'd look up at Sharif with a calm vulnerability, looking like he felt safe and loved. Sharif prolonged these moments well beyond practical necessity.

Waiting for the water to warm at the sink next to the stove, Sharif could feel Adjoua's body heat as her unfocused gaze stayed fixed on the boiling pasta she stirred without pause. He wondered if she thought his coming to the sink was an excuse to impose himself in her space. Maybe it had been an excuse. She stopped stirring when WNYC's radio host gave a breaking news update on Officer Luisa Daniels, the white cop who killed Anthony Augustin, the unarmed Black man Adjoua had been assigned to write about. In an improbable twist, Officer Daniels had been indicted on murder charges by a grand jury. It would soon be decided whether Daniels was convicted of manslaughter or first-degree murder. In the first instance, she faced up to ten years in prison. In the second, up to life. Her future hinged on sentencing guidelines, one judge's disposition, the politics and mediatization of her case, and her ability to show remorse and elicit sympathy. As in, how understandable were her bad choices. How preventable was her negligence. What price should she pay.

Adjoua resumed stirring when the news update ended, not making any comment about something Sharif knew she had feelings about. After cleaning his dog's eyes for a few minutes, Sharif sat crosslegged on the new dog bed they'd received that afternoon. Judy stood over him, visibly perplexed by his presence on his bed, and Sharif coaxed him into some light wrestling and hand gnawing.

Adjoua dumped the pasta in the colander. "Goddammit," she said to herself.

His forearm covered in dog slobber, he said, "What's wrong?"

"Overcooked."

The WNYC news stream was interrupted by a phone call. Adjoua continued staring down at her failed pasta as her phone vibrated on the kitchen island. Sharif stood and saw Aberto's name on her screen. Everything inside him dropped half an inch in concert. He told her who it was and she came alive to answer the call: "Hey . . . Fine, you . . . ? Uh-huh . . . Let me put you on speaker then. . . . " She laid the phone on the table and pushed the button. "Still there?"

"Yep." Aberto's voice filled their kitchen. Sharif looked at Judy, half expecting him to search frantically for the intruder. But Judy never responded to voices on speakerphone or the radio or movies. He'd plunked down directly beside his bed.

"Hi," Sharif said.

"I have news," Aberto said. "In addition to the bodily injury suit they've asked me to file, they decided to go to their local precinct in the morning to file a police report and press charges."

Adjoua said, "What are you talking about?"

Sharif looked at his frightened wife before returning to Aberto's name on the screen. He asked, "What charges?"

"Probably unforced entry and battery against a minor. Paul Lebedev, the neighbor whose apartment you went through, said he'd testify as a witness."

Adjoua said, "Oh my God."

"This is insane," Sharif said, remembering the opioid-eyed elderly neighbor.

Aberto said, "I'd love to stop this from going further. No one would expect you to pay everything up front. It could be a tiny amount every month. It'll be at least a year before the bills get sent to collection agencies. I could petition to extend that further if necessary. I'm certain Emmanuel would accept reimbursement in installments."

The audacity of this prick. This prick who on principle refused to pay back his student loans for the law degree he was using against them.

Adjoua said, "How much is a tiny amount every month?"

Sharif looked at her with open-mouthed shock.

Aberto said, "Depends on a number of things. I'm sure we could get to something like a couple hundred bucks."

"No," Sharif said to Adjoua. "It's not about the money. It's about my not being responsible. How many ways do I have to say that? We don't know what happened to Junior's wrist. He and that neighbor are lying. They must have made some kind of deal." Neither Adjoua nor Aberto said anything to this. He started to feel crazy. "If anyone is in a position to go to the police, it's me. Dozens of witnesses from work say Emmanuel"—he swallowed—"tried to attack me. First they abuse our dog and now this fucking . . ." He searched for the right word for Junior but it didn't come. ". . . *teen*ager and junkie are trying to frame me?"

"Sharif," Adjoua whispered. She put a stiff hand on his back more as a means of shutting him up than comforting him.

Aberto spoke as if Sharif were being childish, wasting everyone's time by dragging this out: "Maybe you were rougher than you recall, man. People often misremember things from high-stress situations."

"If someone's misremembering, it's him! And that neighbor did not see a damn thing. I'm sure of that. He was high out of his mind, inside his apartment the whole time!"

Aberto said, "Fine. I just wanted to give you the update and say that all it would take to stop this train is your verbal commitment to relieve them of their untenable financial burden."

"Okay," Sharif said, "why don't you make that commitment. That would make just as much sense." He stared at Adjoua's midsection, his eyes going in and out of focus, creating a halo of light around her belly. Met with more of Aberto and Adjoua's silence, he found himself losing control of his tongue, rambling: "It's unfair and shitty that they're struggling financially, and that Junior got badly hurt somehow, and it's unfair and shitty that Emmanuel works so much and hardly makes ends meet, and it's unfair and shitty that he was cornered into picking some garbage insurance plan, the world is an unfair and shitty place, that's all I can say right now, a lot of people in this city have unfair and shitty circumstances, and I work with them every day, but like I said, it's not feasible for us to be assigned their financial burdens at random like this."

As Aberto expelled a disappointed breath through the phone, it felt like he was physically materializing in their kitchen that was already too small for them, entering their home and standing by Adjoua.

Sharif needed him out. "Thanks for the update, Aberto. We'll talk it over, all right?"

Aberto said, "Listen, I can pitch another meeting with them and maybe even see if Paul Lebedev, their witness, can join—"

Sharif pressed the red button to kill that awful voice.

Peripherally, he saw Adjoua's mouth drop before saying, "You hung up on him."

"I told him we'd talk it over."

"He was in the middle of a sentence, Sharif."

"He's fine. He doesn't need you advocating for him."

"I'm advocating for *us* by getting as much information as possible." She cupped her forehead. "Jesus. Be strategic, man. It's like you can't think any moves ahead."

Sharif looked up and breathed at the ceiling. Judy was standing now, picking up on the excitement. He leaned his trunk of a neck against the back of Sharif's legs, panting fast. Sharif said, "Aberto's not our lawyer, Adjoua. In fact, he represents the people who want to see me in jail."

"Exactly, so why not mine their lawyer for everything he's willing to share?"

"Why do you think he really called, Adjoua? As some courtesy? Can't you see that he was threatening us?"

She shook her head. "I don't care what you or he thought he was doing. I was gathering information. If you can't keep your cool while I do that, then let me do the talking next time."

"There should absolutely not be a next time."

"You're forbidding me to talk to him now?"

"I'm asking you to stop going along with his manipulations. He's not a friend, Adjoua. He's a wolf."

Her face changed. She looked around the room then came back to him. "So your theory is that he wants to destroy us financially? What would he gain from that exactly?"

"He gets to feel like a hero. No sacrifice too great for his clients, that sort of bullshit. He's obviously an absolutist. An ends-justify-the-means type. But more than that, maybe he likes the idea of making us fail. As a couple."

"I see, okay." She did some dismissive wow-nodding. "This is spinning way out. We're not having a rational exchange. Let's take a step back for a few minutes."

"Yeah. Let's retreat into our corners and stew in silence. I always find that extremely helpful."

"I'm just tired. And overwhelmed." There was a downshift. She tried to smile, but it only made her look sadder. "Zora and I are hungry. Can we try this pasta that I boiled to death?"

After she served two bowls, they sat at the island and stared at the food. The marinara sauce looked like chunky ketchup. Sharif stabbed at the pasta with his fork, and little white-gloved hands of steam rose flamboyantly. "Aberto's trying to scare us. That's all I'm saying."

She crossed her arms. "Well, he doesn't need to try very hard. A man and his son are going to the police with an eyewitness to press criminal charges against the father of my unborn child. That's pretty fucking scary on its own." She rotated her bowl for no discernible reason other than to busy her hands.

"You don't actually think the police would make an arrest based on an incoherent story from a mumbling teenager and an addict, do you?"

"When you say things like that, it tells me you're not registering the gravity of our situation. Of course I think that's possible. It's also possible that we get dragged through some lawsuit that costs us years of our lives, incalculable stress, and more than twenty-six thousand dollars. They have free legal representation and they're playing this aggressively now. So, yeah, there's a world in which settling before this escalates makes sense. I don't want to pay them any more than you do, but we need to assess all options for the one that causes the least damage."

"Paying for something I didn't do isn't some compromise. It's an unacceptable injustice. I cannot comprehend how you're even entertaining it."

Her eyebrows meshed. "And I can't comprehend why you gave some random guy my dog."

He felt blindsided by the directness of her blame despite knowing it had been there all along. "Yes. In hindsight, I obviously see it was the wrong decision."

"A decision that could result in criminal charges and destitution weeks before our baby is born."

"No. Those aren't realistic outcomes. This has all been deception and fearmongering from the moment Aberto called about this. The threats aren't real. I'll secure my raise this week. You'll keep writing and publishing — and pursuing copywriting if you want. And we'll keep it moving like we planned."

"Right. Like we planned," she said despondently. "I sell out to provide a basic safety net for our family while you work the underpaid job you love."

"That's not fair. I've never encouraged you to pursue advertising at the expense of your writing. And this is one hell of a time to tell me you resent my job. I can't quit now, can I? That's our health insurance."

"I'm not asking you to quit without a plan. I'm saying as far as I know, you haven't even entertained the possibility of looking for something else."

"And you haven't once addressed this before."

"I assumed it would dawn on you, Sharif. I guess I'm addressing it now."

"I don't get what you're expecting. If I get my raise and earn fifty-k or more, and you earn about the same, which you're not far from as it is, we'll be richer than half of the people in this city. Do you know what the median income for a family of three is in New York?" It didn't look like she cared. "Fine," he said, "since we're speaking openly, I want to share that I'm happy one of us will be setting the example for Zora of not quitting on your dreams when things get hard. And I'm glad she'll grow up knowing that her father's work creates positive change in people's lives."

"Oh, get over yourself. If we're arguing about money, feeding her cheap food" — she shoved her bowl of pasta away — "collecting coupons, and are unable to afford the clothes or toys or experiences she wants, she's not going to say, 'Well, at least Daddy helps poor Black people for a living.' God, I'm only now realizing how white you are."

She'd never said anything like that before. He said, "What does that mean?"

"It means you think you're entitled to living like an idealist no matter the circumstances. It means you expect everything to work out in your favor regardless of your choices. It means you cannot fathom paying for what isn't your fault."

A terrible calm entered the room. It took him a while to find his footing. "Working at CAPPA isn't some privileged white thing to do. The majority of my coworkers are Black and people of color."

"The majority of your coworkers don't have family wealth. They don't have options like you. They have debt and are one paycheck away from enrolling as CAPPA clients themselves."

"That's not true. Latisha is —"

"Your *one* example! Yes, Latisha went to Harvard Law School and now works at CAPPA, good for her! That's some white shit too, using the exception as your example."

"That's not what I was saying."

"Does Latisha, the one Black person in your office forgoing access to a high-earning career, struggle to pay rent or have a baby with cancer? Oh, you don't know? You don't know the personal circumstances of your favorite example? You and Latisha aren't that close?" Frozen, all Sharif perceived in the pause that followed these rhetorical questions were her enormous eyes and his thumping heart. She said, "I want my daughter to have a few real comforts. She'll be entering this world in extraordinary pain, and I want to exceed her basic survival needs. I want her to have nice things. I want her to have every single advantage that money and privilege and whiteness buys. I don't care if you think I'm some superficial bitch now. It's what I want for my daughter."

He'd been wanting to hear what she was thinking for weeks, and now that he had, it rendered him speechless.

After a long silence, Adjoua said, "I'm calling my parents to see if they'll get us a lawyer."

This reactivated him. He put his hand on top of hers as she reached for her phone, blocking her from picking it up. "Please don't do that," he said. "I cannot express enough how badly I don't want you to do that."

Before this moment, Adjoua and Sharif were committed to self-reliance. Letting their parents cover their basic needs or dig them out of a financial rut had always been out of the question. Crossing that line would threaten the couple's identity in a way they never needed to articulate to each other. They knew implicitly that they didn't want whatever shameful or guilty or fraudulent feelings came from relying on their parents. Smaller gifts were acceptable — a dinner, a birthday present, a toy for Judy, the private room at the hospital since it made Charles and Sylvie's stay more comfortable — but they didn't expect these things, and certainly never requested them.

Large gifts were rejected outright. Earlier that year, for example, both sets of parents had offered to transfer $100,000 each into an account for Sharif and Adjoua to use for a down payment on their first home purchase. The couple passed without hesitation or discussion. They simply exchanged a look of two people noticing a bad smell at the same time, thanked their parents for the generous offer, and said they planned to buy a home on their own when they were ready, feeling proud and aligned.

Sharif's brother, Walid, said: Take the fucking inheritance you're entitled to and invest it in your family's future. If you don't want to start receiving it before they die, then at least get a job that pays a living wage. What do you make now? Fifty, sixty thousand? Walid always represented his brother's pitiful salary with numbers that were higher than what Sharif made. It was unclear whether Walid did this intentionally or if his memory simply couldn't fathom the lower number Sharif had once shared. Sharif said he didn't agree that he was entitled to their parents' money. He said he hopes they give whatever mysterious sum they have to people who actually need it. Mom and Dad have already provided us with more than enough to be financially independent. And as for his nonprofit wage, he explained that salaries are limited by the city contracts CAPPA got. Walid said, It doesn't sound like you understand nonprofit budgets. CAPPA could pay you more if they wanted. Sharif said getting a salary that met Walid's standards would force the agency to hire less staff, serve fewer clients, and ultimately lose future contracts. The whole point is to provide the highest quality of free social services to the greatest number of low-income New Yorkers. Don't worry about me, I know what I signed up for. Walid said, Yeah, well, I bet most of your colleagues would provide higher-quality services if they felt they were earning a dignified salary. And do me a favor, check CAPPA's latest nine-ninety to see what your leadership is making. I bet your bosses are raking in serious bank. It's always like that at these fucking places.

If Adjoua called on her parents now, they'd immediately retain a high-powered attorney and never disclose the cost. Her willingness to relinquish independence and self-sufficiency showed how well Aberto's scare tactics were working. But Sharif wasn't ready to surrender their self-sufficiency because of Aberto's games. He also didn't want his in-laws to learn that this whole drama started because he entrusted Judy to a practical stranger.

Adjoua said, "Well, we need to talk to a lawyer."

"Yeah. I'll, um"—a strange noise escaped his mouth, a belch of apprehension—"check in with Walid."

"Wow," she said. "I don't think I've ever heard you suggest Walid could contribute anything positive to our lives, or to anything really."

"Let's just see what he says."

31.

TO RELAX BEFORE calling Walid, Sharif took Judy on a long walk. For Judy, that amounted to a lap around four city blocks instead of one.

Re: New Adoption Timeline!
Hello, Sharif. Sorry to learn about your circumstances. I've added Vanessa, one of our volunteers, who rehomed the last of a full litter she'd temporarily housed. She may now have space for Judy. I'll leave it to you to connect further. Good luck!

Re: New Adoption Timeline!
Hi Vanessa (thank you so much, Diane — moved to BCC),

What hopeful news! Thanks so much for considering this. Let me know when you have time to chat. For now, let me share a brief description and some photos of Judy . . .

Sharif and Judy entered Seward Park, stopping at the bench where they rested with Adjoua on morning walks. Sharif shared a moment of forlorn eye contact with Judy before dialing his brother.

Walid, who went by Wally outside of the family, was two years younger than Sharif but had long been the one to give unsolicited advice. He informed Sharif on everything from what women really want, to why

New York City is a scam, to why Sharif should pivot to a career in finance. For Walid, if you weren't rich, you were a sucker. The last time they spoke, Walid recommended a book called *Getting What You Want Whenever You Want*.

Walid's head was fat and crowned with an orb of curly hair. He was a close talker too, hogging your entire visual field, eclipsing everything that stood behind him. He had small hooded eyes, round cheeks, and a slim arrowhead of a nose. By looking only at his face padding, you'd have been certain of his pudginess. But when he took off his shirt, he revealed a weirdly perfect physique. He could drink heavily most nights, eat whatever he wanted, and maintain the V-shape and muscle definition of a competitive swimmer by exercising vigorously once a week. This gave him permission to judge overweight people as lazy and self-loathing. He mistook good luck for superiority.

In high school, he started wearing blazers and khakis that gave him a comically Republican look. It stopped being funny when Walid came out as having joined the Young Republicans Club. Their parents blamed themselves, as if teasing him for looking like a Republican turned him into one. Walid had since disavowed the Republican Party, finding a stronger connection with various Libertarian offshoots.

"Fuck me," Walid said after Sharif caught him up on his situation. Lil Wayne played in the background.

"I know."

"Do you? Because what Aberto did is illegal. Lawyers can't even mention criminal charges if it gains them advantage in a civil matter. That's second-degree extortion right there. It's why he said that shit over the phone instead of in writing. Second of all, there's literally no fucking way an illegal alien is going to the police or engaging in formal litigation with you, especially after just getting arrested. Why do you think Aberto keeps everything within these informal mediation sessions? It would be bad for his clients' immigration review if USCIS learned they were tangled up in some legal dispute with a social worker. Believe me, they're more afraid of escalation than you are. You entered that apartment to save your abused dog. End of fucking story. No judge would convict you of shit, not even in woke NYC."

Judy was licking something whitish-yellow off the leg of the bench, either bird droppings or ice cream. Sharif pulled him away and said to his brother, "You're thinking it's all a bluff?"

"It's one thousand percent a bluff. Why would they wait until tomorrow to file their urgent, ironclad complaint? Is the NYPD closed Saturday evenings?"

"I assumed they had a scheduling conflict. If it's a bluff, why not pretend to have a better witness than their drug-addled neighbor?"

"Maybe they thought it'd be a more credible threat to use someone you met that day. Maybe they're just morons. Don't assume that inexplicable behavior from the opposition is part of some brilliant strategy. People are just sloppy sometimes."

"If they're sloppy, then maybe they would go to the police, right?"

"Let's pretend their lawyer is dumb enough to let them go to the police with a supposed witness who's a fucking junkie. No one at any level of the legal system takes an active user's word seriously. They are literally the most unreliable, disreputable, easily corruptible witnesses imaginable. Chances are this guy has a criminal record, too. The poor, older druggies usually do. Have you looked up his record? What's his name?"

"Paul something. I can't remember."

"Doesn't matter. Next time you hear from these people—Aberto, Emmanuel, the kid, the junkie, whoever else wants in on this weak con— you tell them to eat a bag of dicks."

"That's your legal counsel?"

"Yup. Sure is, baby boy."

"Okay. But seriously, do you think I need a lawyer?"

"To tell them to fuck off? Nope, that's for you to enjoy free of charge. And you won't need to pay a lawyer to call the cops if any of these clowns show up at your job or home either. As a matter of fact, if you want this to go away immediately, press charges against Emmanuel for trying to hit you at work."

"That's not what happened."

"Do it and they'll never step to you again. End of fucking story."

Sharif mumbled down at Judy, "That's the second time he's ended the story."

Sharif could hear his brother lighting his nightly joint as he said, "Look, dude. I know this isn't your style, but it's your job to get aggressive when someone threatens your family." He took a long drag of his joint and held it in. He then opened a corked bottle, probably whiskey aged in an arbitrarily complicated way, with charred hawk talons or something. Joint in mouth, he poured a glass.

"You should have called me sooner. This Aberto guy is a joke. I'd run circles around his ass, and this area of the law isn't even my specialization. Let me tell you his next move, because it's the only one he's got. He'll call you back soon to say he talked to his client, managed to calm them down, and thanks to him they're open to letting you pay them in small monthly payments to avoid involving any police or getting into some messy litigation."

Sharif was actually impressed. "He already offered exactly that."

Walid slammed his hawk talon drink on the table, removed the joint from his mouth, and hooted a single "Ha! Of course he did!" He laughed like the winner of a game that had no real importance to him. "That's fucking hilarious to me. Let Aberto pay for it in installments if he wants."

Sharif had basically said the same thing to Aberto. Any overlap with his brother's way of thinking unsettled him.

Walid added, "He's also going to lay on the white liberal guilt real thick. I'll bet you a grand that within twenty-four hours he starts finding ways to detail how sad and terrible these illegal aliens have it."

Sharif needed to create distance. "People don't really say 'illegal alien.'"

"It's literally the term the Supreme Court uses. And you know why the highest court in the land doesn't use 'undocumented immigrant,' brother?

Because it's a totally made-up term used to obscure the fact that these people broke our laws."

"Aren't all terms totally made up?" Sharif said.

"'Illegal alien' came first, and it's objectively more accurate."

It was sport for Walid to make people uncomfortable and then try to convince them that they had no reason to be uncomfortable. His urges to blurt racially coded political talking points increased around Adjoua, taunting her for the chance to deny race played any part in what he said, but Adjoua never gave that to him. She refused to even utter the word "race" in his presence, or express offense of any kind. She also forbade Sharif from advocating for her on these fronts. Walid had yet to tire of the challenge. In fact, the longer he went without getting a rise out of her — let alone achieve his end goal of proving that her pain wasn't real and shouldn't be trusted by even herself — the more his hunger for it grew, and the more steadfastly she withheld it.

Sharif aspired to be someone who didn't judge the ignorant. He didn't think people had power over what they could or couldn't see in a given moment: Everyone's doing the best they can with what they have and what they're able to see in the present. But it felt impossible not to blame Walid for what he didn't know, or for his lack of empathy (another aspect that wasn't a deliberate choice). Sharif couldn't uncouple his brother's ignorance from the structural inequities that rob so many of their human potential. And now here was Sharif, seeking Walid's guidance on a dispute with people disadvantaged by the ideas and policies Walid supported and Sharif despised.

If there had been one constant in Sharif's life, it was being seen as good. He was the kind brother; Walid the selfish one. Sharif's preschool teacher called his parents to say they had never seen a child his age advocate so successfully for the bullied. In third grade, the school janitor, Vince, felt compelled to write Sharif's parents a letter about what he'd observed in their son: how Sharif sought out the unathletic loners for sports when made captain at recess; invited the awkward, shy new kid to his lunch table; picked up other people's litter, held the door for everyone, and saw the janitors, teachers, and admin staff as human beings with lives beyond the school, asking after their children, pets, hobbies, and holidays. Vince wrote that he couldn't remember anyone in his twenty years at the school who exhibited the natural compassion of this third-grader.

Vince's letter was a favorite anecdote in Sharif's family. Adjoua heard it the first time she had dinner with her future in-laws. She loved it, and chastised him for never telling her about this before. She then told his parents why she called Sharif her Little Pope. It started when she asked him how he always had loose singles on him for panhandlers. He explained he'd stolen the idea from an op-ed written by Pope Francis about "giving without worry." Whether a panhandler uses your money on beer or lifesaving medicine shouldn't concern the giver. The giver is usually so far removed from the panhandler's situation that if it's beer they need to get through the next hour, it's not for us to judge.

On average, it ended up costing Sharif about a dollar a day. Some days no one asked for spare change and other days three individuals did on the same train. Giving without worry relieved him of all decision fatigue: Should I give? But I didn't give to the last person, so why does this person get it? Their physical appearance? Voice? My mood? Is it safe to pull out my wallet and check what's in there? What if I only have twenties? Is it respectful or aggressive to make eye contact when telling them no and sorry? Pope Francis turned off all of that noise. Sharif said that giving 100 percent of the time was actually much less stressful. Focusing on the self-serving aspect of his "giving without worry" only caused Adjoua and his parents to celebrate his goodness more.

Goodness was the only thing he'd ever been good at. Everyone seemed to agree it was what made him special. More than an identity, it was his right to be alive. Any cracks in his goodness endangered that right. Lately, he'd been noticing more cracks than before. He didn't know if that was because of an increased self-awareness or a decrease in goodness. A crack became apparent when he noticed he was providing lower quality services to a client because they were boring, or feeling undue rage at Judy's dependency on him, or waiting for the barista to look up before putting a dollar in the tip jar, or binging on porn that was a far cry from anyone's idea of feminist. These private behaviors might not have been new. But they were more obvious, uglier somehow.

His goodness had come to look less like a foundational fact about him and more like an inconsistent faith system. It takes faith to believe honesty and kindness have inherent value; that other lives have equal worth, deserving of equity in treatment and opportunity. All of that is as unprovable as religion, and Sharif's faith in his religion proved vulnerable to fissures of distraction, doubt, self-preservation, virtue signaling, and desire.

He couldn't remember the last time Adjoua called him her Little Pope. Nor could he remember when he'd stopped making a point of carrying loose singles on him.

Walid said, "Let me explain something about lawyers. Playing games is the cornerstone of our profession. Aberto's game is to scare you into thinking that to avoid jail and/or a ruinous lawsuit you must pay for something you didn't do. My game would be to show him that he isn't scaring my client, and that we are, in fact, prepared to initiate our own lawsuit preemptively. This would be communicated via demand letter, clearly stating that if Emmanuel doesn't pay for Judy's vet bills, we'll sue them."

"I've let the vet bills go."

"Hear me out. Not only could being sued interfere with their visa application in its own right and likely result in even more debt for them, but the retelling of events to a judge would expose them to more damaging information: their animal abuse and neglect, Junior's intentionally blocking your escape route with his body during an emergency — which any lawyer worth a damn would indirectly frame as assault — and Emmanuel's attempted assault at your job." He took another gulp of his talon whiskey.

Sharif said, "We don't want to get the courts involved either."

"They wouldn't. It's a play that forces Aberto to accept defeat."

Sharif remembered the fear on Adjoua's face as Aberto talked about criminal charges and lawsuits. It sounded nice to squash all of that. To force Aberto to accept defeat. And to relieve Adjoua of this terrible stress.

He asked Walid, "But concretely, what chance is there that any of this gets picked up by some facet of the legal system and messes with their immigration process?"

"Zero percent chance. Why would Aberto share my letter with any facet of the legal system if he doesn't have to? Look, you don't want this to drag out, but you're also unwilling to press charges against Emmanuel to end this right now. So let me write this letter. It'll take twenty minutes. I'll have my boy Brett who runs a big Manhattan firm send it since it needs to come from a New York–licensed attorney, ideally one who doesn't share your last name. It'll be free, don't worry. Brett's family."

It sounded kind of perfect. He said, "Thank you. But I'd need to talk it over with Adjoua first."

"Spare her, bro. Handle your business. Your wife would never admit this, but all women love when their man presents a *solved* problem. Tell her when it's taken care of and you'll be her fucking hero."

There was some wisdom muddled in with Walid's misogyny. Like most people, Adjoua did like learning that a problem was resolved without energetic cost to her. She found it comforting, sexy even. Something as simple as her coming home to a clean apartment and stocked fridge, or when Sharif handled their plane tickets and housing for one of the weekend trips they used to take, or how Sharif took care of their joint tax return. There was something reassuring and romantic about your partner taking care of things without you. However, it was only last night that Adjoua had explicitly asked him to never leave her in the dark on important matters.

Sharif said to Walid, "I'd definitely want to see a copy of the letter before it gets sent anywhere."

"Obviously," he said. "What's Aberto's law firm called? I want to see his website before I draft this."

"Barbosa and Associates."

Judy shot up to a standing position, hackles raised, tail rigid, and started his pre-growling hum. Sharif followed his dog's line of sight through the park fence, across the street, and saw the owner of the white poodle Judy hated about fifty yards away. Judy's growling wouldn't have been surprising if the man had his poodle with him. The poodle was ferocious, tall, indecently muscular, and had obscene gray balls. He lunged against his owner's leash, baring his teeth at Judy whenever they were on the same block. But he'd never growled at the man walking alone before.

"I'm on his site," Walid said. "Have you seen his About page? What a douche."

Could growling at people be a new development in Judy's senility, or was this triggered by his experience with Junior? Bewildered, Sharif found himself responding to it by speaking to Judy in Adjoua's mobster voice: "Yeah, fugthatguy. Fuggum."

Walid laughed, "That's the spirit!"

Sharif saw no point in clarifying. A father and daughter walked hand in hand in the wake of the lone poodle owner.

"Hey, there's one other small thing. There's this little girl who lives across the hall from Emmanuel. She may have seen what happened that day, and possibly even taken video with her phone. Is there any reason I shouldn't go knock on her door and ask her about it?"

"Don't do that. You don't know her relationship to your accusers."

"Sure, but I'd find out pretty quickly based on her response to me. There's no law I'm breaking by going over there and asking, right?"

"It could easily lead to unintended consequences. Don't take any risk you don't have to. Their side has absolutely no cards to play against you. Save yourself the trip. Wait, is your wife doubting your version of events or something? She's not taking their side, is she?" Sharif heard the eagerness in his brother's voice. Few things would excite Walid more than supporting his brother against Adjoua.

"It's got nothing to do with that."

"Then what would be the point? If both of you know it's a bullshit accusation, and Junior sure as shit knows, who are you trying to prove your innocence to?"

"I'm not sure. I guess I just like the idea of having evidence."

"Unnecessary and ill advised." Walid relit his joint and said, "When we send this demand letter it'll all be over. Have you told Mom and Dad about this?"

"No, and please don't mention it. They're at their retreat. I don't want to worry them."

"I won't say anything." He took a long pull of his joint. "I love you, man."

Judy lay down with a collapsing thump, panting the warm evening air in and out of his old lungs.

"Hello?" Walid said with a long exhale. "I said I love you, bro."

"Thanks. Sorry. I'm kind of tired."

"I know you are, baby boy." He took a couple more puffs. "I'll send that letter over in a minute."

32.

HAVING CHANGED INTO her sapphire boubou and pink headwrap, Adjoua lay on top of the bedcovers, staring blankly at the ceiling. Sharif was catching his breath from carrying Judy upstairs when he asked how she was feeling.

"Good," she answered, in the voice of someone lost in a deep stare.

They had discussed the sacredness of stares before. They're the brain's sensory deprivation tank, she'd said; an enclosed, restorative, floating paralysis that should be as uninterruptible and respected as prayer. When Adjoua stared at something long enough for it to start moving—the brick wall, the swirl of grain in the wooden floors, the uneven ceiling paint—deranged faces emerged from the surface textures. When she saw a particularly obvious face, one she could retrace even after she'd broken the stare, she tried pointing it out to Sharif. The last time she did this, about two months ago, was the first time he'd succeeded at seeing the face. They became so giddy about their historic victory (*I see it! Oh my God, really?! Yes, I see it! I see it! No way! I can't believe it! Oh my GOD!!! It's an asymmetrical Skeletor face! YES!!*) that a ticklefight ensued.

Sharif interrupted her stare now for the second time: "Walid is one hundred percent convinced Aberto is bluffing about them going to the police and about filing a lawsuit."

Her wide, bleary eyes remained fixed on the ceiling. "Walid is one hundred percent convinced of everything he says."

"Yeah." Judy lapped at his bowl of water. Sharif took his jeans off before sitting on the bed next to his wife. The couple agreed that outdoor clothes should never make contact with beds. Especially jeans. Jeans sit on trains, rumple at your ankles on bathroom floors, and can go weeks without being washed. To bring them to bed, even to sit, was a major error. And cleanliness took on heightened importance in a small space.

Still in her deep-stare monotone, she said, "I talked to Aberto."

"Again?"

Trying to maintain her stare, all she managed was "Um."

"Hello? Can we talk?" He put his hand on her thigh.

Jumping slightly, she said, "Your hands are cold. We were talking." She sat up, disoriented and annoyed. "He sent me a video message, and I called him back. Anyway, there's a possible solution I want to run by you."

"Okay." He worried this solution came from Aberto. "Can I see the video message?"

"It's really long. I can summarize it."

The photo of her in Aberto's office flashed in his mind. "I'd rather see it myself."

Clearly reluctant, she said, "Sure," then unlocked her phone and handed it over. He saw a long history of video messages between them he had no idea about, the time markers on all of them seemed unreasonably long. This one was five minutes and forty-eight seconds. It was Aberto walking down the sidewalk, aiming the camera up at his face as he talked: "Hi, sweetie, looks like we got cut off earlier. I know there's a lot going on, but it would be best to have a concrete plan by tonight for obvious reasons. So call me back. Also, I've been mulling over that question you asked about how Emmanuel can be so confident his teenager isn't lying. I wondered if additional context on them might help you understand.

"Emmanuel was a high school English teacher in Haiti. Saved enough money to buy a small house for him, his wife, Léonie, and their baby, Emmanuel Jr. They have this happy life until Junior's about eight, when the 2010 earthquake hits. We're talking the deadliest natural disaster in the western hemisphere ever recorded. Demolished everything in their neighborhood. Emmanuel was walking to the market for cooking oil when it hit and threw him to the ground. For thirty seconds the world convulses, and all he can think is that Léonie and Junior are home in the kitchen. By some miracle, Emmanuel and his neighbors uncover Junior, six hours later, lying virtually unscathed under the rubble of their home. Junior sees his leg has been touching his dead mother's leg the whole time he was buried and can't stop screaming. After that nightmare, a few days of homelessness in their newly ruined world, then moving in with relatives for a couple of years without finding any work, since the school was demolished too, Emmanuel decides they need to leave Haiti. There are no opportunities for them here. And Emmanuel can't stand this place that swallowed up his Léonie anymore. Everything is a reminder. So they join this group taking a boat to Brazil. They need a fresh start. Brazil is loosening its immigration restrictions to fill jobs ahead of the Rio Olympics. But things aren't good for Emmanuel and Junior in Rio. It's unbelievably hard for impoverished outsiders who don't speak the language to build a decent life. Junior goes to a free anglophone school run by missionaries. Emmanuel works construction gigs and does some English teaching on the side. But he mostly ends up teaching fellow Haitians who don't have money to pay him. They sleep in a tiny one-bedroom in a rough favela with two other families.

"Then more bad luck. Brazil is hit with one of the deepest recessions in its history. The work that barely keeps them afloat disappears. They hear of these TPS visas in the U.S. for Haitians and decide to make the trek north, joining one of those caravans our president loves vilifying. They travel over seven thousand miles. Eleven countries. Smugglers, buses, trucks, mostly walking, some swimming. Stopping for weeks at a time, awaiting the next smuggler's promises, working occasionally to save some extra cash. Junior gets malaria while crossing the infamous Darién Gap, their group is robbed at gunpoint, there are rapes and disappearances, people die of exhaustion and thirst through deserts, forests, mountains. They move through one dangerous border town after another as foreigners with nothing to their names.

By the time they arrive at the Tijuana–U.S. border, the U.S. has slammed the door on refugees and asylum-seekers and is even trying to expel the hundreds of thousands of TPS recipients already in the U.S., some of whom have lived here over twenty years: working hard, paying taxes, raising kids. Despite the president's lies, Haiti has not been adequately rebuilt by anyone's standards. There's a reason that a third of Haiti's GDP is still from remittances. So going back there after all they've been through is out of the question, but Tijuana is worse than Rio. They live in an overburdened church with over a hundred other migrants. The only work they find is helping another Haitian sell hair extensions. Junior gets tutored by Emmanuel to keep up with schooling, hoping to test into his grade in the U.S. if given the chance. Emmanuel sees no acceptable future for them in Mexico. They decide to cross in the middle of the night. Emmanuel has a cousin in Brooklyn who says he'll set him up if he can make it here. The crossing itself is another extremely dangerous trek through desolate landscapes. They panhandle and sleep in an emergency shelter long enough to buy two bus tickets to New York. When they arrive, Emmanuel's cousin sets him up with a guy who gets him fake papers. The guy charges loan-shark rates, and it takes Emmanuel over a year to pay off the documents. Emmanuel stays with the cousin, gets Junior enrolled in school, and gets a job as a delivery person, and then manages to land a second job as a wheelchair escort at LaGuardia. He knows how lucky he is that the fake papers got him the job, but is also pretty sure his employer begins suspecting he's undocumented. He needs a safer long-term solution. So he finds me, and we get to work building his asylum case. They were starting to have a semblance of hope before Junior's injury. The loss of Junior's wages alone jeopardizes their ability to pay rent and puts them on an eviction track, not to mention a collection agency could take them to court for the debt and force them to pay or face arrest, all of which would easily domino into the loss of their home, probably Emmanuel's job, and sink any chance of success with their already challenging asylum case, triggering the deportation process. Anyway, all this to answer your question about how Emmanuel can so unquestioningly take his son's word. On top of being a single-father-and-only-child duo, they've relied on each other to literally stay alive through unimaginable danger and loss. The intimate knowledge that comes from a prolonged, shared survival journey like theirs, which they're still on in many respects, creates a bond that is beyond anything we know. Emmanuel has seen who his son is in near-death situations time and again, knows how he behaves when hungry and thirsty and physically threatened; stripped down to his most basic survival instincts. He sees his son's essence. So the idea that he knows when his son is telling the truth isn't far-fetched. I hope that helps shed a little light on it for you, too. Call me to chat as soon as you're able. I have an idea I want to run by you. It's best if you and I discuss it before we present it to the others."

When the message ended, Sharif kept his eyes on the still frame of Aberto on the screen winking goodbye at Adjoua. He in no way felt compelled to speak. Adjoua finally said, "Told you it was long." Ten seconds went by before she added, "And manipulative. And, barely relevant."

A pleasant chill ran across his shoulders and down his back. He'd expected her to defend Aberto and was relieved to be wrong. He turned to her and was somehow caught off guard by her perfect face. He wanted to talk to her about something other than their situation, something that would make them laugh together and feel happiness. He wanted to talk about light things, and how pretty she was, and how much he missed her.

Before he said anything at all, she added, "I also think Emmanuel and Junior are in an objectively rotten situation. And there's a way we could solve everyone's problems."

He struggled to remain present, again worried that whatever idea she was about to share came from Aberto. "Okay."

She frowned. "Do you want me to tell you or not?"

"I said okay. As in, please continue."

"Okay. You just didn't sound open."

"I was. I am. So what did you come up with on your solo call with Aberto?"

She sighed, then said, "An online crowdfunding campaign." She transitioned to a crosslegged position and leaned forward. "I know, hear me out. Remember your mom's friend who raised thirty thousand dollars for her skiing documentary in Kyrgyzstan?"

"Yeah."

"We gave twenty dollars to that. She blew past her funding goal on little donations like ours. All for some personal adventure project that meant nothing to us. Imagine how readily our social network, and our parents' friends, would give to a young immigrant who's fallen victim to our inhumane healthcare system? We can iron out the parameters and phrasing of the campaign itself when we have everyone's buy-in, but there wouldn't need to be any admission of guilt on anyone's part. We can get away from that zero-sum framing." She was getting excited. "Maybe we all agree that Junior fell down the stairs or something. It doesn't matter. The fact is that they need help. We'd call on our community to lift them out of their objectively unfair circumstances."

He was slow in responding. "Whose idea was this?"

An unfocused flatness took over her gaze, not dissimilar to the one she had when staring at the ceiling, seeing deranged faces. Regaining focus, she said, "Does it matter? Aberto brought it up in passing, and I ran with it. I think it's our best option at the moment."

"First he calls to say his clients are in a rush to put me in jail, then he sends that video message about their decade of suffering, and then he plants this crowdfunding idea where his clients suddenly accept a public narrative where we're these heroes saving them." He shook his head. "Walid's right. All the legal threats Aberto has been peppering into these conversations are bogus. The crowdfunder is Aberto's latest method of putting this mess on our shoulders without involving the law. What if we don't raise the full amount? Are we responsible for the rest? And why does it even matter who creates and shares the fiction about how Junior got hurt in order to get money from friends? Why can't Aberto do it? Let him mislead his friends and family for the money."

"Like I said, we can work out the details later, including how Aberto should pitch in and share the campaign with his network. Or yeah, maybe it does come from his account and we share it. Why not? And I agree, we can't be responsible for more money than we help raise, even if it's shy of their needs. But if we can help them put a significant dent in this bill, or raise the whole amount, or potentially exceed it without bankrupting ourselves, then I think it's worth a shot. Don't you?" When he didn't answer right away, she said, "Honestly, I thought this would appeal to your 'give without worry' philosophy."

Whether it was intentionally manipulative or not, her reference to this philosophy shamed him. Did she know he'd stopped giving without worry? He said, "I hear you. I think you make some really good points. And I can probably get behind some version of the idea if they drop this farce of legal threats. I'm not willing to collaborate with people holding a fake gun to my head."

She shook her head. "You're way more confident about the gun being fake than I am. I don't get why you're so sure Walid knows what he's talking about. He's a corporate lawyer in Virginia."

"He predicted all of Aberto's moves. When you revisit Aberto's sequence of communications tonight—the legal threats, pulling on our heartstrings, and the crowdfunder—doesn't Walid's theory check out? Of course Aberto would want to avoid getting his asylum-seeking clients embroiled in some lawsuit, or some back-and-forth of police complaints. I just need him to drop the act. We can't have a cooperative dialogue about a crowdfunder if they think that *we* think we're doing it out of fear of legal consequences." He paused. "Why are you looking at me like that?"

"I'm worried your approach will enter us into some game of legal chicken with Aberto." She looked away. "I'm also concerned that you're willing to take unnecessary risks out of an emotional place, wanting the win more than the safest option."

"Emotional place? Yeah, I'm having an emotional reaction to being falsely accused and threatened. It would be weird if I didn't."

"I meant specifically about Aberto. I don't want there to be any macho or irrationally competitive stuff influencing our decisions."

"I'm feeling clearer and more rational than ever. And I don't see what risk there'd be in my writing Aberto to say that if he quits the legal games, we can have a frank discussion about how to help his clients."

She thought at him for a while with a furrowed brow. "Okay. But I'll do it. I'll write Aberto."

"Fine."

"And one more thing. I've followed up with everyone about Judy. I know it's far from ideal, but if we don't find a home in the next couple of weeks, we might need to consider taking Aberto up on his offer to take Judy in. Crazy as it sounds, we can at least be sure Judy would be in good hands. And that's what matters, right?"

"Why would you say that?" He shook his head. "It's weeks away still."

"Right. But if we don't—"

"I'll get it done. I will. There's a Protect Paws volunteer who's interested. I didn't want to say anything until it was a sure thing."

"Oh. Okay. I didn't know. That's great."

"Yes. I know."

Re: New Adoption Timeline!

Hi again Vanessa! Following up to include some availabilities on our end for you and Judy to have a vibe check! I can make any time tomorrow or Tuesday work that's most convenient for you, with a slight preference for after 5PM when I get off of work (but I can definitely ask for time off during the day too). Please let me know what works best for you, thank you so much!

33.

SHARIF LIFTED JUDY onto the bed next to Adjoua, then went for his nightly shower. His phone flashed on the bathroom sink with an email from Walid:

> I talked to Brett, and he's down with the demand letter. He'll put what I drafted (attached) on letterhead and sign it. Before I forward it to him, I need a copy of the vet bill and Uber receipts. You also need to go through the draft and put info in the XX placeholders.
>
> Don't worry about the 30-day ultimatum. Aberto will read this and beg for you to drop it. You can walk away from this whole thing or tell him you'll allow his client to pay you in installments LOL! The point is, this puts you in control.

Sharif sat on the toilet seat and opened the attachment:

Law Offices of McMaster & Cranston
1300 6th Avenue, 7th floor, New York, NY 10019
June 4th, 2018
Mr. Aberto Barbosa
Barbosa & Associates
1471 Nostrand Ave, Brooklyn, NY 11210

Re: Vet and Transportation Reimbursement

Dear Mr. Barbosa,

This letter has been sent on behalf of our client, Mr. Sharif Safadi, to inform you of a payment owed to him for the following reason: On May 31st, 2018, Mr. Safadi hired your client, Emmanuel XX, to care for his dog for a maximum of two weeks at a rate of $60 per week, for which my client paid the first week in advance. Upon checking in on his dog the same day that he had entrusted him to Mr. XX, my client found his dog tied up on Mr. XX's 14th-floor fire escape, resulting in an injury that required emergency medical attention.

Your client has yet to make any attempt to pay for the veterinary bills caused by his negligence and breach of contract, sealed by verbal agreement and payment. Receipts for the veterinary bills in question, along with the transportation costs of bringing the dog to the hospital, are attached to this letter, totaling $XX.

We at McMaster & Cranston hereby request that your client refund Mr. Safadi the full amount of $XX. If payment is not made within 30 days of this letter, we will take immediate legal action to resolve the matter, and your client may be required to pay all attorney's fees.

Sincerely,
Brett McMaster, Attorney
Law Offices of McMaster & Cranston, LLC

Sharif replied:

Thanks for this. It's a great thing to have, but let's hold off for tonight. Adjoua and I agreed to tell Aberto that we know he's bluffing. If that isn't enough for him to drop it, then we can send this. I really appreciate your time and effort.

Sharif took a long shower, eventually lying down in the tub to get that rained-on feeling he found peaceful as the puddle rose around him. When he came out, he saw that Adjoua had forwarded him the email exchange she'd had with Aberto.

> Hey Aberto,
>
> Sharif and I talked. He's happy to come to discuss the crowdfunder if the police and lawsuit stuff, which he sees as a bluff, gets dropped from the conversation. I'm hoping this can be resolved quickly and diplomatically. Let me know what you think, thanks.

It was hypocritical of her not to consult him about the wording of the email before sending it. Hadn't she demanded total transparency about this yesterday? He called out from the bathroom around his toothbrush, "You couldn't have said *we* think it's a bluff? You make it sound like I'm the problem!"

"What?" she called back from bed. "I can't hear you!"

He shouted, "I said, it would have been stronger to sound united on this!" In addition to the toothpaste foam in his mouth, the bathroom vent fan was operated by the same switch as the light and drowned out sounds.

"I still can't hear! Come over when you're done!" she said.

"Never mind!" he said, moving on to Aberto's reply:

> Hey Adjie Love,
>
> No bluffing here. I only relay what my clients say. If you and I weren't so close, I wouldn't even do that. As an FYI for Sharif: Emmanuel has as much right to go to the police and file lawsuits as anyone. Surprised he thinks otherwise. Regardless, I'll talk to Emmanuel and get back to you ASAP.

It was actually impressive how consistently Aberto managed to insinuate Sharif was some ignorant reactionary. Sharif did some quick research on his phone as he finished brushing his teeth, then marched over to Adjoua, who lay next to a curled Judy.

He said, "Of course Emmanuel has the right to go to the police by local laws, but undocumented immigrants don't do that because they know the federal government can override local sanctuary policies. Some asylum-seekers refuse to even give CAPPA their real names, addresses, or country of origin. According to the American Immigration Council," he now read from his phone, "... *even if sanctuary policy, state, and local officials limit their cooperation . . . they can't actively prevent federal officials from carrying out immigration enforcement duties . . . Sanctuary jurisdictions do not shield immigrants from deportation.*"

Blinking slowly, Adjoua seemed perplexed by the speech and citation, like it had been apropos of nothing. Judy was looking at him uncertainly from his curled position too. Sharif explained, "I'm responding to Aberto's email."

Adjoua said, "All right. Why don't we wait to hear how Emmanuel responds to the crowdfunding idea and take it from there."

"Okay." He looked around what had essentially become Adjoua and Judy's bedroom, feeling stupid and unwelcome. "Do you need anything before I go to bed?"

"I'm fine, thanks."

Re: New Adoption Timeline!

Hi Vanessa, three emails before letting you respond is way too many, I know. And I shouldn't be admitting this, but I Googled you and realized your salon has partnered with my organization, CAPPA, in the past. It looks like some of our clients have been happily employed by Vanessa's Dominican Beauty Salon! Anyway, just wanted to say I was delighted by this little coincidence and look forward to chatting soon!

34.

SHARIF LAY ON the daybed, trying to remember the last time he and Adjoua had sex. Definitely over a month ago. The pregnancy had brought on an excessive arousal in him that he didn't foresee. The second they started, he'd felt the rise of his orgasm and he'd had no choice but to move at tectonic plate speed — so slowly and with so many breath-holding pauses that he was mostly parked inside of her. She pleasured herself while he sat in there, barely holding on. So rousing were her signs of imminent climax — her accelerated breathing, slowly widening mouth, back-of-the-throat whimpers — that it released his pressure valve instantly. When she felt him shrinking, she gave up on getting herself off, turning down his offer to go down on her. The pregnancy had turned sex into a mixture of ecstasy and failure. Yet Adjoua insisted it was amazing when asked about it.

"You sure?" he'd said.

"What do you mean, am I sure?"

"Haven't you noticed how lately you're about to have an orgasm and then I have one and then it stops you from having one?"

"That doesn't always happen."

"It happens at least half the time. It just happened now."

"It's sweet when you can't hold it."

"Sweet?"

"You get excited." She smiled.

"I know, and I either blow it or remain paralyzed."

"I like that I can paralyze you."

"But I want to paralyze you."

"You paralyze me all the time."

"Like when?"

"Why does everything have to be specified? Accept what I'm saying as true."

"Help remind me. Name one time I've paralyzed you."

"How about when we had to be totally quiet at my parents'. That was hot."

"That was a long time ago. And we had to be quiet, so the paralysis was built in."

"Oh, baby. Please don't overthink this. I love sex with you."

He wanted to hear more, that theirs was the best sex she'd ever had. That she'd never imagined it could be this good. That her previous partners paled in comparison. That Aberto was a selfish and boring lover.

"Okay," he said, "but if there's anything you're not getting, or anything you want more or less of, or something you've had before that you'd like us to incorporate, you'd tell me, right?"

"Yeah," she said.

He fished a little more: "Maybe you want dirty talk or something?"

"You give the perfect amount of dirty talk."

"I don't really give any, though. Are you saying you don't like dirty talk?"

"I'm saying nothing is missing. I'm satisfied. And I promise to let you know if I want more of anything."

"Okay," he said, still finding it hard to comprehend being satisfied after not orgasming.

She turned his face toward her with her hand, and placed her parted mouth on his. The heat of her mouth made him hard again instantly. He pulled away as a smile stretched across his face. She looked back at him with the mildly disgusted expression she had when she was horny, and said, "More." She climbed on top of him and kissed him deeply.

35.

SHARIF DREAMED OF a sky lantern floating in their kitchen. He stood marveling at this glowing apparition. It had a small puncture in its side and slowly descended. When it touched the ground, it folded in on itself. The small orange fire suspended in its middle weakened, then extinguished. There was a moment of total darkness before the kitchen combusted into waist-high flames.

Adjoua shook him awake with Judy whining and barking next to her. "It's a dream, it's just a bad dream."

His eyes adjusted immediately to the darkness. But he still felt too discombobulated to ask questions about what she may have heard him shout. At least this time he remembered dreaming something worth screaming about. A second, greater comfort came when Adjoua caressed his head. It amazed him how therapeutic and unclenching her touch could be. When she shuffled back to bed, Judy followed close behind, his long toenails on the kitchen floor sounding like a typewriter. Sharif remembered Judy needed help to get up on Adjoua's bed, so he went over to give him a boost.

Re: New Adoption Timeline!

Dear Sharif,

Oh my God, of course! CAPPA has been an amazing staffing resource for my salon! My oldest and best braider (Cherika) came

214

to us from you all! Yes, I'd love to meet Judy! He looks like such a sweetheart. Before Protect Paws I lost my pitt. He got grumpy with other animals in his twilight years too, so I totally get it. Can you stop by the salon with him Tuesday at noon by chance?

Be well, Vanessa

Feeling vindicated, he replied, Noon on Tuesday is great! Looking forward!

He lay awake for twenty minutes before getting back out of bed and taking Adjoua's laptop from the kitchen island. He wanted to see if Aberto had sent her Emmanuel's response to the crowdfunder idea. Sharif should have been CC'd on that email anyway.

He did find a new email that Aberto had sent her tonight. But it was in another thread from a few nights ago, before the drama with Emmanuel and Junior started. The subject line: NYT Op-Ed (very) Rough Draft.

Hey Sweetie,

Sorry for the delay! Work has been hectic. I'm even sorrier about what's been going on between Sharif and my clients. I still haven't heard back from Emmanuel about the crowdfunder by the way. He seems to only check his email every few days and can't afford to keep his phone connected consistently. Anyway, like you, I hope to end this soon and peaceably. I also don't want what's happening to change things between us. Not sure I could tolerate more distance.

I think one of the ways to protect what we have is to carry on like normal wherever possible. So I hope it's okay that I respond to your op-ed now.

First, about your issue with the title, it's fine as is. The Times always uses literal and expository titles like that. Second, you know how I feel about your semicolon and m-dash use . . .

Sharif stopped there. He wanted to read her piece without Aberto's opinions playing in his head. He scrolled down to her initial email, skimmed through her disclaimers, and opened the draft.

Luisa Daniels Must Be Convicted of Murder, Even If It Wasn't Her Fault NEED BETTER/SHORTER TITLE

On September 12, 2017, a white 34-year-old female police officer named Luisa Daniels drove home after an unusually demanding 15-hour shift. Her day consisted of two drug raids, 9 hours of paperwork, and a dispute on the phone with her boyfriend. That night, she parked on the wrong floor of her apartment complex's garage. She then entered a unit inhabited by Anthony Augustin, a 26-year-old Black accountant. Augustin looked up from the bowl of ice cream he was eating in front of the TV to find Daniels in his entryway. The two had never met. Daniels drew her sidearm and shot Augustin twice in the chest. He died a few minutes later.

There are contested details about what happened that night. Was Augustin's door left ajar as Daniels claims, despite the doors being weighted to shut automatically? Did Daniels ask Augustin to put his hands up before firing her weapon? Did Augustin really respond to this by walking quickly toward her? While such doubts are warranted, none of them suggests an alternative to Daniels's explanation for shooting Augustin. From the moment of her distressed 911 call, to her panic captured on the body cams of the officers who arrived, to her sobbing testimony in court, there is little doubt that she believed she'd entered her own apartment to find a dangerous intruder.

Daniels's defense relies on "inattentional blindness," a failure to comprehend a completely obvious but unanticipated visual stimulus. As both Texas Ranger Michael Albertson and retired police deputy chief David Miller testified today, if we believe that Daniels believed she'd entered her apartment, then shooting Augustin was "a reasonable action under the circumstances." It's unfair and even irrational to punish

Daniels. Within the bounds of her visual and mental perception upon seeing Augustin, killing him was an exercise of her Stand Your Ground rights.

I do not doubt that Daniels made an honest mistake that she regrets. For 33+ years leading up to her encounter with Augustin, Daniels's singular brain had been receiving, interpreting, cataloging, and being literally shaped by a constant flow of sensory information. Her singular brain reacted to Augustin with an inimitable confluence of blind spots, fatigue, personal history, (ADD UNIQUE ANXIETIES/BIASES DATA). At that time, she was a person capable of entering a stranger's apartment and having a fear-based, confused, police-trained reflex to shoot to kill the Black man she saw. Daniels was unlucky to have been the distracted and scared person she was before killing the innocent man in his home. And Augustin was unlucky to be a Black man who forgot to lock the door before eating his ice cream.

In my ideal world, people who make such tragic honest mistakes should pay retribution to society with thousands of hours of community service, a lifetime ban on firearms, and 10% of all future earnings towards victims of police violence. Wouldn't that be more for the common good than locking her up in a taxpayer-funded cage for 28 years (the prosecution's recommendation based on the age Augustin would have been by Daniels's sentencing)?

However, within our purportedly impartial legal system, its pipeline to prisons representing the highest incarceration rate in the world, our penal code's assumption that free will drives criminal behavior, ignoring luck as the single most important factor in a person's life (TOO ABSTRACT/WORDY) — the only defensible response to Daniels's honest mistake is a murder conviction. Here's why:

First, the Augustin family deserves justice. If you haven't already, I urge you to watch the recording of Elizabeth Augustin, Anthony's mother, on the stand last week. Her pleas for justice are a kind of eloquent devastation.

Second, Black America deserves justice. Absolving Daniels for her misunderstanding of the situation is a degree of benevolence absent in the legal structures that govern Black lives. Black people, who also have singular minds shaped by a singular flow of sensory and environmental factors, make up 35% of our prisons despite only being 14% of the general population. There are three possible explanations for that: 1) Black people are biologically and/or culturally inferior, making them more crime-prone; 2) Black people are biologically and/or culturally inferior *and* are hindered to some extent by racism; or 3) systemic racism. Which do you choose? Which one explains the lack of access to quality schools, healthy groceries, reliable health care, jobs, and mentors in low-income Black communities (+MYRIAD OTHER ADVERSITIES STUNTING ECONOMIC MOBILITY) coupled with an excessive and hostile police presence that increases the statistical likelihood of being ensnared in the justice system? Which one explains why Black men get 19.1% longer sentences than white convicts charged with the same crimes who have similar criminal histories?

Black people suffer prolonged, and therefore health-compromising, stress during trials like Daniels's (FIND THAT ARTICLE ON THIS + INPUT MY LIVED EXPERIENCE). It is not merely the stress of anticipating disappointment while being exposed to depressing data about racism from NPR and victim-blaming from Fox News. If we were sure to be disappointed, we might be resigned to it. The stress comes from a sliver of hope that this trial is egregious enough to have a different outcome. We hope, against the odds, that we will see a fair judgment this time, and that our sons and daughters will see it happen a few more times, and their children will see it more still.

I will not feel any personal satisfaction knowing that Luisa Daniels is living in a prison cell. Our carceral system is abhorrent and disingenuous in its claim of rehabilitation. Nor do I believe imprisoning her will beat back American racism. If anything, it will become fodder for more white-backlash politics, making life worse for minorities. The reason she should be imprisoned for murder·is that she entered a stranger's home and murdered him.

The question this trial asks is whether our laws should give police the freedom to enter any of our homes, at any time, on or off duty, and kill us — so long as they were inattentive or afraid. My hunch is that even the most conservative among us, including those rooting for Daniels's release, would not vote on a law that granted police this degree of immunity. And yet, in one trial after another, this is precisely the legal immunity law enforcement officers are granted.

Trials like these are opportunities to reject the legal justification Daniels's defense team is permitted to use (UGH, I SAID ALL THIS ALREADY)................................

-Berto, I've lost steam! This is all so muddled in my head and too long on the page. I'm pretty sure the stuff about free will/how luck dictates individual actions doesn't belong in its current state, but if I'm honest, it's what I'm most attached to. Seems like the only newish and challenging idea to contribute to the conversation. Or maybe I've just been thinking about bad luck a lot lately. Ideally, I would conclude the piece with some clever way to calculate/ weigh every individual's luck factors before judging their criminal actions. New sci-fi novel idea (ha)? God, I'm so scattered and insecure. I feel like the point of the editing process is to find ways to hide my insecurity as a writer.

As you know from our call, my excuse for this mess is that I only started writing tonight while laid up in a hospital bed. In addition to the humiliating false labor, my time here has been peppered with medical racism my parents swear they can't see. Being racially gaslit by your own Black parents is really something. I'll vent more when I see you next.

Thank you for being such a safe space for my disjointed
thoughts. I'm really lucky to have someone I can send these
messy ideas to. Lots of love and gratitude (and eagerness for your
feedback!), Adjie xoxo

Sharif had no idea Adjoua still had the desire, or ability, to communicate such free associative, creative, self-conscious thoughts. He'd been convinced that this facet of her personality got buried by the stressful pregnancy. It devastated him to see it emerge for Aberto. She had sent this from the hospital the night before Sharif had requested to read it. Why didn't she have any interest in Sharif's take on subject matter that impacted the clients he worked with every day? His entire career was a response to systemic racism. He remembered her recent expression of resentment for his job and realization of how white he was. But if his whiteness made him an ineligible reader, why not send the piece to her actual Black friends, which as Sharif confirmed with a quick search, she had not done. Some of her fully Black friends were published authors, activists, and academics. How could her manipulative, lecherous, Sicilian-looking ex be her one "safe space" for her thoughts on racism?

If it were about her not wanting to share her writing in progress with her husband, or even because of his whiteness, Sharif could have accepted that. What hurt was being excluded from her incomplete, exploratory, thinking-aloud, dreamer parts. Her withholding started the day of the diagnosis. It was like she blamed him for their bad luck. Why couldn't she let their shared misfortunes bring them closer? Fired up with defensiveness, he returned to Aberto's latest email response:

. . . There's so much to admire in what you wrote, but I know you
don't like me hanging on what I found dazzling. So I'll get right
to what bumped for me. The first is the luck and free will stuff.
Without loads more context and argumentation, for which there
isn't space, it won't land.

Americans are free will obsessed. Every iteration of the American Dream centers around an individual's right and capacity for self-realization and self-improvement, choosing right over wrong, choosing happiness, choosing hard work, choosing to become a millionaire, and all the rest of the meritocracy bs messaging. I think challenging free will is a subject for a longer essay. But it doesn't belong here. Suggesting that this woman's lethal errors are not her fault, even if you do ultimately conclude that she deserves imprisonment, is confusing and risks coming off as insensitive.

In response to your wanting to publish new and challenging ideas, that's not your job. Your job is to evoke the maximum amount of empathy and rage. This means humanizing the Augustins. Not Daniels. What's needed now is a chorus of writers saying this is wrong, this is racism, and this must be punished to the maximum extent of the law. The stuff about Daniels making an honest mistake and not being in control of murdering Augustin confuses that message.

By the way, since when have you thought like this about free will? It's hard for me to reconcile it with anything I know about you. I think of you as big on personal responsibility. What have you been reading? How can we justify any punishment, or reward for that matter, if no one is responsible for any of their actions?

Anyway, I'm still mad about your night in the hospital. I'm glad we got to debrief a little on the phone. But fuck. The medical racism you described is reason enough to leave the country. Move to Brazil with me:)

Okay, dying to read the next draft. Call me to discuss further. With love and gratitude and eagerness for you too,

Berto
PS I'll call as soon as I hear anything from Emmanuel.

Was this what Adjoua wanted in a reader? Aberto's critique seemed so harsh and unhelpful. Why discourage the free will element that she'd explicitly said she was most excited about? Should Sharif be pushier with her, rougher?

In truth, Adjoua's takedown of free will surprised Sharif too. He had never heard her talk about luck controlling a person's decision-making before. Her parents touted and exemplified the virtues of hard work, discipline, and personal responsibility. They devoted all of their waking hours to preparing Adjoua to earn success: tens of thousands of dollars on private boarding school, test prep courses; turning her high school experience into an onslaught of AP classes, strategic extracurriculars and internships, and pressure around grades.

Their faith in meritocracy had been a strong influence in her life. It was evident in her getting into the Ivy of her choice. It was evident in the way she talked about her writing as "a discipline," something Sharif had never associated with novelists before, imagining them more as flaneurs awaiting lightning bolts of inspiration. Adjoua's belief in free will was evident yesterday when she talked about earning enough money to give their daughter more privilege. Aberto was right. Everything about her seemed anchored in the logic of free will, of a life entirely in one's control. The idea that Officer Daniels couldn't have done better than she did was more inconsistent with the author than the essay itself. Sharif wondered where her new philosophy came from. Was it a deepening nihilism or graceful surrender to their recent circumstances?

He reopened Adjoua's document. His vision blurred against the letters of the title, and he remembered the Canadian truck driver he'd read about who'd mindlessly blown past a stop sign and killed all those people. There was a sudden movement by Sharif's head. The screen of the laptop slapped shut. He actually gasped.

Adjoua's hand lay flat on the closed computer. "What are you doing?"

His heart paused briefly before sprinting. "Oh my God." He breathed in and out loudly. "You scared me." He swallowed. She slid her laptop away and looked down at him. "I——" he said, still mentally adjusting. "I was checking to see if Aberto wrote back. About Emmanuel's reaction to the crowdfunder. And I clicked on his most recent email. I'm sorry." She stood motionless. "I've been feeling far from you, and I thought——"

"You thought violating my privacy would bring us closer?"

"No. Maybe," he said, with increasing self-realization. "I thought it would help me understand what's going on with you. That's all I've been trying to do lately. I've been clumsy about it, I know. But I just want to understand where you're at. And I haven't been sure how to do that." When she didn't respond, he thought he felt some openness and forgiveness emanating from her. He said, "I found your draft really interesting."

She put the laptop under her arm, and said, "Good night, Sharif."

Her openness and forgiveness had been imagined. He spoke faintly to her shrinking back, "Why him? Why never me?" He remained slumped in bed for a moment before the aggressiveness of her nonresponse filled him with rage. He was suddenly standing at her back, almost barking, "What's wrong with you? Your husband says he wants to feel closer, and you walk away? Seriously, what the fuck is your problem?"

When she turned around, her eyes looked like circles of white light in the dark. "I feel actual disgust for my husband right now. Is that what you want to hear? I have never felt so far from you."

Seeing his wife as an enemy for the first time invigorated him. "Do you have any idea how maddening it is to be ignored by your partner? To be with someone who withholds all love and kindness in the face of any challenge? I think you do. I think you know that it tortures me, and you do it anyway because you're cruel, Adjoua. And you can go fuck yourself if you think living some secret life with Aberto on the side is something I'll accept. I'm disgusted too. You've been emotionally betraying me for years. I'm sick of being alone in this relationship."

"*You're* alone! I'm the only adult in this marriage! All you do is ask me to take care of your insecurities. All you want is to be heralded as some savior of the unfortunate even when you completely drop the ball on your own family! I withdraw into myself because you're not doing what needs to be done."

"Watch what you say, Adjoua. You won't be able to take these things back."

"I don't care, I can't live like this! I can't babysit you anymore. I need a grownup, not a little boy."

"And I need someone with a fucking heart! You're a cold — "

"Say it." She stepped closer. "Go ahead? I'm a cold *bitch*, Sharif? Is that it? Let's hear you say it. I'll help you: To me, you're a needy and weak man."

"You're just cold. I won't put up with a dynamic where I'm forced to guess what you think of me from one moment to the next. And when it finally comes out it's these horrible things you're saying now."

"Oh, fuck off. All that matters to you in this relationship is the state of your ego, which you wrap up in this pitiful good guy identity. If you had half a brain, if you ever fucking listened to me, you would know exactly what I think of you and our life together." She shook her head. "You know what, I'm not going to keep explaining this to you. What little patience and respect I had left is gone."

"You're awful. I hate you," he said.

"And I hate myself for being with you."

"Then don't be with me. I don't care. I don't want you either."

"Yeah?" she said. "Okay." She turned around, switched on the lights, and took a bag from under the bed that Judy now stood on. "I'm going to my parents'. Let's not talk again until after the baby is born. We can work out a schedule later."

"That works great for me," he said. "Perfect."

"I'll send for Judy tomorrow."

"Yep, absolutely fine." He went back to lie down on the daybed, staring at the ceiling, listening to her pack up, amazed by how relieved he was to no longer love his wife. What a revelation. It was so obvious that he was better off without her. She made him miserable. How had he been so blind to the toxicity of their dynamic before. Nearly free of the toxicity, and the weight of her mean and brooding presence, he could barely wait another minute until she was gone. When the apartment door shut behind her, he felt a deep sigh of alleviation. Buoyed, he could finally breathe. He was finally light and free.

He went to be with Judy on the big bed and celebrate with him. Five minutes later everything changed, like he'd sunk to the bottom of the ocean. Looking into his dog's worried eyes, he saw that he couldn't let Adjoua go. If he didn't insist on their union, his life was headed toward something he couldn't bear. He ran downstairs in his pajamas, punched the door open and stepped barefoot on the sidewalk. He looked left and right, spotting her on the corner of Canal and Essex, waiting for a car. He ran to her.

When he got there, he said, "Wait. Just, hold on."

She searched his eyes for a long time and then said, "I'm so scared, Sharif."

"I know, baby. Me too. Please come home."

Part IV
DIALOGUE

36.

ADJOUA PUT HER full suitcase back under the bed and changed into her pajamas. They started switching off the lights one by one. Standing in the dark kitchen now, Sharif said, "I'm sorry, Adjoua. For what I did and everything I said. There's no excuse, and I don't stand by any of it. I know things can't go on as they have been. I'm sorry to expose my desperation so nakedly, since I know you don't respond well to that, but the truth is, I have been pretty desperate to reconnect. I can't pretend I'm some traditionally masculine . . . stoic who's comfortable waiting until you feel like opening up. I've lost faith in that approach, and my anxiety around it has made me do dumb shit like go through your email at three in the morning. I won't ever do that again, I promise, but to create a safe, low-stress environment, we need more communication. I've obviously been doing things to alienate you, well before this stuff with Aberto and his clients. We'll eventually need to have a frank discussion about how we can start moving toward each other, and act as teammates again."

He saw her silhouette shift its weight from one hip to the other. "I agree."

"You do?"

"Yeah."

"Okay." He looked around and wondered if some of their mutual courage was thanks to the darkness. There was a passage in Adjoua's debut novel about how light can obfuscate the truth, distracting us with all that's superficially there, and how darkness is the purest revealer. It's why we close our eyes to pray or meditate or dream or feel deeply.

She said, "Are you too tired to have that frank discussion now?"

This caught him off guard. He thought for sure they'd had enough of a breakthrough for one night. "Now is good."

"Is it all right if we lie down and keep the lights off?"

They lay side by side in the big bed with Judy sandwiched between them, something they hadn't done in months, staring up at the dark.

She spoke first. "I talked to my parents about us, about problems in our relationship. This was a couple weeks ago."

He tried to release the embarrassment he felt at his in-laws knowing they had marital issues. "Oh, yeah?"

"I know that's uncomfortable for you, but I needed to talk to someone. Confiding in Julia or Meredith, or any of my other friends, risked making them turn on you in an unhelpful way."

"Why not talk to me?"

"I didn't feel I could. Not productively." She turned to face his profile. "Can I tell you what my parents said?"

"Yes. Please." He shifted around to let some air between his back and the hot bedsheets.

"What my mom said was what you'd imagine: Marriage is a long game, you can't let every disagreement threaten the foundation. You can't expect every moment to be bliss. You have to persevere through the hard times to get stronger."

He heard her turn her head back to the ceiling.

"My dad agreed and added that he wanted to share his secret to a long and happy marriage. I was expecting him to make a bad joke or recite some corporate coaching truism. But he said, the secret to a healthy marriage is to understand that your partner is a different person from you. It didn't seem meaningful at first, but it's been sinking in over the last couple of weeks. You are a whole different person, Sharif." She expelled a self-deprecating laugh from her nose. "The most obvious realizations are the most profound sometimes. You're not some symbol or character in my story, or an extension of my desires. I have no control over your thoughts or feelings or actions. And yet my empathy often only goes as far as imagining myself in your shoes. What *I* would do if my partner were pregnant with our sick child. How *I* would respond to my wife's financial insecurities. What *I* would think of an old photo of my partner in their ex's home office. What *I* would do with white male privilege. When you don't behave as I imagine I would in your shoes, I'm bewildered and disappointed. But true empathy, I'm slowly grasping, goes beyond shoe-wearing. It involves detaching from one's personality and imagining having only experienced the body and mind of this whole other, equally complex person. Their fears and sadness; their unique cognition, childhood, insecurities, traumas big and small, and what arouses their interest and excitement and joy. I'm starting to think this impossible empathy is the worthiest pursuit in life." She faced his profile again. "I was hoping to keep that in mind as we talk. That we're different people."

Sharif heard her smile. He turned toward her too. His eyes had adjusted to the darkness enough to see her face as a blue oval with moving hills. "I've been guilty of shoe-wearing empathy too." Her face, even obscured, was too much information, so he returned to the dark ceiling. "I mean it when I say I want to feel closer to you. We used to speak so freely to each other. Why did that stop? Am I misremembering how it was before?"

"You're not misremembering." She turned back to the ceiling too. "It's hard for me to be free and open with so much instability in our lives. I want to stand in my truth more and be bold enough to say what I'm feeling and thinking in real time. But I'm more afraid of hurting people's feelings than I realized, and I'm afraid of being an angry Black woman. I've spent my entire life softening myself so as not to alienate white people. But I need to remember that you can hear what I have to say and not be put off by it, as long as it's true and natural and not coming out of me after weeks of toxic suppression.

"That said, this is a sad time for me. With the violence of pregnancy, along with the appearance of wrinkles, and cellulite, I find myself having hateful thoughts about my body. I realize I'll never be as thin and pretty as I want to be. And I can't help but blame this body for Zora's illness. Maybe if I had gotten pregnant younger, she wouldn't be sick. On top of that, the whole reason for the delay was to further my writing career, which I see as a failure. It feels like I'll never write my second book. I'll contort myself into some miserable corporate ad woman. I'll be perpetually anxious about my daughter's health. I'll resent and fight with my husband. I'll watch my face slide off the bone as my arms and thighs get fatter and more repulsive, and my body will break down and I'll die. Maybe I'm having a midlife crisis. I know I'm a little depressed, but you'd probably be ashamed of me if you knew how much thoughts like that occupy my headspace. I don't want to dump all that negativity on you. I want to be a happy, healthy partner, and spare you how mean to myself I am."

A combination of love and sadness caused Sharif's heart to feel hugged too tightly. "I've been too self-absorbed to really imagine how difficult this has all been for you. I'm so sorry. It's painful to hear how hard you're being on yourself, but I also really don't want you to spare me anymore. You can offload any thoughts onto me, to process together or just to have someone to say it out loud to." He sighed. "But I have to admit. Times like these I wish you weren't a whole different person and I controlled your self-opinion."

She said, "I'll try to express the bad stuff more, but it doesn't come naturally. When we're hurting or threatened, we revert to wanting our childhood signifiers of love and safety. I think for you it's a need for increased connectedness and intimacy, checking in, being open, words of affirmation, physical touch. Your parents are like that too, so it makes sense. My parents weren't physically affectionate and never talked about emotions. Everything revolved around acts of service, achievements, and planning ways to save more money for my future. I thought I'd transcended their model of money being so important. But when I got pregnant, then found out Zora was sick, forget it. Money became my core need. The way I thought six months ago seems so delusional and far from who I am now. I have to assume that next year I'll look back at my current self and feel the same. Part of me hopes that's the case. I want to keep evolving. But I also recognize it's not easy on you. I really don't expect all this pragmatism and stability I suddenly require to come from you. I'm happy to be the breadwinner like my mom was when I was growing up. But I want a partner who's energized about making our lives better in practical terms, and would sell the shirt off his back to make sure we're cared for. I want our family to be the most important thing in the world to you. I wish we had more conversations about the future.

"You never weighed in on getting a changing table versus using the bed with a changing mat. Or what kind of stroller or diapers we should get. When I bring these things up, you say okay, or yeah, but don't seem present, let alone inspired to take proactive steps. That lack of basic interest in practical planning makes me feel unsafe. And I do shut down. Our free-flowing communication about feelings before had a playfulness to it that I can't tap into when feeling unsafe. This baby seems increasingly abstract to you. Zora's chances of survival are good, yes, but do you ever imagine what it will be like to have a baby who is suffering nonstop for two years? How we won't be able to explain to her why we bring her to some harshly lit, stressful place multiple times a week and connect her to these tubes that pipe in poison that makes her body hurt? Not knowing if you even think about that makes me feel so lonely. It's not that I doubt that you're impacted. You literally scream in your sleep. And that's another thing. I'm angry you're not prioritizing your mental health. Meanwhile, in your waking life, I'm seeing this temper in you that I never knew about before. And I'm noticing how this anger can lead you to making rash decisions."

He said, "I'll call the therapist and continue the process I started. I didn't realize how much it was upsetting you. I'll take care of it."

"Thank you."

"And you're right, I need to engage more on practical matters. Hearing you talk about it makes me realize that I have been pretty avoidant about it, and I want to shake out of that. I hate that you've felt alone. As for my vision for our future, it does start with getting a raise at CAPPA. It's the best job I've ever had. I work really hard there and know I can climb the ranks. Whether it's at CAPPA or another organization I believe in, I aim to be a senior-level director in the next five to ten years. They make between eighty and a hundred and fifty K. Does that sound okay?"

"It's the 'five to ten years' part that is hard given our situation."

"I know. But I can't fathom how changing careers now, with no experience or skill set outside of social work, will bring about an instant pay jump."

"You can't fathom it because you haven't looked into alternatives. You're a white man with a master's degree."

"In social work."

"I'm sure there are higher-wage jobs available to you. My friends from school who make way too much money would have leads if I asked them. Or I could talk to my parents about plugging you into their professional network. Frankly, you could make more as a bartender than what you're making now. I know you're not open to any of that. So I need to work on releasing any resentment toward you because of it. I'm trying. This is where my father's wisdom about accepting that your partner is a whole different person becomes useful."

"Your mother's point about marriage being a long game is useful too."

"Yeah."

"I know I risk sounding righteous or 'white' when I say this, but my one job requirement has always been that it contributes something good to society. I've been consistent about that since we met. And I want to add that I believe in your writing so much. With your talent, you're bound to become a rich and famous author. I wish you'd give yourself permission to double down on your novel while still teaching and doing some copywriting on the side. If I get my raise, don't you think you could try that, at least for a short while?"

"Not when I feel like this. When you say you wish I'd keep writing my book, it makes me feel worse about not being able to."

"That's not my intention."

"I know, but have I communicated clearly and openly enough now for you to stop repeating it?"

"Yes. Absolutely," he said.

"Good. Thank you. You know what else I want to be clear about? That I've never stopped having values, even if I don't have this job requirement to be paid for doing good. You've made me think about this a lot, and I realized that for now it's enough to simply be proud of my behavior. Whether I work at an orphanage or at a hedge fund, Zora will see me behave with honesty, fairness, and kindness toward others. And I'll acknowledge when I slip into unkindness. That's how I'm framing my moral imperative to myself as I turn my back on art and sell out to the highest bidder. And maybe I'll be in a position to give money to worthy causes this way."

"That's a wonderful moral imperative. I know you're a good person. I've never felt morally superior to you, despite how I probably sound sometimes. I had no right to read your op-ed, but your moral sense shines in that piece."

"That draft is chaos."

"I didn't think so. I'm proud of you. I think you're so smart and talented and good."

"Thank you. That's really nice. And also, I still hate what you did."

"Me too. I won't ever do it again. But can I point out that we might be having the longest and most free-flowing conversation in months? How does it feel? For me a pressure valve has been released."

"I think I feel good about it too. I'm too exhausted to know for sure."

"Yeah, let's get some sleep. The sun will be up soon."

"Okay," she said, sounding extremely sedated all of a sudden. "I love you."

A purifying, floating sensation filled him up and down. "I love you too." After a few glorious breaths that made him feel light and strong at once, he put his hand on Judy and sat himself up. "Let me slip out now so I don't wake you later."

"No," she said, almost gone. "Stay, please. Just for tonight."

She went under seconds later. Sharif knew he wouldn't be able to sleep with Judy's clicking and snoring. But he lay back down and smiled at the ceiling as it began to glow.

37.

ON MONDAY MORNING, Sharif carried Judy downstairs like a big baby. Judy's bear-like and cow-like and pig-like head bobbed, his snout facing Sharif's profile and his wet nose brushing Sharif's cheek. Judy took advantage of his situation to give Sharif a long, slow lick and then panted in his face in a way that resembled laughter. Adjoua greeted Judy at the bottom of the stairs, where Sharif had set him down and called him a clever little donkey. Outside, Adjoua took Sharif's hand in hers. An old, liver-spotted man smiled at them as they crossed the street. The sky was bright and clear.

Walking with Adjoua and Judy was to embrace slow motion. Judy, old and overheated. And Adjoua: walking with short, clenched steps, as if Zora might slip out. It was hard to believe they were still five weeks from labor. They stopped at their usual park bench. The Chinese women had congregated by the ground fountain, chatting, holding their long red folding fans at their sides. Sharif tried to support Adjoua as she sat down but she waved him away.

She was grimacing at her cell phone as if in terrible pain. "What the fuck?"

Sharif tensed. "What?"

"Oh my God."

"What's wrong? You're freaking me out."

"They're talking about it."

"Who? About what?"

"About you." She stood. "And Junior. I'm forwarding it to you now."

It was a text message from Adjoua's literary agent: Isn't this your husband? The link in the forwarded message took Sharif to an Instagram page of a high-schooler named Isabella Cervantes, who had 40.6K followers. Isabella described herself as an Afro-Latina hair care influencer and social justice warrior. She had posted side-by-side portraits of Sharif and Junior. Sharif's picture was from his LinkedIn profile. He looked like a generic, unsmiling white man in a passport photo. Next to that, Junior showed off the monstrous metal rig stabbing into his forearm and wrist. He wore a flat-brimmed baseball cap with *MIGHTY* written on the front. The caption said:

Bruh u won't believe this tea @zjunior_fleu just spilled! This dude Sharif Safadi straight up busted into their crib and broke Junior's arm! 😤Sharif broke in thru the window to grab his dog which he paid Junior's dad to watch. When Junior caught him and was like "what u doin here?" Sharif yanked Junior's arm and BOOM snapped his wrist! Then Sharif started going crazy saying the nastiest slurs! 😵 Junior ended up with mad internal bleeding, he had to get emergency surgery. His arm might not ever be the same. 💀💀And guess what? Sharif ain't paying a single cent for the damage he caused! 😤 What even is justice in this country?! 😳 #JusticeforJuniorFleurime #AmeriKKKa

"Slurs? He's telling people I used slurs now?" Sharif said.

Isabella's post had been traveling the internet since 7:38 p.m. the night before. So far, there were 498 likes, over 200 comments, and 997 shares. Even though Isabella hadn't tagged him in her post, Sharif checked his Instagram, which he kept private. Strangers couldn't comment on his posts, but he had received twenty-six direct messages:

straight up inhuman smh!!! ☻

YOU need to drop a bag TODAY!

there is a special place in HELL for heartless assholes like you

☹ I wish ur kids end up with broken bones, abandoned like animals!

I HOPE YOU DIE

I'd say I feel sorry for racists like u, but nah, u don't belong here. Never did. 🐢

bruh kArma IS coming for U.. no one is letting this slide.

Watch ur back in these streets mf. I'll be on the lookout for u. 👀

a broken wrist is the least of your problems rn . . . like the whole block is after you 🧊

on god the disrespect is crazy

imagine being racist today, couldnt be me

Sharif stopped reading there and watched Adjoua pacing with her hand on her forehead. He returned to Isabella's post and reread it. Her characterization of what happened and of him as a person was so antithetical to what he stood for that he searched for the sign of a practical joke.

In a weak attempt to reassure Adjoua, he said, "The people engaging with this are mostly classmates of Junior's and Isabella's, right?"

"My agent sent it to me, Sharif."

"Does your agent have a kid who goes to Erasmus?"

"She doesn't have kids."

"Then how?"

She shrugged in the way of someone giving up. He studied Isabella's page and found a name he recognized: Aberto Barbosa. Aberto had liked the post and replied with a yellow surprise emoji.

Sharif said, "Why the hell is Aberto commenting on this girl's post?"

"He probably saw it through Junior's page."

Sharif said, "I still don't get it. And your agent is friends with Aberto?"

"I don't know, Sharif. I'm going to see if I can report it on Instagram and ask someone to take this down. This is unsubstantiated defamation. No, I'll call Aberto first."

"What can Aberto do about what's on Instagram? It's not even Junior who posted it." He let his head drop between his legs and spoke to the ground. "I can't believe we're getting cyberbullied."

"This won't look like bullying to anyone but us. It looks like activism." Adjoua sat down next to him, bent over her bump, trying to breathe through her stress. "Okay. If we get Emmanuel on board with the crowdfunding plan, Junior can post a correction on Isabella's page. Right?" Adjoua began rocking back and forth. "It'll all go away."

Judy did not appear impacted by these developments.

Sharif said, "Let me be the one to call Aberto." Somehow this idea offered him a sense of control. "I'll call on my way to work. You get ahold of the help admin."

"Okay."

38.

WHILE CROSSING THE Manhattan Bridge, Sharif forwarded the link to Walid and wrote: Any advice on how to handle this?

Walid responded: Motherfuckers. I told you the police stuff was a bluff. Now we know their new game. Same advice: We send the letter and/or press charges for the attack. You know my vote.

Let me think on it. On the train to work.

Stop thinking and act.

When Sharif surfaced at Church Avenue, Adjoua called and asked, "Did you reach Aberto?"

"I left two messages on the way to the train. I'll try him again now."

She sighed. "The site administrators won't remove the post because it's technically reported speech. The most they can do is write her a suggestion that she tone it down. Useless."

Sharif said, "They're a multi-billion-dollar private company. They could do better than the legal definition of slander if they wanted. Jesus. It's like Isabella's done this before."

"Did you see her page? She's far more passionate about trolling than hairstyle tips. Sharif, I think you should respond to her. Ignoring it isn't the right strategy."

"Respond publicly to a righteous teenage girl in front of her forty thousand friends?"

"One succinct statement. You unequivocally deny her baseless accusation. There will be many reactions but you won't engage with any of them. After the crowdfunding thing gets sorted, Junior will back you up. Those will be our terms."

He sighed with dread. "Will you help write it?"

"I'll send you something in a minute."

He felt grounded by Adjoua's confidence, and that they were working as a team. He also realized his brother was proven right again. Junior and Emmanuel hadn't gone to the police. Maybe it was good that they were using social media instead.

Sharif spotted a few old clients on his way to work, receiving warm acknowledgment from all who noticed him. In a state of automatism, he overshot CAPPA, took a left on Flatbush Avenue, and another on Caton. He was behind a block-shaped bush on the corner of Caton and Twenty-First when he saw Junior standing with the same young men who'd helped Sharif get into the building last time. Two of the guys shared a blunt. Junior seemed light and high-spirited, laughing often. Sharif didn't have a plan, so he turned away and speed-walked to work. About halfway there, his phone pinged with a message from Adjoua: Hi Isabella. I was sorry to learn about what happened to Junior too. However, there's no evidence whatsoever linking me to the injury, because I had nothing to do with it. Sharif realized he could have written that himself after all. He posted it on Isabella's page and turned on his notifications. He left another message with Aberto.

Walid wrote again, saying, Give me the info I need for Brett (the XXs) to send the demand letter. They need to know you mean business ASAP or this rumor will spread. There's no reason not to do it at this point.

On the elevator ride up, neither Sharif nor the other CAPPA employee triggered the scripted joke about Mondays. It was 9:15 a.m. and they were nervous about getting caught walking in late by their supervisors. Sharif moved through the lobby without surveying any of the crowd for familiar faces like he usually did. He had to get to his office before Merjem saw him. He felt a tap at his shoulder.

He turned. "Oh, Tanisha, how are you?"

"I'm really good," she said with a bright smile. "I was hoping we could make up our session today."

"Unfortunately, I have clients all day."

"Okay. I left you some messages, and I thought I'd pop in to try and catch you."

"I haven't been at my desk since Friday." He was turning away from her to signal his departure. "But I'll check my calendar and reach out soon about scheduling, okay?"

"Sharif," she said, "I also wanted to thank you for the stuff you said about my situation with my daughter the other day. About taking responsibility, apologizing and all that. I could tell she was really amazed that I could say sorry to her. We both were!" She laughed. "It was kind of a breakthrough for us."

"Oh, that's wonderful." He didn't remember giving any such advice, and started turning away again. "I'll be in touch soon."

"Sorry, I had to tell you." She stopped him again. "The stuff about having the choice to not repeat bad behavior really resonated with me, even beyond my relationship with Jayda. It's like just knowing that has the power to give me second chances. It's so simple but so wise. Anyway, since our session was interrupted by that crazy guy, I thought we could make it up."

"Yes. We definitely will, Tanisha," he said with unmistakable shortness. "I just can't do it today, okay?"

Her smile melted away. She looked left to right. "I understand."

He knew he had hurt her, but he couldn't manage her emotions right now. "I'm sorry, Tanisha, I have to run. I'll call you about an appointment on my lunch break."

"Okay," she said, looking at the floor.

Walking toward the computer room, he saw Merjem. Without slowing her stride, she spoke coldly as they crossed paths: "Message me when you're running late, please. There's a prospective client waiting for you."

"I'm sorry. The trains," he said. What a bad precursor to their ten a.m. meeting about his raise, for which he'd been too distracted to strategize.

He felt flattened by the fluorescent overheads of his windowless computer room office and remembered he hadn't slept. An older gentleman with a fisherman's cap sat in the chair next to his desk, facing the wall cluttered with flyers from partner agencies: free TASC prep, digital literacy training, foster care prevention, youth and education development, eviction prevention services. Sharif greeted him from behind and apologized for being late, again blaming the trains. The man introduced himself as Jurell. Before Jurell explained what brought him in today, Sharif checked his phone and saw a dozen notifications: responses to his response to Isabella's post. The first to fire back was Isabella herself: simply saying, SHAMELESS LIAR. He put his phone down and looked at Jurell, again apologizing. Jurell spoke at length, but Sharif was incapable of paying attention. He snuck glances at his phone under his desk when Jurell was looking away, something he'd never done before. But more and more high school kids were accusing him of a racially motivated assault. And then came the email from Vanessa.

Re: New Adoption Timeline!
Hi Sharif,
Isabella Cervantes is among the hair influencers I follow most closely. I'm not comfortable being involved with you or your dog.
Good luck.

"Hello?" Jurell said, noticing Sharif's downcast eyes. "Do you have somewhere else you need to be?" He had a stooping posture in his seat, a pronounced belly under his sweater, and oily eyes. His neat chinstrap beard climbed up into his fisherman's hat.

"What? Oh, no. I'm sorry, go on." He slipped his phone in his pocket. "Do you have a sense of what kind of job you'd be interested in pursuing?"

"I just told you I have a job. The problem is that it pays fifty dollars over the eligibility requirement for public assistance. Like I was saying..."

Sharif automatically checked out again. He was partially conscious of how negligent he was being, but not enough to do anything about it. He nodded at Jurell while thinking of Judy's unresolved housing, Vanessa's likely assumption that Sharif was a dangerous guy, and this growing group of angry teenagers on their phones at school. Erasmus High, which Junior was probably entering now, was around the corner from CAPPA. Sharif saw these kids walking in slow-moving, backpacked clusters every day. If he were one of them, or really anyone outside of himself, he'd believe Junior and Isabella's account too. It had always seemed improbable to him that a person would publicly identify as a victim under completely false pretenses.

Images of Junior and Emmanuel and Adjoua and Aberto banged around Sharif's head while Jurell said something about housing. Sharif thought he should have confronted Junior this morning to get a better sense of him, what kind of kid he was when his father and Aberto weren't speaking for him. Junior was also a whole different person with his own narrative and inner logic. Maybe Sharif could have connected with him, shown him what kind of person Sharif really was and calmly explained the trouble these lies were causing.

There was a pause in Jurell's speech where Sharif sensed it was his turn to talk. Embarrassingly aware of how little of Jurell's story he'd absorbed, he ventured, "It seems like a housing referral might be a good first step?"

Jurell squinted at Sharif, then sighed. "I guess we could start there, sure."

Sharif asked Jurell to fill out a referral form and let him know if he had any questions, then turned to his computer: Hi Vanessa, I understand your discomfort. But this really is just an unfortunate misunderstanding. Please call me if you're able to reconsider helping Judy. I'm sure you'll agree that none of this could be his fault.

He then searched for the Erasmus High School phone number.

The Erasmus secretary answered on the first ring. Sharif spoke quietly, turning away from Jurell, who was still studying the paper he'd been given.

"Hi there, I'm a case manager at CAPPA and I'm calling about how to get in touch with the homeroom teacher of a student named Junior Fleurime."

"Sure, hold on a second." The secretary clicked around her computer. Sharif glanced back at Jurell and perceived some confusion about what he was reading. Sharif mouthed that he'd be with him in a minute. The secretary returned to say, "Ms. Evans is in class right now. Can I have her call you?"

"Please, thank you. Let me give you my cell."

He hung up the office phone and reflexively checked his cell under the desk again, reopening Isabella's post. He tried to access Junior's Instagram page, but it was set to private. Sharif would have to send him a follow request, and he had the clarity of mind to understand that was a patently bad idea.

Jurell stood up to leave.

Sharif put his phone away and said, "Oh, you finished the form already?"

"That form's got nothing to do with housing." Sharif saw he'd indeed given him an irrelevant employment document. Halfway out of the computer lab, Jurell said, "You hardly listened to a word I said."

"Wait." Sharif stood now too. "A housing referral. I can provide that right now. It'll take me two seconds. I'm sorry, I'm not usually like this. I'm just dealing with a personal emergency."

"Yeah, so am I," Jurell said, continuing out the door.

Sharif fell back in his chair. "Fuck."

After chastising himself, his anger turned toward the Fleurimes and Aberto. He left another message on Aberto's voicemail. "Please make it crystal clear to them that putting an end to this defamation campaign is a nonnegotiable part of the deal, okay?" After a long pause he added, "We don't deserve any of this. We're good people. We're doing our best. Freezing me out like this is really low."

Sharif hung up and stared off into the middle distance without blinking for nearly a minute. Aberto texted: Please stop calling. I'm with a client and need to keep my ringer on for news about her court proceeding. Yours is not the only situation I'm dealing with. I'll get back to you when I can.

Sharif turned to his computer and opened up Walid's email with the demand letter. He inputted and attached all the information Walid asked for and sent it back.

Merjem stood in the doorway, appearing torn between concern and aggravation. "You okay?"

He shook his head no but said, "Yeah."

"I just got a scathing review of our services from a Mr. Jurell Waters."

He expelled the wrong kind of sigh. The self-pitying kind. "I'm really sorry."

"He said you ignored him while he was telling you about the abuse he's been experiencing at the men's shelter on Broadway."

"I'm being terrible. I know."

She came and sat where Jurell had been. "Do you? Because there are two other issues. First, are you aware that there are hundreds of Erasmus High School students out for your blood?"

"Yeah."

"It's all over the internet, Sharif. What the hell is going on?"

"I don't know. It's —"

"Second, the guy who attacked you here on Friday filed a police complaint about you."

His head snapped up from its hanging position. "You're joking."

"That wouldn't be a very funny joke, now would it." She slapped both of her thighs and stood up. "Come on. Let's go talk to Patricia."

"Now?"

"She's in my office now. So, yeah. Now."

A minute later, Merjem, Officer Patricia Dauphne, and Sharif sat wearing sunglasses in Merjem's office.

Patricia said, "The complaint against you filed at my precinct was sent to the DA's office since Emmanuel and Junior Fleurime came with a witness."

Sharif said, "I cannot believe this."

Patricia leaned forward in her chair. "Sharif, why do these people want to punish you so badly?"

He looked at Merjem. "I'm sorry. I didn't want to make a big deal of it." He returned to Patricia. "I met Emmanuel here and gave him a referral, like I told you before, but then we did meet a second time last week at the train station." He shared everything from that second meeting up to his rescuing Judy from the Fleurimes'. "That's it. I have no idea how Junior broke his arm."

"Jesus," Merjem asked. "Why didn't you tell me any of this?"

"I didn't think every embarrassing detail mattered. I thought the only relevant information was that Junior's injury has absolutely nothing to do with me. But I'm sorry. I should have told you the whole story. I couldn't have imagined it escalating to this."

After staring at Sharif with a kind of blank shock for a few seconds, Merjem turned to Patricia and asked, "What can we do?"

Patricia looked around the room and tapped her foot. "I'll add a note to the complaint that the witness, Paul Lebedev, appeared under the influence, which he absolutely did. And that he's got a long record of drug offenses with us, some unruly behavior, aggression toward law enforcement, and more. I'll also mention that I've caught Junior carrying a quantity of marijuana that was barely under the intent-to-distribute amount. I confiscated it and let him off with a warning, but that kid is no angel either."

"That's much appreciated," Merjem said.

Adjoua's revulsion as she watched the Fox News clip on her phone about the marijuana found in Anthony Augustin's apartment flashed in Sharif's head.

Patricia said, "I don't know whether my notes will have much influence, but we'll try." She shrugged. "Other than that, Sharif, get a lawyer if you haven't already. And personally? The first thing I would do in your shoes is file your own complaint for the attack on Friday. You've got a hell of a lot more witnesses than they do, credible ones too. Your coworkers will attest to what they saw, right?"

Merjem answered for him: "Yes, absolutely."

Sharif said, "Would that have any effect on the complaint filed against me?"

Patricia said, "Not in the short term. But it would scare them. Show that you've got some fight in you. I'd be pretty pissed off in your shoes. Putting your dog on the fire escape, attacking you at work, spreading lies, probably paying their junkie neighbor to give a false testimony. Plus, filing against them could give you extra protection in a courtroom, if it ever comes to that."

Sharif remembered the demand letter and decided that was enough in terms of scaring them for now. And of course there was the crowdfunding idea, still the only practical solution they'd come up with.

"I also think you should file the complaint," Merjem said to him. "In the event that you're on trial defending yourself someday, you don't want it to sound like you're retroactively claiming it was a serious incident because of your new legal reality." Patricia nodded along. Merjem added, "One of the security guards can go to the precinct with you now."

The security guards weren't even in the room when Emmanuel supposedly attacked him, he thought. "I don't know."

"You don't even need to come in," Patricia said. "You could write it up here, have your witnesses sign it, and I'll do the rest."

Merjem looked at him, eagerly awaiting his agreement.

Sharif said, "Can I think about it some more?"

He felt Merjem's eagerness slacken with disappointment.

"Don't think too long," Patricia suggested as she stood.

Sharif said, "If I could reason with Emmanuel, I'm sure I could make this go away."

"That's probably not the best idea," Patricia said. "Start with your lawyer talking to their lawyer. Emmanuel is out to bury you now. He doesn't know he's getting bad information from his punk teenager. Frankly, if I believed someone broke my kid's arm, I'd see red too."

"How much time do I have before the DA makes their decision?"

"Hard to say. I've seen them press charges and send us out to pick someone up within a couple of hours. Other times it's taken over a year."

"Okay. I'll decide by tonight."

Patricia left, and Merjem asked Sharif to stay. She said, "This needs to go away."

"I know. I'll take care of it. Please give me until tomorrow."

Merjem would have no choice but to fire him if this dragged on much longer. He couldn't afford to lose his measly salary or his health insurance now. The thought of asking for a raise today as planned was almost laughable.

She said, "You're going through too much." She stared at him with arched eyebrows. "You're unable to be fully present for your clients, as proven by Jurell Waters. So you should head home. Be with your family. I'll handle your appointments."

"Thank you, but I'm fine. I'll be present now. It would actually help me to keep working."

"I didn't mean it as a question, Sharif. Go home."

39.

OUTSIDE, HE TEXTED his brother: They filed a police report.

Ha! Walid replied. These people are dumb. Go file your own

You were sure they wouldn't do this

No, I said they wouldn't if they had half a brain. Brett will send the demand letter to Aberto today

More people, some from outside of Erasmus High, were commenting on Isabella's post, directing their ire not only at Sharif but also at Adjoua. Someone had found Adjoua's Instagram account, which was public, and tagged her in the comments. She was being called horrible names: traitor, self-hater, colonized bitch. Besmirching his name with lies affected him more than he'd have anticipated, but going after his wife ignited a rage in Sharif that made him feel capable of random acts of violence. When he called her, she sounded more depleted than after learning of Zora's diagnosis. She said, "Just like that, I'm part of the problem."

He said, "You're not part of any problem. These comments don't represent any majority opinion. They represent a few full-throatedly ignorant cowards getting a cheap thrill."

"People I know personally are sending direct messages of concern. Coworkers from Mercy College posted on my page that they're 'troubled' by what they read. I can't blame them. If I'd read Isabella's post without additional context, I'd believe it was true too." He heard her collapse on the bed, smashing the side of her face into a pillow. "I want to crawl into a hole."

He wasn't going to share the bad news about Emmanuel filing the complaint now, or about Judy's rehoming falling through. "We'll get through this, Adjoua."

She said, "I wish I didn't care what people said about us. But I really do."

He imagined himself walking down this avenue with a baseball bat. People scattering, terrified to be near him, begging forgiveness for disrespecting his wife. "I know, baby. Did you write a single, unequivocal statement for yourself like you did for me?"

He heard her lift her head. "Not yet."

He stood wide-eyed on the train platform, feeling so angry he was afraid to speak. He finally managed to ask how Judy was doing, and she joylessly described him curled up like a croissant beside her.

He said, "I hate that we're waiting for Aberto to let us know if his clients give us permission to raise money for them. I had a letter sent from one of my brother's friends. It's called a demand letter——"

"Oh, no," she interrupted. "You've got to be fucking kidding me." She was responding to something else.

"What?"

"I can't deal with this." She began to cry.

"What happened?"

Through tears she said, "The editor. I'll forward it. I have to go." She hung up.

He opened the forwarded email:

Hi Adjoua,

I'm so sorry about what's going on with you and your husband. I'm sure it's complicated and stressful beyond description. Given the attention it's getting, we thought it best to put a hold on your op-ed. Perhaps having a little relief from deadlines is welcome

right now? Please be in touch when this blows over. Above all, best
of luck with the baby!

Stephanie Diaz
Opinion Editor

Sharif did not take the train. He left the Church Avenue station and
marched headlong toward Emmanuel and Junior's. He needed to find that
little girl who saw — or possibly even filmed — what happened.

On the corner of Caton and Twenty-First, he stopped behind the
block-shaped bush on the corner and observed the same young men in front
of the building. They were probably familiar with Junior's online narrative.
But Sharif couldn't let their presence stop him. He refused to let his wife's
and his reputation depend on whether Emmanuel agreed to their crowdfunding terms. If Sharif obtained definitive proof from that little girl, or
even heard what she witnessed, it would give him control. No longer would
they be held hostage by Emmanuel's capriciousness, Aberto's games, or
Junior's lies.

He received a call from an unknown number. His first thought was that
it was Vanessa calling about Judy. "Hello?"

"Hi, this is Kiara Evans. Junior Fleurime's homeroom teacher."

"Oh, yes, of course. Thanks for getting back to me."

"No problem. I didn't know he had a caseworker."

He felt a quick stab of fear, suddenly realizing he was on the verge of
crossing a serious line. He said, "I wanted to touch base to get a fuller picture of how he's doing."

"Sure. I'm really glad he's getting support. And it doesn't hurt that
CAPPA is such an amazing organization. Okay, what can I tell you about
Junior. You probably already know that he's shy, until he's not. He'll be
completely silent for weeks on end but when he opens up it's like this over-
flow of expression." He heard her smiling. "You suddenly realize he's been

paying close attention all along. Of course, he's been quieter than usual lately. I know he's taking pain medication."

He said, "Right," looking around, lowering his voice. "Did he mention how he injured himself?"

"Well, it's strange. Last week he said he'd gotten jumped by what sounded like a gang. But then this morning I caught wind of a different story going around the internet that someone broke into his home. This is all secondhand information. I don't really go for social media, so I haven't had a chance to see the post myself. But it's quickly becoming the story of the day around here."

"I see." He swallowed. "And did you have a chance to ask him why there were two versions of the story?"

"I did briefly in the hall. He shrugged, mumbled something. Looked embarrassed. For what, I don't know exactly. I plan to follow up later. What else can I tell you about him. Academically inconsistent. By that I mean, he'll have three weeks of exceptional output and then a month where he doesn't do any work. Math is his favorite subject. He loves drawing and painting, too. He's always doodling cartoons on his notebooks."

"Any"—he cleared his throat—"disciplinary issues at all?"

"Not recently, no. There was a weird incident at the beginning of the year, though." Kiara described security footage that had caught someone vandalizing a classroom door. Although the video didn't show his face, everyone agreed it resembled Junior. "We searched his locker and bag but didn't find any markers or anything. We called his father, who became quite defensive. He watched the video and said that was absolutely not Junior, insisting on a difference in the slope of the shoulders. No one else seemed able to see it, but he was really adamant." When Junior returned the next day, Kiara said that he gave them the name of another student who he said had done it. "We searched that other student's bag and found markers that matched. But they looked brand new, like they'd never been used before." Kiara described how the student started sobbing and swore he'd never seen those markers. "He claimed someone had planted them. His body type didn't match that of the hooded boy in the security footage, either. Some teachers believe Junior planted the markers. But we couldn't be certain about any of it. We decided punishing an innocent student by accident was worse than letting both boys off with a warning. Neither student has been in trouble since."

The young men in front of the building were listening to the cinnamon stick guy say something animatedly. Once he'd finished, they walked as a tight and determined group up the block toward Prospect Park.

"Ms. Evans," Sharif said, "this has been really insightful. Thanks so much for your time."

"It's my pleasure to speak with you. If there's anything I can do to help you help Junior, please let me know. I hope working with you will brighten him up a little. He's been in a bit of a funk lately."

He said goodbye, watching the young men disappear around the corner. Then he advanced on the building.

40.

AS SHARIF STEPPED on the walkway of the building, feeling trepidation begin to weaken and confuse his resolve, he spotted Wesley Michel, an old client. Wesley had exited the neighboring building carrying a number of full trash bags. When they met eyes, Wesley dropped the bags on the sidewalk and shouted, waving at him, "Sharif! Hi! It's me, Wesley!"

"Hi, Wesley," Sharif said much more quietly, not wanting to invite attention.

Wesley was a muscular man of about forty who'd enrolled in one of CAPPA's job programs two years earlier, when Sharif taught job readiness workshops. Wesley was well liked for his enthusiastic and friendly manner. He made everyone smile despite how difficult it had been to find him a job. The workshop Sharif had him in was called Acing the Interview. No matter how many times Sharif taught Wesley the structure of answering the classic interview question "Tell me about yourself"— 1) give relevant work experience; 2) highlight skills applicable to the job; 3) explain what you're looking for on your "career journey" (in which students were to indirectly describe the job they were interviewing for)— Wesley systematically answered by 1) stating his name; 2) sharing something personal and irrelevant, like how many brothers and sisters he had; and 3) that he was a hardworking, honest man who would be the best worker ever. He always concluded with a magnificent smile. After six months of daily visits, his job developer finally managed to find him a position as a porter at the five-star Royalton Park Avenue Hotel. Wesley was thrilled. He bought his job developer flowers and wrote a number of people, including Sharif, effusive thank-you cards.

Sharif said, "How are you, man?"

"I'm good, I'm good!" He walked away from the trash bags to come give Sharif one of those handshake-hugs.

Sharif looked Wesley's maintenance worker jumpsuit up and down, and said, "Looking great. You work in that building now?" He motioned toward the building Wesley had come out of.

"I do, I do!" He sustained his usual, jovial shout, putting Sharif a bit on edge.

"Are you still at the Royal too?"

"That ended months ago!" Wesley laughed. "My boss was a *crook*! He had me pay for porter certifications that I found out were fake! My sister told me he was scamming me, so I quit."

"That's awful. I'm sorry."

His smile remained huge. "Everything happens for a reason! Are you out for a walk?"

"Well, sort of." Sharif became even more self-conscious and hushed. "I'm hoping to visit someone in here." He gestured toward the building's door.

"I work in there too!" He laughed.

"Really?"

"Yeah, yeah! I do maintenance for four buildings!"

"No kidding."

"Yeah, it's the greatest job! I love it!" He laughed again before counting out the four buildings for which he was responsible: "This one, that one, that one over there, and the one after. The sort of red one."

"Wow," Sharif said. "Must be a lot of work."

"Yeah, yeah, and I'm friends with everyone in all *four* buildings!" He laughed.

"That's great, Wesley." They smiled at each other for a few seconds. Sharif looked up and down the street, feeling he'd been lingering for too long. Then the thought of Adjoua crying in bed returned to him. It rocked him from side to side before turning into bright arrows shooting outward: He had every right to stand on this sidewalk for as long as he wanted, and there was nothing wrong or illegal about going in to speak to that little girl. He had to do this. "Do you happen to know the family who lives in apartment 14D in here?"

Wesley squinted and stroked his shaved chin, "14D, 14B——"

"14D."

"Oh yeah," he laughed. "14D, 14D, 14Deeeeeęe." He clenched his eyes more tightly, then shot them open. "Yes! My friend Samantha lives there!"

"Really? That's the little girl's mother?"

"No!" he laughed. "It's the little girl!"

"What luck. That's who I was hoping to speak with today. Do you think she or her mother will be home?"

Without requiring more information, Wesley said, "Samantha's always home. Come on, I'll go up with you! Samantha's the best!"

Sharif reminded him of the bags left on the sidewalk, and Wesley ran to throw them in the dumpsters between buildings. As Sharif waited, he found himself looking up and down the block again, thinking of the five young men who'd left and the hundreds of Erasmus teenagers who associated him with pure villainy.

After running back to Sharif, Wesley unclipped the large set of keys from his belt and used a key fob to open the front door. As Sharif entered, Wesley jangled the keys in his face. "Samantha gave me this!" Sharif guessed he meant the braided piece of neon plastic string on the key chain.

Halfway to the elevator one of the five young men from earlier caught the front door and walked in behind them, having obviously run back. It was the drill-dancing guy from that first time. He entered the elevator with Wesley and Sharif, making it such a tight squeeze that it was hard not to be touching. The young man kept glancing back and forth between Sharif and his phone, angling the screen away from view. Sharif's heart rate increased. Wesley had a big grin on his face the whole ride up, like they were on a fun ride, repeating, "Samantha is the best!" He laughed. "She's so funny."

When they got to 14D, Sharif looked back and saw that the young man had held his head out of the elevator to see where they were headed. He and Sharif locked eyes briefly and the young man retreated back into the elevator. Sharif felt he didn't have much time. He could also feel Emmanuel and Junior's door breathing behind him. Wesley knocked on Samantha's door with a *tock, tock, to-tock tock . . . tock tock*, then put his ear to the door and wiggled his eyebrows at Sharif. "That's our secret knock." The door cracked open. A woman of about sixty with dark circles around her eyes, an orange headwrap, and a green boubou looked at them. The smell of lamb or goat stew wafted out. Wesley said, "Gloria, it's me, Wesley!"

"I know that, Wesley. Hello." She wasn't nearly as excited as him. "Everything okay?"

"Everything's great!" he said.

She looked at Sharif then back at Wesley, "What is it then?"

"Can Samantha come out to say hi?"

The woman glanced at Sharif again before saying, "She's doing schoolwork."

"Oh," Wesley said. "My friend Sharif needs to meet her." His eyebrows mashed together and then he turned to Sharif. "Why do you need to meet her again?"

Sharif tried not to sound nervous. "She may have taken some videos of my dog that I hoped to look at."

Gloria said to Sharif, "So you're who they were asking about." She crossed her arms, gripping herself at the elbows. "I already told them we didn't see anything."

"But maybe Samantha did," Sharif suggested, hearing his voice quicken.

"The child doesn't speak."

"The thing is, there's a chance she filmed what happened on her phone."

"She doesn't have a phone. Not anymore." She squinted at him long and hard. "What do you want exactly?"

"I'm a caseworker at CAPPA. There's been a misunderstanding with your neighbors, the Fleurimes. I'm trying to get information to clear it up."

She relaxed. "CAPPA. That's God's work right there."

"Yeah, it's a good place to be."

"They're the best thing that's happened to this community. Come on." She opened the door and let them in.

Huddled by the closed door, Sharif asked, "Samantha doesn't have that phone anymore?"

Gloria said, "She went to do laundry downstairs and came back crying. That's when I learned someone took it."

"Did she see who?"

"Nope. She put it on the table behind her while changing the wash. When she turned back it was gone."

"Has anyone else come asking to see it?"

"Oh yes. Not ten minutes before it disappeared, that boy across the hall, Junior, came asking for it. I told him Samantha was doing laundry and that she'd be right back, but he left. Then Samantha came back up crying her eyes out."

"Did Junior come back asking to see the phone?"

"No, he did not. Then his poor father came asking if we'd seen anything about how his boy got hurt. I said no and told him about how the phone was stolen right after Junior came asking after it. He got mad I was implying his son was a thief. Poor man's delusional. Thinks his son is some attendant of God. But that boy is headed down a bad path. I see him hanging around front with those older boys."

Sharif said, "Would it be all right if I tried asking Samantha a few questions about that day?"

She chuckled. "I told you. She doesn't speak to anyone but me when we're alone, and even that's only happened a few times in the six months she's been here. She's my foster child. I've never seen her say a word to anyone but me. Sometimes I think I imagined it. But when this one comes around"—she motioned toward Wesley—"she laughs and laughs. Doesn't speak, but sure does laugh. Isn't that right, Wesley? I feed her, make sure she does her homeschooling, because there's no way you can keep this girl in a school. She runs home the second the teachers turn their back. She basically homeschools herself. I check her work. She's a clever girl."

"Would you mind if Wesley and I tried talking to her anyway?"

She shrugged. "Can't hurt to try." She knocked on the closed door a few feet behind her.

The apartment was the same layout as Emmanuel's, though looked more lived in, especially the kitchen: considerable cookware, cooking oils, knickknacks, bags of rice and beans, spices, stew bubbling on the stovetop.

Samantha cracked her door open and Wesley celebrated, "Samantha!"

Samantha smiled at the floor, letting the door hang open a bit more.

"Hi, Samantha," Sharif said. "Do you remember me? You met my big dog, Judy, the other day."

She didn't respond. Gloria said, "I told you."

Sharif spoke to Gloria in a happy tone, for Samantha's sake: "She came out every single time Judy was in the hall. She was so fascinated by him, and she used her phone to make these short films that I bet are great."

"She does love her animals," Gloria said, matching Sharif's tone. "I remember that big dog." Gloria pushed Samantha's door open wider and pulled Samantha's chin up for eye contact. "Don't you, darling?" Samantha let her head be angled upward but kept her eyes cast so low that they were almost closed. Gloria said, "Tell me something you liked about that dog. And did you see any funny business that day?"

As soon as Gloria released her chin, Samantha tucked it back to her chest. A breath later, she stepped back and shut the door.

Gloria sighed and turned to Sharif and Wesley. "You hungry?"

Wesley said, "Yes, please!"

Gloria called over her shoulder on the way to the kitchen, "How about you, sir? You want some stew?"

Sharif was wondering how he could get something out of Samantha. "I just ate, but thank you. It smells delicious."

A piece of paper shot out from under Samantha's door. Sharif picked it up to find a pencil drawing of Judy. Sharif thanked her through the door and said it looked just like his dog. Gloria had finished serving Wesley a heaping bowl of steaming rice covered in a brown meaty stew, then came toward Sharif with her hands on her hips. "I can try asking her again on my own. What was it you wanted to know specifically?"

"Anything she saw as I carried my dog out that day. I'm trying to confirm that Junior did not break his arm at that time."

"He's saying you did it so they don't have to pay the bills?" She shook her head, clearly disgusted by Junior's strategy. "Okay, I'll try one more time. But like I said, she's unlikely to open up while you're here." She knocked on the door, entered, and closed it behind her.

Sharif stood by the door, listening. Gloria said, "Hey, my darling. This is important. We have an opportunity to reveal the truth. And you know there's nothing more important than the truth, don't you?" She waited. "Nod if you understand. Ah, you see. That wasn't so hard, was it? So can you tell me what you saw that day the man came to pick up his dog?" After nearly thirty seconds, Gloria said, "Okay, sweetie, how about we start simple. Tell me. Is that man out there a good man, a bad man, or a so-so man? Good means he's nice and never hurt anyone. Bad man means he did hurt someone. And so-so means you're not really sure or that he seems normal. So, which is it? Do you think he's good? Bad? Or kind of so-so?"

During the long and taut silence that followed, Sharif wanted to propose that Samantha write down what she saw happened instead of this excruciating and irrelevant good, bad, or so-so question. It surprised him how much it melted his heart to finally hear Samantha's tiny, dry voice say "Good."

Sharif smiled.

"Wow!" Gloria said. "Now we're cooking with gas! I'm so proud of you, darling!"

There was a banging at the front door, and Sharif jumped.

"Ms. Gloria!" a voice called. "It's me, Lucian!"

Gloria burst out of Samantha's room and looked through the peephole. "What is it?"

"Hi, Ms. Gloria. Mind if we come in for a minute?"

She turned to Sharif as she answered the young man. "I'm busy."

"We need to talk to your guest."

Sharif looked through the peephole and saw all five of the young men. The one speaking, Lucian, was the cinnamon stick guy. Sharif turned to Gloria, who mouthed, "Bad."

Lucian said, "We need to talk to him, Ms. Gloria."

She whispered to Sharif, "They're dangerous. Go out the back."

He mouthed, "The back?"

Lucian said, "Come out, we know you're in there. We just want to talk."

Gloria said, "The fire escape. Go. Now." To the young men she said, "Leave me be. I told you I was busy."

Sharif whispered to her, "Really?"

"Yes, go!"

Another young man said, "Open the door, Ms. Gloria."

Sharif was halfway out the window when he heard Gloria say, "Go away! It's just me and the girl here!"

"And me!" Wesley announced with a mouthful of food.

Gloria said through the door, "We don't want any of your trouble here."

They pounded on the door again, and Sharif shut the window behind him. He looked out at the overgrown lot behind the building. Broken bottles and trash littered the grass, and five or six skinny cats lay about. He looked down and couldn't believe what he was doing. As he hesitated whether to go back inside and talk to those guys, his eyes scanned three spray-painted phrases on the opposite building: *Chucky; 21st Street; Fuck White Supremacy.* He hadn't done anything wrong. Why should he run like a guilty man, he thought as he descended the first flight of rusty stairs. By the time he was at the final landing, he heard someone call to him from above. "Sharif!" It was Wesley. "They say they just want to talk!"

He'd already come down too far. He waved at Wesley in a vague way, then he unlatched the ladder so it slid loudly to the grassy lot. The cats scattered. He climbed down, trembling, not trusting himself on the thin and bent rungs. Once he dropped into the lot, he cut across to a narrow alley leading to Flatbush Avenue. He looked left and right before stepping onto the sidewalk. After a few dozen paces, a voice shouted, "Hey!" at his back.

He glanced over his shoulder and saw two of the young men. How could they have gotten here so fast? He sped up, unable to distinguish between the thumping of blood in his ears and their quickening footsteps. A bus had pulled up to a stop in the middle of the block, about to close its doors after taking a new passenger. One of the young men yelled at him again, but Sharif sprinted without looking back. He climbed into the bus, not knowing where it was headed, panting as the doors shut behind him. He walked to the back and heard hands slapping frantically at the windows. One of the young men was shouting for the bus driver to stop. Sharif yelled, "No! Don't let them on!"

Everyone looked back at him. The bus driver shrugged, then drove off. When Sharif took his seat and looked out the window, a guy he'd never seen before wearing a McDonald's uniform was cursing the bus. No one had chased Sharif. The group of young men he'd seen behind him on Flatbush weren't the same ones. Of course not. They couldn't have ridden down the elevator and made it around the block that fast.

His head spun with confusion and shame for fleeing like that. He should have stepped out into the hall and talked to those guys. He might have heard more from Samantha afterward or gotten her to write it all down.

In what felt like two minutes, but must have been forty-five, the bus arrived at Avenue V, Marin Park. He couldn't get Samantha's small, dry voice out of his head, labeling him good. He was convinced that she was the answer, the star witness.

Waiting for the return bus, he called Patricia. "Hi, Patricia, it's Sharif. I was wondering if you could help me out with something."

"You ready to file that complaint?"

He explained about Samantha. "Would you be willing to get her testimony? She isn't comfortable talking, but she might be willing to write it down. If we get what I think she saw that day, this whole thing stops."

"Text me her details. I might be able to swing by after my shift."

"I'm sorry to add more work to your plate. I can't tell you how much I appreciate this. Thank you."

"No problem," she said. "Happy to serve."

41.

AT HOME, ADJOUA listened and said, "I really wish you'd talked to me before you did all of that."

He said, "Junior stole Samantha's phone for a reason. I think she's the key to all of this."

"I hear what you're saying, but I'm uncomfortable with the idea of sending a cop over there."

"I know, but they're not in trouble or anything. Gloria's all about shedding light on the truth. And Patricia is a good person. She believes in real community police work, supports what we do at CAPPA, and is Haitian too."

"So?"

He didn't actually know what her being Haitian should imply. "Patricia isn't going there to dig up dirt or harass or arrest anyone. She'll get a sense of what the girl saw, and leave."

"The mere presence of a cop will make residents nervous." Sharif wondered how she could be so sure about that. He could imagine a resident like Gloria enjoying an increased police presence. Adjoua then said, "Were those guys knocking on the door threatening you at all?"

"No. They just said they wanted to talk."

"But she thought you should sneak out the fire escape?"

"She insisted on it."

Adjoua tapped an unnerved beat on the kitchen island with her fingers.

He worried she'd ask him to call Patricia to cancel the favor. "I wish I'd discussed everything with you first. But when we spoke, you seemed so down after that *Times* email."

Her phone lit up and she read the message. In an inscrutable deadpan, she said, "Aberto wants us to come over at six p.m. to discuss the crowd-funder with his clients. He says Emmanuel's interested."

"Okay. And are we still interested? I admit, the idea of raising money for that con artist is getting harder to swallow. I told you, it sounds a lot like Junior tried to frame his classmate for vandalism. Planting evidence and everything. This is something he does."

"Yeah." She drew out the word slowly as she squinted at him. He could feel her apprehension and guessed it came from her discomfort around his calling Junior's school.

It was now that he disclosed it: "They filed a police complaint with that witness today."

"What? Why wasn't that the first thing you told me? You were sure they wouldn't."

"I know. It's why I've been more aggressive about finding evidence."

She closed her eyes and focused on breathing for a while. Then: "So what's going to happen with the complaint?"

"I don't know. It depends on if the DA cares to pursue it. But Patricia said their witness is a known liar, criminal, and addict. She said he came in visibly high. She believes they paid him to do it."

Her hand went to her mouth, and she touched the tiny scar above her lip with the pad of her finger. He'd never seen her seek it out before. She said, "I do think we should meet with them to discuss the crowdfunder. Have you seen the number of comments and shares of Isabella's post?" She looked at Judy. "I put out my statement. And apparently people have a lot to say in response. I had to make my page private. I don't want this kind of attention. I want this nightmare to be over."

"Me too. Okay, we'll talk to them. I'm with you."

"I want them to pull everything back tonight. It's gone way too far." She nodded, a vacant look in her eyes. "For now, I need a bath to collect my thoughts."

"Sure, of course." The bathroom was the only place in their minuscule apartment where one could be truly alone.

When he heard the bath running, he went online to read her statement:

> Anyone who has spent 15 minutes with Sharif Safadi would find these accusations impossible to believe. He is the definition of a mensch. A pacifist with a religious devotion to honesty, fairness, and personal responsibility. This is apparent in his dedication as a social worker, his generosity with friends and family, his gentleness as a husband and soon-to-be father, his care for animals, and his kindness toward strangers. We are shocked and saddened by these lies. We believe false accusations like this are incredibly rare, but they do occur. This is one of those extraordinary instances. There is no evidence whatsoever of my husband hurting Junior Fleurime. We respectfully request the privacy and space needed to uncover the truth. Thank you.

42.

ABERTO'S OFFICE HAD a funereal tone. Emmanuel greeted Adjoua and Sharif with solemn, conciliatory handshakes that suggested an intention to put an end to this. Junior, however, did not stand to greet anyone. He remained slouched in his chair, like last time; his legs stretched in front of him, his metal-rigged forearm cradled. The swelling had gotten worse. His skin was marbled a violent purple, red, blue, and green. Sharif said hello and asked how he was feeling. Junior mumbled what could have just as easily been "[something something], thank you" as "[something something], fuck you," followed by an exaggerated sniffing sound. Sharif wondered when loud sniffing had become cool.

Aberto spoke with a practiced serenity from his throne.

"And here we are again," he said, rubbing his hands together. "This time, to discuss a practical strategy for the financial burden of Junior's injury. Adjoua had the fantastic idea of raising money online. I'm here to support her however I can."

Sharif noticed that the corkboard with the picture of Adjoua and Aberto on it had been moved, angled to face Sharif's chair more directly. The pettiness of Aberto doing this inspired an almost supernatural calm in Sharif. There were other reasons for Sharif's extraordinary composure: the renewed connection with Adjoua since early Sunday morning, and her unequivocal alliance to him in her online statement. But also the voicemail from Patricia that had come through while they were on the way to Aberto's office:

"Hey, so I talked to Samantha. Well, her foster mom talked to her for me. I proposed your writing idea, but that didn't take. Anyway, the good news is that she confirmed that you did not hurt Junior. I asked if Junior lied about you hurting him, Gloria repeated the question, and Samantha nodded yes. I said, 'So Sharif did *not* cause Junior's injury, are you sure?' and she nodded yes again. The bad news is that neither of them will file the 'testimony' in any official capacity. Gloria doesn't want any more trouble with her neighbors. All I can do is add what I learned to the electronic file sent to the DA. I hope it helps. And it goes without saying that I'll testify to what Samantha communicated if needed. Call me if you have any questions."

Sharif had played the message for Adjoua, who listened with a furrowed brow. After handing back the phone, she took a big breath that seemed to be what blew life into the dazed expression on her face. He asked if she was okay. She nodded blankly and said she was fine. After taking their seats on the 2 train, she said she didn't see any need to mention the voicemail in the meeting. She wanted to carry on with the crowdfunder pitch as planned. Sharif agreed easily, simultaneously understanding why this was complicated for her and empowered by the mere knowledge of the voicemail in his pocket. He then made a commitment to remain poised and unreactive at the meeting. He wanted to show Adjoua that he'd heard her concerns about his temper and rashness. And so far, maintaining his composure had cost him nothing.

Aberto said, "Adjie, you want to take it from here?"

She turned to Emmanuel. "The idea is that we give a bit of background on you both, tell the story of the criminally expensive insurance premium you were cornered into selecting, and the loss of wages due to the injury, leading to an urgent need for twenty-six thousand dollars. Then, all of our friends and family"—she pointed at Aberto with her whole hand, holding his eyes and nodding at him for a beat—"donate and share, and then *their* friends and family donate and share. I have no doubt that our combined social networks"—she looked at Aberto again—"will respond generously to such a campaign."

After a long silence, Emmanuel said, "This is like charity."

Adjoua said, "You know the expression 'It takes a village'? It's that. People who are moved by your story and believe in a world where a stroke of bad luck shouldn't get in the way of good people's success will feel good about contributing and requesting others to do the same."

"You think this can really make twenty-six thousand dollars?"

"Yes. If we do it right, the donations will pile up quickly. Sharif and I know people who have raised far more for far less compelling reasons. I suggest we set our fundraising goal at thirty thousand to create a bit of cushion, in case unexpected costs crop up for you."

Emmanuel looked at Aberto before leaning back and crossing his arms. "How will it impact our asylum case?"

Aberto shook his head. "I don't see why it would. Even if USCIS saw this crowdfunder, which is extremely unlikely, being supported by dozens or even hundreds of Americans would only suggest higher community integration."

Emmanuel asked Adjoua, "How long will it take to receive money?"

"Once we go live, people have thirty days to give. The money is in your account within a week of the campaign ending."

Emmanuel looked satisfied. Sharif felt no need to weigh in. Adjoua was doing beautifully.

She said, "I could draft something for everyone's review tonight. Of course, our stories will have to align. This requires withdrawing the police complaint and posting a corrective statement through Junior's social media. I'm happy to draft language for that too."

Emmanuel gave a nearly imperceptible nod before asking, "What if you don't succeed at raising the money?" He turned to Aberto. "We make another complaint and put everything back online like before?"

Aberto nodded. "That's within your right, yes."

"This won't exactly help me with the bills," Emmanuel said.

"Actually"—Adjoua sat further up on her chair—"while I'm confident we'll raise more than you need, we can only use the full force of our social capital once the police complaint and social media retractions are made total and permanent."

Emmanuel looked at Aberto. "If they fail, then what? We're on our own?"

Adjoua was still on top of it: "That won't happen. It'll be apparent whether we're putting our best foot forward. We'll write up a contract that holds us to certain benchmarks. We'll put hard dates for when the campaign is drafted, published, minimum number of contacts who receive it, et cetera. I trust that after a week of seeing me work on this, and when the money starts coming in, you'll be happy."

Sharif could now picture Adjoua in a corporate environment, running meetings at her advertising firm, dazzling her bosses with her unflappable resolve. Despite his disdain for corporate America and his wish for her to prioritize her novel, he found this business mode of hers exciting.

Emmanuel said, "Okay, why not meet in the middle? For example, we make some kind of statement online, say we're in the process of working together to make this right, we're optimistic, and so on. This allows us to come up with the story for the crowdfunder everyone can support. And we keep this police complaint until we get the money."

Sharif noticed a small shake in Adjoua's confidence when she said, "I can't ask our network to donate money under those conditions. First, I won't do this under duress. Second, if my husband gets arrested during the crowdfunder, it's unacceptable to us and a huge risk for you. People won't be comfortable donating. This can only succeed if everyone's all in."

Emmanuel's head hung in contemplation before he looked up at Aberto. "What do you think?"

Aberto said, "I think her position is understandable. However"—he turned to Adjoua—"I'm sure you get why my clients want concrete safeguards beyond goal-setting and promises. I propose using guarantors who can commit to bridging any gap between the crowdfunder and my clients' needs." He looked back and forth between Sharif and Adjoua. "Maybe someone's parents."

"This again," Sharif said.

Adjoua said to Aberto, "You couldn't have mentioned this before?"

"I didn't think of it before," Aberto said. "But Emmanuel makes a good point. It's a huge risk to do this without any contingency. I'm as confident as you are that the crowdfunder will work. There's little chance of needing to rely on guarantors, right? So it's not a big concession."

Emmanuel nodded in agreement. Adjoua stared at Aberto, wide-eyed. The more fight and tension emanated from her, the less reactive Sharif felt. A counterbalancing mechanism seemed to exist between them where only one person responded angrily toward a third-party antagonist at a time. Nine times out of ten it was Sharif who had seethed throughout this conflict, but now it was Adjoua. That's not to say Sharif was pleased. He sat back inside himself, feeling a woozy, ink-in-water sensation at the thought of engaging either set of parents in this muck, especially his in-laws. Charles and Sylvie thought of him as the mensch Adjoua described in her online statement. To them, he was uncomplicatedly good. His hand reflexively went to touch his phone through his pants, soothed by the memory of Patricia's voicemail.

Then Junior spoke up more emphatically than ever before: "I already wrote something anyway."

Before everyone could recover from Junior speaking so clearly, Emmanuel asked, "What do you mean?"

"A letter," Junior said. "You can read it to them if you want."

"If you wrote it, you should read it."

It was the first time Sharif had detected impatience from Emmanuel toward Junior.

Junior looked at Aberto, who agreed with Emmanuel: "Yeah, let's hear it."

Junior unfolded his arms, sat up straighter, and carefully dipped the fingers of his uninjured hand in his pocket to retrieve his phone. After opening it, he reclined back into his chair and did that exaggerated sniffing thing again. Only then did Sharif connect it to something boxers do before the ring of the bell.

Junior read loudly and with a pronounced tremor: "Dear Mr. Sharif and Ms. Adjoua. I wish this wasn't so crazy. I'm sorry I put the dog on the fire escape. I thought he could go to the bathroom if he had to. When I came home, it was crazy. The dog was on the floor crying. Then Mr. Sharif started shouting at me about hurting him. I didn't know who he was even. I said I didn't do anything." Sharif started shifting in his seat, agitated.

"When Mr. Sharif said he was leaving with the dog, I asked him to please settle his bill with us. My dad said if I looked after the dog, I would get the other half of the money for a Nintendo Switch. I've been wanting one for a whole year. No one told me it was bad to put the dog on the fire escape, and I didn't hurt the dog. Then everything got really crazy. Mr. Sharif said, 'Get the F out of my way' and ran at me with this crazy look. His dog started growling with his teeth out. Mr. Sharif was trying to put those teeth on me. He came at me so fast. I froze up. It was crazy. And suddenly they were on me, trying to take me down. I dodged the dog's teeth but Mr. Sharif used his elbow to shove me into the apartment over his leg, so I got slammed on the ground. I landed on my left hand first and heard this cracking sound. It was so crazy. Then Mr. Sharif started saying stuff like 'G-damn you, mother F-er.' Then he ran away, and I was lying there thinking my wrist looked all wrong. My neighbor came over and told me Mr. Sharif forced himself into his home to break into ours and that I should go to the hospital. I was worried it would be too expensive, so I said no thank you. But the next thing I know, I wake up in the ambulance. The doctors and nurses said I was dying. It was crazy. I'm grateful to God that I'm still alive. Every day is a blessing. Emmanuel Fleurime Jr."

Without expression, Emmanuel gave Junior's shoulder a perfunctory squeeze.

Sharif thought: First, I grab him by the shoulder and somehow throw him. Then I yank his arm down before shouting some slurs. And now I shove him backward with my elbow. He touched his phone through his pants again. It was best to let Junior's inconsistencies linger. Everyone here was smart enough to notice them on their own.

Adjoua put her hand on Sharif's thigh, signaling for him to remain calm, but it was she who had a broiling undercurrent to her voice when she said, "Thank you, Junior. If you send me . . . that . . . I'll see what pieces I can borrow for my draft. But the final narrative would have to be quite a bit different overall. The cause of the injury would be unconnected to us. It could be framed as a sort of accident. Falling down a stairwell, for example. Or we could leave it vague. I'm open to suggestions."

After a long silence, Aberto said, "What about the guarantors suggestion? Your guarantors sign the contract and all complaints are immediately withdrawn."

This increased the rigidity of Adjoua's posture. "Sharif and I can discuss it in private, but to be honest, I don't think it's fair to delay this further while rumors about us are spreading like wildfire."

Junior spoke unprompted again. "I already posted it."

The room briefly turned into a paused movie scene. Then everyone reanimated, reaching for their phones. Emmanuel grabbed Junior's. The letter he'd read had been posted on Junior's Instagram a few minutes before the meeting started, with Adjoua and Sharif tagged. It had already been shared by 446 people.

Emmanuel was the first to break the silence, asking his son something in Creole. He waited, then switched to English. "Answer me. Don't you see how this makes this more complicated?"

Junior spoke to the floor: "He called my school."

"What?"

"He told Ms. Kiara he was my social worker. He asked her about me. Now she thinks I'm some loser."

Emmanuel looked at Sharif with more hurt than anger, as if learning of a friend's betrayal. "Why did you do this?"

Sharif was thrown by Emmanuel's pain. He'd thought Emmanuel had come to see him as an irredeemably craven and self-serving man, unable to further shock or disappoint. Sharif couldn't quite remember why it had made sense to call Junior's school. In hindsight it wasn't necessary. "I never said I was his social worker," Sharif explained. "I called to get a better grasp of Junior and why he was doing all this."

Aberto stood from his throne. "Sharif. Adjie. A quick word in the kitchen, please?"

On their way out, Emmanuel spoke to his son in a rapid, reprimanding whispered Creole.

Aberto shut his clients in the office and walked to the farthest corner of the kitchen. He sighed. "Adjie, I need you to stay calm. We're really close to making a deal that everyone can live with."

Adjoua said, "I've been extremely patient. Between you springing this guarantor thing at the eleventh hour and that kid's unbelievably destructive impulses, I can't remain the only diplomat in the room."

"You guys are playing this pretty aggressively too." To Sharif, Aberto said, "Calling his school? In addition to it being triggering for Junior and deeply unproductive, you could lose your license for letting his teacher believe you're his caseworker. Even if you didn't say it explicitly. And that demand letter wasn't helpful either."

Adjoua asked, "What demand letter?"

Sharif said, "I told you about it. It's a civil thing to say we'll take them to court if they don't pay Judy's vet bills."

Aberto interjected, "No, it's to threaten my undocumented immigrant clients with court involvement. I didn't even mention it to Emmanuel because of how counter it is to the de-escalation I thought we wanted. If you reel in the retaliatory tactics, we can resolve this tonight."

Adjoua said, "Tell that to the little sociopath in there. I can put on a brave face before going back in there if you want, but let me be clear: There's no world in which we accept anything less than a full retraction of all of this online bullshit and the permanent withdrawal of the police complaint. Does your resolution assure that tonight?"

"Yes, with a guarantor. As soon as either of you call your parents, I'll email them a contract to sign and return. Once I have that, we're done."

Adjoua put her hands on her hips. "Every time we engage with you on this, we get blindsided by some new obstacle or demand. You're the one allowing this charade to escalate, Aberto."

"No, I'm advocating for my clients. That's what I do. And I've tried to consider your well-being as much as possible along the way."

"Really? Because you know what this whole guarantor idea sounds like to me? It sounds like you want me to call my parents and explain that we need them to provide a twenty-six-thousand-dollar safety net so we can lie to our community to get donations to pay off what amounts to blackmail. They're not idiots, Aberto. They know that guarantors aren't needed to raise money for a charitable cause. I mean, do you really not see how humiliating and unfair and unethical and fucked that is?"

"If I'm understanding correctly, you don't mind paying off blackmailers. You just can't tolerate your parents knowing about it."

"Can you drop the law school, philosophy of logic, snarky bullshit? This isn't a game." She took a small step toward him. "This is my family you've been threatening from day one of this farce."

"Sure." Aberto looked offended in a way Sharif had never seen. "And can you not let your ego, or your concern over how this makes you look to your mom and dad derail this process?"

"*My* ego?" Adjoua scoffed. "You're delusional. You pretend you're driven by ethics, but all you have ever cared about is winning. Looking strong and heroic and righteous by any means necessary."

Appearing even more stung, Aberto nodded. "You forget that I know you. I know what makes you see red. You can't handle how all of this has made you look to your little online writing community, how it challenges this image of you being married to some Jesus figure you posted about online, or how your parents might judge you as a weak, foolish girl if you ask them for help. Or maybe you're worried they'll believe my clients over your blameless husband. They really don't know anything about this?" He saw the answer on her face and angled his head higher. "My asking for guarantors has nothing to do with embarrassing you. It's a totally reasonable request, not blackmail. But that's always been your trigger. More than the police complaint or the money, what you're really struggling with is these threats to your image."

While still staring up at Aberto, she said, "Sharif, please play that message from Officer Dauphne. I want him to hear it now."

Sharif hesitated for a beat, then pulled out his phone and played it. Aberto stared at Adjoua with a stunned look the whole time they listened.

When it ended, Aberto said, "You sent a cop to question a foster child in their NYCHA building?"

Adjoua's chest began rising and falling more quickly. Sharif didn't know if she was about to shout or cry or run. She seemed unable to speak, retroactively startled by her decision to play the message.

Sharif said, "We need this to end, Aberto. You heard it yourself. That little girl saw the whole thing."

"You may remember, my clients have a witness too. One who did file their testimony in an official capacity."

"Come on. You know he's not reliable. Look, have your clients retract everything and we'll do the crowdfunder, okay? That's more than generous at this point."

Aberto stared passionately at Adjoua and repeated his question. "Did you agree to sending the cop over there? I have to know." Sharif now saw that the reason Adjoua couldn't speak was that she didn't want to expose being on the verge of tears. Aberto too had a crumpled, pained expression. "I was literally responding to your piece about hostile police presences in poor communities of color this weekend. I've shared articles you've posted about police abolition. And you asked a cop to go into a NYCHA building as some personal favor?"

Sharif said, "Officer Dauphne's visit was my idea, and she didn't harm anyone."

Adjoua looked up at Aberto, her strength recollecting rapidly. "Don't you dare cast aspersions on me, Aberto, or shift the focus. We've exercised tremendous restraint up until now."

"Is that so?"

"Yeah. But you know what, what you and I think of each other isn't important. This is the last time I'll say it. Unless they retract everything that endangers my family's safety and well-being—which, yes, includes defamation to our images that inhibits us from earning an income—not only does the demand letter stand, but we'll have no choice but to press charges on Emmanuel. Do you understand?"

Aberto had also transitioned from despondency to strength. "Don't threaten me."

"I'm not. I'm informing you. We've reached our limit. The crowdfunder under the precise terms we presented, or we take protective measures."

Adjoua and Aberto were staring each other down, seeming to grow more powerful with every inhalation.

"Okay," Sharif said, trying to break out of his riveted state. "Can we pause, please, and take a step back?"

But it was like he wasn't there. Aberto said to Adjoua, "Don't go down this road."

"Or what?"

"You know I know people at every level of this city. I will not hesitate to pull on those levers to protect my clients."

"Have you lost your mind? You're going to use your connections to take us down? You're a fucking mobster."

"You're the one having a cop run personal errands for you."

Sharif now stood between them, the three of them sandwiched awkwardly together, Adjoua's belly touching his hip. The office door flew open behind them, and they broke apart to turn and see Junior rushing out. His face was twisted up and wet with tears. He carried his injured arm like a dying thing.

Emmanuel shouted for him to come back here right now as he followed him. Junior opened the front door and swung around to say to his father, "We don't need these people. Forget them. I'll get the money myself." He then glared at Sharif, clearly wanting to look dangerous, but, for the first time, appearing utterly childlike.

Part V
THRESHOLD

43.

ON THE RIDE HOME, Adjoua asked Sharif why he'd been such a bystander at the meeting. He asked if she was serious, then said he'd tried to calm things down multiple times but no one listened. "Anyway," he said, "you were saying everything I was thinking. I wasn't going to start yelling to be heard saying the same thing. I thought that was exactly what you didn't want."

"I don't know what I want."

"Well, do you really want to press charges?"

"I said I don't know what I want."

"Okay."

"What I want is for you to take the lead."

"Meaning what?"

"Meaning stop asking me questions. I don't want to be the decision-maker anymore."

"You got it." Then, "You don't have to respond to this, but to paraphrase my understanding of what you're asking: you want me to make unilateral decisions, but only if they're decisions you'd have agreed with had you been privy to them. If you disapprove of my decision after the fact, you'll wish I'd checked in with you first. Is that the idea?"

"That's pretty much it, I'm afraid."

Sharif placed a hand on her thigh. "As long as we're on the same page."

"Maybe you can announce the decision you've made right before actually taking action to see if I stop you."

He nodded. "Sure, I can do that."

She rested her head on his shoulder and side-hugged her belly with her outer arm.

At home, Sharif helped her down so she could lay spooning Judy on the new dog bed. An hour later, he said, "Should I take Judy out for a spin before dinner? Sorry, I mean, I *will* take him out now."

Into the back of Judy's neck, she said, "Go with your papa, bubba," squeezing him more tightly. Judy farted from the squeeze. No one laughed, but everyone found it funny.

Outside, Sharif and Judy crossed paths with the heavily tattooed Japanese barber, Hiro, on their block who'd given Sharif the best haircut of his life two years ago. He'd never returned because it was too expensive. Hiro petted Judy while laughing about the dog's cuteness, no words exchanged, just laughing and petting and nodding. Sharif thought of Adjoua's insight about cuteness being inherently funny. Judy's cuteness used to make them laugh a dozen times a day. How quickly expressions of mirth could be vacuumed out of a home.

Turning onto Orchard Street, he realized he'd forgotten to bring poo bags. That's when Judy stopped and, with a curved back and trembling head, took a massive shit in front of the laundromat. The laundromat owner stared in horror from the doorway. Sharif told her he'd forgotten his bags and asked if she had something he might be able to use. She said no in a way that showed the question revolted her. Sharif experienced an emboldening anger and said, "Fine, have it your way," leaving Judy's shit in front of her business.

Ten seconds later, a man with a cartoonishly thick Brooklyn accent yelled at Sharif's back, "Real nice, buddy! Beautiful fucking work! Hey, maybe the Met wants your dog's shit sculpture for their next show, asshole!"

Sharif didn't turn around or speed up. In fact, he slowed down to show how little the man's indictment affected him. Leaning into this strategy, he stopped at Scarr's, the overpriced but delicious pizza parlor, a few feet later and ordered a slice through the street-facing window.

He looked at his phone and saw a text from Patricia that had come in: Pal at DA's says complaint of no interest. Doesn't look like criminal matter to them. Civil case if anything.

Thank you, this is such incredibly great news!

He forwarded it to Adjoua, who replied: Oh my god! I could cry with relief! I feel a hundred pounds lighter!

I know! Finally, some fairness coming our way!

Also, some of Junior's classmates are pointing out the obvious inconsistencies in his story!

These sudden improvements to his and Adjoua's luck filled him with a gust of optimism and faith that good things do happen to good people. When the pizza came, Sharif took a big bite and looked at Judy. He sat in a posture of overperformed obedience, stopped panting, and shifted his weight from one foot to the other. Sharif smiled at his beloved drooling dog and gave him the rest of the slice. He asked himself why he had ever deprived his dog of this before. Judy clearly felt a thrill from pizza that no human experience could match. Who cared that it upset his stomach? Look at his purposeful joy. One day he'll be gone, and Sharif will regret not giving him more experiences like this. He vowed to get Judy a giant ice cream tomorrow. This decision empowered him, replacing any lingering, righteous anger he'd felt toward the laundromat owner and shouting man, which segued into his making another decision: He would drop Judy off, grab some bags, return to the laundromat, and clean up the mess. He didn't want to be someone who refused personal responsibility out of spite or pride. Not only was it the right thing to do, but once he did it, he'd be free of dread or shame or defensiveness next time he walked down Orchard Street. Doing the right thing by others protected him. This decision to clean up, and its many benefits, gave him yet another boost, ushering in another decision. Once upstairs, he announced it to Adjoua: "I'm going back to work tomorrow."

44.

SHARIF KNOCKED AND entered Merjem's blinding office before being invited in. Shazeeda sat across the desk from Merjem with a notepad, twisting to face Sharif with her sunglasses. Merjem pushed her shades up her nose and said, "Sharif. Hi. I wasn't expecting you."

"Hi," he said, stepping in and shutting the door behind him. He grabbed the pair of green glasses he'd worn before. "How are you?"

Merjem paused. "Fine."

Shazeeda said to Merjem, "I can come back later."

Sharif said, "No need. I'll be quick. Merjem, I want to come back to work today." The strength in his body flowed through his voice. He didn't know where the strength came from, nor did he need to know. "I've put my clients and this agency first for years. I accepted teaching the workforce readiness classes instead of the job for which I applied and am credentialed with a master's degree. Like most of my colleagues, I've taken little pay for a lot of work. That's because I believe in doing whatever is needed for CAPPA to serve the most disadvantaged. I believe in striving for equity, correcting for bad luck one person and one family at a time. But today, my family is in a precarious situation due to some bad luck of our own: an awful, false accusation made against me. I'm here to ask if I can count on CAPPA to support me through this crisis. If you believe I've been wrongly accused, I ask you to stand by that belief, defend it when challenged, and let me do my work. I understand that optics matter. But so does right and wrong. Your employees are an essential part of the CAPPA community too. It aligns fully with CAPPA's mission to be brave for us, to fight for us in our greatest time of need the way we fight for our clients."

Her mouth open, Merjem appeared pinned to her chairback. Shazeeda's eyebrows were lifted high above her shades. She had a barely perceptible smile and seemed to be nodding slightly. Merjem said, "Shazeeda, could you excuse us after all?"

"Of course," she said.

They watched her go. When the door shut, Merjem said, "That was clever. Shazeeda will share your speech with two people. By lunchtime, the whole agency will know."

He sat down. "I wasn't being clever. I just want to do my job."

"I can't have any more scenes here, or any clients complaining about case managers."

"Has anyone other than Jurell Waters had a good reason to complain about me?"

"One is too many, Sharif."

"I agree. But one second chance isn't. I should have enough credit with you for that."

"You are a representative of this organization. You know how word of mouth spreads in this neighborhood. If people start complaining about our services, claiming we're disrespectful, especially when the case manager is white, prospective clients will stop coming. We won't meet our numbers. Funders won't renew contracts. That could be devastating for us, but more importantly for this community."

"I know. I wouldn't be here if there was any risk of me not doing my job well."

She sighed. "I assume you filed your own complaint against Emmanuel?"

"No. I'm not going to do that."

"Why not? Patricia was clear about how it could help."

"Two reasons. The first is that Patricia said the DA isn't interested in Emmanuel's charges. The second is that I have no reason to think Emmanuel was going to act violently that day. He came to talk, albeit heatedly, because he thought I'd hospitalized his son. I can't claim he was trying to attack me if that's not what I experienced."

Shaking her head, she said, "So principled and so young," as if these were character flaws. She smiled at him. "That's great news about the DA. And have you been keeping up with the online chatter? Erasmus students are pointing out the wild discrepancies in Junior's story. The character assault on you is losing traction."

"Yes, it's fizzling out. None of it will impact my work. Or CAPPA's reputation." Without allowing her to respond, which she'd opened her mouth to do, he added, "But we also need to discuss my next raise."

"Excuse me?"

"A raise. Once my daughter is born, my salary will no longer be a living wage. I need a minimum increase of ten thousand dollars to continue working here."

She put her elbows on her desk and leaned forward, searching his face for signs of the joke. "You're getting ahead of yourself, Sharif. I'm still contemplating letting you work here at all." She watched his face again, perhaps expecting it to lose its resolve.

"Merjem, I don't want to find something else. I love CAPPA. But to meet my family's basic needs, I need that raise. I wanted to be transparent about that."

He'd never seen her on the back foot. It was in the small, befuddled movements of her head and hands. "I understand what you're saying. I do. But for now, let's see how today goes, all right?"

Her conceding that he could work today wasn't enough. "I'll need to know whether it's a possibility by the end of the week."

Awestruck by his unflappable insistence, she said, "Well, it's possible that I bring it up with Brionna." Brionna was CAPPA's president and CEO. "But beyond that——"

He remained still and indomitable in the pocket of silence she'd created. Waiting.

She swallowed and picked back up with "She and I are catching up Friday. I'll let you know what she says. Okay?"

"Thank you, Merjem." Sharif got up, tossed the sunglasses in the bowl, and headed to his office.

45.

FOR THE REST of the week and into the next, Sharif carried that confidence he'd had in Merjem's office. He possessed a calm and invigorating focus, feeling agile and fully present for every task and person. He even felt this way during Adjoua's final scheduled checkup at the hospital. Sharif found it easy to see past Dr. Ballou's clownish, vague manner and embrace what mattered: Adjoua was doing fine; everything seemed normal. It wouldn't be long now. The treatment plan for Zora was clear and would almost certainly eradicate the disease in her body.

He followed up with Merjem about her conversation with Brionna. She said Brionna wanted to discuss opportunities with him next week. Merjem would propose meeting times soon.

At home, during this time of heightened poise and courage, Sharif had set aside an hour each night to discuss practical matters with Adjoua. Their discussions ranged from lists of baby supplies received, forthcoming, and needed, to their current finances and financial goals. He listened to her strategy for building her advertising portfolio, never mentioned her novel, and found appropriate windows in which to share his workforce development knowledge. As a team, they'd considered when and how Sharif should follow up again with Merjem about the raise if she didn't get a meeting on the books soon, what he'd say during the meeting, and where in their lives that extra income should be invested: savings, hospital bills, baby formula depending on Adjoua's milk production and Zora's latching, and so on. And what they would do if he only received $5K. She helped him polish up his résumé, and he sent it out for a number of director positions at other non-profits. If Merjem or Brionna was resistant to giving him the raise, he'd get a higher-paying job offer to present to them as something they needed to match.

He and Adjoua were a team like never before. He realized that he too benefited from the security of pragmatic strategizing and assurances. Their admiration for each other increased by the day. Adjoua began sharing her most free associative and emotional and affectionate self with him. Something about having worked through this episode with Aberto, Emmanuel, and Junior instilled a patience and assurance in Sharif that made him feel capable of anything. Adjoua and Sharif started having sex again.

Within those same two weeks, Sharif received two pieces of good news about his clients. Nneka, who he'd been helping prepare for the Con Edison entrance exam for months, aced the exam and her subsequent interviews. She was now being onboarded as a meter reader. The job gave her access to higher wages and better benefits than she'd ever dreamed possible, offering her and her children a whole new tier of opportunity.

The second piece of good news came after Sharif's makeup appointment with Tanisha. He worked closely with her and a job developer to land Tanisha an interview for an NYC Department of Sanitation job, running logistics for cleanup crews out of their headquarters in Lower Manhattan. As with Nneka's new job, a position like this was a chance for Tanisha to achieve a new income bracket. Sharif scheduled daily thirty-minute mock interview appointments with her leading up to the real interview. He recorded their sessions, him drilling her on her résumé and interview answers, and they analyzed them together like an Olympic athlete and her coach. He referred her to a nonprofit that offered free styling and professional attire. Sharif was Tanisha's first call after the interview. She said, "No matter what they decide, I know that I could not have done any better in that interview. No regrets. That's the best feeling. Thank you for all your help." The wobble he heard in her voice gave him chills. It was these rare opportunities for upward mobility that had the power of breaking cycles of generational poverty. Sharif's small role in the process was deeply fulfilling.

At the same time, Junior had launched his own crowdfunder, so far raising less than thirty dollars. In it, he wrote the story of Sharif's break-in and violence and cursing in yet a new and more absurd way, further weakening his defamation of Sharif. He'd made too many mistakes, including lashing out at people who questioned the flagrant inconsistencies. The tipping point occurred when Isabella Cervantes herself admitted to her 40.6K followers that she didn't understand why Junior's story kept changing. When Junior "showed his tru colors," as Isabella put it, with insulting posts about her that the administrator had to remove, she announced that she had blocked and no longer supported him. Once she'd flipped, there was a domino effect in Junior's disfavor. On the one hand, it was a relief for Sharif and Adjoua. On the other, it was terrifying that one high-schooler could have this much influence over what thousands believed was true.

As Sharif felt increasingly fortunate and optimistic and Junior spiraled downward, he began wanting to help Junior and Emmanuel. Regardless of the teenager's many missteps, the U.S. healthcare system was still a moral failing. Sharif had called his brother after learning from Patricia that Emmanuel's complaints wouldn't be going anywhere and asked him to tell Brett not to act on his threats in the demand letter. Walid pushed back at first but ended up agreeing, begrudgingly. With Adjoua's blessing, Sharif left a message on Aberto's phone about how they remained open to their initial crowdfunder proposal if his clients were interested. Remembering how Aberto had made the executive decision of not informing his clients about the demand letter, Sharif also called Emmanuel and left the same message.

46.

WALID CALLED SHARIF repeatedly one night at eleven, waking both him and Adjoua. Walid said, "Yo, finally! What the fuck are you doing over there?"

"Sleeping," Sharif replied as Adjoua waddled into his room.

"Well, wake up, bitches! Is your girl there? Put me on speaker."

She was rubbing her eyes. He said, "Really? No."

"Is she there or not? She'll want to hear this."

Sharif turned to his squinting wife. "It's Walid."

In her barely awake voice she said, "Oh. I thought you were having a bad dream."

Sharif put him on speaker, and Walid told them, "I solved it."

They waited.

"Solved what, Walid?" Sharif said.

"I have the abso-fucking-lutely perfect solution for your dog problem."

Adjoua became more alert. "What do you mean?"

"An Australian."

"Okay?"

"His name's Andrew. Incredibly rich. Made zillions selling shrimp in Venezuela and sold it hours before the country fell apart. He is one of those freaks who gets on all fours and shoves his face in every dog's business he sees in the street, wrestling with them on the ground. Parking lot, sidewalk, whatever. He's stupid and perfect for this situation."

Sharif said, "And he's open to taking Judy? He knows what he's like and everything?"

"I had him swear full commitment before I called you. He's got an insane apartment with a courtyard in Lower Manhattan, no other pets, an elevator service that goes up to his penthouse, lawn space on the roof, and someone is always home. Judy will never be alone."

Adjoua repeated, "Judy will never be alone."

Walid said, "Maids, cooks, fix-it guys — there's always someone looking after the place, even when Andrew is traveling. Judy will live in nonstop, total luxury." After a pause, he said, "Hello? You hearing any of this?"

Adjoua said, "Yes, sorry. I worried if I spoke too soon my voice would crack with emotion. This sounds better than anything I could have dreamed, Walid. Thank you."

"Of course, you're family. You're my fucking sister. I'll forward you the email now. Love you guys."

The email from the Australian included his address and a short message:

> 100% excited and onboard, mate! Seems like a real legend! I grew
> up with grumpy old-timers. Special place in my heart, you know.
> Can't wait to bunk up with the fella! Cheers to you and yours, mate!

He was a twenty-three-minute walk from their apartment. Adjoua said they needed to meet this Australian first. Sharif agreed wholeheartedly, and soon put Judy in a loose headlock, kissed him hard on the head, and announced, "We did it, mate!"

47.

BECAUSE OF HOW many clients came through Sharif's computer lab office, it had never felt right to keep personal effects on his desk. The one exception was a glass mug that Adjoua had bought him as a gift years earlier. It had a bright white rubber band around the center to protect it from the heat, and a copper base forged into the glass at a stylistic tilt. It looked like an Apple product, or something from a Sharper Image catalog. Not at all Sharif's aesthetic. He was embarrassed by how expensive it looked and relegated it to being a pen holder. Now it reminded him of Junior's struggle to raise money for his medical bills. The glass mug's design team had raised $700,000 through an online crowdfunder to manufacture these dumb things. With the fifteen-dollar donation Adjoua contributed, because she went to college with the co-founder, they received one of the first 10,000 mugs manufactured.

Turning the mug of pens in his hand, Sharif wanted to see it break. How shameful to be the richest country in the world that lets residents be financially destroyed by medical misfortune. It had been three days since he'd left messages with Aberto and Emmanuel about revisiting the crowdfunder idea, and he'd resolved to call them again between his appointments today. Despite Junior's online antics making something like that trickier, they'd figure it out. If Sharif didn't get ahold of them by phone, he'd swing by Aberto's after work.

Stanley, a new client of his, announced himself. The others poured in from behind: Iryna, Paul, Denise, Latoya, and Osman. They must have ridden the elevator together. They exchanged teasing jokes, laughing like old friends. They were here for Sharif's cover letter workshop that he'd gotten permission to set up.

"Good morning," Sharif said as he stood, feeling a genuine fondness for these smiling faces. "Why don't you all log in to a computer and pull up a draft of your cover letters. Don't worry if you don't have one yet. Just log in and open up Microsoft Word."

Denise said, "Since when was not having one an option? Tell me again why I was working on mine at one a.m.?" She laughed.

Latoya echoed the same sentiment. "Aww, come on, man! You could have told us and saved us the homework."

They were in high spirits, and Sharif felt liked when he was lightly teased by clients.

As if Sharif didn't get it, Stanley explained, "They're messing with you, man. But truth be told, I am trying to submit my cover letter to that employer by tomorrow. So I hope whoever doesn't have their draft won't slow me down, you know what I'm saying?" He chuckled but was quite serious.

"Not to worry," Sharif said, enjoying a bit of paternalism. "We'll get everyone's done." He distributed the handouts he'd made that gave an overview of the purpose and steps of a cover letter. Sharif started reading off the bullet points, providing supporting examples and answering questions. He spoke with enthusiasm, firing on all cylinders, fully aligned with his effective leader self.

Osman shyly announced having no cover letter draft as of yet, and Stanley shook his head in unsubtle disapproval. On account of Osman's low English level, Sharif anticipated doing most of the writing. He got Osman a draft form that provided the basic structure of a cover letter with generic language and blank spaces for Osman to fill in with personal details. Osman would complete the form and Sharif would help type it up. Twenty minutes later, all of his clients were up and running. He was making his rounds from computer to computer, providing individualized support and assigning the next task in the process that they should complete before he circled back. There was a collective sense of progress, of people believing in what they were doing, having fun and laughing along the way. Things were flowing. Everyone was engaged. Sharif loved his job.

The flow was interrupted when he noticed Merjem in the doorway. Her eyes were snapped wide open on him, red marks on either side of her nose from the sunglasses now on her head. Her expression was one of alarm, but maybe her face was making a mistake. Maybe she was admiring the synergy of his workshop. Couldn't awe and alarm look similar? The clients sensed her stiff, wide-eyed presence too. One by one, they turned to look at her.

Merjem said, "Sharif, can you come out here, please?"

"Sure," he said, and half jogged over. He stepped out into the hall with her. Patricia leaned on the wall, staring at the floor. Next to her stood a fat white police officer with a puffy face that sucked back his small green eyes. Heat rose to Sharif's head and his mouth fell open. "Where's Adjoua?" he said, feeling like he was standing on the edge of a blustery cliff. The next gust would be life or death.

Merjem's forehead stayed creased. "No. It's not about her."

The fat white cop, whose name tag read Jones, said, "Sharif Safadi, you are under arrest for criminal trespass and two counts of assault against a minor." Jones had him face the wall as he read him his rights and cuffed him. Sharif's body was emptying itself of the initial fear for Adjoua as it simultaneously filled up with another fear, saturated in confusion and shame. Coworkers and clients came out to see what was happening. He felt his own clients in the computer lab hovering by the threshold, right around the corner from the wall his eyes were inches from. He saw every distinct bump in the wall's paint. His pulse made them dance, jump up and down, everything vivid but nothing settled.

Merjem whispered angrily, "Patricia, are you out of your mind?" Getting no response, she tried with a pleading deference, "Please. Let's go to my office and discuss this quietly, okay? Patricia?"

Jones turned Sharif around and told Merjem, "We don't give special treatment, lady. Right, Officer Dauphne?" His smirk was audible. Something about Jones's rhetorical question caused Patricia's posture to become unnaturally straight, like a soldier at attention being scolded.

Sharif had seen her two days ago idling in her car across the street from CAPPA. He called her name through the morning mayhem before entering the building. It looked like she'd made direct eye contact with him before donning her aviators and driving off, but he told himself she must not have heard or seen him after all. Now he knew it was more than that.

"Oh my God," said Denise from the computer lab when she saw Sharif in handcuffs.

Merjem was still staring at Patricia, who was still ignoring her and standing unnaturally erect. Merjem returned to a reprimanding tone: "Really, Patricia? Here? You do this here, when you know exactly how it hurts the agency? How it hurts the community? *Your* community."

Tanisha appeared at the end of the hall carrying a pastry box with a red bow. She didn't have an appointment. She came up and said, "If this is about what happened with that crazy guy a couple weeks back, Sharif didn't do anything wrong. I was there that day."

Merjem said, "Well, Patricia? Is that what this is about?"

Patricia finally faced Merjem. "Take a step back and let us do our job, ma'am."

"*Ma'am?*" Merjem said.

Jones pushed Sharif down the hall, past Tanisha, and into the crowded lobby. The sight of Sharif created a domino effect, tipping people over into gawking silence. At the elevator, Sharif continued to feel all of those crushing eyes at his back.

Once they'd stepped into the elevator, Merjem blocked the door with her forearm and said, "Patricia, at least tell me why you're pretending you don't know me."

Patricia said, "Let go of the door, ma'am."

Merjem's glare softened into hurt feelings before letting them go down.

Sharif had trouble breathing inside the elevator. Everything felt so real that it didn't. "Where are we going?" he said.

"Precinct, then Central Booking," Jones said.

Sharif turned to Patricia. "What happens after Central Booking, Patricia?"

She retracted her chin into her neck, and he saw that calling her Patricia was a mistake.

Jones answered, "You'll be driven to criminal court for your arraignment." He sounded smug, as if he'd been trying to take Sharif down for years and finally got the son of a bitch. The elevator made its mocking ding, and the doors opened to a group of more clients and colleagues on the ground floor, half of whom had received his recent dog care email, and one of whom was a client he had an appointment with in twenty minutes. Some people greeted him normally before understanding, then their jaws dropped as they parted for him and his detainers. Someone said his name. Others, Oh my God. And, Jesus. On the sidewalk, more people stared and exclaimed, a few filming him on their phones as he was escorted to the double-parked squad car.

Sharif had been walking up and down Church Avenue five days a week for over four years, working closely with hundreds of local families. People recognized him. He was the nice white man who helped poor people in crisis. Now they'd think they were witnessing the unveiling of some pernicious corruption he'd been hiding all along. He was a man with depraved secrets that had finally caught up to him. A bad man.

Part VI
CONTROL

48.

PATRICIA WALKED SHARIF to the center of the precinct's chaotic open office space. She sat him in the chair opposite Jones's desk and hovered while Jones went for a cup of coffee. Alone with her for the first time, Sharif said, "Pa—Officer Dauphne. I'm sorry if I've caused you some kind of trouble. Can you please just tell me what happened? Maybe I can help."

She glanced in the direction Jones had gone, then over her shoulder. Hardly moving her lips as she spoke, she confirmed his suspicions: "That lawyer you gave my name to threatened to sue the NYPD for my misconduct. I'm on probation. They're talking about an internal investigation. I could lose my job."

"Jesus." They had sent her to CAPPA with Jones during rush hour to prove her loyalty, or as some perverse humiliation tactic.

"You want to help?" Patricia asked. "Please don't address me again."

"I won't. I'm sorry. I had no idea this would happen."

Jones returned and she went to her desk in the corner. He asked for Sharif's basic information—full name, address, date of birth, social security number—writing it down with the impatience of doing someone he resented a favor. He huffed and shook his head when Sharif requested a phone call. Somewhere along the line, Jones must have decided that treating the people he arrested like scumbags made the job more satisfying.

When Adjoua picked up, Sharif could tell she'd just woken up. A movie played in the background. He said, "Hey, how are you feeling?"

"Where are you calling from? I almost didn't answer."

"The police station. In Flatbush."

He heard her sit up in bed. "What? Why?"

He briefly wondered if there was a way to soften the blow. "I've been arrested." During the silence, he visualized CAPPA's lobby full of eyes. "Something changed." He spoke slowly, keeping his voice as steady as he could. "The DA decided to press charges."

"Aberto," she said.

"Yeah."

"Fucking shark. He actually leveraged his connections. I can't believe it." She started moving quickly, throwing off the bedcovers. "I'm coming."

"Hold on. Let me ask what the plan is here." To Jones he said, "Excuse me, sir? Approximately how long am I likely to be here before getting moved?"

Jones kept filling out his paperwork without acknowledging Sharif.

Adjoua said, "Moved? Where?"

"Hold on a second, baby." He tried Jones again: "Excuse me, Officer Jones? Sir?"

Without lifting his eyes, Jones said, "What?"

"I was wondering if you'd be able to tell me how long I'll be here?"

"Depends."

Sharif looked over at Patricia's desk and caught her watching them before averting her gaze. Sharif said to Jones, "If you could provide a general sense of what to expect, that would be very helpful."

Jones dropped his pen on top of his papers and pinched the bridge of his nose before saying, "I told you. We move you to Central Booking next. I have to finish this paperwork, then do the fingerprinting and photographing. That can take an hour or all day, depending on how many times you interrupt me. Anything else you want to discuss before I get back to work?"

Jones's combination of power and immaturity made for a novel experience of unfairness for Sharif. The indignation it spawned in him came with the strongest violent impulse of his life — involving a fantasy, bordering on hallucination, of clubbing Jones with the legs of his chair — but also the strongest commitment to appearing submissive before the tyrant controlling his freedom.

To Adjoua he said, "It sounds like I should call you when I get to the courthouse."

"Okay," she said. "I'm calling my parents. We need a good lawyer."

His immediate reaction was of acceptance and relief. He then wondered if he should get a free public defender instead of letting his in-laws pay some ungodly sum for a case that shouldn't be complicated to defend. But the way these precinct walls were squeezing him — the officialdom and severity and bitter unfairness, the loss of Patricia's alliance, the power-tripping pettiness of Jones — raised the stakes into trenchant focus. Innocent people really can end up in prison. He felt that novel indignation again. His future and the well-being of his wife and child were on the line. Pushed in this corner by no fault of their own, they must fight with every tool available to them. They must leverage every advantage. They must win.

49.

AFTER TWO HOURS in the precinct and one at Central Booking, he was placed in a holding cell behind the courthouse. None of his five, then six, then eight cellmates were intimidating, as Hollywood had conditioned him to expect. There was no discernible hierarchy in the fluorescent lit cage they shared, no threat of violence. These were simply other men also having one of the worst days of their lives. They slumped on the bench, stared off wearily, stood to stretch their cramped bodies, paced, and expelled distressed breaths.

The lawyer Sharif's in-laws retained arrived after about three hours. His name was Yann Doumbia. He was a tall, slim, handsome man in his early forties with a calm confidence and an expensive-looking suit and briefcase.

Yann and Sharif were escorted to a windowless room with a table and chairs.

Once the door shut, Yann said, "It may sound strange under the circumstances, but I've heard a lot of wonderful things about you."

"Oh, really? Thanks."

"Charles and Sylvie talk about you all the time." Sharif nodded, feeling a little awkward for having never heard of Yann before. Yann continued, "They have done more for me and my siblings than we could ever repay. They covered my school fees back home, my student visa here after I left Côte d'Ivoire, and my college tuition. All this to say, I won't bankrupt them." He smiled. "They told me you might be concerned about the cost. But there's no need to worry. This is an honor for me." Sharif nodded without knowing if this meant Yann's services were completely free or at some family discount. "Let's focus on getting you out of here. Okay? Good." He took out a leather folder from his briefcase. "I've read all the relevant files and spoken to the arresting officers. Based on what I've seen, their case sounds extraordinarily thin."

Yann spent about ten minutes explaining the charges and what to expect at today's arraignment. He then asked Sharif to recount the whole story with the Fleurimes in his own words. Yann listened attentively, took some notes, and asked a couple of succinct, clarifying questions. When it was over, he slapped his folder shut and said, "Unless there's a massive piece of information I'm missing, I see no reason why you won't be home for dinner."

Sharif was made to sit in the holding cell for another hour before getting moved to an empty carpeted room adjacent to the courthouse. As soon as he was brought into the courtroom, he spotted his beautiful and worried Adjoua. She'd taken out her braids. Her luscious natural hair stood tall in an updo. His longing to be home with her and Judy overflowed into shivers running down his back and legs. She sat with her parents, as well as Merjem and Tanisha. His attention on them was stolen by Aberto, who, incredibly — but perhaps not unpredictably — sat at the prosecutor's table, writing on his legal pad.

Sharif was escorted to Yann, who stood behind a podium facing the judge. On the other side of Yann was the deputy DA prosecuting the case.

The bridge officer announced a series of long numbers followed by the stomach-hollowing words "*The People versus Sharif Safadi.*"

The officer then asked Yann if he "waived the reading."

Yann answered, "Yes."

Sharif didn't understand the implications. Yann hadn't prepped him on it. Everyone stood silently, watching the judge read something for a long time. She then asked the lawyers for any notices. The DDA said a 190 50 was being served and brought the judge a piece of paper. Sharif didn't know what that meant either. Yann responded by saying he had a cross 190 50 and brought whatever that was to her. Why hadn't Yann walked him through this jargon? Couldn't he imagine how frightening it would be to have your fate decided in a foreign language?

"Good morning, Your Honor," the DDA said, which seemed out of the blue since they'd been standing there ten minutes already. "Before we begin, I would like to enter an appearance for Mr. Aberto Barbosa, an attorney in private practice, as co-counsel in this case. He has joined me at counsel table and will be delivering our reply to the defendant through counsel if given the opportunity."

"That's fine," the judge said in a monotone, still reading papers on her desk. The judge then removed her bifocals, looked up, and addressed Sharif directly: "Mr. Safadi, do you understand that you have been charged with one count of criminal trespass, one count of third-degree assault against a minor, and one count of second-degree assault against a minor, and that you are facing up to fifteen years in prison?"

Yann had coached him on this part, but hearing it from the mouth of a judge made him nearly collapse. Yann had explained that the criminal trespass was for entering the Fleurimes' apartment without permission. The second-degree assault was for Sharif's supposed attempt to use his dog's teeth as a deadly weapon against Junior. When that didn't work, Sharif apparently resorted to third-degree assault: hitting Junior to the ground, causing the three breaks in Junior's forearm and wrist.

Sharif answered the judge in a dissociated state, like he was speaking from within a glass jar: "Yes, Your Honor, I understand."

"And how do you plead to those charges?"

"Not guilty."

Yann leaned over and told him to specify "Not guilty on all counts."

Sharif repeated the words from inside his jar.

Yann said, "Your Honor, my client has no warrants or criminal history whatsoever. He's never so much as received a parking ticket or jumped a turnstile. Furthermore, he has significant ties to the community. His wife, who is eight and a half months pregnant, is here today with her parents." He turned to gesture toward them. "They sit alongside Mr. Safadi's supervisor from the social services nonprofit CAPPA, where he is employed, and one of Mr. Safadi's clients who came out of personal concern. As a devoted caseworker, helping hundreds of low-income New Yorkers achieve life-stabilizing careers a year, Mr. Safadi makes an unusually positive impact on the community. It is no exaggeration when I say that over a thousand Brooklyn residents would jump at the opportunity to vouch for Mr. Safadi's character and share their story of how he improved their quality of life. He is known for his commitment to equity, honesty, kindness, and consideration.

"But that's not why these charges brought against him are outlandish. Your Honor, Mr. Safadi did make one serious mistake recently. He trusted that Emmanuel Fleurime would honor his commitment of taking care of his dog so he could tend to his wife's medical emergency. The same day that Mr. Safadi left his elderly arthritic dog with the Fleurimes, he found him tied to a fourteenth-floor fire escape in a state of absolute neglect, abuse, and distress mere feet from a gaping hole in the fire escape's handrail. Hearing his dog's cries and no one answering at the Fleurimes', he knocked on the neighbor's door. This neighbor, Mr. Paul Lebedev, let my client into his home. It wasn't long before Mr. Safadi discovered his injured dog on the fire escape Mr. Lebedev shares with the Fleurimes. Since the elderly dog was tied to the radiator inside of the Fleurime's apartment, Mr. Safadi's only way to untie him was to go inside. Emmanuel Fleurime's son, known as Junior, entered the apartment at that time. Junior proceeded to shout and physically obstruct Mr. Safadi from leaving the apartment until he was paid sixty dollars for 'looking after that dog.' While Mr. Safadi made light contact with Junior to exit the blocked doorway, after demanding three times that Junior clear the way, it could not have resulted in anything resembling the severe injury described in the complaint. In addition to its being preposterous that Mr. Safadi would have used his elderly, senile, injured dog as some kind of toothed battering ram, or been physically capable of hitting Junior to the ground behind him while holding the one-hundred-and-fifty-pound dog, there happened to be a little girl across the hall who filmed the whole thing. Despite her phone mysteriously disappearing twenty minutes after Junior came asking for it, the little girl confirmed with the NYPD that Junior was not injured in Mr. Safadi's presence. It was said that Junior continued shouting about the sixty dollars he believed he was owed for 'looking after that dog' when Mr. Safadi and his injured dog had made it inside the elevator."

"'It was said'?" The voice came from the prosecutor's table. Everyone turned to look at Aberto, including the DDA. Aberto added, "By whom *was it said*, Mr. Doumbia?"

The judge said, "Mr. Barbosa, do not interrupt."

"Certainly, Your Honor. My apologies," Aberto said, yet he stood abruptly enough to make his seat bark against the floor, and slowly approached the podium to stand with the DDA. The judge asked Yann to continue.

"Thank you, Your Honor," he said, adjusting his tie for a bit too long. "As I mentioned, my client's wife is over eight months pregnant. What I have not yet shared is that their child has been diagnosed in utero with leukemia. This requires additional medical supervision and care, as well as familial support leading up to the birth. I present this as yet another reason for Mr. Safadi to be released to his family immediately and on his own recognizance. Mr. Safadi is not a rich man. These accusations are completely unfounded. He has an irreproachable record as a law-abiding citizen. His ties to the community, investment in the community, and personal circumstances make it clear that he poses no flight risk. He is committed to proving his innocence and clearing his unfairly tarnished reputation. My client has every motive to stay and fight these lies with every fiber in his body."

Aberto came to be the only one standing at the podium for the prosecution. The DDA was sitting at the prosecutor's table behind them, possibly checking his phone under the table.

Aberto said, "Your Honor, may I reply?"

The judge took a long, sizing-up look at Aberto. "I'm listening, Mr. Barbosa."

"Thank you, Your Honor," he said, almost flirtatiously. "First, I'd be remiss not to redirect a few of Mr. Doumbia's misleading statements and correct the patently false ones. Mr. Doumbia mentioned a little girl who saw, filmed, and confirmed the defendant's innocence to an NYPD lieutenant. If you look at all the filings and notations, you will see that this nine-year-old girl, Samantha Williams, has made no statement supporting Mr. Doumbia's claims. For all intents and purposes, Samantha Williams is mute. There is no record of Samantha uttering a word to anyone about what happened between the defendant and Junior Fleurime. The defendant's friend, Officer Patricia Dauphne, lieutenant in Brooklyn's Sixty-Seventh Precinct, deviated from NYPD protocol by going to interrogate Samantha, a child, as a personal favor to the defendant. Despite being off duty, Officer Dauphne showed up at Samantha's home wearing her police uniform. Under these false pretenses, which have since resulted in Officer Dauphne's reprimand and job probation, as well as an internal investigation, she then elicited vague head nods from Samantha with a series of leading questions. I will not waste the court's time describing every detail or concern I have regarding this egregious abuse of power, other than to say Mr. Doumbia has absolutely no business saying Samantha Williams confirmed any facts about this case. At present, the prosecution is the only side with a formal witness."

Yann said, "Yes, a witness with an expansive record of stealing, lying, illicit drug abuse and sale, illegal gambling, and one sexual misconduct conviction."

Aberto said, "Your Honor, I hope you'll agree that disparaging our witness is grossly inappropriate."

Yann said, "Mr. Lebedev's police record is an objective fact."

The judge said, "Gentlemen. Do I need to explain what an arraignment is? Witnesses are not relevant. I am also warning you both against haphazard argumentation. This has already dragged on longer than necessary. It's the end of the day, others are waiting, and I'd like to be home before nightfall."

They both apologized.

Aberto said, "I'll cut to the chase, Your Honor. Mr. Safadi is being charged with breaking into a private resident's home and committing multiple counts of violence against a minor. The prosecution can also show that these acts of violence were accompanied with racially motivated verbal abuse."

"I'm sorry," Yann said. "Could you define 'racially motivated verbal abuse'? I'm not familiar with that terminology."

Aberto turned to Yann and said, "I'm not done speaking. Wait your turn." The judge was shaking her head but seemed to prioritize moving things along over pausing for another scolding. Aberto continued: "Your Honor, there are myriad examples of individuals without criminal records committing acts of violence against socioeconomically and disadvantaged minorities. It is more important than ever that this court shows it will not tolerate the mistreatment of our most vulnerable community members. Letting the defendant back out on the street tells our low-income communities of color that their safety doesn't matter as much as the comfort of individuals like Mr. Safadi. The defendant works mere blocks from where the Fleurimes live. I can't help but be concerned by the consequences of them meeting out in the world before this is resolved. The defendant presents a clear and present danger to my clients and other community members."

"Thank you, Mr. Barbosa and Mr. Doumbia." She signed some paper on her desk and handed it to an officer, who left the courtroom with it. Then she examined Sharif's face for an agonizing moment. "Mr. Safadi, the charges against you are quite serious. However, you have not been proven guilty at this time and you have no prior criminal history. So I've set bail at twenty thousand dollars. Trial commences in six weeks."

50.

HALF AN HOUR after his in-laws paid for his release, he was in front of the courthouse hugging everyone. His last hug was with Charles. Enveloped in those strong yet soft arms, he let himself go limp and be gently swayed. At the same time, Sylvie slapped his back with a loud and precise rhythm. Tanisha and Merjem huddled close, nodding along. Adjoua had been smiling with more love and fear than he'd ever seen, tears streaming down her cheeks.

Charles spoke into his ear: "I'm sorry these people are doing this. It's so wrong. I'm stunned by Aberto's involvement. What a disappointment. But don't worry, we'll beat this nonsense. I only wish you had called on us earlier."

As soon as Charles released him, shame started polluting Sharif's gratitude. This insane progression of events had activated his support system, making him a burden to his loved ones. Their lives were massively disrupted by his problems. They would devote substantial time, energy, and resources to get Sharif back to a pre-crisis baseline. He'll come out of this hell feeling indebted to his people.

As if reading Sharif's mind, Sylvie took his face between her hands and said, "The number one thing to avoid in these situations is self-pity. Don't start boo-hooing for yourself, okay? Call me if any of that poison creeps in. I'll snap you out of it." He nodded and she let his face go. "I haven't had any luck getting ahold of your parents at their retreat. Have you? They turned off their phones for a whole month?"

"Yes, Mom," Adjoua said. "I've explained this."

"Well," Sylvie said, "what if something comes up? An emergency, for example. Anyway, they're going to be so sick about this."

Sharif had hardly considered his parents. He had this way of forgetting they existed. He still imagined no benefit to involving them. They would insist on flying in to support him, but their helpless presence would only inject more stress into Sharif and Adjoua's life, for which Sharif would have to pretend to feel thankful. He'd field their endless questions, assuage their fears, explain every decision he'd made up until now and why his parents' alternative solutions wouldn't work. He and Adjoua would indirectly be in charge of their accommodations and most meals. They'd give him their credit card to "book something simple," saying, "You know what we like." Despite knowing that they would never cease feeling hurt that he didn't call on them in his time of need, he had no capacity to even continue thinking of them now, and so they disappeared.

Adjoua said, "Walid wants to come out, but he's in court himself for work. He's going to pitch in remotely."

The attention shifted when Charles started clapping, repeating, "There he is," as Yann exited the courtroom and joined them. Sylvie started applauding too, telling him what a marvelous job he did.

Yann's broad, bright white smile got wiped off his face when Adjoua asked, "What are the chances of Sharif doing time?"

Yann said, "I can't give an exact percentage, Addie, but I'll tell you this. I have never lost a criminal case." Sylvie clapped and cheered again. Yann continued, "And I assure you, I'm going to do absolutely everything to prevent Sharif from spending another minute behind bars."

"So you can't give a general likelihood. Okay." She then asked, "How can Aberto Barbosa be allowed to work with the prosecution? Did Sharif tell you about him?"

Yann said, "Oh, I'm familiar with Aberto. He's quite well known."

"I'm not talking about his professional reputation," Adjoua said. "I'm talking about the fact that he's the Fleurimes' personal immigration attorney, my ex-boyfriend, and the lawyer who contrived biased and disastrous mediation sessions with us and the Fleurimes."

Yann was visibly shocked. "You're kidding."

"No. At the end of our last mediation, he literally told us he would pull on levers to get the DA to press charges. Not only did he apparently do that, but he's somehow weaseled his way inside the courtroom."

Yann looked at Sharif then back at Adjoua. "I was not informed of that."

Sharif said, "I didn't know he'd be in there."

"Addie," Yann said, "I'm glad you told me. You're absolutely right. His involvement is a clear conflict of interest. Frankly, an astonishingly audacious one. He's known to challenge norms, but this is unacceptable. Arguably illegal. I'll file a motion to have him dismissed from the case immediately."

Charles transitioned into his Big Man voice to say, "That's good, Yann, that's very good. Walk with me for a moment now." He put his hand on Yann's shoulder to guide him away. "Let's talk."

"Um, no," Adjoua said, and followed them.

"Addie!" Sylvie said to stop her, but then followed her to the men.

Sharif used this time to talk with Merjem and Tanisha, who'd been standing at a slight remove.

"Thank you for coming," he said to them. "It means so much."

Tanisha said, "I can't believe any of this is happening. To you, of all people."

"Yeah, it's been overwhelming," he said. "But talk to me about something else. Did you follow up with the sanitation job with a thank-you letter like we talked about?"

Tanisha started smiling bashfully. "That's actually why I came by this morning."

"No way!" Sharif said, "Really?" The good news now beamed from her smile, nearly making him cry. "This is so wonderful!"

"Yeah," she said, her joyous tears spilling over. "It still doesn't even feel real. Every time my phone rings I think they're calling to say they made a mistake."

"They didn't. They're so lucky to have you. You're going to be great."

Again starting to appear bashful about celebrating herself, she said, "I got you a cake this morning, but me and Jayda ate it since I didn't know when I'd see you next. I'll get another one though."

"I can't wait," he said.

"Anyway, thank you. Really. I owe it all to you. You'll say that's not true, but it is. It wouldn't have happened without you going above and beyond to help me. No one has ever believed in me like that before. Ever." She glanced at Merjem to say, "I wouldn't have even thought to apply for a job this good if he didn't push me. This could really change things for me and my family."

Sharif said, "I'm so happy for you."

Tanisha said, "Well, I wanted to say that if there's any way I can help you with what's going on, I'll rush to the opportunity."

Merjem added, "Tanisha and I could still file that complaint against Emmanuel."

"Hell yes," Tanisha said.

Sharif shook his head. "I don't see what it would fix at this point. I really appreciate your wanting to help though."

Merjem said, "Ask your lawyer about it. It might help at the trial."

"I will," he said unconvincingly.

Tanisha suddenly realized the time and said she was going to be late picking up Jayda. She gave everyone another hug and jogged off.

Sharif and Merjem watched her go for a while before she said that Brionna wanted to talk to Sharif tomorrow if he was available.

"She does? Do you know what she's going to say?"

"Ha, you think she tells me?"

"You really don't have a clue about where she stands on this?"

"Honestly, none. We haven't talked about it. I can see her being proud to stand by her staff in times of trouble just as easily as I can see her wanting to put as much distance between you and the agency as possible."

"She's going to fire me. She has to, right?"

"Maybe. But why would she want to do it herself? She's always made me do it. There is one other thing, but I'm hesitant to tell you."

"Oh, come on. Now you have to."

She really did look hesitant, a rare expression for her. She shifted her weight from foot to foot, then finally said, "She's wanted to find time to talk to you since I told her about your raise request. There's this big change coming. It hasn't been announced yet, so it absolutely must stay between us, okay?" He silently communicated his word. She said, "Jamal wants to retire as soon as possible. That's actually been the case for a while, but Brionna has been ignoring it." Jamal was the director of economic development, one level down from Merjem. She cupped her forehead, appearing to feel some regret. "You really can't tell anyone this, okay? But Brionna prefers to hire internally, and when I brought up the unusually large raise request, she asked if I thought you could do Jamal's job. I gave my two cents, and she said she wanted to interview you. As of my last conversation with her, yesterday, you were the only candidate."

In that role, Sharif would earn at least twice his current salary, possibly more, while easily doubling his impact. He shook his head with a surrendering smile. "Wow. So as I was getting arrested at work, our CEO was considering me for my dream job."

"I'm an idiot." She was squinting now. "It was cruel to tell you. I was desperate to tell you something positive, but I see now that it's not positive since we don't know why she wants to talk. Look, I'll send you a few times for a phone meeting tomorrow. I'm sorry, Sharif. I shouldn't have said anything."

"It's okay. It's—flattering. And I would have been nervous about the call no matter what."

"Ugh. Okay. Say goodbye to your family for me." Still looking regretful, she walked off quickly.

He joined Adjoua and her parents. They were side by side now, looking down the block. He followed their collective line of sight leading to Yann and Aberto. The two men faced off at the corner of Schermerhorn and Boerum, too far away to hear, having an animated discussion.

"What's happening?" Sharif said.

"It's being handled," Sylvie said. "The right way."

51.

IT WASN'T UNTIL Charles and Sylvie drove them home in their BMW X5 that Sharif learned about his in-laws' strategy. Outside of the courthouse and on the walk to the car, they'd only used cryptically optimistic language, like *Good things are coming. You'll see.* And *Once you understand what the other side really wants, you're halfway to victory.* And *It's the simplest solution that works the best.*

From the driver's seat, Charles opened with a bit more vagueness: "We can't leave anything to chance."

"That's right," Sylvie added. "Yann could probably get you off, but there's no guarantee. And one of those plea deals is out of the question." She craned her neck around the passenger seat to show Sharif the severity of her expression. "There can be no doubt in anyone's mind of your innocence." Facing forward again, she said, "We need you both as far away from this as possible. No compromises."

Charles glanced at Sharif in the rearview before spelling it out for him: "Yann has instructed Aberto to propose a simple contract to his clients."

Sylvie added, "Simple but ironclad."

"Okay," Sharif said, "what kind of contract?" Adjoua took his hand and looked out the window. She seemed to already know and accept the plan.

Sylvie said, "The kind where that silly boy withdraws every lie about you and confesses publicly to making false accusations."

Charles said, "He and his father must also go to the police station and retract their complaint. What their supposed witness claims to have seen will be nullified."

Sylvie said, "The DA will have no witness, no victim, no proof. They'll have to drop the case."

Sharif knew the answer to his next question but asked anyway, "And why will the Fleurimes do all of this?"

Charles gripped the steering wheel a little tighter. "Because these people will get what they've been after all along. Money."

"Guaranteed, fast money," Sylvie said. "Not some online charity plan. I can't believe you were going to do that, Addie! How could you have waited so long to call us? Haven't we taught you better than that?"

Sharif asked, "How much are you offering them?"

Sylvie said, "It's an offer they can't refuse, and a small price for us to end this."

Sharif didn't insist on a number. Instead, he asked, "Aberto agreed to this?"

Sylvie said, "It's not up to him. Yann made clear that he had to tell his clients about it. And his clients will agree. Money is all they want."

Sharif said, "I'm really grateful for your help. I can't tell you how incredibly lucky I felt seeing all of you in that courtroom." This wasn't true. The feelings he'd had were of fear and desperation, not thanks. "I can't imagine going through this alone." He had been receiving squeezes from Adjoua's hand, little pulses of love. "But I must admit, it's uncomfortable to think of you spending your hard-earned money on this. It shouldn't be your problem to solve."

Charles flicked his eyes at Sharif in the rearview, looking insulted. "That is our daughter and grandchild next to you. The greed of these people is jeopardizing this family's well-being. Of course it's our problem. Addie already lost a job with the *New York Times* because of them." He shook his head. "And you're at risk of losing your job. Right before having this baby. Both of our families' reputations are on the line here."

Sylvie was nodding along. "And Aberto," she said. "How could he? I never, in a million years, would have guessed he was capable of such behavior." She made disapproving tuts with her tongue, saddened by who Aberto turned out to be, and perhaps a little frightened by what it meant to be so wrong about a person. She said, "You'll have to show me how to block his number, Addie."

"He doesn't still call you, does he?" Adjoua said.

"At least once a month."

"Are you serious? Why didn't I know about this? What could you two possibly have to talk about?"

"He says he wants to check in, see how we're doing. But the real reason is to show off with these long stories about all the needy people he's helping, hoping it'll get back to you. Speaking like he's living some moral pilgrimage when all it takes is finally understanding that he's lost you for him to turn wicked. You see, that's the problem with you altruistic, godless people. When you're not accountable to Him, you bend the rules whenever it suits you."

Hearing his in-laws depict Aberto as a snake didn't give Sharif the satisfaction it might have under other circumstances. As they crossed the bridge to Manhattan, Sharif said, "If the Fleurimes accept this deal, I hope you'll at least let me pay you back."

Charles answered with a snort, as if disregarding light insolence, or a bad joke.

Sylvie then said, "People like them, these Fleurimes, make it worse for the rest of us."

Sharif felt the muscles in his face clench.

"Yes," Charles said. "They make it harder. They make us all look bad." In the rearview mirror, Sharif caught a strip of revulsion on his father-in-law's face.

If Adjoua's parents had said these things a week ago, she would have jumped on them, firing off counterpoints to their misguided logic. Today, neither Sharif nor Adjoua betrayed so much as a sigh of disappointment.

When he looked over at her, and they briefly made eye contact, he saw that she felt it too. Principles that mattered a great deal to them had been extinguished. They were no longer the same couple.

Turning onto Essex Street, Adjoua said to Sharif, "I didn't tell you. Judy and I visited the Australian's." She nodded. "It's going to be really great for him. He'll be so happy there," she said sadly.

52.

ADJOUA WOULDN'T LET Sharif out of her sight. She accompanied him on all errands and dog walks. She asked where he was going as soon as he got up for a glass of water or to use the bathroom. She wanted him to sleep with her and Judy that night and assured him before he could respond that she'd happily take the inside of the bed against the brick wall. She could wake him if she needed to get up for any reason. She didn't know why they'd never thought of it before. And it would be easier to rescue him from bad dreams this way too. So the three of them lay with touching limbs all night, hardly sleeping.

On their morning walk, he told her about the call Brionna and Merjem scheduled with him for nine a.m. He admitted to being nervous. Then he shared everything Merjem told him about being considered to replace Jamal as the new director, explaining what that could have meant for them financially if this other problem hadn't interfered. Adjoua became more energized and optimistic. She said, Well who knows, maybe that offer is still on the table. She reminded him that Merjem said it would be unprecedented for Brionna to fire someone herself when she could outsource it to Merjem. Adjoua then started coaching him on how to sound calm on the call. How he should pause before speaking, and to talk twice as slowly as he thinks he should.

"Slowness lets every word sink in for them and allows you to hear what you're saying so you don't repeat the same stuff over and over. It'll give you space to only say what you mean, and sound confident. A writing teacher told me this before I did my first public reading."

"Isn't there a risk of talking too slowly? I don't want to sound sleepy."

"That's unlikely when you're nervous. Trust me, go more slowly than feels natural. And like I said, lean into the pauses. They always feel longer for the speaker than for the audience. It'll be empowering, I promise."

Sharif recalled how she expressed resentment for his job less than a week ago. Now she spoke of CAPPA as the solution to all their problems. She wouldn't be wrong about that. If her parents helped resolve things with the Fleurimes, and Sharif became director, all of their problems would actually be solved. Maybe he shouldn't have gotten her hopes up. It was fanciful to imagine the directorship would come up at all on this call. But keeping exciting possibilities from her, especially ones that flattered him, felt beyond his control. Her excitement made him feel like a man capable of saving his family.

53.

AT 8:58 A.M., Sharif helped Adjoua lie down on the dog bed behind Judy. He dialed into the meeting and put himself on speakerphone as she'd requested. Pacing the kitchen, he held the phone face-up to his mouth, like it was a hotdog he was about to bite into. It put an awkward strain on his wrist, but he was delayed in imagining an alternative. It rang. He paced. Adjoua and Judy's eyes tracked his movements from below. Merjem answered and gave a suspiciously chirpy greeting. He turned the phone to hold it like a mic.

She thanked him for meeting on such short notice, and, in an attempt at levity, told him that Brionna happened to pick the same green sunglasses he'd worn last time he'd been in her office!

"Is that right?" Sharif said, trying to match her lightness. But he was thrown by the fact that Brionna had come into the office at all. Having only ever seen her twice in the flesh at CAPPA, he'd assumed she would be calling in too. She worked remotely. Her presence was mostly felt through stories staff had heard about her, or through Merjem's reported speech about a change Brionna wanted. No one asked questions when Merjem said Brionna wanted something done. Even when it didn't make sense to anyone, it always ended up being good for the agency. Her ability to understand the inner workings of CAPPA better than anyone who actually spent time there gave her a supernatural mystique. Staff whispered her name as if she could hear them no matter where she was physically. Others believed Brionna's ideas were really Merjem's and Merjem used Brionna's name to get things done without pushback.

But Brionna had been a legend well before Merjem was hired, earning a reputation across Brooklyn for her unmatched foresight about the shifting needs of the community. She had put CAPPA on the front lines to serve families who'd lost vital incomes during New York's crack era, the HIV/AIDS epidemic of the nineties, the economic catastrophe following 9/11, the Great Recession of 2007 to 2012, the mass dislocation caused by Hurricanes Katrina and Sandy and Maria, and the ongoing affordable housing and homelessness crisis. She had creative and practicable solutions to the city's biggest problems and a talent for advocating for them to elected officials, grantmakers, community leaders, philanthropists, nonprofit partners, and the press. Even Aberto sounded impressed when her name came up at the work function where he and Sharif had first met.

Most recently, she had persuaded New York's Eighth District representative to provide $10 million of community project funding through the House Appropriations Committee process so CAPPA could launch Brionna's Career Navigation program in East New York. Whoever replaced Jamal as director of economic development would be in charge of this program. It was designed to target disaffected youth who had aged out of high school and foster care, lacked pathways to self-sufficiency, and were in crisis (homelessness, substance abuse issues, involvement in the criminal justice system, living in unsafe or abusive situations, and so on). Creating meaningful career paths that lead to economic stability and mobility for these young adults would have myriad positive impacts on the community, from boosting the local economy to reducing crime rates. Brionna had cleverly housed the program across community centers inside of five NYCHA buildings, each one a short walk from the other — a crucial detail for young residents who struggled to leave their neighborhood out of fear for their safety. In that part of East New York, young people inherited territorial tensions automatically based on their address. Whoever replaced Jamal would likely be based at the Church Avenue site and make weekly program visits to East New York. It was hard to imagine a title, job, responsibility, and salary that would make Sharif prouder.

The three main criticisms of Brionna were that 1) she employed cut-throat tactics to get what she wanted, something Sharif thought all women in positions of power were accused of at some stage; 2) she took a $500,000 salary, originally based on the 1 percent budget formula she'd used when founding the agency in 1977 from her kitchen table with a $50,000 grant; and 3) her whiteness. Sharif acknowledged that the second and third criticisms were valid, but felt they were dwarfed by her contributions to society. He even felt a little starstruck the two times he'd seen her in person. She represented everything he wanted to be.

"Sharif," Brionna now said. "Let me start by saying how sorry I was to learn about everything you've been going through."

He glanced down at Adjoua and Judy's unblinking faces and said, "Thank you. It's been a pretty confusing and challenging stretch, but we'll get through it."

"I really admire how gracefully you've been handling what must be an absolutely maddening situation. I'd be pulling my hair out."

Slowly, Adjoua mouthed to him. His eyes dropped to where her belly touched Judy's back, and he repeated, "Thank you," into the phone.

Brionna sighed and said, "When I was a young girl, my father was engulfed by a false accusation too. The short of it is that some complete stranger filed a slip-and-fall suit against him. The man claimed he'd sustained his injuries by slipping on the wet floor of my father's corner store. This was before every shop and street corner had surveillance cameras. The lawsuit dragged on for a decade, consuming most of my dad's attention and finances. It felt like such a profound, almost impossible injustice to us children. Some random person can point a finger at *Dad?* Our *hero?* He won in the end. It turned out the accuser had never even set foot inside his store. But none of my father's time or money could be reimbursed. His accuser was broke. The experience altered my father's worldview. Permanently.

One desperate stranger made my previously cheerful dad a bitter man. He saw everybody as a threat after that. All this to say, your situation hits home. It was important to me, on a personal level, to express my sympathy."

After using Adjoua's pause guidance, he said, "I really appreciate it. And I'm sorry your father dealt with that for so long."

"Thank you. Me too." There was a long gap in time that Sharif would have liked to close, but he managed to remain quiet. "I also wanted to tell you how valued you are at this agency. You work well with your coworkers. The clients love you. And senior management sings your praises."

"Oh, wow. That's so nice to hear."

"It's long overdue," she said. "And how about Tanisha? The fact that she showed up to support you in court speaks volumes, let alone this life-changing job you helped her get. Since your circumstances hit a nerve for me personally, and your work has been so immensely appreciated, it felt only right to communicate the following directly. While we must initiate your separation from the agency at this time, I hope you'll consider returning to us once you've cleared this matter."

"Oh," he said, feeling blood leave his face, and his shoulders and back curling forward. "What kind of separation exactly?"

"Unfortunately, administrative leave isn't possible. It would have to be a full, at-will separation. There's been too much buzz. Staff and clients have been talking nonstop about the arrest, and you know how that goes. A couple of journalists have reached out to us already. No major outlets yet, but the *Daily Eagle* contacted Merjem, and I received an interview request from them and *The Haitian Times*, which I'm sure you know we use for program outreach. Has anybody contacted you yet?"

"No," he said, his top half folded over and supported by his forearms on the kitchen island.

"Check your social media and work phone. I imagine that's what someone would find if they looked you up online. Anyway, there's a chance that a bigger publication takes an interest, and next thing you know, I'm fielding questions from electeds, funders, partners, et cetera. I need to get in front of all that. But I want you to know, Sharif, that the only things I plan to say about you are positive and that we'll have to trust that the legal process will reveal the truth about this case. I wish I could do more for you. But you know as well as anybody that CAPPA's ability to provide essential services depends on our good name, which must be earned every single day in this community. There isn't an individual in this world for whom I'd risk that, including myself."

Sharif finally had the courage to lift his head from the table and check on Adjoua. He couldn't stand the information coming from her face for longer than a glance. Her eyes were round with fear, like a child looking up from the bottom of a well. He stood straighter and turned his back to her before asking, "What happens to my health insurance?"

Merjem said, "It's valid until the end of the month."

He closed his eyes.

"I know," Brionna said. "It sucks. The whole thing really sucks. I'm sorry, Sharif. Given your wife's pregnancy, I encourage you to enroll in Cobra or Medicaid today."

"Okay," he said with his deadened voice. They couldn't afford Cobra. He pressed the home button on his phone. It was June 12th. 86 degrees Fahrenheit. Adjoua would need to put the air conditioner on soon. A news notification read: Syrian Forces Move into Strategic Town, Tightening Grip on Rebels. The thought of an energy bill they couldn't afford floated by. He watched his hand clench and unclench. It didn't seem like a hand he'd seen before or had any control over. It was a creepy, autonomous thing. He heard himself ask, "What about my caseload?"

It sounded like Brionna was smiling when she said, "That says everything I need to know about you. Even now you're thinking of your clients."

Merjem said, "Don't worry, Sharif. We'll handle your caseload. Just focus on getting past this."

Adjoua had gotten up by herself at some point. The call had ended, and she was rubbing his back in a circular motion. She said, "It's okay, my love. I'm actually not feeling discouraged by this."

"Really?" he said, looking to see if any of the fear from before was still in her eyes. Not a trace.

"Really. Brionna genuinely admires you and feels a personal connection to our circumstances. And the fact that she honestly spelled out the politics behind her decision shows that she trusts and respects you. I think it was implicit that once this is over, they'll take you back and consider you for that promotion."

"I hope so." He shook his head. "I get why she's putting the well-being of tens of thousands of people over one man. But I cannot understand how I came to be that one man."

"Unjustly. That's how. She knows you're a deeply good man. So many people know that about you."

"Thank you." He felt an unexpected softness spread across his face. "You're deeply good too, you know?"

54.

BEING A RECIPIENT of public assistance carried a different weight for Adjoua than for Sharif.

"If it weren't for this," she said, tapping her belly, "I'd sooner fix my own broken leg than go on Medicaid." She shook her head with a bitter smile. "Too many people have sacrificed too much for someone like me to be a ward of the state. I truly never thought I'd see the day. But it's fine! It's just temporary, right?"

"Yeah," he said, deciding to spare her the enrollment process. He took Judy out and first called New York–Presbyterian to confirm their doctors would accept Medicaid. After twenty minutes on hold, Sharif learned that three of the six doctors on rotation in Adjoua's ward accepted it. If the doctor on duty happened to not take their insurance, staff would locate a doctor who did. However, the hospital couldn't provide an estimate for how long that would take or tell him if the doctor would come to Adjoua or have her moved to a different wing, floor, or possibly even building.

The Medicaid process through the NY State Healthline lasted nearly three hours, and Sharif couldn't spare Adjoua's involvement after all. The enrollment specialist had to speak to each adult applicant individually. Adjoua's face was bereft of expression as she answered the specialist's questions in monotone. It would take three weeks to learn if their applications were approved, at which point coverage began on the first of the following month. Since there would be a gap between their private insurance and Medicaid, the hospital would bill them directly. They would then have to apply for a retroactive Medicaid reimbursement for those bills. However, qualifying for reimbursement depended on qualifying for Medicaid in the first place, which they probably wouldn't know before the baby came. When Sharif expressed his concern to the specialist, noting that an uncomplicated vaginal delivery alone cost $11,900 at New York–Presbyterian, to say nothing of the cost of one month of postnatal treatments for Zora, she explained that if their application was denied, they could always reapply.

Such messages from administrative personnel caused a new kind of internal wear and tear on their bodies. Adjoua took a bath. Sharif lay on the carpet next to the daybed and called the Department of Labor's unemployment line. The split second of hope he felt every time the hold music stopped, only to again hear the pre-recorded voice say his call was important to them, was torturous. He turned to his social media page for distraction and saw direct messages from two journalists at the same papers that had contacted Brionna and Merjem. They wanted to know if he had time to talk this week, so he blocked them and lay with his eyes closed. Judy lumbered over and licked his unreactive face.

When Sharif was finally connected to an employee at the unemployment office, he learned it would take three to six weeks before receiving his first check, assuming he qualified in the first place. The estimated amount would be $384 a week, down from the barely manageable $604 he'd been getting as a full-time employee. They'd have to use Adjoua's book advance for this month's rent. Then they'd most likely need to live with his in-laws in New Jersey for a while.

55.

WITH ADJOUA STILL wrapped in her bath towel, he said to her, "You know what? Come with me."

"Come with you where?"

"Over here. I want to show you something." He opened their front door. "I should have done this a long time ago. Go ahead, stand right here." He pointed at the threshold between the doorframes.

"Can you close the door?" she said.

"I want to show you the staging of it all. I want you to see how it happened." He took her by the arm and walked her to the open door.

"There's no reason to do this."

Sharif placed her in the doorframe and said, "Turn ninety degrees." When she didn't comply, he slowly but firmly turned her by the shoulders. "There. That's exactly how he stood when I asked him to move out of my way. Now stay like that." He went over to Judy and picked him up.

"Put him down, please."

"I pick him up like this every day."

"Not right after he ate. Let him digest." She stepped back into the apartment and began shutting the door.

"This is important to me, Adjoua!" he shouted. Then he said, "I'm sorry. Please. This is important to me."

"My feet are all dirty now." She meant because her bare heels had been in the hallway.

"Let me just show you how it happened, and we can move on." Begrudgingly, she reopened the door and resumed her position. "Now watch what happens when Judy and I try to exit with you standing there. And keep in mind, Judy was freaking out at the time so it was even more impossible."

"Yes. I know all of this."

He slowly exited, keeping Judy tight to his body. "Okay, stay right there," he said, all three of them squeezed in the doorframe.

"Please be careful."

"I *am* being careful!" he shouted again.

"What's going on with you? I don't need you to show me this."

He tried to quickly free one hand from holding Judy to push Adjoua into the apartment, but he could only let go of Judy for a split second without having to return his hand to support Judy's weight. "See? Now move any which way you want. See how I have no ability to shove or pull or yank or throw or whatever the hell else he claimed?" Judy started fidgeting, and Sharif rolled him up higher to avoid his dangling legs from touching Adjoua. "See? See how I don't have any power from here?" Rolled up nearly to Sharif's shoulders, Judy started bucking to get down.

"That's enough," Adjoua said, putting her hands up to protect her face from Judy's kicks. "I'm done."

"Wait!" He put his knee up to block her from going back into the apartment. "How about with my elbow? Now that I'm partially past you, do you see how I couldn't have done any damage even using my elbow?" Judy's struggle was harder to contain. "And it's too tight for me to put my elbows out at all, forget squeezing behind you somehow and pushing so hard as to launch you to the ground."

"Let me out!"

Adjoua started moving into the apartment. Her shoulder caught on Judy's front legs. Sharif tried to pull him up even higher, but Judy's backside slipped out of the hold. "Stop!" Sharif yelled, but it was too late. Judy's bottom half swung down like a pendulum, kicking the side of Adjoua's belly.

She was crouched on the floor in the apartment now, the towel unwrapped, holding her naked stomach, gasping.

Sharif dropped Judy and kneeled on the floor with Adjoua. "Are you hurt? Tell me you're okay."

Her shoulders shot up. "Get away from me!"

He felt the door across the hall open behind him. He glanced over his shoulder and saw at least four young men, each at various stages of putting on police uniforms. They looked over and around each other from their doorframe to better see the scene. Judy lay half in the apartment, staring at Sharif with shiny, frightened eyes, holding a toy fetus in his mouth, enveloped in slime. Then everyone was out on the sidewalk. The young police officers carried a hogtied Judy upside down on their shoulders. Adjoua was screaming that Judy didn't mean to, he'd been afraid, please, he didn't know what he was doing!

When Adjoua shook Sharif awake, he was saying, "I'm sorry. Oh God. I'm sorry!"

She held his head against her chest. "You're okay." She caressed the side of his face. He'd have to lie if she asked him what his dream was about. But then it started smoking away on its own. He was observing himself forget, and within a few seconds it was all gone. In its place was a simultaneously empty and heavy feeling, as though he were a large, inanimate object.

Adjoua then said the most unexpected thing. "I have some very good news."

56.

SHE HELD HIS FACE in her hands in their bed, and said, "They agreed to end it. Aberto and the Fleurimes."

"What do you mean?"

"My parents, Yann, and Walid have been working out a deal with them nonstop since the arraignment." When Sharif's face didn't move in light of this revelation, she said, "They kept us out of the process to protect us. Baby, this is good."

"Yeah, I'm just still waking up. What deal was made exactly?"

"My dad emailed us both the terms. Walid participated remotely, but apparently his help was invaluable."

Everyone was to convene at Aberto's home office tomorrow afternoon. Three checks would be written out to Emmanuel, each for $20,000. They would be given to him one at a time, upon completion of three tasks. The first task was to be completed before the meeting. Emmanuel must hand deliver a written withdrawal of his police complaint, explaining that the initial complaint was based on false information. Yann would accompany him to the precinct, and hand him the first check afterward.

The second task required Junior to recant his accusations online, unequivocally absolving Sharif of responsibility with a text prepared by Yann and Walid. The text stated that Sharif was nowhere near Junior when he hurt himself. This must be posted on all of Junior's social media pages during the meeting. The final task was for the Fleurimes to sign a contract and nondisclosure agreement that prevented them from undoing the previous tasks.

Without complaint, plaintiffs, witnesses, or evidence, the DA could not prosecute. Sharif and Adjoua would be free of all legal and reputational risk. And the Fleurimes would be $60,000 richer.

After finishing the email, Sharif put his phone down on the bed and stared at the ceiling.

Adjoua was the first to speak. "I know this has blown up at every hopeful turn, so I don't want to jinx it. But this feels different. After tomorrow, I really think this will be over." Emotion caught in her throat. "Sorry, wow. I'm so relieved."

"Me too," he said, without feeling it. It hardly seemed possible that his life could drastically change this many times in a week. He had been considered for his dream job, arrested and charged on three felonies, arraigned and bailed out of jail, fired from his job, become desperate for public assistance that would cut his family's standard of living in half, and now this. Without his or Adjoua's input, others had swooped in and negotiated a radically improved future for them. The past week, then month, then years of his life skipped around his head as if someone else were flicking through television channels.

Adjoua said, "What's wrong?"

He looked down. "Nothing." She waited. "Some part of me can't believe it might really be over. Maybe because I got arrested last time I let myself believe that."

She nodded. "Of course, my love. There's no rush to let your guard down. If anything, my relief is the anomaly. And probably imprudent. But I can't help it. Taking the literal nightmare scenario of you going to prison off the table makes all of our other problems feel so manageable." She shook her head and smiled self-mockingly. "Listen to me, making a speech about gaining perspective. I thought I was the pessimist."

Sharif suspected that her optimism came from her parents' involvement. She implicitly trusted their ability to fix whatever they said they could. He said, "To be honest, I think I'm also feeling a little ashamed that your parents are saving us. It's stupid, I know, but I wish I could have been the one to save us."

"I get that. It's not stupid."

"It's like every significant turn in this has been triggered by something beyond my control. It was totally arbitrary that I ran into Emmanuel the day you went to the hospital, and that he happens to have this confused teenager who happens to come home when I'm getting Judy out of there, and they happen to be working with Aberto. It's just as arbitrary that I happen to have in-laws with the money and desire to rescue me, and on and on it goes like that." He felt his eyebrows mashing together so hard that it started to hurt. "I'm overwhelmingly aware of how much dumb luck defines me. You talk about this way more eloquently in your op-ed draft. But it feels like my choices don't matter."

"That wasn't exactly what I meant in the piece. But yes, luck is probably the foundation of all unfairness, advantages and disadvantages alike. That said, when good luck saves us from bad luck, like my parents saving us from this crazy shit, it can change us for the better. This experience will cause us to make more informed decisions moving forward. You're probably less likely to give Judy to a complete stranger. Sorry, too soon?" She nudged him teasingly with her elbow. "Seriously, good luck can give us a second chance. We'll be more careful and thoughtful and poised in the face of future adversity, and hopefully more grateful and relaxed people. That's our latest draw of luck. Listen, I don't know about you, but I'm a hell of a lot more zen about last month's set of problems that are waiting for us on the other side of this."

"You're so smart," he said in earnest.

"Oh please, you've always known this. I learned it from you."

"No you didn't."

"Of course I did! Your awareness of the all-powerful nature of dumb luck is why you're so dedicated to helping people with worse luck. Believe me, I couldn't have married a privileged Midwestern man if he didn't see his abundance of good luck."

"A privileged Midwestern white man," he corrected. "It's okay. God will forgive you for marrying a white guy. You have so many other redeeming qualities."

"I refuse to acknowledge such heresy."

Soon there was laughter, and the warmth expelled from her nose as she kissed his cheek made him feel so safe and loved. There was some play-fighting and nuzzling after that. With her head in his lap now, facing Judy at the foot of the bed, she said, "I've gotten so swallowed up by fear that I forgot how much your goodness and your commitment to helping others means to me. The relief I'm feeling around getting rescued by my parents makes me want to rediscover that worldview. I miss my romanticism. I miss being idealistic. I like myself so much better that way." She quickly covered his mouth with the palm of her hand. "*Shh!* Don't you dare say a word about my writing. I know you're thinking about it!"

"Oh, you're a writer? I had no idea."

"Don't!"

"What sorts of things do you write? Anything I might have heard of?"

They play-fought and laughed and nuzzled again.

He said, "I can't believe it. If I'd known all I had to do was get framed and arrested for you to flirt with me, I would have done this months ago."

"You really should have."

Holding her, he said, "I think I'm experiencing some of that relief you mentioned earlier."

She stiffened, then whispered with urgency, "Give me your hand." She guided it to the side of her belly, where Zora thumped against the inside of the wall.

57.

Merjem: A man named Paul came in asking after you . . . wanted me to give him your cell . . .

Sharif: Did he give a last name?

Merjem: Nope . . . Not a journalist or past client either . . . He claimed he has something of "significant value to you . . ."

Sharif: Weird. What did he look like?

Merjem: . . . White . . . 60s . . . greasy long hair . . . scruffy and unkempt . . .

The addict, Sharif realized. Paul Lebedev. The Fleurimes' fake witness and neighbor whose apartment Sharif had to go through to get to the fire escape.

Merjem: . . . he left his number . . . I'll send it in case it matches one of your saved contacts . . . let me know if you resolve the mystery . . . I'm curious now . . . !

Sharif: Will do, thanks!

Sharif sat on the information. He knew Adjoua would say there was no point in hearing from some lying addict now. They had a plan that everyone had agreed to. They were no longer desperate. Whatever this Lebedev wanted to say was irrelevant. But Sharif couldn't suppress his curiosity. Maybe Lebedev's conscience had gotten to him, and he wanted to confess how and why he'd lied to the police about Sharif. Maybe Junior had shown people the video from the phone he stole from Samantha and it got back to Lebedev. Maybe Junior showed Lebedev himself. What harm would there be in hearing him out? Who knows, Sharif could learn something that would prove useful for tomorrow's meeting if things got contentious. Having some privileged information up his sleeve would give him a fragment of control instead of forcing him to sit on his hands while his in-laws arranged his rescue. Even if Lebedev had nothing, what did it cost Sharif to make a phone call to confirm that?

Getting away from Adjoua wasn't easy. She still wanted to accompany him on every walk. So he waited for her to take a nap before stepping out on the fire escape attached to the half bedroom to call Lebedev. He landed on his voicemail, left a simple message, then followed up with a text fifteen minutes later. It wasn't until three a.m. that Lebedev called him back, leaving his own message. Lebedev's croaky voice instructed Sharif to meet at eleven thirty a.m. at Four Seasons Bakery & Juice Bar. Sharif knew the restaurant: a Guyanese vegan spot on Church Avenue, five minutes from CAPPA. From seven to nine thirty, Sharif snuck three texts to Lebedev, but none showed as being delivered. He called again from the bathroom, which only confirmed Lebedev's phone was off. He wasn't going to turn up for some completely unnecessary meeting with some profoundly dishonest man without knowing the purpose.

By ten his curiosity had turned to obsession. He told Adjoua that Merjem wanted an impromptu meeting at eleven. Adjoua asked why, and when he said he didn't know, she said she'd head into Brooklyn with him and wait nearby. This way they could walk to the meeting at Aberto's together.

Whether it was good or bad news, she wanted to be there with him afterward.

"Baby, please. That's so sweet, but I won't be long. Stay and keep Judy company, okay?" he said, hugging her. "I'll come back and we'll go to the meeting together." As she sighed into his armpit, he tried to rationalize his deception by telling himself he was protecting her. That didn't work. She had too recently communicated her disdain for men who lied about important things that impacted her life under the guise of chivalry. Still working to alleviate his culpability on the train to Flatbush, he argued to himself that Adjoua was impossibly inconsistent. Sometimes she wanted transparency and collaboration, and other times she really did want the antiquated gender roles of a man who took care of things without her input. But by the time he got off at Church Avenue, he knew to only be mad at himself. Of course she'd be upset if she found out about what he'd done. They had gone through too much and come too far to commit such pointless transgressions. Don't fuck things up now, he said to himself as he speed-walked to the restaurant.

58.

DESPITE THE UNINSPIRED name, Four Seasons Bakery & Juice Bar had excellent food. Sharif occasionally treated himself to one of their small combination plates, which changed daily based on seasonal ingredients from the market that morning. Unfortunately, the indoor dining environment was starkly at odds with the culinary quality. It felt like a storage space. There were more mismatched tables and chairs than could fit comfortably. If you pulled one chair out, it invariably blocked another. To the right of the overcrowded furniture was a shallow counter for eating against a mirrored wall. The stools for this counter were too high, which was why the man eating there now with his forehead inches from the mirror looked like a giant insect hunched over his Styrofoam food container.

Having begun to internalize the likelihood of getting his job back, and possibly a substantial promotion, Sharif treated himself to an organic parsley orange juice with a shot of ginger. He pulled a chair out to sit, pinning the chair behind him under its table, and surveilled the front door.

Paul Lebedev entered looking as Sharif remembered: greasy silver hair, gray stubble and gray-blue eyes, wearing a yellowing white tank-top. Only this time he had a beige trench coat on top, ill-fitting jeans, and dirty white sneakers.

"Sharif?" he said.

"Hi."

"Nice to meet you. I'm Paul."

They shook hands, and Sharif said, "We've actually met before."

"Yeah. My memory is crap. Sorry about that." He looked at Sharif's juice. "Would you mind getting me a little something too? It's been a while."

"Okay, um — sure."

By the time Sharif stood, Paul had already fired off half of his order with the cashier: large Combination Plate ($15.00), side of Roti Skin ($3.75), Fried Eggplant Fritters ($1.00), Macaroni Pie ($3.00), and a Power Maxx-Protein Energy Shake ($8.70). He turned to Sharif and said, "God, I love this place. I'm going to hit the head. Be right back."

Sharif paid $31.45, already regretting his decision to come.

Paul returned and sat across from Sharif. He had apparently washed but not dried his hands. They were dripping, making a small puddle on the table underneath his interlaced fingers. He smiled at Sharif. "So! Tell me about yourself. Where you from?"

"You said you had something to tell me?"

"Oh, all right. You want to jump right into it." He lightly slapped the water on the table, as if hearing a joke. "You're a social worker but talk like a businessman." He laughed. "No, no, I mean that as a compliment. You got to be efficient if you want to make progress in this life, right?"

Sharif stared at him. He couldn't believe he'd lied to his wife for this man. "Paul. Why are we here?"

"Yes. Let's get to the point. Sometime recently, I headed down to the laundry room in the basement of my building." The server came and put down the first half of Paul's feast, needing a second trip for the rest. Paul rubbed his hands together and said, "Ah! Good tings, mon."

Sharif glanced up at the server, who appeared more amused than offended.

Paul removed his phone from his pocket and placed it on the table. Then he took several heaping spoonfuls of rice and stew and added two fried plantain pieces from the combination plate. Through his second bite he said,

"So. Recently, I headed down to the laundry room in the basement of my building."

"Yes, you said that."

"Actually, let me back up. It started before that, when I heard my neighbor moaning. You know who I mean. That young guy, Junior. At first I think it's an animal dying or something. I go knock on the door, and he opens it all slowly. His forearm looks like a crowbar, broken at a ninety-degree angle. His face is white as a ghost. I mean, as white as a Black guy gets, you know?"

"Do you remember what day and time this was?"

He rapidly took a few more bites. It was as if he could only speak with his mouth full. "Honestly, no. Definitely a weekday. But I'm not one hundred percent on that. Anyway, I tell him he better get to the hospital. He's saying he doesn't want to go. And I'm like, Okay, don't go then. Free country. But then his eyes kind of roll back like he's about to faint. I take ahold of him, walk him inside his apartment, and put him on the couch. I ask him what happened but he just passes out. So I call the ambulance myself. I wasn't going to let him die. So the EMS folks come and take him away. They make pretty good time too." He took a long sip of his smoothie and then immediately shoved more food in his mouth. Two of the many pieces of rice that tumbled back out got caught on the stubble of his chin like Velcro. "It's a different day that I'm down in the laundry room," he said, appearing to be affirming the fact while also presenting it to himself as a new and relatively strong theory.

Sharif checked the time on his phone. He'd have to be at Aberto's in about two hours. "All right. Anything else?"

"Hold on, I'm getting to it. For a while, the kid's dad is doing his rounds, asking everyone in the building what they saw. He comes to my door and I tell him I saw whatever he wants me to for a little grocery money. He says some hoity-toity bullshit about honesty. He comes bugging me a couple more times, asking me the same questions in different ways. I tell him we've been over this a million times. I didn't see shit until after the fact. Then I remind him I'll say whatever he wants if he helps me out.

He turns me down, but not as fast as the first time." He ate for a while, and Sharif stared in silent awe at this man's lack of shame. "So the second or third time, maybe fourth time that day, or maybe over a couple days, he says okay. You can tell it pained him. Like he was doing some evil thing that would take him straight to hell." Lebedev looked amused. "I even went to the precinct to make it official and all that."

Sharif couldn't remember ever feeling such disgust toward a person. "You don't even remember meeting me. How much did they pay you for this?"

His face changed, darkened. "When you interrupt me, I lose my train of thought. So don't interrupt, okay?" He looked up at the ceiling, squinting in thought, making a show of finding his place in the story. When he returned his eyes to Sharif, he had partially resumed his cheery affect. "So I go down to the laundry room, like I said. Sometimes people forget coins or singles down there. Lo and behold, that little mute girl is doing laundry, and her phone is on one of the machines behind her, by the door where I'm standing."

"*You* took the phone?"

Paul wouldn't be interrupted this time. "It's a nice phone too. So I bring it to that phone repair shop right by here, what's it called? The one between St. Pauls and Ocean. Something like We Fix You Buy. But they won't fix or buy nothing from me unless I have some kind of passcode or receipt or proof that the phone is mine. I know damn well they don't ask everyone for that. They see some ugly old white man and assume I'm a bum. Now *that's* racist profiling. It cuts both ways, fucking hypocrites."

Sharif gestured toward the phone on the table. "Is that her phone?"

"No," he said, as if offended by the idea. "Can I finish my story, please?" he said. "So, I go home and take my medicine. I figure I'll relax for a bit and then head to the pawnshop and see what they'll give me for it. But I end up losing track of it for a couple days." More food was stuffed into his mouth. "Then one day I come home from the park and see Junior's dad, the one I went to the precinct with. He's standing in the hall, talking with the little girl's foster mom. The foster mom talks fast, and it's kind of hard to understand her with her accent and all. But the gist is something about it not mattering what was on the little girl's phone since it's gone missing. I feel kind of bad about taking her phone and all, but I can't really deal with it at that moment, so I go inside to rest a bit."

"Did you ever give it back to her?"

This time his eyes widened with anger. "I'm going to tell you this at my own pace or not at all. You understand? That's the last time."

"Sure, Paul," Sharif said.

Paul said, "So, later, I hear those little thugs from outside banging on the foster mom's door, asking after some man inside. A sexy Black lady cop comes at some point asking what the little girl saw. It's all kind of muddled but it's the kind of stuff that makes me re-remember that *I* have that girl's phone! But I can't remember where I lost it. I finally find the damn thing underneath the radiator! Must have gotten kicked under there by mistake. So I decide it's time to take action and go to the pawnshop. They say they'll buy it for twenty dollars, but only if they can unlock it. This young Indian or Paki or whatever-type guy goes into the back and then comes right back out saying it's unlocked. I ask him how he did that so fast, and you know what he tells me? He says he always tries one-two-three-four first. About one in twenty people use it as their passcode!" Lebedev laughed open-mouthed, mashed food covering his tongue. "It's like that movie where that guy's suitcase code is one-two-three-four. Come on, you know it. Everyone knows it. I can't remember what it's called. Funny as hell though." He drank from his smoothie and swallowed the buildup he'd shown off. "So the Paki guy asks if I want the twenty dollars. I say hell yeah I want twenty dollars, but then I think, Hold on a second, Paul. Let's just see what's on this thing, you know? And besides, you never know what you're missing until you take the time to take a look. I'm a pretty curious guy. So I take the phone from the Indian and start snooping around. I know what that little girl filmed isn't any of my business. I don't need you to teach me about what's private. But I'll tell you this, my friend. You'll thank me soon for making it my business."

Sharif sat up straighter, trying to stretch out of the physical discomfort he was experiencing in Lebedev's presence.

Paul smiled. "Glad you came?"

"What did you see on the phone?"

"Well"—he stuffed his mouth some more—"lots of things, honestly. A ton of pictures and videos, mostly of animals. Hundreds, maybe thousands of animals—pigeons, alley cats, dogs, rats, skunks, squirrels, worms, ants, spiders, you name it. Most of it got filmed from a window in her apartment. But then I stop on these images of this huge fucking brown and white dog, and I'm like: *There*. Boom. Light bulb, you know? I think that right there is important. The dad had mentioned a big dog at some point. Now I'm really curious and ask the pawnshop guy how to make it play. He looks kind of pissed but says he'll go as high as twenty-five dollars, last offer. Then this lady waiting behind me steps in and shows me how to watch the videos." He paused, and then in an almost mean, taunting tone, said, "That little girl is like a pro. Steady hand, you know. The first couple are of you and the dad coming and going. But it's the last one that I think has the potential to really clarify things, if you know what I mean."

Sharif restrained himself for as long as he could, which couldn't have been more than a few seconds: "Where's the phone?"

"You know"—Paul leaned back and pushed his food away, like it suddenly repulsed him—"I was never one to pass what they call the marshmallow test. You ever heard of that? It's to test if someone can wait for a better thing. Usually a child. I never had that kind of patience. But I don't know. This time, lady luck made things play out in a way that made me able to see the opportunity in my hands for what it was," he said with pride. "I swear, if I had brought the phone to the pawnshop a day before, maybe even an hour before, I definitely would have taken twenty-five for it, even twenty. But something about that specific moment let me see I should hang on to the phone for just a bit longer." He grinned with excitement.

"What now, Paul?"

"Give me your phone number."

"Why?"

He shook his head, breaking into a full smile. "That Russian chick you work for was funny about your number too, like you're some celebrity or something. I've been trying to send you these videos, man."

"I'm not giving you any money, if that's what you're looking for."

He mimed a frowny face, then spoke in a baby voice through his pout: "Can I send you her little movies or not?"

Sharif gave his phone number, and Paul pulled out a second phone from his pocket. He spent a long time entering Sharif's number under the table.

Sharif finally received the video. It was eight seconds long and showed Sharif, Emmanuel, and Judy walking down the hall, toward the Fleurimes' apartment. Sharif looked up and said, "That's it?"

"It's a progression. A story."

Sharif eventually received and played the second video that came in. About twelve seconds long. Emmanuel, Judy, and Sharif leaving for the practice walk. Then a third video of similar length of Emmanuel, Judy, and Sharif returning from the practice walk.

It wasn't until the fifth video delivered to his phone that Junior appeared. In the still frame of the video was Junior's back, filling the doorframe. The sight transformed Sharif's physiology, speeding up his heart. He felt like a jaguar inside, so eager to pounce that he hit play three times in succession, inadvertently pausing it. He quickly forced a slower breath and gently tapped play again.

59.

SAMANTHA'S SUBJECT REMAINED the dog. She filmed Judy's hind legs, which could only be seen through a sliver of space between the left side of Junior's body and the doorframe. As soon as the video played, Sharif heard a voice yell, "Get the fuck out of my way!" It was the first thing that baffled him. He didn't understand who had said it. It wasn't Junior, but it couldn't have been him either. His heart drummed faster, and he reflexively turned the volume down with his thumb and swiped the progress bar at the bottom of the screen to start the video over. Recognizing the voice as his own, then rewinding and hearing it again as his, it still seemed unbelievable. He had no memory of saying that.

Junior made these rapid, micro shifting motions in the doorframe — side to side, forward and backward, diagonal — vibrating with indecision. His inability to pick a direction was so evident from Samantha's perspective, yet it appeared as completely new information to Sharif.

The video then showed Sharif bursting through that sliver of space Samantha had focused on to capture Judy's hind legs. Sharif had turned his back to Junior, covering Judy, and exited shoulder first. Junior was spun by the impact and slammed against the opposite frame post. The two men were momentarily stuck in the doorframe, hip to hip, with Sharif's left elbow and Judy's front half in the hall. Sharif twisted out of it explosively, using his triceps and elbow to propel himself off Junior's back and into the hallway, causing Junior to drop out of view at shocking speed. Junior vanished so fast that it seemed like a video editing trick. When Sharif rewound and played that moment slowly, he could clearly see Junior dropping from the frame, as if through a trapdoor.

Samantha was forced to take a step back inside her apartment as Sharif stumbled into the hall, barely catching his fall to prevent Judy from crashing to the floor.

"Goddamn you!" yelled Sharif, and then separately, "Mother*fucker!*" He had no memory of saying these things either, but he could tell he was yelling at the situation, at his and Judy's near fall, like someone cursing a stubbed toe. But it made sense that Junior would think Sharif had aimed this language at him. Sharif started running toward the elevator. Samantha stepped back into the hall, her camera briefly sweeping across the Fleurimes' open door before shooting Judy. During that brief sweep, Junior was lying on the floor. Sharif paused and zoomed in on Junior to look for clues of injury, but it was too blurred.

She kept the camera trained on Sharif's retreating back for the next six seconds, zooming on Judy's head. Junior yelled, "Hey, wait, come back here!" Sharif entered the elevator without looking back. Samantha's camera returned to Junior. It was then that Sharif saw the unmistakably — and horribly — broken bone. Junior had sat himself up on the floor. He cupped the elbow of the injured arm with his other hand and stared at its unnatural bend like an ugly, threatening object he'd never seen before. He was repeating, Hey, come back here, with a weakening voice, as he stared at the arm. Samantha turned around to go back into her apartment. The recording ended with a frame of the orange rug of her entryway.

60.

REWATCHING THE VIDEO, Sharif experienced a kind of progressive disintegration. His middle had vanished already, and the mind and body around it were turning to vapor, clinging to the hole where his center had been, desperately trying to stop his memory of what happened from being displaced by the video evidence. He had to reinstate his previous reality. But doing this was like commanding himself to hang on to a dream that was slipping further away with every waking second.

He tried to revive the truest feelings and convictions built off of the dissipating dream-version of events: his moments of true rage toward Aberto, Junior, Emmanuel; his singular commitment to justice and truth and fairness at every turn; his resentment for the stress this all put on Adjoua; then, his refusal to press charges against Emmanuel, and his willingness to raise money for them. But it had all been tethered to dreamed-up facts, nearly pure smoke now. *No, no,* he fought it. Junior had changed his story too many times. Even his classmates publicly called him out. What about that bizarre smirk on Junior's face at the meetings? And his teachers who suspected he'd framed a classmate for vandalism. Some of it had to be pertinent. Some of it had to mean something.

He had heard of this. He had seen the films and true crime series and documentaries and procedurals with false memories. He had read articles and watched clips and listened to podcasts about innocent people spending decades in prison because of faulty eyewitness testimony, or people swearing to amnesia for a violent crime. He'd always known memory was fallible. But no secondhand information can prepare you for being wrong about an important event that you experienced directly. What amount of cognitive distortion could have made him so certain of something so inaccurate? And where did the cognitive distortion begin and end? Just how unreliable was his mind? He returned to existential dissolution as he stared at the final frame of the video, the orange rug at Samantha's.

No one would believe it was an accident and that he'd simply misremembered. And if they did, it still wouldn't excuse him. This video would be enough for the DA to prosecute even if the Fleurimes pulled out. Aberto and his friend at the DA's office could still put Sharif on trial as some lying racist. A shot of adrenaline caught his breath. He suddenly thought of his mother. The unbearable sadness she'd have in her voice when saying that telling the truth and taking responsibility was the right thing to do. He'd always done the right thing.

But it wasn't so simple. There was the tug of his self-preservation too, creating an impossible conflict between his moral self and his intense desire to be spared harsh consequences for an honest mistake. The inner conflict was physical, triggering a dizzying pulse around his eyes that quickly turned into full-bodied, panting waves of anxiety. The restaurant shrank and quieted around him, then abruptly grew extremely loud and bright. A gentle note in the Guyanese song playing in the kitchen became a shriek. Footsteps, chatter, dishes, laughter competed and bounced off one another, overlapping, exaggerating, glitching, tangling. His torso was a giant, throbbing heart that joined the delirious soundscape, panning back and forth, thundering from miles off, then forty feet away, then inside his pounding eardrum. His eyes were open, yet somehow he was also fainting and coming to again and again, fainting and waking back up in this sensory nightmare. His body could not handle the present.

His phone rang and the swirl of destabilization slowed. He saw Adjoua's name, and his senses realigned. The world provided information in its familiar, balanced, untrue manner. My Adjoua, he thought. He silenced his ringer, deciding to call Walid for advice as soon as his wife got sent to voice-mail. But then he changed his mind and held down the power button. The screen went black, and he was left staring at his monochrome reflection. When he looked up, he saw another desperate man. This one grinning with pleasure.

Part VII

SACRIFICE

61.

AT ABERTO'S, SHARIF took the empty chair between his wife and in-laws. If anyone nodded hello, he wouldn't have noticed with his eyes downcast. Babs didn't get up from her bed. There was no chatter. Emmanuel sat motionless in a faded blazer on the other side of Sylvie, who had the posture of someone in charge. Aberto stood behind his desk, looking down at a stack of papers. Distractedly, he said they'd get started as soon as Junior was out of the bathroom. Adjoua sat erect and heavy, as if wearing a medieval suit of armor. This was all peripheral knowledge. Sharif hadn't faced the questions he knew he'd find on his wife's face if he looked at it directly: Where have you been? How could you make me worry at a time like this? We were supposed to come here together.

When Lebedev had said that the video on the phone he'd stolen from Samantha was the only copy in existence, a look of regret washed over him. He seemed to realize as he spoke that he should have made a copy. He shrugged off the missed opportunity and said he'd be willing to part with the phone for two hundred dollars. Sharif went to the same ATM he'd gone to with Emmanuel that first day and withdrew the cash from Adjoua's book advance money. He'd have to come up with an explanation for that, along with one for what happened at his meeting with Merjem that morning, then another for why his phone was still off. There would be a learning curve to managing the little lies needed to uphold the big lie.

Charles leaned over to quietly inform Sharif that the police complaint had been withdrawn. Yann had accompanied Emmanuel to the precinct this morning before heading to work. Sharif gave the barest of nods to the news. Neither Charles nor Sylvie would have found it strange that he didn't ask them a single question about today's deal, or really spoken at all since arriving. His withdrawn state matched their self-serious business mode. They were people who believed serious things should be decided upon without emotion, as if cold logic could be the underlying motive behind any decision.

Sylvie said, "Okay! Let's go. We can't wait around all day. That boy doesn't need to be here for us to begin."

Aberto sat on the throne Charles and Sylvie had once given him, and said, "He goes by Junior." His voice sounded ragged, like he hadn't slept the night before or was feeling ill.

"That's fine," Sylvie said. "Can we start?"

Unexpectedly, Aberto gave in. "Sure." He then asked Charles, "Do you have the checks?" Sharif could now hear that Aberto's raggedness was disappointment, maybe even sadness. But sadness about what? Not getting to see Sharif behind bars, stripped of his reputation? Or was it about losing Adjoua? Sharif looked at the corkboard over Aberto's shoulder and saw that her picture had been removed. He was peripherally reminded of his statue of a wife and returned his eyes to his hands.

Charles neatly placed the two remaining checks on Aberto's desk. Aberto talked at the checks, giving a monotone overview of today's agreement. Then Aberto was suddenly standing in front of his desk, two feet from Sharif. Sharif had missed how he'd gotten there, and it startled him enough to catch his breath and pull back as if from a ledge. But Aberto was only distributing copies of the contract. Sharif redirected his adrenaline toward his commitment to seeing this thing through, to giving himself and his wife a fresh start. He wouldn't face felony charges. Their names would be cleared. He would get his job back and help thousands of people a year while earning a salary that provided a decent life for his family.

Sharif felt a new body enter the space from behind. Aberto spoke over everyone's head to say, "Hey, Junior. Want to take a seat?"

There was a beat before Junior said, "Nah," and walked around the chairs toward Aberto's desk. Sharif blinked slowly at the metal pins swaying at Junior's side.

He caught his wife's statue in the corner of his eye again. He couldn't imagine ever again looking at her directly. She might always remain a hard shape at the border of his senses. Junior faced the semicircle of adults and said, "I'll read the statement."

Aberto said, "Oh, no. You don't need to do that. That's not part of it."

Junior said, "I want to."

Sharif felt a sharp, inward constriction, like his very soul was being squeezed. He stared down at the contract in his hands, the letters blurring, as he told himself that this deal was the only acceptable option. A clean break from the situation was all he could offer Adjoua. It's what she deserved. He had to push through one last, horrible moment. The Fleurimes were receiving life-changing money. A confession from Sharif wouldn't be good for anyone.

Junior took his phone from his pocket, saying, "It's copied here. Ready to post." He began reading the prepared text: "I, Emmanuel Fleurime Jr., spread false information about how I broke my arm and wrist on May 31st, 2018. Mr. Sharif Safadi is in no way responsible for any part of this injury."

Junior was doing this to challenge Sharif. Punish him. "On May 31st," Junior continued, "I took the stairwell to visit a friend one floor down. I tried jumping some steps but fell. The injuries to my wrist and forearm were caused by that fall and nothing else. Mr. Safadi was nowhere near me at the time."

Sharif started feeling that pulsing in his eye and those panting waves of anxiety that had so disoriented him in the restaurant. That war between morality and self-interest, good and desire, identity and feral survival.

"I blamed Mr. Safadi when I woke up in the hospital because he yelled at me for putting his dog on the fire escape, and because I knew my father and

I could not afford the hospital bills. Once I lied about it, I was too scared to take it back."

Needing to do something with his hands and attention, anything at all, Sharif turned the page of the contract, as if looking for the statement to read along. And that's when it jumped out at him:

SECTION 4 ADDENDUM. <u>Confidentiality of Video Recording</u>

4.7(a) I, the undersigned, shall not at any time directly or indirectly, in any way, reveal, report, publish, disclose, transfer or otherwise disseminate or use the video recording described above or any copy of . . .

The lines danced hysterically on the page.

. . . 4.7(b) In the event that a third party directly or indirectly . . . disseminates said video recording, or any newly discovered video recording . . . I agree to submitting a second public statement in support of, and drafted by . . .

They know. They all know.

62.

INSTEAD OF SEEKING information from people in the room, Sharif turned his phone on. Junior was still reading when Sharif saw the dozens of calls and messages from Walid, Charles, and Adjoua. Aberto had forwarded them the video. Of course Lebedev hadn't waited for Sharif to try selling it. Adjoua had written, How can this be? Where are you? What should we do? CALL ME BACK. In the less than two hours since the video had made the rounds, Sharif's in-laws, Walid, and Yann had managed to incorporate the new evidence into the contract, bumping one of the checks to $40k, making the total $80k.

A voice in Sharif's head told him he should act surprised. He should interrupt Junior and say, Wait, hold on, what is *this?* What video is this addendum in reference to? He should shake the contract in dismay and perform the shock of learning of the video. He should demand to see it, to see what the hell they were talking about, and then show them more shock as he watched it for the first time. He should make absolutely clear that he had no idea about this. The shoulds multiplied frantically, becoming mirrors that reflected his inescapable shame back at him. Junior's voice contained the censoriousness of a mirror too. His wife's statue was a mirror. His in-laws, Aberto, Emmanuel. The room, the objects inside it, the air itself, all mirrors. All exposing him. Reflections of reflections of him, seemingly endless lines of reflections in every direction. He couldn't get away from them. He felt he was dying.

Then he heard a distant crack in Junior's voice. And then another. The cracks shifted something inside of Sharif. The reflections of reflections of himself were no longer infinite. He saw that each one absorbed only some of the light from the previous one, darkening imperceptibly until eventually they faded into invisibility. The bottom fell out of Sharif's panic as he gravitated toward that point of invisibility. He lifted his eyes and could still see beyond his reflections when he looked at Junior. Something opened in him that had never been open before. Floating outside the small, mostly unknown confinement of himself, he could not only see Junior as if for the first time, but could actually feel him. He felt the magnitude of Junior's fragility in this moment. It was an evolving fragility, one that radiated steady ripples into the air around them.

Sharif could see that Junior was never reading the statement to challenge or punish him. Of course not. Sharif didn't exist. Junior had been reading to his father. "Again, I'm deeply remorseful for any suffering I caused and for misinforming my community." Sharif felt Junior trying to speak the words angrily, wanting to shame his father for making him do this, but only fear and loneliness were coming through.

Going off-script, Junior looked at his father directly: "After Mom. After everything we went through, keeping each other safe all those nights, and all that talk about truth and integrity, and how He sees everything, and how important it is to keep my good name—" He fell off. He looked down to take a breath. Sharif felt a shift in the fragility Junior radiated. Junior became more determined somehow, the ripples of energy coming off him faster. "I used to pray every single night to be brave and good like you. This"—he shook the phone—"is a lie."

"I don't see a better way," Emmanuel said, his voice sounding like it had traveled from deep inside an empty cave.

"I do," Aberto said. "We can still stop this." But he too felt distant and defeated to Sharif. "You don't have to do any of this, Junior." They'd obviously been over this many times. "I'll fight for you."

Junior made like he hadn't heard Aberto, but Sharif could feel that he had. Then the anger Junior tried to find and aim toward his father flared to life. "Go to hell," he said to Aberto, a gust of defiance filling his chest. He stood tall now, emanating vitality. "You only fight for yourself. You only ever cared about beating some punk who took your girl. Oh, you didn't know I saw all that, huh? Yeah. But you know what? It's all good, because I don't need you to fight for me." When Adjoua shifted in her seat, Sharif felt the crosscurrent of her shame and Junior's newborn rage. Junior looked at her and his anger billowed out across the room, his voice expanding with it. "And I cannot *wait* to never see this bitch again."

"Watch your tongue, young man," Sylvie snapped. Sharif's unprecedented awareness picked up on the underlying tremor of fear flowing from Sylvie despite the sharpness of her words and gestures. "You think you can insult us and then take our money?"

"Oh, this lady!" Junior blustered. "At least you're not fake like the others. You don't even try to hide how selfish and soulless you are."

"Ex*cuse* me?" she said, leaning forward, but maintaining even less control over the jittering vibrations Sharif was able to feel so clearly.

Charles put his arm across his wife like a seat belt to make sure she didn't stand up. He said, "Let's everyone hold on a minute." Charles was deeply afraid; Sharif felt that too.

Adjoua said, "No, you're right, Junior," with a nakedly pleading tone. "This whole thing. It's. The truth is, I could never begin to tell you how sorry—"

"*Keep* that shit in your mouth!" Junior boomed. "You think I give a *fuck* about your sorry?" Junior's power became increasingly large and frenetic. He started pacing in front of the desk, his waves of energy overwhelming the room, everyone caught in the undertow. Aberto took a few steps back. Adjoua pulled in her chin and covered her belly with her forearms. Sylvie and Charles pinned themselves to the backs of their chairs.

"You and your man's whole life is fake as fuck," Junior said. "Walking around trying to *look* like good people. It's so fucking sad and pathetic. *I'm* the one who is sorry for *you*. Sorry for that baby inside you too. Having you as a mom is going to be hell on earth. But you know what? I should actually *thank* you. Yeah, I should thank you for showing me exactly how *not* to be!" His pacing was speeding up. "Because I *know* I'll be different. I *know* I'll be better than all of you!"

Emmanuel said, "Junior."

"No, *fuck* these people!" His arm gestures were taking up more space, undeterred by the pins stabbing him, throwing his warlike vibrations left and right. Aberto stepped farther back, putting himself in the corner of the room, and raised his hands as if to show he was unarmed. But Junior couldn't be calmed; his voltage was too strong. "This is what they want, Dad! For me to post some shit that makes me look like a dumb, greedy, lying fucked-up kid from some shithole country! Well, I don't give a fuck! I know what I am! I know I'm better than these bitches! I don't need anyone to fight for that! I *own* my shit!" His energy shifted into something more sinister. He laughed loudly and humorlessly, then abruptly stopped pacing and swiveled around to face the frightened adults. He brought his phone up and out to the side, like he was gripping a rock he was about to bring down on one of their heads. Sharif felt everyone in the room flinch, preparing for Junior to strike. But Junior was still only staring at his father, holding on to the hum of his rage as long as he could, but quickly losing purchase, his thumb hovering over the phone's screen like it was a detonator. Keeping the anger in suspension to the brink of his capacities, a broken cry burst forth: *"WHY WON'T YOU PROTECT ME!"*

Sharif felt all of the crosscurrents in the atmosphere abruptly change. Something resurged in Emmanuel, causing him to leap up and catch his son in his embrace. "I am, son, I am. I'm doing this to protect you. You have to believe that." Junior sobbed on contact. Emptying, emptying.

Emmanuel held him through convulsions, then quaking, then trembling, then shivers that grew farther apart.

Junior was now small and fractured as ever. He said, "I can't go back to school with everyone thinking this about me, Papa. Don't make me, Papa. Please."

Emmanuel held Junior through another wave of sobs. The vibrations Sharif could feel coming from Emmanuel were muted, blocked by thickening walls of forced invulnerability, stuffed deep down into himself. His pain was too great to release into more realness. When Junior had quieted down, Emmanuel whispered calmly but firmly, "It's okay, son. You can do this. I know you can."

A terrible stillness followed.

Junior pulled back to look at his father, his eyes round and his mouth open. The face of innocence betrayed. He slowly closed his mouth. And like a kind of death, Sharif saw the childhood drain from his eyes.

63.

SOON SHARIF WAS drawn back into himself, no longer able to see past his own reflections or tune into the large, vague, shifting vibrations of the people around him with any clarity. The universe was again limited to his enclosed heart, a beast running through its cage of darkness and mirrors. It would be years before he'd glimpse beyond those mirrors for a second time.

First, he will receive a hero's welcome at work. A literal ovation. They'll celebrate him like a wrongfully accused man winning back his freedom, the most admired kind of victim. His moral fraudulence will lodge a hard ache in his throat. It will then melt and start to spread like illness as he shadows Jamal to be the next director of economic development, earning triple his former salary. Junior will receive brutal contempt from his peers online before making his social media pages private, then deleting them a week later.

At home, Adjoua will emanate a powerful sorrow that Sharif will be unable to address. It won't be the shame of what they did that blocks their communication. It will be the horrible awareness that they would do it again under identical circumstances. There is no path toward acceptance or forgiveness, or any fantasy of restorative justice, without simple regret. They will dislike themselves for this, both individually and as a couple.

Sharif will collapse into uncontrollable lament when dropping Judy off at the rich Australian's. The maid will rub his back, telling him how well

Judy will be cared for here, eventually telling Sharif he should go, his wife needs him at the hospital now.

When the nurse hands him Zora, he'll be shocked by the strength in her tiny body, mesmerized by her ancient face and toothless scream. In a zombie-like state, they'll move into the fully furnished three-bedroom, two-bathroom apartment in a new Flatbush development that Charles and Sylvie bought without asking permission. Sharif will sleep on the sofa in the living room. His night terrors will get so bad that he'll have to medicate them into submission. The couple will be more at ease at the hospital for Zora's treatment than at home. Receiving clear directives from doctors and nurses will spare them any collaborative decision-making.

His mind will beg itself for a way of explaining to Zora that her aching and nausea and fatigue will not be her whole life. Turning corners in his head, he'll run into Junior's face as it was rung dry of childhood, of feeling protected by the adult he trusted most in the world.

Zora will go into remission after the induction phase, but it won't be cause for celebration; 95 percent of patients like her achieve this. The more intensive consolidation phase will overlap with the end of Sharif's paternity leave. His workweeks will quickly ramp up to seventy and eighty hours, leaving Adjoua and Zora alone.

They'll learn to anticipate the side effects of medications: the one that turns her skin yellow, the one that makes her gums bleed, the one that lets them sleep for three consecutive hours. They'll talk only of logistics and scheduling, cleaning, medical appointments, safety precautions for trips outside of the apartment, restocking medical supplies and diapers and creams; changes in urine and stool, lip dryness, eye coloration, nail density. Grandparents will follow strict hygiene protocols when they visit. Sylvie will cook a month's worth of food each week, mumbling offended comments as she throws out leftovers from the time before. Sharif will not find a trace of the Fleurimes through search engines or Aberto's social media, where he sees Adjoua has been erased. He will call Erasmus High School and learn that Junior is no longer enrolled there. He will track down his old client Wesley and learn that the Fleurimes no longer live in that building.

They will host a friend for the first time on the patio when Zora is a month and a half. Adjoua will hold their grayish, bald baby at a safe distance. Answering their guest's question, Sharif will describe witnessing Adjoua's labor as the closest thing to war he will probably ever experience — the blood and screaming and danger of it all. Adjoua will sharply interrupt the guest's fascinated head-nodding by saying only a man would associate a bleeding pussy with violence. Sharif will feel he's been slapped in the face. The guest will hide in a glass of water, then pivot to asking about Sharif's new job. The shock of Adjoua's slap will transition into a kind of invigoration. A fierce wakefulness lengthens Sharif's spine and widens his eyes. A bit aggressively, he tells their guest that his new job sucks. He hardly ever interacts with clients anymore. Feeling another gust of wakefulness, he adds that places like CAPPA shouldn't even exist. The government should staff their own social service delivery departments and take direct responsibility for the basic needs of residents. Instead, they outsource it to private nonprofits in this disconnected, fiscally idiotic, cumbersome way. Adjoua becomes lively and contributes her own teardown of government and nonprofits like CAPPA. It will be the most connected the couple has felt since before the last meeting at Aberto's.

Cynicism will be their bridge. Everyone will be a hypocrite. Coworkers, parents, radio personalities, writers, philanthropists, doctors and nurses, friends: Sara posts constantly about the Yazidi women taken by ISIS but is deafeningly silent on the reporting about forced child labor used to mine the cobalt for her smartphone. How does Mathew defend paying taxes into the systemically racist and warmongering country he says he can't stomach? If Ben is so worried about the climate, how does he justify all those flights for work?

Sharif will start showing impatience with coworkers. Adjoua will help him edit excessively long emails to Merjem, and then to Brionna, detailing the domino effect of their minor oversights. Merjem will express concern at first, then advise him to come talk to her before sending anything like that ever again.

The *New York Times* will re-invite Adjoua to submit a piece on the ten-year sentence Officer Luisa Daniels received for killing Anthony Augustin. She will mostly write about the victim's brother, Joshua Augustin, who pronounced forgiveness for Daniels at her televised sentencing. Adjoua will argue that Joshua's pronouncement only reinforces the undue absolution cops receive for murdering unarmed Black people, deepens the historically rooted expectation of Black people suppressing their pain and forgiving white people implicitly for any harm caused, and is otherwise an improbable shortcut to forgiveness. One cannot bypass the deep inner acceptance and healing that true forgiveness requires by simply saying the words out loud on TV. The editors at the *Times* will be uncomfortable publishing a critique of Joshua's way of grieving and will reject the piece. She and Sharif will share a newfound hatred for the triumphant liberalist newspaper. A paper so obsessed with appearing objective and fair that it hires a climate change denier to their editorial staff to represent "broader perspectives." A paper enjoying a 66 percent increase in revenue by giving central coverage to every one of the president's idiotic comments, tirades, and lies — which they don't even have the courage to call lies even when proven as such, and which is why that loathsome man was elected in the first place.

Adjoua will turn against her writing ambitions more broadly, especially against her fiction. How delusional to think writing a novel is a practice in empathy. Spending years contemplating characters created from parts of the author's self is the height of narcissism.

The couple's negative power source will start burning out. They'll lose the shielding torque of pessimism and feel more threatened by the external environment. A to-do list or an inane conversation or a politician's face will push their bodies into the blind anxiety of survival mode. They will start turning against thinking itself, the volatility and restlessness of thoughts, the transience of memories and voices and images that light up islands of discomfort in their bodies. Then the nihilism will become so total that even expressing it will feel pointless. There will only be a deep, croaking desiccation left. Just as they hit absolute bottom, Zora will smile, and a line of electricity will pass across their black sky.

It won't instantly overturn their unhappiness, but it will move something. A light kick off the ocean floor. The slow ascension will continue with Zora's laughter, then babbling, then face-touching. For months, Sharif will work on teaching Zora to look at the object he's pointing at instead of at his finger. It will be proven false that parenting flies by. Around six months, a brightening, buoying in-loveness will start creeping in. They'll forget that their experience is different from that of parents with healthy children. Zora will mirror more nuanced facial expressions. They will mirror her mirroring. Silliness and giggling will be increasingly common. Zora will point and understand pointing simultaneously. They will be desperate to get her to sleep then find themselves watching videos of her twenty minutes after she's down. Zora will learn to walk like a drunk before learning to crawl.

Sharif's breath will catch every time he thinks he sees Junior, but it won't be him. Walid will mention what happened with the Fleurimes exactly twice, both times in the tone of someone recalling a crazy night out with friends. Their parents will appear to only know as much as Sharif's coworkers.

Zora will be two and cured of cancer. Sharif won't feel awkward around his in-laws anymore. Judy will be ten and move in with them. Zora will conflate the words Judy and doggie and Daddy, saying, "Are you a good boy, Daddy?" Sharif will drop a dish in the sink. He will make Zora cry when he tells her it hurts Judy when she hangs on his neck like that.

Zora will enjoy two and a half months of normal childhood without hospital visits before the world becomes a dystopian sci-fi film. They won't take risks with Zora catching the virus, so they pay others to take them by delivering items to their closed door. They will stay locked inside, wash everything that enters their home, wear masks and gloves when they take Judy out, avoid contact with others. Sharif will have to lay off half of his staff by phone and Zoom. Six employees and twenty-three clients will suffocate to death in isolated hospital beds.

Zora's face will look impossibly old when the story that convulses the nation breaks on the radio. She'll have surely heard the strain in her parents' voices when they discuss how to support the protests. The marches are too dangerous. Sending money is the most helpful thing they can do. Sharif will intercept a returned envelope from the Offices of Aberto Barbosa and Associates with a check Adjoua wrote out to Junior. The attached note will read: *I have no contact with the Fleurimes. No idea about Emmanuel. Last I heard, Junior went back to Haiti to live with his aunt. I doubt he'd want this or anything else from you anyway.* Sharif will not share any of it with Adjoua.

The president will be voted out of office. He will catalyze his supporters to attack the Capitol. The ugliest aspects of the country that the ex-president emphasized will remain emboldened. He will be voted back into office. Zora will suddenly know how to read by herself. She will write the words *baby sister* and *puppy* on the grocery list on the fridge. She will ask why some people's lives are harder than others. They'll be amazed by her sophistication when she describes the embarrassing emotion of feeling annoyed that someone is annoyed with you. Sharif and Adjoua will tell people how fast it all flies by. Adjoua will get a full-time job at an advertising firm and sound defensive when telling people how fun it is. They will not have sex for three months and agree to marriage counseling, but neither will make the first appointment. Judy will crawl under Zora's bed one last time at age sixteen. Zora will be permanently changed by the loss. A crater will be felt in every corner of their home. Adjoua will get pregnant and cut off all of her hair. Zora will start telling lies at school about being a homeless orphan. They'll sell their apartment and buy a bigger one in the same building.

The two sets of grandparents still won't be themselves around each other. They'll sit on opposite sides of the living room, smiling as Zora and her three-year-old brother, Moussa, run between them, as if their small bodies are the conversation. Adjoua will become someone who loses her wallet, phone, or keys daily. Sharif will start needing glasses and become knowledgeable about imported coffee beans. He'll stop caring when he feels his butt crack exposed from bending over. Moussa will ask his father if he can be a girl like Zora when he grows up since girls don't die. Adjoua will read luxury real estate newsletters and buy more expensive clothes. They'll receive the *New York Times* twice a week, then seven. They'll tell friends who never asked that the only reason Zora and Moussa go to private schools is because their school district is truly bad. The best part of Sharif's job will be when the older youth in his East New York Career Navigation program greet him enthusiastically during his site visits.

Sylvie will die in her sleep. Charles will be permanently changed by the loss. The only person who will brighten him up will be Zora. He'll be visibly uncomfortable around Moussa. Adjoua will commit to writing fiction on the weekends and then quit again after six months. She'll say she seems to only find meaning in her anxiety about the kids: How can we get Zora to care more about schoolwork? How can we teach Moussa bravery and self-possession so I won't have to hear of his being bullied again? She'll drink more wine than usual at a dinner party and weep about how her love for her children feels like sadness, like mourning.

In high school, Zora will be disgusted by how little her parents have done about climate change and racial justice. Her father's career will be as much bullshit to her as her mother's. Her anger will simmer to a quieter, more toxic cynicism. Everyone will be a hypocrite. Parents, teachers, politicians, celebrities, classmates. She'll reject her closest friends, seeing them as phony and shallow. She'll fall into a depression. She'll fall in love. She'll have her heart broken. It will happen three more times. She will study film and marry an architect. Moussa will go to college without a major and become ever more inscrutable. No matter how much alcohol Moussa consumes at dinner, Sharif will see no change in his affect. Zora will miscarry and deny being affected, as if caring were somehow anti-feminist. Moussa will drop out of school and move in with a friend he will deny is his lover. But that will only be Sharif and Adjoua's best guess.

Sharif will be frightened by how little he knows the people he knows best. Despite knowing how they'd behave and what they'd say in most situations, there will hardly be any sense of their inward experience. He won't feel seen in this way by them either. The walls of himself will isolate him almost entirely. And even within his own borders, it will remain mostly dark and unknown to him. Seeing so little of himself and others will make him feel unreal somehow.

He will receive a terminal diagnosis a week after his sixty-third birthday. Over the next two years, he and Adjoua will move through a stunned and withdrawn state, anger and cynicism, depression and nihilism, and acceptance. Sharif will see that his life has been a series of grief cycles, mourning some loss or another, most of them small. But near the end of this cycle, he will be transported by a heightened openness. It will bring him to the limits of himself, to a kind of disappearing point. From there, he'll feel how the walls of his isolation are pressed against and defined by the walls of those he loves the hardest. He'll be attuned to the vibrations passing through. The vibrations won't only be an emotion. They'll be much more. They'll be all of the inner richness at once — all of the emotions and voices and imagery and humor and memories and sensory perception, millions upon millions of pieces of information that neither the mind nor language could ever capture — resonating as one unified chord. His capacity to receive the vibrations of that chord will allow for a depth of connection with his loved ones he never imagined possible. He'll finally experience the whole, separate, complex being of another person. He'll only wish it happened before learning he was out of time.

It will take him weeks to realize why this wonderful ability of his feels so familiar. At first, he'll assume it's because it's a capacity he's always had beneath the noise of his roles and self-image, then that it must be some foreshadowing sense of what's to come. But later he'll remember Junior Fleurime. It happened briefly back then too. It happened just before the moment he perceived Junior's childhood leave him, and stopped afterward, which he now recognizes as the moment Sharif and Adjoua's idealism died. And here it is again, happening as his body dies. Oh, he thinks, imagine how harmless my life could have been had this happened from the start.

He will ask Adjoua to find Junior for him. She'll tell him not to worry about the Fleurimes. She's been in touch with them all this time, sending money, supporting Junior's children's schooling. They're all doing really well, they're all so happy. And Emmanuel is the proudest grandfather, happily retired and remarried. Sharif will be touched by her lies. He'll ask her to please pass along a short message to them on his behalf. "Tell them I said: It's little, I know, but I finally regret it all."

The walls will soon dissolve completely. He will open fully and merge with all those vibrations. In his final moment, Zora will be eight months pregnant. But when he shuts his eyes and pictures her, she will be nine years old again. She runs across Prospect Park's Long Meadow, her gait elongating with each stride, her two dark braids whipping the air. She's flying now. When he pictures Moussa, he will see him as five years old again. He is throwing fistfuls of soil into a crackling river like flung seed, mouthing something to the sinking soil. When he looks up at Sharif, his face breaks open with joy, believing that whatever he imagined was also seen by his father. When Sharif pictures Adjoua, it will be how she looked a moment ago: gray-haired and smooth-skinned, sleeping on the cot next to his hospital bed, dreaming just beyond his closed eyes.

ACKNOWLEDGMENTS

Thank you:

To my agent, Emily Forland, for her care and advocacy. I'm so lucky to have you in my corner. To everyone at Little, Brown and Company. To Ben George for acquiring the book. To Vivian Lee and Maya Guthrie for their deep engagement with this story. To Allison Kerr Miller and Michael Noon for their careful eye. To Katharine Myers, Chloe Texier-Rose, Kayleigh George, Sabrina Callahan, and Marieska Luzada for giving *The Uproar* their curated and expert support. To Gregg Kulick for the striking cover. To Abe Koogler, my trusted first reader for over a decade. To Nadim Dimechkie, Lea Beresford, Dan Sheehan, and Corey Miller for the resuscitating encouragement and conversations about fictional people. To Ben Weiss and Jillian Buckley for the close read and guidance on all matters related to NYC social service delivery and culture. To Lyse Pamphile for the insights on Flatbush's Haitian community. To Art Omi for the time, space, and support to write. To CAMBA for giving me the social service experience I needed to tell this story. To the activists who let me interview them about the personal motivations behind their work: Zach Hollopeter, Tom Rosenberg, Summer Michele Plum, Steve Lambert, Stephen Duncombe, Pat Beetle, Mink Rose, Lisa Raymond Tolan, Laura Mannino, Jonathan Rodriguez, Felice Brenner, Dread Scott, and Ben Shanahan. To Margaret Garrett, Nicholas Klein, and Tom Schmidt for applying their legal expertise to my fabricated world. To doctors Emilia Hermann and Sarah Yu for patiently and generously discussing the medical catalysts that shaped my plot. And to Nana Afua and Ramzi — my heart, my home, my greatest fortune.

ABOUT THE AUTHOR

Karim Dimechkie's first novel, *Lifted by the Great Nothing*, was praised by NPR, the PEN/Hemingway Foundation, and Oprah.com. Dimechkie was a fellow of the Michener Center for Writers at UT Austin, and has held residencies at MacDowell, the Anderson Center for the Arts, and the Ucross Foundation. His writing can be found in the *New York Times*, the *Saint Ann's Review*, and *Empirical Magazine*'s "Best of" anthology. Like the protagonist of *The Uproar,* Dimechkie spent more than five years working in New York City's social services in Flatbush, Brooklyn, while writing and serving as an MFA thesis adviser at Columbia University. He now lives in London and New York with his wife and son.